Blind Passions

Acclaim for Miranda Lee, Rebecca Winters and Emma Goldrick

About Miranda Lee
"Miranda Lee pens a sensual tale with a potent conflict and energetic characters."
—*Romantic Times*

About Rebecca Winters
"Rebecca Winters is a woman for all seasons with her ability to write fantastic romance novels."
—*Affaire de Coeur*

About Emma Goldrick
"Emma Goldrick's light, humorous touch combines with delectable characters giving readers a wonderful lasting impression."
—*Romantic Times*

Blind Passions

THE RELUCTANT LOVER
by
Miranda Lee

BLIND TO LOVE
by
Rebecca Winters

IF LOVE BE BLIND
by
Emma Goldrick

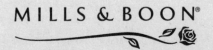

MILLS & BOON®

MILLS & BOON and MILLS & BOON with the Rose Device are registered trademarks of the publisher.
Harlequin Mills & Boon Limited,
Eton House, 18-24 Paradise Road, Richmond, Surrey, TW9 1SR

BLIND PASSIONS
© by Harlequin Enterprises II B.V., 1999

The Reluctant Lover, Blind to Love and *If Love Be Blind* were first published in Great Britain by Mills & Boon Limited.
The Reluctant Lover in 1991, *Blind to Love* in 1995
and *If Love Be Blind* in 1987.

The Reluctant Lover © Miranda Lee 1991
Blind to Love © Rebecca Winters 1989
If Love Be Blind © Emma Goldrick 1987

ISBN 0 263 81533 1

05-9901

Printed and bound in Great Britain
by Caledonian Book Manufacturing Ltd, Glasgow

Miranda Lee is Australian, living near Sydney. Born and raised in the bush, she was boarding-school educated and briefly pursued a classical music career before moving to Sydney and embracing the world of computers.

Happily married, with three daughters, she began writing when family commitments kept her at home. Miranda's first novel was published by Mills & Boon® in 1990 and since then, more than ten million copies of her books have been published worldwide.

Miranda likes to create stories that are believable, modern, fast-paced and sexy. Her interests include reading meaty sagas, doing word puzzles, gambling and going to the movies.

THE RELUCTANT LOVER
by
MIRANDA LEE

CHAPTER ONE

APRIL slid open the glass doors and stepped out on to the wooden decking. She moved over to the railing and leant against it, letting her tired eyes feast on the serene beauty before her. The clean white sand, the clear blue-green water... The Pacific Ocean at its best!

Uncle Guy had been so right. A couple of weeks up here at his beach-house, all alone, was exactly what she needed before getting back to the grindstone of her last year at university.

She glanced idly down to the other end of the secluded cove, to the only other house for miles, calm in the knowledge that its owner would not be in occupancy.

'Oh, no,' she groaned. A light was coming from one of the windows of the cliff-hugging dwelling. And yes... there was a man standing at the water's edge.

Her stomach twisted. Uncle Guy had said that Max had gone overseas. She wouldn't have come otherwise.

April strained her eyes in a vain attempt to recognise the man, but he was too far away.

The distant figure turned and began strolling towards her end of the beach. April shaded her eyes from the rays of the setting sun and peered hard.

His hair colour was similar to Max's. Fairish. And he looked just as tall.

Her agitation grew. If it *was* Max she would turn right round and drive back to Sydney.

The man drew nearer. Any moment now she would be able to see who...

'Oh, my *God*!'

April's mouth remained open after her startled exclamation. Any relief she might have felt at finding out it wasn't Max was forgotten as she stared at the approaching stranger. Her heart began to pound, her eyes almost popping out of her head.

For the man was *naked*. Starkers! Wearing nothing but a tan and a pair of wrap-around sunglasses.

Her heartbeat quickened appreciably as her startled gaze skated over his undeniably impressive form. He drew nearer. And nearer. He seemed to be heading right for her uncle's place!

Good grief! Her mother had warned her when she went to live with Uncle Guy in Sydney not to talk to strangers. She imagined *naked* strangers would rate decidedly stronger measures!

Her retreat from the sun-deck was hardly graceful. She lurched backwards, stumbling through the open sliding doorway and falling on to the nearby divan.

Had he realised she had seen him? came the disturbing thought. It was hard to imagine that he hadn't noted her arrival, since she'd had to park the car at the top of the cliff and lug her suitcase down the steep path to the beach-house.

Her face flamed with the possibility that his decision to walk along the beach in the buff was some sort of male ego-trip. True, he was male perfection personified, but surely he wasn't going to come along and introduce himself like *that*!

April's fluster turned to panic. Maybe he was a weirdo, a rapist even. She quickly closed and locked the sliding door then returned to huddle on the divan.

Finally, a type of morbid curiosity drove her to lever herself up on to her knees and peep through the curtained window.

Relief made her head spin for a moment. Her unwanted visitor had stopped, and was now facing out to sea, watching the horizon. Clearly he was unaware of her presence, his whole attitude preoccupied.

She let out a long-held breath but noted with some annoyance that her hands were still trembling, her pulse still racing. Perhaps it was not right to watch him but April could not seem to tear her eyes away, nor stop the erratic thumping of her heart.

Yet there was nothing lewd or obscene about his naked body. In that setting, with the fading light dispatching softly caressing lights, his nudity seemed very natural.

And he *was* beautiful.

Wide bronzed shoulders tapered down to a trim waist and slim hips, well-muscled legs supporting the taut buttocks. It was impossible to see details of his face from that distance but he had a well-shaped head and an attractive thatch of tawny-coloured hair.

April was still staring in spellbound fascination when she saw his shoulders stiffen, his fists suddenly clench at his side. He reminded her of a wild animal, with an animal's tense, unpredictable type of stillness. Any moment he might spring.

So when the stranger's head unexpectedly jerked around to glare up at the house, shock made April bob down. Had he seen her at the window? she flustered. Or was it some sixth sense that made him feel he was being observed?

That must be it, she reasoned more calmly, realising that she couldn't possibly be seen behind the drawn curtains. Rather gingerly she took another peek, comforted to find the man was no longer looking in her direction. In fact he was already turning to walk back the way he had come.

With an ever-increasing compulsion her eyes followed him till he disappeared up the cliff steps into Max's beach-house.

April immediately reached for the phone and dialled, willing that her uncle was at home. He answered on the second ring.

'Guy Richards here.'

'Uncle Guy? It's April. I've arrived safely.'

'And broken the record getting there I would say,' he teased. 'I hope my little Datsun comes back in one piece.'

April laughed. Her uncle was such a dear, insisting on her taking his car, vowing that he rarely used the Datsun anyway, much preferring taxis around the unparkable-in city.

'Had a swim yet?' he asked.

'Well, actually, Uncle, no... You see...'

'Don't tell me you forgot your cossie! Not that you need one up there. No one's to see you if you go skinny-dipping.'

'Well, that's it, you see. There is.'

'There is what?'

'There is someone to see. In fact...' She bit her tongue, stopping short of telling her uncle about her neighbour's state of undress. For a bachelor who'd had as many lady friends as April had fingers and toes, he took his responsibility of looking after his niece with surprising seriousness.

'It seems Max has lent his holiday house to someone,' she informed.

'Really? Who?'

'I don't know, do you?'

'I can't think... Let's see...'

April could hear orchestral music in the background, a sure sign that her uncle was working on one of his articles. She waited patiently.

'Oh, yes.' His sigh carried self-exasperation. 'Max did mention something about letting Hugh Davies use the place while he was away. Sorry, love, I forgot.'

'It's all right,' April hastened to assure him. 'It just gave me a bit of a fright, that's all, seeing a strange man on the beach. By the way, am I supposed to know this Hugh Davies? You sounded as if I should but I could swear I didn't recognise the man.'

And I certainly wouldn't have forgotten this individual, she thought drily.

'Dear heavens, April, surely you remember Hugh? I took you to his exhibition at Max's gallery last year.'

'The sculptor?'

'That's right. You met him, didn't you?'

'I didn't actually speak to him.' April vaguely recalled glancing across a very crowded room at an indifferently dressed man with long brownish hair, a pale complexion and a totally introverted expression. He'd been there, yet not there, clearly uninterested in the gushings of the guests.

'I even bought one of his pieces,' her uncle was saying. 'The one I put on the hall table.'

'Oh, yes... that's right.' It was a curious piece. Quite small, made of grey streaked marble, and shaped into a type of bowl with a curved handle. Around the handle were two rings that could be moved and positioned as one liked, but could not be removed. They'd obviously been carved from the original block of stone, along with the main section, for there were no joins anywhere.

'Well, he must have a friend with him,' April decided aloud. 'The man I saw on the beach is definitely not Hugh Davies.'

'Not everyone vants to be alone,' came her uncle's Greta Garbo impression.

'You would if you'd just spent the entire month of January minding two fourteen-year-old monster brothers twenty-four hours a day.'

Actually, April had been only too glad to do it for her parents. They'd had a difficult year, with her father suffering a nasty bout of shingles and then her mother having a cancer scare. Luckily, the lump in her breast had turned out to be benign, but by Christmas her father had insisted on taking her mother for that overseas holiday they'd always dreamt about and never managed. Of course April's mother had started worrying about leaving the boys, till April had stepped in, promising she would not let the rascals out of her sight.

She hadn't. But it had proved much more wearing than she'd imagined. Worth it, though, when she saw her parents so happy and relaxed on their return.

'You are a noble creature, April Jamieson,' her uncle was saying. 'Almost as noble as a certain long-suffering uncle I know. Now get off this phone before I charge you extra board to cover the bill!'

April grinned, and did as she was told. The truth was that her uncle refused to take any board from her at all. Her parents were not wealthy, and the government student subsidy barely covered the cost of her books, fares, lunches and clothes. But she did repay him by doing most of the cooking and housework.

No sooner had she hung up than her smile faded, to be replaced by a thoughtful look. So the man on the beach was a friend of Hugh Davies, eh? An arty type, no doubt, who probably thought nudity was the way to commune with nature.

April gave herself a mental shake, but she couldn't seem to get the memory of the naked stranger out of her mind. Not that she totally blamed herself. It would have been an odd female who could so easily dismiss such a sight.

Shrugging lightly, she swung away from the phone table and strode across to the small box-freezer, pulling out a steak for her dinner while telling herself quite firmly that she was silly to let her reaction to the man bother her. This wasn't the first male she had found physically attractive in her life. Neither would he be the last.

It was hard to dismiss, though, the fact that he was virtually staying on her doorstep. His presence could prove distracting, and she had come here to have a restful holiday, to use the peace and quiet to refresh her weary spirits for the tough year ahead. She was determined to get the very best pass she could in her final exams, repaying the faith her Uncle Guy had shown in her.

Knowing her ambition to be an economic journalist, he had, after she'd completed the first year of her economics degree with distinctions, approached connections of his at the *Herald*, and they had agreed to take her on when she finished. But then last year...

April squeezed her eyes tightly shut, the memory of what had happened still having the power to upset her. It wasn't that she was still infatuated with Max. She despised the man now. But nothing could wipe out the dismay at her own behaviour, which, while excusable considering her age and Max's undeniable attractions, had still been incredibly naïve. Fancy thinking a thirty-five-year-old playboy would really care about her, particularly a man like Max who was a well-known connoisseur of young women. April knew she had acted like a silly little fool, both during her stay up here last summer—and afterwards...

She shuddered, recalling only too well that she had almost destroyed her future in one fell swoop. How she'd passed her exams last year she would never know. Her uncle had not said anything when she'd only scraped passes in all her subjects, but she had known he was disappointed. And so was her family.

Just thinking about where her adolescent emotions had led her hardened April's heart against her disturbingly attractive neighbour. No way was she going to let her youthful hormones play havoc with her this year. No *way*!

She marched into the main bedroom and heaved her suitcase on to the king-sized water-bed, re-affirming her resolve that men were not on her agenda this year!

She snapped back the zipper and began lifting her clothes out on to the bed. But try as she might thoughts about the man on the beach kept infiltrating. Who was he? How old was he? What did he do for a living? Was he...?

April sighed. The stranger's undeniable appeal seemed to be irrevocably planted in her brain.

And her body...

With a rueful shake of her head she tried defusing her interest with sheer logic. Didn't she realise that a male as attractive as that would have some female in tow? If not a wife, then a girlfriend. Maybe hordes of them! And even if by some miracle he was single and unattached, who was to say that he would find her just as attractive?

Why, he probably likes tall, willowy blondes, she decided, not petite brunettes!

Not that colouring and size were the only factors that turned some men off, she acknowledged with feeling as Max's cruel words of a year ago catapulted into her mind.

'You must be jesting, April. A *virgin*... At *nineteen*?' He had managed to look disbelieving and bored at one and the same time. 'Look, darling, initiations were never my scene. I think you'd better run along, but by all means come back after the big event, then I'll be only too willing.'

April cringed as she remembered Max's taunts. She cringed even more as she thought again of her immature reaction at the time.

She had gone back to university, defiantly determined to become the sort of sophisticated woman Max would be interested in. She had even gone on the Pill. Another of his caustic suggestions.

Thank the lord that despite engaging in constant partying and socialising, and having countless offers from some of the best-looking guys on the campus, when it came down to the nitty gritty she had kept running a mile.

It had finally dawned on her that she was acting like a little fool, and that Max was a thirty-five-year-old creep!

April had decided then and there that her first sexual experience was going to be something special, with someone special. She wanted it to be part of a true romance, a love-affair where she was carried away with passion.

Passion.

April turned her head to stare at the window. The thought insinuated into her mind that with the man on the beach she could feel passion...

Her frown was swift and dark. This was getting ridiculous, she thought irritably.

With quick angry movements she began unpacking her suitcase. When she pulled out her skimpy red bikini she gave the sexy garment an honest appraisal then stuffed it back in the suitcase, drawing out instead a sensible black *maillot*. Now that was more like it!

When she finished unpacking, April hurried around, opening windows, turning on lights and generally making a lot of noise. She turned the radio up full blast. One thing was for sure. She was going to make certain her neighbour, or neighbours, were well acquainted with her arrival, and would hopefully put some clothes on in future.

Night came slowly, February still being cursed with daylight saving. Tired from the long drive, April retired early, though she found it hard to get used to her uncle's water-bed. On other visits she had slept on the convertible divan. But gradually weariness took hold of her body, the sensations of disturbing movement slowly changing to soothing, lulling rocking. As April slipped over that edge from semi-consciousness to oblivion, one final thought infiltrated.

His eyes would be blue...

CHAPTER TWO

When April awoke the next morning, she was disorientated for a few seconds, wondering why she was in a strange bed. Realisation of where she was and what had happened the previous afternoon brought a nervous flutter. Would she run into her interesting neighbour today? And, perhaps more to the point, would he have some clothes on?

She was to have her answers the second she stepped outside for her morning jog.

Yes. To both questions.

He was lying low in the sand, not far from where the stone steps led up the cliff to Max's beachhouse. April might have missed him except for a slash of royal blue in the middle of his tanned length.

At least I succeeded in getting him to wear a swimming-costume, she thought, trying hard to control an irritating surge of adrenalin.

Damn it all! This was not what she had in mind for her holiday. She'd been looking forward to quiet swims, relaxing sunbathing, hours of reading and music, all by herself. It was annoying to have to worry about sharing the small beach, particularly with this macho male who kept bombarding her thoughts and disturbing her equilibrium.

She pulled her bright pink T-shirt well down over her black costume and set off across the sand, re-

affirming her resolve not to encourage any un-
toward developments. All she had to do was make
some innocuous greeting when he saw her and keep
on running. Nothing hard about that.

The morning breeze was unexpectedly sharp,
causing goose-bumps to spring up on her arms.
Shivering, she hurried down to the firmer sand at
the water's edge and broke into a light jog. As she
drew closer to his outstretched form her heart began
to pound in unison with her feet. Any minute now
he would become aware of her.

But he didn't!

Or didn't seem to.

He just lay there, staring upwards, the opaque
sunglasses firmly in place. If he noticed her going
by he certainly gave no indication of it. Neither did
he acknowledge her presence when she turned and
went by again.

It was an oddly peeved April who returned to her
uncle's beach-house a few minutes later.

'Well!' she exclaimed, dropping down on the
divan. 'How do you like that? Not even so much
as a twitch. No recognition whatsoever.'

It took all of an hour and three cups of coffee
for April to get over the feeling she had been well
and truly snubbed.

But another explanation of events finally dawned
on her. He was asleep! That was it. Out like a light.
She could imagine how warm and comfortable it
was nestled low in the sand, out of the wind.

With the third, nearly empty mug cradled in her
hands April found herself standing at the window,
watching him again. Somehow her decision not to

let this man's presence intrude into her life had been forgotten.

Shortly he got up, stretched, then put himself through the most rigorous workout of exercises April had ever seen. It was awe-inspiring. So many push-ups! Then he strolled down to swim lazily in the almost waveless water.

Watching him exercise had made her feel hot and sticky but April was loath to join her neighbour in the water. Yet the longer she stayed in the house pretending to herself she was not watching him, the more unsettled she became.

It was all so silly, the way she was building him into a mental fantasy. OK, so he didn't appear to have a female—wife or girlfriend—with him. But so what? Up close he was probably not so good-looking. He was also probably as thick as a brick. Unintelligent men always bored April to tears, no matter how handsome they were.

Before she could think better of it, April stripped off her T-shirt and picked up a towel, fully intending to go for a swim, and, if the situation arose, to casually introduce herself. But by the time she covered the distance between her uncle's beach-house and the water, the man had left the water and was towelling himself down. And once again he seemed to be deliberately ignoring her, for he didn't look up or give any indication of her approach.

Exasperation made her decide to go right up to him and say something. Otherwise she would be nervy and self-conscious every time she came down for a swim. Even now, as she walked towards him, her stomach was full of butterflies.

She was almost on top of him when suddenly his head jerked upwards to face her. The cold, hard glare from behind those opaque shields would have unnerved the most confident female.

April froze. Then bristled. How she detested those sunglasses! The type that allowed the wearer to see out but no one to see in, the type so often worn by male movie stars.

But there again, she realised sinkingly, this fellow *was* movie star material. While not classically handsome, he was still very attractively male with a strong nose, a wide firm mouth and aggressive chin. Even with his hair wet and slicked back, he looked good.

The strain of his icy stare finally got the better of her. 'Hello, there,' she chirped. 'Been in for a swim, I see. Is the water cold?'

'Yes. Quite cold.' His voice would have been rich and deep if he hadn't clipped his words short in barely held irritation.

April swallowed and went on bravely. 'My name's April Jamieson,' she said, though making no attempt to hold out her hand. 'I'm staying at the other beach-house.'

'So I gathered,' he said without even looking up. He just kept on towelling his legs dry. 'One would have had to have been deaf to have missed your arrival last night.'

Such unexpected sarcasm took April aback for a second, but perhaps she *had* overdone things last night. Still, it was a comfort to know he didn't realise she had arrived in time to see his nude stroll. 'Yes, it took me all day to drive up from Sydney,' she rattled on brightly. 'This is my uncle's place. I'm living with him, you see, while I'm——'

'Really, Miss Jamieson, I——'

'Oh, do call me April,' she cut in carelessly.

'April,' he ground out through clenched teeth. 'Look, if you don't mind I'd rather not hear about your living arrangements. All I want is to be left alone.'

There was a limit to April's good-natured tolerance, a line over which she would not allow others to cross. This excuse for a person had just put his big male foot over it. Her chin lifted defiantly, her nostrils flaring. 'Suits me,' she returned coldly. 'Who would want to talk to someone as rude as you anyway?' And with that she whirled round and began to stride away, her angry feet stamping into the sand.

'Miss Jamieson...April! Stop!' he shouted after her.

She kept on going.

'Please?' he added.

She ground to a reluctant halt. 'What?' she demanded, her face still flaming with fury and self-reproach. She should have known better than to even speak to such an individual. There was not one overly good-looking male of her acquaintance who wasn't insufferably arrogant and opinionated.

He lifted his shoulders in a careless shrug. The morning rays glinted on his now drying, sun-streaked hair. 'What can I say? That *was* unforgivably rude of me.' His smile was wry, and damnably attractive. 'Would you accept an apology, humbly delivered?'

Humbly delivered, my eye, she thought, and remained mutinously silent.

'Come back and sit down,' his voice beckoned with that seductive quality she just knew it could possess.

Despite still feeling annoyed, she began to walk slowly back. He settled down where he was and patted the spot beside him. 'Come on,' he said, glancing up at her. 'Sit down. The sand's pleasantly warm.'

'Oh . . . All right.'

This friendly about-face dissolved the last of April's anger. Perhaps this chap was the exception to the rule. She did as he asked, sinking down into the sand with a winning smile on her previously scowling face.

Nevertheless, it didn't take her long to realise that she was wasting her smiles. The man beside her didn't respond in kind or give her a second look. He hunched forward, knees raised, arms wrapped around shins, and stared blankly out to sea. She found his indifference quite hurtful.

'I haven't been well,' he said simply, as though that excused everything.

April's eyes flicked over the rippling muscles, the healthy glowing skin. 'You certainly look well,' she voiced without thinking. Then flushed.

He didn't seem to notice. 'Really?' The word had the oddest inflexion. It was vaguely sceptical.

There was a moment's awkward silence.

'Max told me that Guy Richards owns the other beach-house,' he finally said, still not looking at her. 'I've met him, I recall. He's an art critic.'

'Uncle Guy does do some art reviews,' she explained, just managing to hide her uncustomary pique, 'but I wouldn't call him an art critic. He's a freelance journalist and writes up all sorts of things, from sport to cooking competitions. He did do an article on your friend though.'

He turned his head towards her, a frown forming wrinkles on his high, wide forehead. 'My what?'

'Your friend,' she repeated. 'Hugh Davies...'

The frown deepened. April longed for him to take off the glasses so she could see what he was thinking.

'But.I...' He hesitated, cocking his head to one side in obvious puzzlement. 'What makes you say that?'

She blinked her surprise. 'Well, I thought... Uncle Guy said... I mean... You *are* a friend of Hugh Davies, aren't you?'

Suddenly the frown dissolved and he laughed. The sound had a disturbingly mocking edge. 'Sometimes.'

'Isn't he staying here, then?' she persisted, feeling totally confused now.

'Oh, yes,' he agreed. 'Hugh and I go everywhere together. We're old, old friends.'

'I see,' she murmured, not seeing at all. 'Are you both sculptors?'

'Yes and no.'

She stared at him. 'What does that mean?'

He smiled. Or at least his mouth did. April felt certain that, even if she could see his eyes, they would not be joining in. 'Never mind. Yes, I'm a sculptor too. Or, at least, I might be, some day soon...' His lips compressed into an impatient line and finally the penny dropped for April. He was obviously a protégé of Hugh Davies, still learning his craft, still tortured with doubts about his own ability. Her uncle had many aspiring artist friends and they were all like that. Torn, intense, full of insecurities. Till success came. Then they were simply arrogant.

A thought struck. At least Hugh Davies had not seemed arrogant. April slid a surreptitious look at her companion. It was unlikely that *this* individual would be similarly unaffected, she decided, if he ever hit the big scene. She could imagine it now. Women dripping all over him, flattering him, propositioning him...

His face half turned towards her and her gaze drifted from his stubborn-looking mouth to the sunglases... Darn, but she wished he'd take those infernal things off! Even up close they were complete blinds.

'Tell me, April, what do you think of Hugh's work?' he enquired. 'Or haven't you seen any of it?'

'I went to one of his exhibitions once,' she confessed. 'He's obviously very good, and I love that streaky marble he uses, but I have to admit I found him a trifle off-putting.'

'You've *met* Hugh?' The question carried so much astonishment that April felt peeved. Was it so unlikely that a mere mortal had met such a rising star?

'Not actually,' she tossed off. 'But he was there, drifting reluctantly from group to group and looking as if he wished everyone would disappear.'

His laughter was dry. 'That sounds familiar. Antisocial through and through. One thing intrigues me, though. When we met just now you automatically assumed I wasn't Hugh. Yet I've been told we could be mistaken for one another.'

It was April's turn to laugh. 'How ridiculous! You don't look anything alike. Why he's...he's... Well, he's... And you're...'

April floundered. She was not going to boost this man's ego by saying he was God's gift to women whereas Hugh Davies was... well... She frowned, realising that she couldn't really recall what Hugh Davies looked like in any detail. All her attention had been focused on Max that night. Nevertheless...

'I can assure you that no one would mistake you for your friend,' she went on with conviction. 'For one thing you're bigger. And your hair's a different colour. Fairer.'

'Oh?' His eyebrows lifted up over the rim of the sunglasses and he ran an absent hand through his hair. It was fully dry now, the blond streaks lightening it to its attractive tawny colour.

'What *is* your name, by the way?' April asked.

'My name? Oh—er—Harold... Harold Chambers.' His lips curved slowly back into an odd smile. 'But you can call me Harry.'

Harry? He was called *Harry*? It just showed you, April thought ruefully, that appearances could be deceiving. There she was thinking he'd be called something forceful like Blake or Leon. Even Hugh was better than Harry!

'OK,' she said with a sigh. What did it matter what he was named or what she called him? She followed her companion's idea and wrapped her arms around bent knees. It was a surprisingly comfortable position. And the sun was warming up, beating down on her head and shoulders with a drugging heat.

'So you quite liked Hugh's work, did you?' he persisted.

'His smaller pieces were particularly nice,' she said.

'*Nice*? What does nice mean, for God's sake?' he said so sharply that April's mouth dropped open. Her surprise quickly became resentment. Who did he think he was, talking to her like that?

'It means *nice*!' she retorted. 'Like in pleasing to the eye. I happen to like the word nice. It's better than those pseudo-intellectual adjectives art people come up with. When I say his smaller pieces are nice that's meant as a positive, complimentary statement.'

'Hmm.' Harry looked as thoughtful as he could with sunglasses on. He stroked his chin and turned to look at her. 'Why the smaller pieces especially?'

She shrugged. 'I don't know. I guess it's a pleasant change to find a sculptor who creates art that can be picked up and admired, and can be placed in the ordinary home. Modern sculpture is usually so unwieldy.'

'Unwieldy,' he repeated slowly.

'Yes. You know, only fit for massive concrete courtyards and such. What good are they to a small collector who lives in a two-room flat? Look, I know you're a sculptor too, but can I be frank?' She was rather enjoying herself, giving vent to her plebeian ideas. She firmly pushed aside the notion that she might be acting like a woman scorned.

His mouth twitched in one corner. 'I get the impression you always would be.'

She gave an irritable sigh. 'I just wish people would be more honest about art and stop following the so-called experts' opinions like sheep. I don't mean to offend you——' Oh, yes, you do, April Jamieson, her conscience inserted '—but I find most sculpture a bit of a con. Pieces of metal thrown together then given some airy-fairy title like "Survival". People come along and rave over it and they use words like dimension and perspective, but no ordinary person has a clue what they're talking about.'

She waited for him to come back at her but he didn't. He just sat there, silently nodding. It rather took all the wind out of April's sails.

'From what I heard,' he said slowly, 'some of the international critics didn't overly like those smaller pieces you mentioned.'

'See what I mean? What would they know? If you ask me, Hugh Davies would do well to stick to making smaller pieces. Uncle Guy bought one and he's got excellent taste.'

'Which one?'

'The oddly shaped bowl with the curved handle and the two rings. Fascinating, I find it.'

'Fascinating?'

'Yes. Occasionally when I go past it I slip the rings into another position and it makes it look entirely different.'

'You mean it gains a different perspective,' he teased.

April couldn't keep up her attack. She burst out laughing and so did he. But she stopped abruptly when she found herself staring at his mouth and wondering what it would be like to be kissed by it. It perturbed her how much she wanted this man to fancy her, particularly since it was clear that he did not.

'Hugh!'

They both spun round on their bottoms at the sound of the loud shout. A giant of a man was standing on Max's concrete balcony. He was totally bald and reminded April of one of the henchmen from a James Bond movie.

'Breakfast's ready,' the voice grated out. 'Come on, Hugh. Hurry up or the steak'll be cold.'

'Coming.'

April stared as the man next to her stood up. 'But . . . but . . .' she squeaked. 'Is that man calling to *you*?'

He looked back down at her and the sudden silence was electric. 'Afraid so,' he said at last. 'Well, April? I'm waiting for you to tear strips off me. Don't disappoint me.'

April gaped up at him. The realisation that this actually was Hugh Davies looking down at her, Hugh Davies she'd been talking to, Hugh Davies who had drawn her into making such outrageous statements, made her blush furiously. She supposed someone must have pointed out the wrong man to her at the exhibition.

'You should have told me,' she blurted out. 'Oh, God, I've never felt so embarrassed in all my life!'

'Embarrassed? *You*?' His laughter was mocking. 'There's not an embarrassed bone in your body, April Jamieson! Besides, you've only got yourself to blame. You kept insisting that there was no way I could be mistaken for Hugh Davies.' He chuckled. 'Come on.' He held out a conciliatory hand to help her up.

April groaned, put her hand into his solid palm and levered herself up on to her feet. 'But you said your name was Harry,' she accused.

'A little white lie. That's Harry.' Hugh nodded towards the man who'd called out.

She could feel the heat of his hand seeping into her own. Her blood began to race, her skin to tingle. 'That wasn't nice,' she muttered.

His smile was oddly cynical. 'I don't claim to be nice. Anyway, at least I got an honest criticism. You've no idea how hard that is to come by.'

'For Pete's sake, Hugh,' came the impatient bark from the beach-house. 'Shake a leg, will you?'

'Fancy some breakfast?' he asked, and dropped her hand. April felt instantly chilled.

She glanced up at the big man on the balcony. His face was grim, his whole bearing formidable.

'Er—no, I don't think so. Your friend looks...um...'

'Don't worry about Harry. He's not too keen on women but his bark is worse than his bite.'

'Another time maybe,' she murmured.

'Fair enough. Well, it's been interesting talking to you, April. Most...enlightening.'

Enlightening.

April thought about that word as she wandered back along the beach. She supposed that by enlightening he meant he'd gleaned a frank opinion of his sculpture, even if it was inspired more by pique than the need to be honest. She wished she felt similarly enlightened about why she kept being attracted to the wrong men. The only consolation was that Hugh was quite a bit younger than Max. Late twenties, she guessed. How ironic, though, that with Max she hadn't been able to get him to keep his hands and eyes off her body. Yet with Hugh she could hardly get him to look at her at all!

She was back at the beach-house before the memory hit her. And it quite took her breath away.

It had been Max who had pointed out the sculptor to her at the exhibition. And Max would not have been mistaken.

The situation was so puzzling, so perplexing that she just had to telephone her uncle again.

'So soon, April?' Guy joked.

'I've just run into Hugh Davies,' she said straight away.

'Yes?'

'Could you tell me what he looks like?'

There was a moment's silence before he came back on the line, sounding worried. 'Is this some sort of joke, April?'

'No, of course not,' she said hurriedly. 'It's just that he doesn't look the same. He's...different from the man I saw at the exhibition. Do me a favour and describe him for me.'

'Really, April!'

'Please...'

He sighed. 'OK. Reasonably tall, very lean, brownish hair, attractive but anaemic-looking. Interesting eyes. Deep-set, bluish grey. Won't make the world's ten best dressed this year,' he finished with a laugh.

'That's not him,' she said bluntly.

'Not him? What do you mean, not him? Of course it's him, I've met him more than once.'

'I mean that's not the man on the beach, claiming he's Hugh Davies.' April shivered. Fear rippled down her spine.

'April, are you sure?'

'Yes...' Her voice was barely a whisper.

'Look, April, hang up and lock the door. God knows what's going on but I'll ring Max's gallery and speak to his assistant. Then I'll ring you back. If you're still worried then you'd better come home, OK?'

April paced the floor, waiting breathlessly for him to call back. She wanted to believe that the man on the beach had been a genuine individual, but strange things happened in this world. There were all sorts of confidence tricksters in operation, most of them handsome men preying on vulnerable women. She prayed that was not the case this time.

When the phone rang she snatched up the receiver. 'Uncle Guy?'

'Breathe easy, love. It is Hugh Davies. Seems he was in a car accident soon after the exhibition. No life-threatening injuries but he does look different, I gather. His jaw was broken and had to be re-wired, for one thing. And it seems he's employed some sort of trainer chap to get him fit and healthy for more surgery. Apparently he's built his body up considerably, which makes him look bigger and taller. Would that explain the changes?'

April struggled to take in the surprising news. Accident, hospital, surgery... But it did all fit, she supposed, particularly the bit about the trainer. That had to be the bruiser on the balcony.

'Well, yes, I guess so...' Her mind flew to his hair colour till she remembered that weeks in the sun could have bleached it at the same time as it had turned his previously pale skin into bronze. And yet...

'Oh, and Max's secretary says he's become a pain to deal with, not the quiet self-contained Hugh of old. But I can understand that. Hell, it can't be easy having to put your creative urges on hold. It's all very well for doctors to say that something is only temporary. If it were me I'd be damn worried, I can tell you.'

'What do you mean?' April asked. 'Is there something wrong with his hands?'

'Didn't I say? No, it's not his hands. It's his eyes. They were damaged in the accident. He's temporarily blind.'

CHAPTER THREE

APRIL'S mouth dropped open. She blinked a few times. 'Blind?' she repeated, shock rippling through her. 'But he can't be! I mean, he…he…' Her voice trailed away as the truth of her uncle's news sank in. It explained so much. The impenetrable glasses; his failing to notice her jog along the beach; his avoidance of looking at her; that confusing 'yes and no' comment about being a sculptor.

'Oh, Uncle Guy, how awful for him,' she groaned. To be suddenly locked in a world of dark helplessness would be dreadful at any time. For a man like Hugh it would be utter torture.

'Yes. Very frustrating, I would imagine. But at least he should recover. Eventually.'

Eventually… What a ghastly word for Hugh to come to terms with! Even in the short while she had known him April sensed that patience was not one of his virtues. As for living without his sculpting… She recalled how in her uncle's article Hugh had come over as a loner, a man who lived and breathed his art, claiming he was lost when not working.

'I have to go, April. There's someone at the door. Have a nice time, and give my best wishes to Hugh, will you? I gather he's to have an operation in the not too distant future.'

'All right. Will do.'

An hour later, April was seated at the small kitchen counter, her toast going cold in front of her, her mind still preoccupied with the startling news.

Blind.

Poor Hugh. What he must have gone through—was *still* going through. Her heart turned over as sympathy welled up again inside her. Thank God it wasn't going to be permanent. At least... A momentary doubt sliced through her, making her feel almost ill. Surely the doctors wouldn't give him false hope, would they?

April gave herself a mental shake. She refused to think like that, refused to be pessimistic. Hugh was going to get his sight back. He *was*! The alternative didn't bear thinking about.

But a frown came to her face as she wondered why he hadn't told her about his blindness, why he... Oh, of course, she thought, and nodded resignedly. He wouldn't want pity. Not a man like him.

Yes, April felt very sorry for Hugh. Very sorry indeed. And she felt ashamed of herself for the way she'd been trying to attract his attention. Her romantic fantasies seemed juvenile and selfish in the light of the great personal trial Hugh was facing. The last thing he needed was some female throwing herself at his head. A friend he might welcome. Nothing more.

April sighed. But then shrugged. Be honest, she lectured herself. Isn't that all *you* want at this time in your life? Aren't you just a little relieved that something has come along to put a halt to those rapidly escalating feelings of yours?

'Too right!' she pronounced aloud, and stood up to make herself some fresh toast.

The rest of the day promised to be hot, a perfect day for swimming. And the cove was made for swimming. The reef that stretched across between the rocky headlands broke the waves and the water inside held only the barest of swells. April had always preferred it to the open surf which she found tiresome and inevitably crowded. No one came to this place.

After breakfast April went straight from the house into the water, not intending at that point to venture down Hugh's end of the beach. She could appreciate that most of the time he probably did want privacy, but she believed that being alone all the time was not healthy for the mind. Perhaps she would go along and talk to him later. After his initial aloofness he had seemed to appreciate her company.

The water was cold at first, but she soon got used to it. And when she tired of stroking up and down she turned over and lay on her back. Closing her eyes, she stretched out her arms and floated, the warm rays beating down on her cooled body. It was infinitely relaxing and she must have stayed that way for longer than she realised, for when she lifted her head it was a shock to find that she had drifted way down the other end.

'Hey, April!' came a shout across the water. 'Harry said you should watch that rip. You might get carried on to the rocks.'

It was Hugh, standing at the water's edge, his hands cupped around his mouth. April waved and shouted that she was OK, but when she began to tread water she suddenly felt the dangerous pull around her ankles.

Swallowing her panic, she started heading towards the beach, all the time fighting against the treacherous undertow. It was slow going and by the time she made dry land she was exhausted. She dragged herself up on to the sand, her lungs bursting, her breath gasping.

'April?' Hugh was instantly there, reaching down and pulling her bedraggled wet form up against his warm but equally scantily clad body. 'Are you all right? April? Say something!'

'I'm fine,' she expelled shakily, her skin breaking into goose-bumps as he rubbed her arms up and down.

'You're terribly cold.'

Her teeth began to chatter. But there was nothing cold about the sensations charging through her at Hugh's touch. And she had thought sympathy for his condition would dampen the sexual attraction she felt for him! Evidence to the contrary made her heart turn over with dismay.

'You silly girl,' he reproached. 'Look, my towel's over here.' He guided her across the sand, unerringly making for the brightly coloured towel lying in the sand. He picked it up and wrapped it around her shoulders, then flicked the wet strands of hair out of her eyes and smoothed them behind her ears. All she could do was stare up at him, her mouth open.

'But I thought you were blind?' she blurted out.

He stiffened, his jaw clenching tight, the muscles twitching along the base of his cheeks. 'So you've found out about that, have you? Pity. I was rather enjoying your refreshing lack of sympathy.'

'But ... but you saw this towel on the sand just now,' she accused. 'I'm sure you did.'

'In a fashion,' he conceded curtly. 'I can recognise light and dark to a degree, and bright colours. In the sunshine here I can just make out your vague outline. Your very short outline, might I add.'

It was a sore point with her—her height. Her twin brothers had shot up past her at age eleven. And never ceased to tease her about it. For a second she lost any urge to act sympathetically. 'I'm almost five feet four!' she declared.

His mouth pulled back into a wry smile. 'Who do you think you're kidding, sweetheart? I'm a sculptor. I felt you.'

She blushed at the memory of his hands in her hair. 'OK, so I'm only five two and a bit. Just because you're a giant!'

He gave a dry laugh. 'Five eleven—*and three quarters*—is hardly a giant. But I'm glad to see my blindness is not warranting any special treatment. I should have known it wouldn't with you.' He laughed again, and this time the sound had lost its cutting edge. 'You know, April, I think you're good for me. You amuse me. I haven't found much to laugh at lately.'

'Want to hire me as your court jester?' she suggested cheekily.

'Are you expensive?'

'Frightfully.'

'Too bad. I was hoping you'd donate your time for nothing as a charitable gesture. I'll have to count my pennies now that I can't...' The ready smile faded, a black cloud sweeping across his face. 'Good God, what am I doing? Making stupid damned jokes about it when for all I know I might never see again, might never——'

He broke off and slammed heavily down on to the sand, taking up the same position as before, knees bent, arms wrapped around shins. But where then he had seemed reasonably relaxed, now he was a taut bundle of anguish and anger. 'For heaven's sake, go!' he threw up at her. 'I'm not fit company for anyone at the moment.'

April ached to put her arms around him, to hug him and tell him everything would be all right. But she knew he would hate that, would see it as a sign of pity. 'What a grouch you are, Hugh,' she said with feigned intolerance. 'But you don't frighten me. I have two brothers who make your bad temper look like kindergarten playtime.' She plopped down on the sand beside him. 'I have no intention of going till I find out exactly what's wrong with your eyes. I was talking to Uncle Guy on the phone and he told me you'd had some sort of accident, and that an operation can fix you up, but that's all I know.'

'And, being a typical female,' Hugh snarled, 'you want to know all the gruesome details!'

'But of course.' She laughed.

'Tough. I don't like to talk about it.'

'Can't you at least tell me when the operation's scheduled? And where?' she persisted.

'Why do you want to know?' he asked suspiciously.

She shrugged before she remembered he couldn't see the gesture. 'Wouldn't you like visitors?'

'Not particularly.'

'Tough. I think I'll come anyway.'

She could see he was startled. 'Why would you want to do that? We hardly know each other.'

April fell silent. He was right, of course. From his point of view, they were only mild acquaintances of very brief duration. He wasn't to know that already she was being carried along by a tide of feeling for him too strong to deny. Even sitting here next to him was an insidiously pleasurable experience. She could watch him, let her eyes feast upon his lovely male body without the chance of being caught.

'How old are you, anyway?' he asked abruptly. 'Seventeen? Eighteen? Harry said you were young. You sound young.'

People had even mistaken her for sixteen. It was her stupid height, she knew. Thank the lord she had well-developed breasts. 'I'm twenty,' she announced firmly.

'Twenty,' he repeated, shaking his head and sounding as if twenty were still a baby.

'Twenty's not so young.' Her voice was defensive. 'I'll be twenty-one soon.' When he made no comment she said, 'Well? How old are *you*?'

'Old . . . very old.'

'You don't look old.'

'Ah, yes, but there are two kinds of old. The one I'm talking about is in here——' he pointed to his head '—and here.' The finger indicated his heart.

Suddenly he looked so bleak. It moved her unbearably.

'Tell me more about yourself,' he insisted.

She sat back on the sand and sighed. She would rather have talked about him. He still hadn't told her anything about his blindness. Or how old he really was. 'What would you like to know?' she asked.

'Hair colour?'

'Black.'

'Eyes?'

'Blue.'

'Job?'

'University student. Sydney. Last year economics degree.'

He whistled. 'Smart too, eh?'

'What do you mean, smart too?'

'Smart as well as beautiful.'

She was thankful he couldn't see her blush. 'I wouldn't call myself beautiful. Anyway, I thought you could only see a vague outline.'

He laughed. 'Harry has twenty-twenty vision and he says you're a looker.'

Compliments always flustered her. 'I think your Harry's an exaggerater.'

'Could be, April. Could be...' He turned his head slightly towards her. 'He seemed to think you might fancy me?'

'*Fancy* you?' April repeated, her throat constricting.

'Yes. Apparently I qualify as a ladies' man now that I boast a few muscles and a tan. Not to mention my sexy sun-streaked hair,' he added sarcastically. His mouth pulled back into a startlingly bitter grimace. 'Perhaps if I'd had them a few months ago, my darling fiancée wouldn't have been so swift to decamp after the accident.'

April struggled to handle a whole host of emotions. Not the least of which was dismay at finding out Hugh had been recently engaged. Yet hadn't she known there would be a woman somewhere? And while his relationship with this unnamed woman was apparently over, his feelings for her obviously were not.

'Well, April?' he prodded caustically. 'Is Harry right? Do my newly acquired superficial attractions appeal to your adolescent eye?'

April bristled. It was the second time Hugh had sounded condescending about her age. Clearly he thought that any female who'd just left their teenage years couldn't have a sensible thought in their silly, shallow, empty heads. She could see that even if he weren't blind, even if he hadn't still been hurting over a broken engagement, such an attitude ruined any hope of a relationship between them.

This last realisation hurt far more deeply than she had been prepared for, her dented pride and heart making her answer with an offhand flippancy. 'You don't have to worry about me on that score, Hugh.' She laughed far too brightly. 'If there's one thing a university is full of it's good-looking, superficial males. The only thing they think about is sex, sex, sex! It really gets to be a bore after a while. That's why I came up here to this place. To get away from that sort of thing for a while.'

For a few elongated seconds he sat in grim silence.

April was aware that, in her anxiety to sound unaffected and sophisticated, she had overdone it, actually sounding like the immature flip he obviously thought her to be. She regretted it immediately, but the damage had been done. When Hugh next spoke his voice held a sardonic note.

'It sounds as if nothing's changed since my days at university. The favourite game then was musical beds.'

'Not everyone is like that,' she muttered irritably.

'No?' he scoffed. 'I dare say there's the odd exception, but somehow I don't think that would be you, April, my love. You don't sound like the prim and proper type.'

'There's a vast range between being prim and proper and promiscuous,' she pointed out indignantly.

'Is there? I doubt that these days. Still, I guess you can't put an old head on young shoulders.'

'Will you stop talking like Methuselah?' she said sharply. 'Good grief, you couldn't be older than twenty-seven or -eight at the most.'

'Well, well! I must congratulate Harry on his exercise programme. I'm thirty-four.'

She was shocked. That meant he was only one year younger than Max. Good grief, why was she always attracted to older men? 'You don't *look* that old,' she argued futilely.

'Sceptical? Let's see, I left school at eighteen, spent three years at Sydney University, four years in London, one in New York, another two in Italy, then it took me six years of solid work getting ready for that exhibition. How are you at maths?'

'It happens to be my second-best subject,' she retorted, irked that Hugh seemed hell-bent on making their age-gap seem wider than it was! 'Thirty-four, eh?' she tossed off with obvious exasperation. 'Oh, well, only twenty-six more years and you'll be getting the pension. How time flies!'

His laughter was genuine this time. 'I do sound like an old pain, don't I? Can I claim mental stress as the excuse?'

'You can claim it,' she countered, 'but I won't believe it. I think you're just jealous!'

'Jealous?' He appeared genuinely astonished.

'Yes. Jealous! You've lost the art of having fun, but you don't like others to have it.'

'And you think leaping into bed with every Tom, Dick and Harry is fun? Haven't you ever stopped to think of the possible consequences?'

'Oh, don't be such an old fuddy-duddy,' she declared, frustrated at having been so misunderstood.

'A *fuddy-duddy*?'

'Yes. A fuddy-duddy!'

He burst out into rollicking laughter.

'What's the big joke?'

April's head jerked up to see Harry looming over them, his bulk blocking out the sun. A chill invaded her.

'April thinks I'm an old fuddy-duddy.' Hugh chuckled.

Harry gave her a sharp, suspicious look. It sent shivers up her spine. 'Time for your massage,' he growled.

'OK.' Hugh levered himself up on to muscular legs. April stood up too, knowing that she had just been expertly dismissed by the watch-dog.

'Oh, Harry, this is April Jamieson, Guy Richards' niece, the chap who owns the other beach-house.'

'Miss Jamieson.' Harry nodded coldly.

'April, meet Harry Chambers, fellow sculptor, truck driver, nurse, gym instructor, chauffeur, and my all-time best mate.'

April was taken aback, by Hugh's words and the flash of true warmth that leapt into Harry's world-weary eyes, a pleasure that died when he glanced back at her. 'You forgot to mention ex-con.'

Hugh's mouth thinned. 'I didn't forget, Harry, but that's over now.'

'I just like to have it all out in the open,' Harry persisted grimly, 'and then people don't get any nasty surprises later on. Do you want to know what I was in there for, girlie?'

'Harry...' Hugh warned.

'I don't mind knowing,' April said, 'if you don't mind telling me.'

'Grand larceny. Then escaping lawful custody. Served eleven years.'

There was a charged silence.

April kept her eyes steady, feeling suddenly sorry for the big, brusque man with the hard, wary eyes.

'As Hugh said, Harry——' her voice was low and gentle '—you've paid your debt to society...' She held out her hand. 'And any friend of Hugh's is a friend of mine.'

Harry's expression betrayed a grudging surprise but he shook hands. 'Yeah, well, some people don't look at it that way.' He dropped her hand, turned and stalked off. 'Mornin' tea's ready if you want some, girlie,' he growled over his shoulder.

Hugh reached for and found her shoulder. He leant close. 'That was sweet, April. Really sweet. And, believe me, there's no harm in Harry.'

April was no longer thinking about Harry. Her mind was solely concentrated on the touch of Hugh's hand and the warm whisper of his breath on her hair.

'Well, come on...girlie,' Hugh said teasingly, his fingers finally slipping off her shoulder. 'Help me find my suntan lotion. It's here somewhere.'

'Really!' she huffed, relieved that he had moved away. 'I thought you didn't want any special treatment! You've been getting around pretty well all by yourself and now you can't find a little itty-bitty tube.' The light banter hid a still thudding heart.

'That was before I had a female around to wait on me,' he countered. 'Harry makes me fend for myself. Found it? Good. Take my hand and lead me home.'

Leading him home proved quite an experience, particularly when he insisted on more solid support up the steep steps that had been cut into the cliff-face. They were still damp, he said. He slipped an arm around her waist and the side of her breast brushed up against his ribs.

Immediately a rush of heat invaded her body and she was quick to move away from him as soon as they reached the overhead balcony. The intensity of her response to a mere accidental contact was disturbing.

Harry opened the door for them and led Hugh to a stool at the vast breakfast bar. Max's house was a far cry from her uncle's simple wooden dwelling. This was spacious luxury, made of concrete and glass, with stark leather furniture and all mod cons. She had been very impressed last year when Max had invited her inside. Now she saw it for what it was. An expensive, characterless building reflecting the taste of an expensive, characterless man.

'Want a biscuit?' came the blunt question as Harry plonked two mugs of tea on the marble counter.

'No, thanks,' she murmured.

Hugh patted the stool next to his. 'Sit here next to me, April, and tell me some more about yourself. First of all, why are you living with your uncle? Where's your family?'

'They live in Nyngan.'

'Aah, a country girl. You're from the country, aren't you, Harry?'

Harry grunted.

'And this is your last year at university? What are you going to do when you leave?'

She took a sip of the tea. 'I have a job lined up at the *Herald*, as a cadet journalist in the business section.'

'That's a bit serious for a girl like you, isn't it?'

Again, Hugh's patronising tone rubbed April up the wrong way. 'I don't think so,' she said sharply.

'You don't have to get all uppity!'

'Then don't talk down to me. You sound just like my father.'

'Well, I'm nearly old enough to *be* your father, aren't I?' he said predictably. 'So tell us, April, how long will you be staying up here?'

'Two weeks.'

'Exactly the time I've got left before I have to go back to Sydney for my operation. I think we could just about stand her for two weeks, don't you, Harry?'

The big man busying himself in the well-appointed kitchen issued another grunt along with a guarded glance.

April groaned silently. Two weeks. Two long weeks of a sort of masochistic torture, being near this devastatingly sexy man and having him treat her like a naughty adolescent. And, in the background, his henchman, watching her every move.

'I couldn't last two weeks without knowing what happened to your eyes,' she said defiantly.

Hugh chuckled. 'Fair enough. Simply put, I was in a car accident. A collision at an intersection... The windscreen in my car shattered and some splinters of glass apparently penetrated my corneas and spilt the vitreous humour—the transparent jelly inside the eyeballs.'

April was grateful that Hugh couldn't see the appalled look on her face. 'How are they going to fix that?' she asked.

He shrugged. 'Apparently the surgeon puts in a probe and sucks out the damaged jelly. Then down the same tube he trickles this solution of salt and chemicals that compensate for the lost jelly. And presto! Vision instantly restored.'

April felt squeamish just thinking about it. But she knew it was imperative she sounded confident about the success of the operation. 'Isn't it marvellous what they can do these days?' she enthused.

Hugh agreed, then quite unexpectedly took off his sunglasses and rubbed his eyes.

April could not help staring. After what Hugh had said she had been expecting some sort of damage, or scarring. But there was none. Not a scratch. His eyes were deep-set and quite beautiful. Not strictly blue. More a grey with a dark blue rim. But there were some lines around them and he did look older with his glasses off.

'Shouldn't you be leaving those on?' Harry growled. 'You know what the doctor said. Any glare is bad for you.'

Hugh grumbled. But he replaced the glasses.

April slid off the stool she was sitting on. 'I must go,' she said. 'I have plans to read at least four novels while I'm here, not to mention the acquiring of a tan. Thanks for the tea, Harry. And the loan of your towel, Hugh.' She slipped it from her shoulders and placed it on the counter.

'How about reading to me some time, April?' Hugh asked as she turned to leave.

She stood still. 'Oh...of course...if you like. What?'

'Anything you've got would do.'

She thought of the novels she had brought with her. All sexy, pacy best-sellers, not the sort of thing she would want to read aloud to Hugh. 'I'll see what Uncle Guy has in his bookshelves.'

'Fine. When?'

April bit her bottom lip. How could she refuse? 'I could come back some time after three. I don't like being out in the sun in the heat of the day. We could lie on the sand and I'll read to you.'

'Fine! She's a great girl, isn't she, Harry?'

Harry grunted again. It was amazing the range of Harry's grunts. This one was definitely a 'we'll just wait and see' grunt.

'I'll walk back with you,' Hugh offered, getting to his feet.

Fluster claimed April. 'Oh...you don't have to.'

'I know.'

It was clear he was determined to come with her for he was off the stool and out of the door in an instant. April breathed deeply in and out before following. As long as he didn't want to hold her hand again, she thought anxiously.

Hugh began speaking as soon as they were alone walking across the sand. 'I wanted to explain about Harry,' he started. 'I know he seems rude but there are reasons for his behaviour, April, reasons I'd like you to know.'

She couldn't find it in her heart to tell him she would rather not know, that all of a sudden she wanted to run away from Hugh and everything associated with him as fast as her legs could carry her.

But as her gaze slid hungrily over him, and her heart contracted, April knew that she would stay. She would stay and listen, she would stay and read to him, stay and let nature take its cruel, inevitable course.

CHAPTER FOUR

HUGH'S story about Harry proved very touching.

The poor man had had a dreadful childhood. Drunken, abusive parents. Repeated beatings. Interrupted schooling. No love and little chance at life.

At fourteen Harry had run away from home, and, being a big lad, was able to get a job as a builder's labourer. When he was old enough to secure a driver's licence he'd taken to driving interstate trucks. By the time he was twenty-five he had saved enough to buy his own truck. This in itself had been rewarding, but his need to have a family of his own was great.

He'd married a pretty blonde waitress and begun working doubly hard to provide a nice home for his wife and future children. He hadn't minded the long hours he'd had to put in, because he had a goal—a purpose in life.

But his new wife had not been so patient to get the good things in life. She'd introduced her husband to a friend of hers who had ideas on how to get rich quickly. Harry had reluctantly agreed to take part in a robbery at an empty millionaire's mansion, only to be caught. No sooner was he gaoled than his wife had begun divorce proceedings. Desperate, he'd attempted a foolhardy and disastrous escape. This had only increased his sentence and did nothing to stop the inevitable divorce.

Hugh had met Harry ten years later when he was asked by a Salvation Army chaplain to conduct art classes at the prison. Harry had surprised the warders by signing up for the sculpture section. Yet for six months all he had done during class, Hugh told April, was sit down at the back of the room, his arms folded, never saying a word. Then one day he'd come up to Hugh and said, 'I'd like to make something ... in that stuff,' pointing to a piece of marble Hugh had brought in.

It had taken him ages but the simple form of a dog Harry fashioned was the best piece any student of Hugh's had ever produced. Their friendship had blossomed alongside their working relationship and Hugh's promise of a job and a room had helped obtain his early release.

Hugh's car accident had happened a couple of days before Harry got out of prison. He'd come to the hospital straight from the gaol, refusing to leave Hugh's bedside. When Hugh had needed someone to look after him in the long months of recuperation, Harry was the natural choice.

'I pay him of course,' Hugh remarked. 'Though I'm sure he'd do it for nothing.'

April agreed. There was more than a touch of hero-worship in Harry's feelings for Hugh. And she could understand that. Hugh was probably the first person to ever extend him a genuinely kind hand.

'I get the feeling, April,' he went on quietly, 'that, underneath his grunts, he quite likes you.'

April had to laugh at that. 'I don't think so.'

'I beg to differ. When he doesn't like someone he's very vocal. The things he said about Cynthia would make your toes curl.'

April's heart flipped over. 'Cynthia?'

'My fiancée,' Hugh announced, then laughed. It was not a happy sound. 'Wrong word... my *ex*-fiancée.'

They had come to the base of April's steps. When Hugh's hand reached out to hold the railing, she noticed his fist was clenched tightly around the wood, his knuckles white. 'There's no reason why you shouldn't know. Cynthia was driving when the accident occurred, ran into a car at an intersection. She wasn't hurt, except for a few minor bruises. It appears she was at my bedside for a couple of days. I was in a semi-coma so I don't remember. When the doctors told her I was blind she apparently took off the ring and left. I haven't seen her since.'

He let go of the railing and dragged in a deep breath, expanding his already broad chest. 'I think my experience has reinforced Harry's wary attitude to females. I'm sure that given a few days you and he will get along famously. He likes genuine people. And I feel that, despite your youthful impetuosity, you *are* genuine, April Jamieson. Very genuine indeed.'

His right hand found and tipped up her chin. Then he bent to brush her forehead with a light, very platonic kiss. 'Thank you,' he said warmly. 'For bringing me out of my shell, for offering your friendship when I needed it.'

April tried to speak, but couldn't. The lump in her throat was in danger of melting into tears.

'April?' He was frowning down at her. His hand had slipped down her slender neck to rest on her shoulder. 'Is there something wrong?'

She cleared her throat. 'No. Should there be?' Even to her ears she sounded strangled.

His frown remained. 'I guess not.'

'Well, then. I'll see you on the beach around three. OK?'

She turned from him without waiting for an answer and hurried up the steps.

April set off back down the beach shortly before three. Hugh was already sitting on the distant sand and as she approached she could see he was busily applying a sunscreen, first one arm and then the other.

She had the crazy urge to creep up on him and place her hands over his sunglasses while saying 'guess who?', knowing that it would make him laugh. But she didn't dare, fearing it might backfire on her if she touched him. Better to keep her hands right off!

How different the situation had been on this very beach last summer, with Max. He had been all hands, inviting her touch, seducing her with his sophisticated charm, making his intentions very clear.

April had been secretly infatuated with Max for some time—one of the reasons she had accompanied her uncle to exhibitions at his gallery so often. But Max had never noticed her till suddenly he had found himself alone at his beach-house last summer after his latest dolly-bird had left in a huff. April had been staying at the cove with Uncle Guy, whose idea of a holiday was to read and sleep a lot, leaving her to her own devices.

Stupid, naïve April had not realised till long afterwards that it had hardly been honourable of Max to try to seduce the young niece of a friend. But she now appreciated what a lucky escape she'd had from his lecherous clutches.

April's gaze raked over Hugh's beautiful, semi-naked body as she dropped on the sand beside him. Instinct told her that Hugh would not scoff at her virginity as Max had done. It made her unhappy that he thought her loose in that regard.

'Aaah.' A wide smile split his face as he turned towards her. 'Florence Nightingale has returned. Now what splendid tome have you brought to read to me? Harold Robbins? Jackie Collins?' His insinuation was clear. A modern young girl like herself would only read books whose characters reflected *modern* values.

April was hurt. Then defiant. He had no right to judge her so harshly. Nor did he have to keep on mocking and teasing her. If he kept it up, she vowed, he might find a hard-cover edition of *Hollywood Husbands* stuffed between his perfect teeth!

'Sorry,' she said sweetly. 'I've already read all the Harold Robbinses and Jackie Collinses at least three times. I've even marked the juicy bits for repeated perusals.'

'*Touché,*' Hugh muttered. 'All right, what *have* you brought?'

'*High Stakes.*'

'*High Stakes*? Who wrote that?'

'Dick Francis.'

'I haven't read any of his.'

'Neither have I.' He was a favourite author of her uncle, so April figured a man should like the stories.

Hugh squeezed some lotion down his legs and began massaging it in. April looked away. 'Shall I begin?' she suggested briskly.

'In a sec.' Now he was smoothing the cream over his shoulders. 'Got your sunscreen on?'

'Yes.' She always applied hers while naked if she planned wearing a bikini. And there seemed no point in not wearing hers now.

April glanced down at the skimpy red garment with a certain irony. At least Harry couldn't accuse her of dressing to seduce a blind man. But she had quite deliberately not put on any perfume. Somehow she sensed that old eagle-eye would notice the slightest suggestive move she made towards Hugh, which seemed ridiculous considering Hugh's attitude to her.

Yet despite her irritation April was moved by the big man's protective devotion. It bespoke a caring nature beneath his tough, gruff exterior.

'Here!' Hugh extended his hand with the tube resting in his palm. 'Put some on my back, will you? I can't reach properly.'

She stared aghast at the outstretched object for a moment before taking it. 'And what did you do before I came along?' she almost snapped.

'Contortions.'

'Really!' She squeezed a large dob into her palm and slapped it on his back.

'Hey! That's cold,' he protested. 'You could have warmed it up in your palm for a while.'

'Oh, for goodness' sake! What a baby!' She did, however, stop lathering it on quite so ruthlessly, slowing her hand movement to a more reasonable speed.

But with the slowing came the dreaded heightened awareness. His skin was so smooth. And hairless. Like satin. Cool, silky, sensuous satin...

April found herself swallowing hard, trying not to let her fingers linger on his rippling muscles longer than necessary. 'I think I've put too much cream on,' she said in a choked voice. 'It won't sink in.'

'Just keep doing what you're doing,' Hugh sighed. 'It feels marvellous.'

Against all the dictates of her conscience and common sense, she knelt up closer behind him, kneading and caressing, smoothing and soothing till the nerves in her stomach had turned into other more disturbing sensations.

There was no fooling herself. She was becoming sexually aroused. Totally. Thoroughly.

She had known she would if she touched him. Known it from her first sight of his naked beauty. And as she continued to touch him, her throat grew drier. Her body ached. Her fingers trembled.

'You're ripe and ready for a lover, April,' Max had told her after she'd confessed her lack of experience. 'Just be grateful I didn't take advantage of the fact...'

She hadn't been grateful at the time.

'I could take this treatment forever,' Hugh murmured dreamily, stretching back into her hands.

The sudden contact of his shoulder-blades with the hardened points of her breasts shocked April. She pushed him upright. 'That's enough. I came here to read to you, not be your personal slave!'

Oh, God, she groaned silently, let me be your personal slave. Let me...

'Very well, o, callous one.' Hugh rolled over and stretched out on his front. 'Read away. But don't blame me if I go to sleep. I feel so relaxed now.'

He might feel relaxed. *Her* nerves were at screaming-point!

April took her time, finding a comfortable position in the sand before opening the paperback at the first page. Taking a deep breath, she began to read. Typical, she thought grimly, a few pages later. A novel about rejection.

'Surely that's not all?' Hugh joked when she hesitated.

'Oh, shut up, or you can get Harry to read to you.'

'Impossible.'

'Nothing's impossible.'

'Harry can't read.'

April's heart sagged. Once again she felt guilty, once again she had allowed herself to become consumed with her own feelings when the people around her had major, heart-wrenching problems in life to deal with. A broken engagement, blindness, illiteracy.

She felt terrible. 'Oh, Hugh... The poor man...'

'Yes,' he agreed. 'I was going to teach him before this damned accident happened. He wouldn't go to night-school. He said he couldn't bear to be laughed at.'

'Don't tell me any more or I'll cry.'

He leant over and patted her arm. 'You really are a softie, aren't you? Better toughen up, love, or the world will eat you for breakfast. At least...that's what Harry's advice always is.'

'And what's your advice?' she asked, her voice catching.

'I wouldn't be looking to *me* for any advice on life's problems just now if I were you,' he said with a wealth of self-mockery. 'Though funnily enough I used to think I had all the answers, that I knew exactly where I was going and what I wanted from life. I watched the poor decisions others made with their choices in careers and life partners, and I was sure I had successfully avoided all the pitfalls. There I was, making a name in the art world and about to enter into what I thought was the perfect marriage, when whammo! Everything went black—in more ways than one! Believe me, April, going blind certainly gives you a new perspective.' He laughed at his own sick joke. 'Though at least you find out who your real friends are!'

'Don't you have any family, Hugh?' she asked, upset by the lonely bitter sound in his voice.

'No. My parents were middle-aged when they had me. They've been dead a few years now. I have a couple of distant cousins scattered around Australia. But no one close.'

'How did you start sculpting?' she went on, hoping to get his mind off his accident, and its subsequent unhappiness.

'Both Mum and Dad were artists. Dad, a painter. Mum, a potter. One of their friends was a sculptor—and a fascinating man. When I was thirteen I used to go over to his studio, pretending I wanted to learn his craft, just to hear the stories he told. But before I knew it I was hooked.'

'He sounds an interesting man.'

'He was. But he's dead now. Cirrhosis of the liver, the death certificate said. A broken heart, more accurately,' he finished sharply.

'What happened?'

'He fell in love with one of his students—a girl over twenty years younger than himself. Married her after a whirlwind courtship.'

'And?'

'The inevitable happened, of course. After six months the honeymoon was well and truly over. At least for her! She simply upped one day, said he bored her to death, and left, moved in with another of his students, a twenty-year-old. Garrick was simply devastated. He started drinking and didn't stop till he was six feet under. Such a rotten waste, and all because he let his heart rule his head! He was crazy to marry such a young girl. Simply crazy!'

April blinked at Hugh's virulence, understanding dawning at why he was so scornful of the young. And students in particular. Obviously his mentor's decline and death had made a lasting impression on his teenage mind, making him think all young people were not to be trusted in matters of faithfulness. His being an only child to elderly parents would also have contributed to what she thought was an overly serious turn of mind.

But what good was this new understanding of Hugh's attitude? If anything, it underlined the futility of feeling anything for him other than friendship. She dragged in a deep breath, letting it out with a weary sigh.

'Something tells me,' Hugh said drily, 'that Dick Francis is not going to get a good hearing today. What say we have a siesta instead?'

April pulled herself together, determined to concentrate on being the friend he needed. 'Definitely not!' she declared. 'We're going to reach page one hundred by five o'clock. Then tomorrow we'll finish it. Now... I'll begin again...'

CHAPTER FIVE

APRIL was wrong.

They finished the book that day, both becoming so engrossed that they couldn't put it down. Even when Harry insisted they come up to eat, the book went with them, April reading while they devoured hamburgers and beer.

Harry said they were 'bonkers' to let a book get them in like that, and left to do some night rock-fishing.

April finished the last line with a satisfied sigh shortly after nine. 'Our hero showed those baddies a thing or two, didn't he?' she said, glancing over at Hugh who was stretched out in an armchair, ankles and arms crossed. It looked as if his eyes were closed beneath the sunglasses. 'You haven't gone to sleep, have you?'

'Nope,' came the curt answer. 'Just thinking.'

'About the book?'

'About the book. And life...'

Her chest tightened, knowing instinctively that Hugh was thinking about his fiancée, about how she had left him when he needed her most.

April's heart turned over. What hell he must have gone through! To wake up in hospital, broken and blind, desperately needing the comfort that could only come from family and loved ones. But there'd been no family to hold his hand. And no loved one...

'What about life?' she asked softly, half hoping that he would confide in her.

He sat up straight, tension in every line of his body. 'A young girl like you doesn't want to have serious discussions about life.'

'Will you stop saying things like that?' she snapped. 'I've told you before. I'm almost twenty-one. A lot of women my age are already married and having babies.'

'Unfortunately true,' he scoffed. 'And in a few years they'll be divorced, with problem children on their hands.'

April could only shake her head at Hugh's continuing outbursts of cynicism. She understood that he had reason to be bitter over what Cynthia had done. And she accepted it wasn't easy for him during these countdown days to his operation. But it wasn't doing him any favours if she let him use her as some sort of whipping-boy.

'You really have to stop lumping people together into boxes, Hugh,' she debated firmly. 'Not all young people are flighty. Or unfaithful. I don't know what gets into you sometimes, picking on my age as if it's a dirty word. I suppose your Cynthia was young, was she? Like that girl your teacher fell in love with?'

His laugh was very, very dry. 'Cynthia happens to be thirty-two. And, before you add two and two together and make five again, she's also intelligent and cool and calm and independently wealthy. As I said before, she was perfect...'

April was stunned. And even more confused. Why, then, had Cynthia left? Was it just an inability to accept a husband who was handicapped, even temporarily? What kind of love was *that* if it disappeared so readily? April accepted it wouldn't be easy to deal with blindness—one could see how difficult it had made Hugh—but she felt instinctively she couldn't have left her fiancé if she had been in Cynthia's place, even if he'd been permanently blind.

'She couldn't have loved you very deeply, Hugh, if she left you like that,' April voiced aloud. 'You're better off without her. Some women——'

'For God's sake, leave it alone, will you?' Hugh bit out, leaping to his feet. He went to move forward and immediately banged his shin on the edge of the coffee-table. He swore volubly and bent down to rub his leg.

April's first instinct was to race over and help him. But some inner voice warned her not to do so.

'I don't know how you can stand yourself, Hugh Davies,' she reproached. 'You're not the first person who's been dumped in this world. You should be grateful that you're not going to be permanently blind as well. If it weren't for my feeling sorry for Harry having to put up with you, I'd walk out of here right now and never speak to you again, let alone read you any more books!'

There were a few moments of charged silence. Then suddenly, Hugh tipped back his head and laughed. 'My God, but you're precious! I honestly don't know what I would have done if you hadn't come along.'

'You'd have kept breathing and hopefully stopped feeling sorry for yourself!'

He chuckled again. 'What did you say you were going to be? An economist? I would have thought the army would have suited you better. Stand up straight there, Hugh Davies. Chin up, stomach in, eyes straight forward.' He did just that, holding his body to attention. 'How's that, Sarge?'

April swung her eyes away from his taut muscles. 'Just passable, for such an old, *old* soldier.'

'Ouch.'

Just then, Harry made an appearance on the balcony outside, a couple of fish on his line. 'Harry's back,' April informed Hugh. 'I'd best be going.'

'Do you have to? I was just beginning to enjoy myself.'

'Is that so? You mean you didn't enjoy all those hours I was reading to you? That's gratitude for you!'

'Why don't you stay for supper?' he urged.

She ignored the desire to do just that, fearing how this man made her feel by just being in the same room as he. 'I don't think so, Hugh. I'm rather tired. I'll see you tomorrow afternoon. About three again? On the beach?'

'You'll bring another Dick Francis with you?'

'I'll certainly bring something.' Much safer all round to have something concrete to do, she thought ruefully. 'Bye.' She walked over and kissed him on the cheek, thinking to herself that it was the bravest, most stupid thing she could do. 'Good-night. Sleep tight.'

'You too.'

But of course she didn't sleep tight. She didn't sleep till sheer exhaustion won the day near dawn.

'I thought you weren't coming!' Hugh accused when she finally made an appearance down his end of the beach around four the next afternoon. 'Did you bring another book with you?'

'No.'

'Why not?'

'Absence makes the heart grow fonder,' she tossed off, thinking ruefully that never a truer word had been spoken. In the hours she had been away from Hugh she hadn't stopped thinking about him. 'Dick Francis will appear on every second day,' she added firmly.

He groaned. 'You would have made a splendid SS Kommandant, April Jamieson.'

'Good! Then obey orders. Today we are going to do a cryptic crossword.' She had come fully armed, with an old newspaper. Not to mention a dictionary, two biros, and a beach umbrella. It was far too hot to sit in the sun indefinitely, she decided. Neither was she going to torture herself every day putting on Hugh's sunscreen.

With businesslike efficiency she arranged everything, making Hugh sit in the shade. 'Now,' she began firmly. 'One across: stolen near the equator...three letters...'

* * *

It turned out to be a surprisingly enjoyable two weeks, with both April and Harry conspiring together to take Hugh's mind off his coming trauma. Between the Dick Francis books and the crosswords, they swam, sunbathed and fished. Harry cooked them all sorts of interesting foods, once again surprising April. She discovered that, though illiterate, he was a man of many talents, with a huge capacity for kindness and caring. Soon, they were firm friends.

Her feelings for Hugh were still not clear-cut in her mind. Oh, they were firm friends too. There was no doubt about that. Hugh obviously liked having her around, even though he continued to tease and patronise her in the most irritating fashion.

She gave as good as she got, but she was finding it harder and harder to control the sexual side of her feelings. On the whole she had successfully buried her urges—except in her dreams—but occasionally her body betrayed her, and she would find herself staring at him with a very real and fierce hunger. Mostly she hid it, even from Harry's sharp eyes. But she was grateful that Harry was not present during the incident that occurred on the last afternoon of their stay at the cove.

Harry had driven into town to buy some Chinese food for their final meal together and, since it was stiflingly hot, April and Hugh went swimming. When they emerged from the sea at around four o'clock, it was still too hot to lie in the sun, so the two of them made for the cool of inside.

Hugh went confidently ahead, forgetting perhaps that the soles of his feet were still wet and that the stone steps could become slippery. April was right behind him when, half a dozen steps up, he lost his footing. Arms and legs flailing, he crashed back on to her so that they both went tumbling backwards.

Whether by design or accident Hugh was able to grab April's arms then spin her round so that he, not herself, took the brunt of the fall, his back hitting the sand first with her body being cushioned by his. She landed sprawled half sideways across him, her breasts pressing into his stomach, her lips brushing a male nipple, one of her hands up around his neck, the other wedged firmly between his thighs.

For a second they lay winded, with April not daring to move that hand from its embarrassing position.

'Are you all right?' Hugh asked.

'Y-yes... Are you?' Her voice held a breathless, husky quality.

'Fine... I think...'

Her cheeks flamed as she lifted her head to stare down at the precariously placed hand. Its side was pressed against his swimming-costume and as she shakily withdrew it she could do nothing to prevent her index finger and thumb grazing across the damp material in an intimate retreat.

The gasp was Hugh's, not hers.

'Hell,' he muttered, his body leaping into arousal with startling speed.

Mortified, April scrambled to her feet, not knowing where to look or what to do. Her heart was thudding painfully in her chest, her throat dry. Best to ignore it, she thought frantically. Pretend she hadn't noticed.

'Here...take my hand,' she offered hurriedly.

His grip closed warm and firm around hers, but when he hesitated she said, 'Are you sure you're all right?'

He made a sound deep in his throat that could have been impatience, or frustration. 'No permanent damage,' he growled, then put his weight against the pull of her hand. April was relieved to see that by the time he rose his body was almost back to normal.

'Perhaps I'd better help you up the steps,' she suggested, not really wanting to but knowing she should. Her heart was still pounding from the incident, her palms uncomfortably clammy.

His refusal was swift and sharp. 'No, thanks. I can manage.'

He was angry. Angry, and embarrassed.

Another time, with another woman—Cynthia perhaps—his arousal might be a wished-for occurrence. With her, it had been an annoyance.

The thought depressed April. Unbearably. But, as she lifted unhappy eyes to his grim face, another more devastating realisation hit. She loved Hugh, loved him with all the boundless love her young heart was ready to give. There was no denying it. It surrounded and consumed her, making everything she had ever felt for anyone else seem shallow and worthless.

It was a realisation that brought real pain, a pain that contracted her heart, twisted her stomach, made her want to cry. How could she have let it happen? He would never love her back. Never! Not only that, it was the last thing she wanted for herself this year, the very last thing ...

April's gaze travelled over him as he turned to place a careful foot on the first step, the knowledge of her love making her want to touch him more than ever. How wonderful it must be to make love with someone you loved, she thought yearningly. To be able to kiss them, hold them, caress them, join with them ...

April was thankful now that she had not thrown her virginity away on someone like Max. But what dismayed her unbearably was that she would never get an opportunity to give herself to the man she loved, this man who even now was walking away from her, who tomorrow would go back to Sydney, and a life that was unlikely to have a place for her, even as a friend.

'Hugh!' she called out as he reached the balcony.

He stopped, and turned slowly.

'I don't think I'll come up just now. I'd like to shampoo my hair before tonight. Harry wants me over here by seven at the latest, he said. You didn't need me for anything, did you?'

He said nothing for a couple of seconds, setting her nerves on edge. She hoped and prayed he didn't need help with anything.

'No... You go on. I'll see you later.'

Relieved but still miserable, she turned away and hurried across the hot sand.

CHAPTER SIX

IT WAS terribly hot.

April stood naked in the bedroom and tried to decide what to wear. Finally she dragged on a pair of white shorts and a red T-shirt, hating the touch of any clothing at all on her sticky skin.

She didn't bother with a hair-drier, letting her freshly shampooed curls lie in damp relief around her neck. She had no intention of bothering with make-up either, since Hugh couldn't see, and Harry wouldn't give a hoot.

But when the thought crossed her mind that one day soon Hugh would no longer be blind, she walked over to stare in the dressing-table mirror, wondering if it would make any difference when and if he saw her.

She had attractive hair. Everyone said so. Thick and black, layered to take advantage of its natural curl, it framed her oval face, touching her shoulders, dipping slightly down at the back. Her eyes were her next best feature, being dark blue and widely set, with long black lashes.

She frowned at her mouth, never having felt happy with it since the headmistress at school had called it pouty.

And then of course there was her figure. What a shame she was so short. April had always thought that more height was needed to carry her overgenerous curves. She didn't regret her full bust, but there was much too much bottom, she considered with a grimace.

A sudden wave of depression took hold of her, making her sink down dejectedly on to the water-bed. She knew in her heart that her looks would not sway Hugh. He had spelt everything out very clearly. She was too young for him. Besides, she had the awful feeling he wasn't over the break-up with Cynthia yet.

April sighed and stood up, absently picking up a bottle of perfume that was lying on the dressing-table and spraying herself with it. It was called Destiny, an exotic musky fragrance, obviously left behind by one of her uncle's lady-loves.

Hugh and Harry were lounging in deck-chairs, drinking beer, when she arrived. Harry got up immediately, telling her to take his chair while he got her a glass of the white wine she preferred.

'Thanks,' she murmured as she settled next to Hugh. He was wearing bright Bermuda shorts and nothing else, a fact that had April staring resolutely out to sea.

'You're wearing perfume,' he remarked in an abrupt tone. 'You don't usually wear perfume.'

She found his brusqueness upsetting. Most men complimented a woman's perfume, not castigated it. 'I'm sorry you don't like it,' she said irritably. 'Shall I move further away?'

'That might be a bloody good idea!'

She stared at him. 'What's got into you tonight?'

'It's this heat,' he growled, and downed the rest of the beer. 'Would you believe Harry wants to play poker after dinner? I told him it was impossible but he said you and I could collaborate. You're supposed to sit next to me and tell me what cards I'm holding.'

The idea of sitting close to Hugh all night brought a squirming sensation to her stomach. 'I'm not sure that would work,' came the hesitant comment. She looked across to see Hugh's forehead wrinkling in a dark frown, so she added with a quick laugh, 'I'm a good poker player myself and we might argue over what cards to throw in.'

A short, impatient sound rumbled in his throat.

Harry reappeared with her drink. He handed it over before disappearing again. April glanced across at Hugh, her gaze unconsciously drifting down to his powerfully muscled thighs. The memory of what had happened that afternoon brought a tide of heat to her cheeks.

'What are you thinking?'

April jumped at the sudden question. 'Oh ... I— er——'

'Come on. Be honest.'

Her laugh was self-mocking. 'I don't think you'd really want to know.' She took a large gulp of the wine.

'I'm game.'

'Are you?' She couldn't help the heavy irony in her voice. Hugh picked up on it immediately, for his head jerked round to glare at her. With the sun having set he had taken his glasses off, and the impact of his sightless yet intense gaze was unnerving.

'You really think I'm an old stick-in-the-mud, don't you, April?'

She was in no mood to humour him. 'If the cap fits...'

A flash of fury swept over his features. 'That's so easily said, isn't it? Would you prefer I do as this modern generation does? Give in to every whim I get, every urge I feel?'

She was shocked by his unexpected anger.

'Do you know how I feel tonight?' he went on quite savagely. 'Tomorrow we head back to Sydney, and in two days I'll be in that bloody hospital, having that bloody operation. I hate the uncertainty, the doubts. Hate the way it all makes me feel. Weak, helpless!'

'Oh, Hugh, you shouldn't...'

'Shouldn't what?' he snapped. 'Shouldn't swear? Shouldn't worry? God, April, I'm going *mad* with worry, not to mention...' He broke off and ran a shaking hand through his hair. 'I crave... distraction. What do you suggest I do? Race you off for a quickie?' He was gripping his beer glass with finger-bruising strength. 'If you're as sexy as you smell, I'd surely sleep afterwards!'

Harry popped his head outside. 'Chow's on,' he informed brightly. 'Come on, Hugh, April.'

April scrambled to her feet immediately and went inside, her face white, her insides trembling.

The tension at the beginning of the meal was palpable and in the course of things April drank more wine than she should have. Hugh was not slow on imbibing either and by the time they had finished their banquet of several dishes he was even more caustic and cynical than usual.

Harry gave April a frowning glance, and suggested they begin the poker as soon as he had disposed of the dirty dishes. They did so, but it was as bad as April feared, sitting so close to Hugh. Their bare thighs were pressed together along one side, and she had to whisper in his ear to prevent Harry from knowing what cards they held.

The third deal of cards saw Hugh and April disagreeing, ostensibly over what cards to discard. April had her way, keeping a pair of kings instead of going for a flush. Unfortunately the first card she drew was a club, the very suit she would have needed if Hugh's will had prevailed. There were no further kings, however.

'See what I get for listening to a female?' Hugh scoffed. 'I think I should take her over my knee and paddle her backside.'

Harry's shaggy eyebrows shot skywards. 'I think you've had too much to drink, mate.'

'Who, me? My partner here's the one who's sloshed.'

April sighed and stood up, her whole body tense with suppressed emotion. 'I think we'd better give the cards a miss, don't you? How about I make us some coffee?'

Harry yawned. 'None for me, thanks. I think I'll hit the sack. Wine does strange things to me.' Which was patently clear when he nearly walked into his bedroom door as he left the room.

'Well, Hugh?' she said tightly. 'Coffee for you?'

His negative grunt was the last straw.

'In that case I don't want any either,' she snapped. 'I'm going for a swim then I'm off home. It's a long drive back tomorrow.'

His brooding silence had her shaking her head and leaving, her emotions only just in control. She marched down to the water, stripped off all her clothes and plunged defiantly naked into the sea, swimming out into the dark waters like a person possessed.

After a few minutes Hugh surprised her by making an appearance at the water's edge. 'You shouldn't be swimming on your own, April!' he shouted wearily. 'You might get a cramp. I could hardly save you. And Harry's out like a light.'

'Go to hell, Hugh!' she shouted back.

'Can't,' he growled. 'I'm already there.'

His obvious wretchedness totally defused her anger. What on earth are you doing, April? she asked herself. Hasn't the man got enough troubles? OK, so he drank too much and was beastly and rude. So what?

She sighed and began swimming back to shore. At least she was sober now. She hauled her naked form from the water and after a slight hesitation began walking towards him. The moonlight showed every inch of her nudity and she had to keep telling herself he couldn't really see. A nervous flutter rose and fell in her chest as she drew up to him, for he appeared to be looking right at her breasts.

'Aah, so there you are,' Hugh muttered, sensing her presence. 'Well? I suppose you're waiting for an apology.'

'Not really.'

'Then what are you waiting for?'

She swallowed. 'You're standing on my clothes.'

He froze for a moment, then bent down and picked them up.

April watched, shivering, as he felt each piece. Shorts, T-shirt, white lace bikini briefs. 'You don't wear much.' The words sounded thick.

She stepped forward and held out an unsteady hand. 'Would you give them to me, please?' Her damp skin was breaking out into goose-bumps. Her stomach was in knots. 'Please, Hugh...'

He just stood there, not making a move, not saying a word.

What devil was it in her that made her do what she did next? Who knew? All human beings were good and bad, light and dark. And love made one daring...

With tremulous fingers she took the clothes from his hands, then dropped them on the sand before bridging the final space between them. Hugh's gasp of shock sent a hot jab of arousal through her body.

'Hugh,' she whispered in a voice reserved for sirens. It was low and husky. Sweet and inviting.

Her arms slid up around his neck, the contact of her swollen nipples with his chest making her shiver. But not with cold now. She moved against him, sending more currents of electric pleasure all through her.

Hugh groaned, and for a brief ecstatic moment held her close. Then suddenly he was disengaging her arms, pulling back from her. 'No, April. No...'

'Why not?' This time she wrapped her arms around his waist and sank into his warmth. 'I want to touch you. Don't you want to touch me too?'

'Oh, God,' Hugh rasped. 'This is madness. *Madness*, I tell you!'

'Then let it be madness,' she urged, raining moist kisses on his chest. Her hands slid up over his back in a sensuous trail.

'You don't know what you're inviting!'

The blood was pounding in her veins and the words came—mindless and passionate. 'Yes, I do.'

The tip of her tongue grazed over his skin and he groaned again, a tortured despairing sound, but his hands were already reaching to hold and lift her face, his mouth searching for hers, finding it, forcing it open. His kiss probed and plundered without mercy, demanding an equally uninhibited response, sweeping aside all April's misconceptions that her first time would be a tender, sweet experience.

There was no persuasion or seduction in Hugh's actions. Somewhere in the back of her dazed mind, April knew that, while he was taking what she had so blatantly offered, his lovemaking had a harsh, angry quality to it, as though despite being devastatingly aroused he was hating himself for it.

His hands grazed down over her shoulders, down, down, till they were moulding her buttocks, cupping them so as to press her into him, then half lifting her till she fitted his body to perfection. Her thighs had parted and her hot aching flesh curved around his thinly clad loins. She was feverishly aware of his pulsating hardness, pushing, demanding, and the urge to blend her body with his was so strong that their union seemed inevitable.

'Yes, Hugh,' she panted, dragging her mouth away from him. 'Yes... Please, yes.'

His breathing was as heavy as her own. He let her go, her body sliding down his till trembling toes touched the wet sand. He pulled back a fraction, then slowly his hands began to roam over her body, tracing her curves, as though imprinting her shape on his mind.

She stood still, breathless with pleasure as his hands caressed her breasts, moaning with disappointment when they moved on. But she was not to be disappointed for long. His slender, knowing fingers had a more devastating goal, making her cry out when they slipped between her thighs. They found and explored her moist womanhood, stroking and caressing with considerable expertise till soft, panting sounds were coming from her throat. Her own hands had closed over his shoulders, their bruising grip echoing the growing tension inside her. When she suddenly dug her nails into his flesh, he dragged her hands away.

'Here... touch me,' he commanded, holding her palm against his own throbbing need.

Somehow they had moved into the shallows, but April was oblivious of the water lapping around their legs. She was without thought, her whole being concentrating on what lay beneath her hand. She thrilled to Hugh's moans when she caressed him, each muffled cry sending fierce flames of desire through every vein in her body. Before she knew it he had discarded his shorts and was guiding her hand back to hard, naked flesh.

But even as her fingers moved to touch him once more he pushed them aside, sweeping her up into his arms and carrying her to the shore, stretching her out and covering her. She, in turn, opened eagerly to his imminent possession, already moving her hips in a slow, sensuous rhythm.

It never crossed her mind that her body, her ignited excited body would feel any pain, and when it ripped through her like a knife slicing into her flesh she could not stifle the instinctive cry nor prevent the involuntary recoil.

'What the...?' Hugh froze, then abruptly withdrew.

April grabbed him by the shoulders. 'No, don't stop! Please, Hugh...'

But he abandoned her, cursing. 'Good God in heaven, girl!' His voice was shaking, as was his body. 'Why didn't you tell me?' He rolled away then sat up, his breathing heavy and laboured, his face in agony.

Her disappointment at his stopping was almost as acute as her distress at his anger. 'Hugh, please...'

His groan was tortured. 'That's all I need, you begging me to go on.'

A ghastly dismay was creeping into her heart. 'But Hugh, I...I wanted you to make love to me. I still do.' She reached out to touch his thigh but he angrily swept her hand aside.

'That much was obvious, girlie.'

'Don't call me that!' she cried. I'm a woman, she wanted to scream at him. A woman. And I love you...

'And why not? That's all you are! A girl, a silly young girl, and a virgin to boot. What in the hell did you think you were playing at here tonight? Good God!'

'But Hugh...' She was struggling for words. 'I'm almost twenty-one. I... I can't stay a virgin forever.'

'Well, I've got no intention of being the one to start you on your merry way!'

April's heart plummeted. What was the use? How could she say that she wanted him to be her first lover even if he didn't love her back; that it would have been a memory she would have treasured forever?

Shattered, miserable, she dragged herself up into a sitting position. Her muscles were beginning to stiffen and there was a dull throbbing in her temples. 'Well, you didn't, did you?' she murmured, pressing her hands against the sides of her face. 'You stopped,' she repeated dully.

'And thank God I did! What if you'd got pregnant? Did you think of that? No, of course not. As I've said before, just a silly little fool looking for kicks without considering the consequences.'

'I'm on the Pill,' she said in a weary, wretched fashion. She had continued taking it even after she had seen the light about Max, for the simple reason that it alleviated her extremely painful periods.

'I might have known!' He shook his head in total exasperation. 'What gets into girls like you? Do you all go on the Pill as a matter of course, just in case you get the urge one night? Then what, April? Another lover, then another and another, till you can't remember their names or what they did to you?'

'Who are you to pass judgement, Hugh Davies?' she shot back at him. 'You would have taken me, if I hadn't been a virgin. Stop being holier than thou.'

'Much to my discredit, I assure you,' he returned bitterly. 'My only excuse is that I've been drinking. And it's been a long time since I had sex.'

A shudder went through April. The heat of passion was gone, cooled by cold, hard reality. Hugh had not desired her, April Jamieson. Frustration and alcohol had made him vulnerable to her provocative advances.

'I suppose I should apologise,' he muttered. 'Though damn it all, April, you were asking for it.'

'I don't usually act that way,' she said in desperate defence. 'I had too much to drink, too.'

'Well, keep off it in future! Exercise a little control.'

His preachy attitude was beginning to infuriate her. 'Oh, don't be ridiculous! I've had a few drinks before and not tried seducing the first male in sight. But it's inevitable that one day I would want to sleep with a man,' she tossed off, ready to say anything except that she loved him. 'I'm at that age.'

'And what stupid age would that be?' he growled.

'You know very well. The age of sexual experimentation. It happens to everyone, sooner or later,' she continued. 'There comes a time when you just have to know what it's like. I went on the Pill as a sensible precaution, not as a free ticket to promiscuity.'

'But that's what it will become, April, don't you see?'

'Look, Hugh, you're my friend, not my keeper. I don't have to answer to you, OK? Let's just forget any of this happened. I'm freezing and tired and I'd like to go to bed.' She scrambled to her feet and began dragging on her clothes.

It was only when she was fully dressed that she remembered Hugh's shorts. Oh, dear, she thought wearily, spotting them lying in a soggy heap at the water's edge. She supposed she'd have to go and get them. She couldn't get out of helping him back up to the beach-house but there was no way she was going to do that while he was still nude.

'Your shorts,' she said, red-faced, as she handed them over. 'They're wet, I'm afraid.'

'No hassle.'

She looked away while he put them on. 'Here's my hand,' she offered once he was dressed. They walked in silence and, despite holding hands, Hugh kept his distance and did not ask for extra support up the steps.

'April...' He turned to her once they reached the landing. 'I've been thinking... When we get back to Sydney... I'll understand if you don't want to see me again. Please don't feel you *have* to visit me in the hospital.'

Her heart took a nose-dive. She'd already accepted that their friendship might eventually dwindle away, but she hadn't been prepared for such a swift severance. She couldn't let him go. Not just yet ...

'But why, Hugh?' she asked in the calmest voice she could muster. 'Surely not because of tonight?'

'Yes ... because of tonight.'

Her laugh portrayed a light attitude. 'Don't be silly, Hugh. We both had too much to drink, as you said, and got carried away, that's all. I don't blame you one bit.'

His face was grim as he turned and moved slowly away from her, his hand reaching out till it found the railing. 'Well, I do. I shouldn't have let it go that far. I almost used you as nothing more than a sex object.'

'But you didn't, Hugh,' she argued. 'You wouldn't do a thing like that.'

He gave a short, sharp laugh. 'Don't go giving me too many virtues. You're not in my body just now.'

She blushed and the silence between them lengthened.

'I suppose I am being a touch melodramatic,' he said at last.

'You certainly are. Besides,' she went on, adopting a lighter note, 'you don't have that many friends that you can afford to throw away one as tolerant as me! Look what I've put up with these last two weeks. Nothing but patronising put-me-downs and never-ending teasings. "Oh, but April, what would you know, you're so *young*!"' she mimicked.

He grimaced. 'Bad as that, eh? Well, you certainly didn't *feel* young tonight, my friend,' he admitted. 'That's the problem.'

More heat zoomed into her cheeks but she said nothing.

'I don't want to hurt you, April.'

'You...you wouldn't hurt me, Hugh,' she rasped.

'I might if I made love to you without loving you.'

'I see,' she choked out. 'And what if I said I wanted you to make love to me, whether you loved me or not?'

He sucked in a startled breath.

'Just testing,' she joked. It was amazing how carefree one could sound, even when one's heart was crumbling into pieces. 'See you in the morning.' Then without waiting for a reply she said goodnight and moved swiftly down the steps, her feet breaking into a run as soon as they reached the sand. She ran and ran, tears blinding her way, but even as she ran, faster and faster, she knew that was no escape from the hopeless love that burned in her heart.

CHAPTER SEVEN

THE drive back to Sydney the next day was long and hot. April had a difficult task keeping her mind on the road, which wasn't wise since it was Sunday, and the weekend flow of traffic was heavy.

She hadn't seen Hugh alone that morning, having stopped by the beach-house only long enough to say goodbye and to promise to come and see him in hospital on the Tuesday evening. He was to be operated on that morning, and, from what she'd been told, should be fit for visitors by then.

She might have been imagining it but she thought he'd been rather stiff in his manner towards her, Harry being the one to make most of the conversation. Perhaps he'd felt embarrassed by what had happened the night before. Guilty, even. April had made an extra effort to act her normal breezy self, but it hadn't been easy, and she was almost glad to get away.

By the time she pulled up outside her uncle's terrace-house in Balmain several hours later she had resigned herself to her so-called friendship with Hugh fading away once he got his sight back. He would plunge back into his work and totally forget about her, his need for the distraction of her company no longer there.

Feeling depressed, she was relieved when she let herself inside to find that her uncle was not at home.

He had left a note for her on the kitchen table, saying he was attending a society afternoon tea. There was a postscript announcing that last week he had secured a contract to write a gossipy by-line in one of the dailies.

A small smile came to her lips as she put the note back down on the table and began making herself a cup of tea. She could just see him now, dressed in his best Pierre Cardin suit, eating cucumber sandwiches and charming all the ladies, while extracting the most intimate and personal details with the ease of a magician pulling a rabbit out of a hat.

Her uncle loved gossip, loved to hear the latest scandal, and people seemed to like confiding in him. Perhaps it was because he was such a good listener, and never acted shocked by whatever people did.

April frowned. Would he be shocked if she told him what had happened up at the cove between herself and Hugh? How would he have reacted, she wondered, if Hugh had reciprocated her feelings and they had by now become lovers?

The answer came back immediately. He would definitely not approve of her becoming involved with a man of Hugh's age and experience.

April's sigh was agitated. Perhaps her uncle would be quite right. As Hugh had been right. Perhaps she *was* too young for him. She had to forget that he didn't look his age. The fact remained that he *was* thirty-four, a serious-thinking man with a conservative outlook—not a dolly-chasing trend-setter like Max. Hugh clearly found a twenty-year-old girl juvenile and childish by comparison to the sort of women he was used to going out with. The dreaded Cynthia had been thirty-two. Unlike Max, Hugh obviously didn't want to indulge in one casual affair after another. He wanted a lasting relationship, with a mature woman, as evidenced by his engagement the year before.

Tears pricked at April's eyes and her chin began to quiver. It was all very well to work things through sensibly. What had sense ever had to do with matters of the heart? She loved Hugh, age difference or no, and she felt positive it was a true and lasting love.

But what did any of that matter? He didn't love her back. He had said so.

April sank down on to one of the kitchen chairs and cried, cried till there were no tears left. Then she dried her eyes and stood up, feeling fractionally better. Lifting her chin and taking a deep breath, she turned and resumed her tea-making. April was not one to bash her head up against a brick wall. Nor did she intend to be one of those girls who made fools of themselves by chasing shamelessly after a man. She resolved that once Hugh had had his operation and was back on his feet she would leave it totally up to him if and when they ever saw each other again. Meanwhile, she would go back to university and get on with her life.

Uncle Guy swept in shortly after seven that evening, his flushed face and high spirits showing that the afternoon had not been confined entirely to tea. He was looking well, April thought, though his grey hair and portly figure made him look every one of his fifty-one years.

He raved about April's tan and listened interestedly while she told him a carefully edited version of her holiday and her friendship with Hugh and Harry.

'So, our famous sculptor's being admitted into hospital tomorrow afternoon, is he?' Guy said over a strong cup of coffee.

'That's right.'

'Awful places, hospitals. I remember when I was having my gall bladder operation. The night before I didn't sleep a wink, despite a sleeping-pill. Then the next morning I lay there for what felt like an eternity waiting to be wheeled down into theatre while everyone else was busy eating breakfast and making beds, et cetera. It was sheer hell. I read the whole of *Hunt for Red October* that day. No mean feat, I can tell you.'

'Well, I'm afraid Hugh won't be able to read,' April sighed. Really, she wished her uncle would shut up about Hugh and the operation. She had started feeling nervous about it all again. Over the last two weeks she had pushed aside her initial worries about whether it would be a success or not, trying to take a positive attitude for Hugh's sake. But now that the moment was at hand all her doubts and fears came rushing back. She could imagine how Hugh would be feeling at this very moment, how tense and nervous. It made her want to rush to him, to comfort him. But she had to stay away. She just *had* to!

'I know what!' her uncle exclaimed. 'I've got a couple of talking cassette books in my desk somewhere. You could take them over to Hugh tomorrow morning. You don't have to go back to university till next week, do you? Where did you say he lived? Mosman ... Not the best place to get to by public transport. I'll lend you the car again.'

April went to protest, but once her uncle decided something was a good idea there was no stopping him. And if she was strictly honest with herself, deep down, underneath all her common-sense reasonings, she wanted to go.

April swung the Datsun Bluebird carefully into the left-hand lane so that she wouldn't be caught behind the cars turning right at the next big intersection. The lights proved to be green so she sailed through, swinging left slightly on to The Spit Road. She had her street directory open on the passenger seat in case she became lost, but the way to Hugh's house had been etched into her brain after staring at the map for an hour the previous night.

Driving slowly, she easily located Hugh's street on the right and turned into it. Large old trees shaded the footpaths and April noticed that most of the houses, though in faultless condition, were just as old.

Mosman was not a new suburb. It had nestled against the shores of Port Jackson for many decades and the coveted home sites and their solid, family-sized homes had been passed on from generation to generation. During one of their chats up at the cove, Hugh had volunteered the information that his parents' estate had provided him with the family home, along with enough investments for a modest private income.

April's nerves began to get the better of her once she finally spotted number twenty-two. It had a high white-brick wall which totally obscured the house. All she could see as she parked at the kerb was a pitched iron roof and the tops of several leafy trees. A narrow wrought-iron gate stood guard in the centre of the wall.

She had rung the previous evening to say she was coming, and why. Harry had answered, sounding pleased to hear from her. 'Great,' he said. 'You can mind the patient while I pop down to the shops. Hugh needs pyjamas and a new toothbrush for his stay in hospital.'

Levering herself somewhat reluctantly from behind the wheel, April got out and walked over to the gate. There was a buzzer located next to it just above the built-in mail box. She pressed it three times and, as the seconds passed, she became restless and fidgety. It was a cloudy day, but very humid. She pulled her multicoloured top from the waistband of her white jeans, flapping the bottom to let some cool air pass over her sticky skin.

The sudden appearance of Harry's bald head pressed up against the bars nearly gave her a heart attack.

'Hi, there,' he said, slipping the lock and throwing open the gate. He was dressed in a pair of navy surfer shorts and a navy singlet, his fierce-looking face softened by a welcoming grin. 'Hot, isn't it?' he said, dabbing at the perspiration on his forehead with a handkerchief. 'I've been mowing the lawns all morning, and trying to get the place in order.'

April glanced around the large front garden as they walked towards the house together, noting the freshly cut lawn, the neat edges, the perfectly kept garden beds. Harry had shown himself to be a meticulous housekeeper up at the cove and she didn't doubt he'd been working like a dog since his return yesterday. She knew how unkempt a place could get after a few weeks away.

'Everything looks great, Harry,' she complimented, lifting appreciative eyes to run over the stately old home. White-brick and single-storeyed, it had the wide cool front veranda inherent in federation-style homes, with bay windows on either side of a most attractive front door. Such beautiful stained-glass panels were rarely seen these days, not to mention the elegantly carved brass door-knocker.

'Where's Hugh?' April asked casually once they reached the front door.

'Would you believe he's still sleeping?' Harry pushed open the door, revealing a long cool hallway with an exceptionally tall ceiling.

'At eleven o'clock?'

Harry sighed and shook his head. 'He didn't sleep last night, the poor thing. I heard him at three still pacing up and down, so when he finally dropped off I didn't like to wake him. He'll have to get up soon though. Admission at the hospital is between two and three this afternoon.'

'I see,' she murmured, her stomach turning over at the mention of what Hugh was about to face. 'Well, lead me to the kitchen, Harry. I'll wake him with some coffee while you do that shopping you've got to do.'

'You're a life-saver, girlie. A real life-saver!'

Harry moved into the cool of inside, with April following. Despite the home's basic quality, she was surprised to see that the walls needed painting and that the strip of floral carpet running down the hall had seen better days. It was typical of Hugh though, she conceded, that he wouldn't think to spend money on maintenance of his home. He would have other priorities, such as great chunks of marble!

Several shut doors blocked any views of the rooms on either side of the hall and they eventually emerged into an enormous, though old-fashioned kitchen. April was not surprised, however, to see that it was spotless, since Harry was in charge. Hugh, she suspected, would be a typically messy bachelor if he didn't have someone to look after him.'

'Where do you keep the coffee?' she asked, putting her bag on the floor and approaching the myriad cupboards.

Harry opened one of the head-high cupboards that lined the walls. 'And here's the crockery,' he indicated, opening another.

'Thanks. Now off you go. I'll manage.'

'Don't mind Hugh if he's a grouch,' he warned.

'I won't.'

Harry gave her a grateful look, and left.

April smiled ruefully to herself as she filled the rather ancient jug with water. The grouchier, the better, she decided. It was rather hard to feel tender and loving towards a grouch.

Ten minutes later, with a mug of steaming coffee cradled carefully in her hands, April made her way down the hall in search of Hugh's bedroom. Her heart began to thump erratically at the thought of invading such an intimate domain, and as each opened door failed to find Hugh her jumpiness increased.

One room was clearly Hugh's studio, her gaze passing over many more chunks of marble than even she had imagined he might own. Large and small, rough and smooth, all different colours, the room was full of them. Only the large wooden work-table was free of their presence, though it was littered with all manner of things from tools to books to old newspapers to a selection of empty mugs.

April lifted her eyebrows and moved on. The next door on the right proved to be a bedroom, but, it being empty and tidy, she decided it had to be Harry's.

Now there was only one door left. Gingerly she twisted the brass knob, pushing it just far enough to see inside. Hugh was sprawled across a king-sized bed and...

Oh, no, April groaned silently. Once again he was stark naked!

Fortunately, he was lying face down and, while his tanned back and taut buttocks had an undeniable appeal, they were not as disturbing as certain other parts of Hugh's anatomy. April moved closer, her grip on the mug increasing. Keep your cool, girlie, she kept telling herself. It's only flesh and blood.

Yes, she thought drily. *His* flesh and *your* blood, pounding like a hundred drums in your head.

As carefully as shaking fingers would allow, she put the mug down on the bedside table next to his glasses and ever so slowly pulled the sheet out from under his feet and up over his body. She let it drop, as if she were dropping it on a sleeping snake, at waist-level.

She tapped him on the shoulder. 'Hugh...'

He stirred, rolling sideways so that the sheet wrapped tightly around him, outlining the contours of his lower body. Oh, God! April looked away sharply, then back, this time at his face only. There was stubble on his chin, shadows around his closed eyes. His thick tawny hair was in disarray. He looked vulnerable yet very, very sexy.

'Hugh!' This time her voice was louder and her hand not so gentle. Was she angry at herself or at him? she wondered.

'What?' He woke with a fright and lurched upright.

'It's all right, Hugh,' she reassured hurriedly. 'It's only me. April.'

'April?' One hand ran unsteady fingers through his hair while the other grabbed rather roughly at the sheet. 'What in hell are you doing here at this hour?'

'It's gone eleven,' she said far too shakily, and firmed her jaw. 'Harry said it was time you were up.'

'Eleven?' Hugh flicked his sightless gaze towards the open door. 'Where *is* Harry, then?'

'He popped down to the shops to buy you some pyjamas. You have to wear such things in hospital, you know. You can't sleep in the raw.'

His head snapped towards her.

'Don't worry,' she said drily. 'You were reasonably decent when I came in.'

His sigh of relief irritated her. What did he think she was going to do? Take unfair advantage of him? Maybe he thought she had deliberately come into his bedroom to feast her lustful eyes on his body.

'Watch it!' she cried when he reached for his dark glasses, almost upsetting the coffee. 'You almost spilt the coffee I brought you,' she said, handing him his glasses, then the mug.

An awkward silence descended while he drank it down. She had the oddest feeling that he was watching her over the rim of the mug, though she knew he couldn't see her at all from where she had moved back to. Agitated, she started looking around the room, admiring the lovely old bedroom suite which looked almost of antique status. 'I like your furniture,' she said for something to say. 'What wood is it?'

'Walnut, I think. It belonged to my grand-mother, passed down to Mum, now me.'

'I like your house too. It has character.' And so have you, came the sudden clear thought. What other man would have stopped the other night on the beach, particularly if as frustrated as Hugh had admitted to being? Most other men wouldn't have cared about her virtue or the consequences. Max had called a halt to their possible affair merely because she wasn't experienced enough for him.

'That was good, April,' Hugh said, holding out the empty mug.

She reached for it with both hands, her fingers curling around his. An electric charge pulsated up her arm, but it was Hugh who jerked his hand away, who spun around to sit on the side of the bed, the sheet still firmly in place. She stared at his back, and the way the muscles across his shoulders were stiff with tension.

Heat suffused her skin as she recognised this tension for what it was, and what had caused it. Her touch. Her soft, feminine touch.

But April found no joy in this realisation. Hugh had been perfectly frank about his physical frustrations. He wanted a woman, *any* woman. He had admitted as much up at the cove. The inadvertent brushing of her flesh against his had probably aroused memories of what they had done on the beach together and of what his body was missing. He wouldn't have been human, or the male he was, if such thinking hadn't affected him.

'If you wouldn't mind doing a quick exit,' he said gruffly, 'I'd like to have a shower.'

A *cold* shower, no doubt. But she was only too willing to go, her own body having leapt in response to her thoughts. She too couldn't forget what had happened between them, how he had been able to make her feel before that moment when he had pulled back.

'As long as you can manage,' she said shakily as she made for the door.

'Necessity is the mother of invention,' he growled after her. 'I know where every damned tile, towel and tap is in that blasted bathroom. I spent weeks doing nothing but going from here to there and back again!'

She closed the door on his burst of ill temper and took a deep breath. It was hard not to feel angry, both with herself and him. She could understand his irritation, but that didn't make it any easier to put up with. A moment ago she had wanted to lash out at him, to tell him to go to hell and take his prickly moods with him.

But that would hardly be the action of a friend. And Hugh desperately needed friends, people he could rely on in this time of trial, particularly after his experience with Cynthia. Harry had confided to her that most of Hugh's so-called friends had drifted away during his blindness. Max had lent him his beach-house but Max was, after all, only a business associate. So April was in a no-win situation. If she abandoned Hugh she would feel terribly guilty. But by staying in his orbit she was opening herself up to continuing heartache. And a frustration that would rival anything Hugh was feeling.

April returned to the kitchen, rinsed out the mug, left it to drain on the sink then wandered out on to the back veranda. She stood there for a moment, blinking in the sudden glare of outside before letting her eyes rove around the enormous back garden, a far cry from the ten-by-ten-foot yard behind her uncle's house. One could almost see a cricket match being held on the expanses of lawn.

April sat down on the steps in the shade of wide eaves. What a lovely home this was, a home just right for a whole horde of children. She had always wanted a lot of children, despite her wish for a career as well. Somehow she'd always thought she could juggle both. Now, she didn't think she would have to bother. A deep wretchedness swamped her. It just didn't seem possible that she would ever fall in love again, after Hugh . . .

A sudden breeze lifted her hair, and April glanced up to see darker clouds gathering on the horizon. The southerly change that had been predicted for later that afternoon seemed to be arriving early. Her attention was drawn to the assortment of clothes flapping on the line. She stood up and walked across, and began unpegging the items, putting them in the trolley under the line.

'April! Where are you, dammit?'

April swung round at the sound of Hugh's voice. He'd come out on the back veranda and was leaning with one hand high on a post, the other clutching a towel around his waist. Freshly shaven and showered, he looked even more breathtakingly handsome. His bronzed torso gleamed where droplets of water still clung, the glistening skin giving extra definition to the well-honed muscles that rippled just beneath the surface.

'I'm here, Hugh. Getting in the washing.'

'I can't seem to find my shorts. Did you pick them up? They were on the floor beside my bed last night.'

'I can imagine,' April grumbled under her breath. 'It looks as if Harry's put them in the wash,' she said more loudly. 'I'll bring them to you. They're quite dry.'

But when she stood on the bottom step and handed up the brightly coloured shorts he seemed to glare down at her. 'I heard that first remark,' he said in a low, curt tone. 'I'll have you know I put the shorts there so I'd know exactly where they were! For pity's sake, April, do you think I like being like this, depending on others to do things for me? I hate it!'

April counted to ten. 'I can understand that,' she said with creditable calm. 'But you won't have to worry about such things after tomorrow, will you?'

'Maybe,' he muttered. 'Maybe...'

His patent doubt softened her heart, but she said firmly, 'You have to be positive, Hugh. The doctors are confident, aren't they?'

'Aren't they always?' he mocked.

She thought of her mother and how the doctors had kept telling her the lump in her breast was most unlikely to be cancerous. But what if it had been? Wouldn't they have been guilty of giving her false hopes?

Still, it wouldn't have done Hugh any good if she told him about that.

'Would you rather they be negative?' she pointed out. 'I wouldn't think so. Besides, I'm quite sure the doctor wouldn't say your operation has an almost one hundred per cent success rate if it hasn't. And Hugh, it's important for you to go into surgery with an optimistic attitude. The mind is a powerful thing. It can make one feel sick even when there's no physical reason to be so. We had a dog once who had its tonsils out. The next day it was fine, simply because it didn't know it should be otherwise. If you go into this operation thinking it isn't going to be a success, then it probably won't be.'

Her lecture finished, Hugh said nothing for a few moments. Then he shook his head. 'You'd better watch it, April,' he drawled. 'If you keep talking sense like that I might forget how young you really are.' And, with that, he turned and stalked back into the house.

April was left staring after him, her mouth suddenly dry. She wasn't sure if she was relieved or not when she heard Harry's voice calling out to them from the front of the house. Hugh's tone and words had conveyed a type of intimate threat that had brought goose-bumps to her skin.

She spun away and strode over to get the washing basket and carried it inside, determined to distract her over-active brain and body with some ironing. But all she could think of was what might happen when and if they were ever alone again, particularly after her got his sight back.

April was not a vain girl but she was honest. And she knew men found her sexually attractive. If Hugh was as frustrated as he claimed to be, would he always be able to resist what she might recklessly offer him once more? She doubted it, doubted it very much.

The thought didn't do much for her peace of mind or her earlier resolution to let Hugh make the running.

'That's some frown you've got there, girlie,' Harry commented as she set up the ironing-board.

She glanced up at him. 'I was just thinking about tomorrow,' she muttered, grateful that Hugh had retreated into his room.

Harry sighed. 'Speaking of tomorrow...'

CHAPTER EIGHT

APRIL had a blinding migraine. She knew the cause. Tension. But it didn't make the blurred vision or the sick pounding in her head any easier to bear. For the umpteenth time she got up from the chair and paced around the hospital room.

'For Pete's sake, April, sit down,' Harry growled.

'I can't.' She continued to walk up and down, up and down. 'I'm worried sick.' April's stomach gave a sudden heave and she dashed into the bathroom that adjoined Hugh's private room. When she returned, she did sit down, white-faced but slightly better.

'Boy, you really meant it, didn't you? About being sick,' Harry said. 'Is there something I can get you?'

She gave him a wan smile. 'No, nothing. I . . . I feel better now.'

'I guess I shouldn't have asked you to come and stay with me today. It wasn't fair to you, under the circumstances.'

'U-under the circumstances?'

Harry gave her a look that was remarkably affectionate. 'You don't think I've been blind too, do you, girlie? I know you're in love with Hugh. And I know the fool treats you like some sort of kid.' Harry sat down on the side of Hugh's empty bed, picked up April's hand and patted it. 'Don't worry, he won't think you're such a kid for much longer.'

A flurry of activity in the corridor outside had both April and Harry on their feet. A trolley-type bed was wheeled into the room by a blue-uniformed man, a nurse alongside. Hugh, with eyes bandaged, was lying still and grey-faced under a mountain of blankets.

'Why has he got all those blankets on?' April asked Harry in a worried voice.

The nurse heard, however, and answered while she helped the porter move Hugh into his own bed. 'He woke up in the recovery-room shivering,' she said matter-of-factly. 'Some people react to anaesthetic like that. The body temperature plummets.'

April swayed on her feet and Harry grabbed her. 'Is that dangerous?' he asked as he lowered April back into her chair.

The nurse smiled. 'Not usually. Of course we don't leave them that way, hence the blankets. As you can see, once he felt comfortable, he drifted off to sleep again. Thanks, Warren,' she said as the porter departed with the trolley.

April finally found her voice. 'The operation went well?'

'As far as I know,' the nurse murmured, busying herself taking Hugh's blood-pressure.

'When can we speak to the doctor?' Harry joined in.

'He'll be in theatre for a few hours yet. You might not see him till he comes in later this afternoon to take off the bandages.'

'So soon?' April was astonished.

The nurse began packing up. 'Oh, yes. In this type of operation sight recovery is instantaneous. Once they've replaced the damaged jelly with the synthetic solution, the patient should be able to see.'

'Should' being the crucial word, April thought nervously.

The nurse wrote something on Hugh's chart at the foot of the bed then looked up. 'I have to go now but you can stay as long as you like. If you need a nurse for anything, ring the buzzer.' She lifted Hugh's pillows to show the buzzer lying underneath then moved towards the door, turning briefly before she left. 'Oh, I've left a bowl there on the side-table just in case Mr Davies doesn't feel well when he wakes. If you can't manage, just ring.'

For a few moments all Harry and April could do was stare down at Hugh's unconscious figure. He looked pitifully vulnerable, lying there between the antiseptic sheets, his tanned skin having acquired a pasty, sickly colour.

'Dear God, let him be able to see,' April prayed, and it wasn't till Harry answered her that she realised she had spoken aloud.

'Amen to that,' he finished. 'Can you stay with Hugh for a while, April?'

'Yes, of course.' Wild horses wouldn't have been able to drag her away.

'I thought I might go and get some flowers.' His cheeks went a shade of pink. 'I know that sounds a bit wimpish but I want Hugh to see something bright and beautiful when they take those damned bandages off. Not just white walls and polished floors.'

April found his gesture unbearably touching. This rough, gruff man loved his friend, with a love that urged him to do something he would normally find embarrassing.

'I think that's a wonderful idea,' she said warmly. 'I wish I had thought of it first.' And I wish I shared your faith in the operation, she added privately.

'Hugh won't think it...silly?'

'Oh, no, Harry. He'd really appreciate it, I'm sure.'

Once Harry was gone April moved her chair closer and reached to stroke the damp strands of hair away from Hugh's forehead. He was sweating profusely. Surely he was too hot? She glanced at the numerous blankets and wondered if she should ring for a nurse. Common sense told her it wouldn't hurt if she removed just one. She did so, then turned the other blankets back from his neck.

He stirred. 'Thirsty,' came the raspy whisper.

April saw the jug of iced water on his traymobile and quickly poured a little into the plastic cup. She pressed it to his lips, thinking he would just take a sip, but he gulped down a couple of mouthfuls. It was a mistake. Immediately he retched, and she reached for the bowl in the nick of time. Once he had finished and was lying back, pale and drained, she pressed the buzzer.

A nurse bustled in, saw the problem, and advised no more water for a while. She did, however, take off another blanket. 'After a while he can suck some ice, and, if he doesn't bring that up, then he can have a few sips of the water.' She bustled out with the bowl, returning immediately with a clean one.

'I'm sorry, Hugh,' April said softly.

'April? Is that you? I thought you were a nurse.'

'Hopeless nurse I'd be. I shouldn't have let you drink so much.'

A faint smile flittered at the corners of his parched lips. 'We always seem to be having a problem with drink,' he murmured.

She stiffened at the memories his words evoked, unable to continue. The silence was both awkward and extended.

'You still there?' he asked, a tentative hand reaching along the bed.

She only hesitated the tiniest second. 'Yes, Hugh,' she said, taking his long slender fingers in hers and giving them a reassuring squeeze. I'm still here, she said silently. I'll never leave you. Not unless you tell me to go.

He did not tell her to go, nor did he let her hand go. It rested in his on the mattress, palm against palm, fingers entwined.

'Harry was here when they brought you back to your room,' she said evenly, not at all betraying the way her heart was racing. 'He went out to buy you something.'

'Oh? What else is there for him to buy?'

'It's a personal present, a surprise, and I'm not going to spoil it by telling you.'

'You and Harry are already spoiling me with all this attention. Shouldn't you be at lectures, or something?'

'Nope. I don't go back till next Monday so you'll have to put up with me for the rest of the week. And Uncle Guy said he'd drop in at the weekend, if you're still here.'

'God, I hope not! I've had enough of hospitals to last me a lifetime. But I would like to thank him for those cassettes he sent over. They were a godsend last night.'

'I'll pass on your thanks,' she offered.

'You're a good friend, April. I don't know what I would have done without you and Harry.'

Tears hovered in her big blue eyes. Oh, Hugh... I don't want to just be your friend...

He licked obviously dry lips. 'Could I have a chunk of that ice, do you think?'

She quickly blinked back the tears. 'Just a small piece.' She slipped a bit on to his tongue, but by moving she'd had to drop his hand, and when she sat back down it seemed too forward for her to pick it up again. The feeling of closeness that seemed to be growing between them disappeared with the loss of physical contact, melted away like the ice.

She began to wish Harry would return but by noon he was still absent. A lunch tray came for Hugh, but he said the very thought of food turned his stomach. The meal, a mild curry and rice, looked quite appetising and when April said as much Hugh suggested she have it.

She was indeed hungry, worry having made her skip breakfast, and it didn't take much encouragement for her to give in. Besides, it was something to do and, while eating, she was almost glad to see Hugh drift off to sleep, his head lolling to one side on the pillows. A fortuitous happening, as it turned out, for Harry popped his head in the door shortly afterwards.

'Asleep, eh? Good.' His head disappeared, only to be replaced by the most enormous arrangement of carnations she had even seen. Pink, red and white interspersed with greenery. And that wasn't all. There followed a basket full of delicately hued orchids and then a massive spray of yellow and orange gladioli.

'Couldn't find any blue flowers,' Harry complained. 'The violet in the orchids was the closest I could get.'

'Oh, Harry... Harry... They're lovely.' April gave him an enthusiastic kiss on the cheek.

'Cut that out! Keep the kisses for Hugh.'

April went bright red. 'Harry! Ssh... Hugh might hear you.' Now she was completely flustered.

'So? Do him good to know you love him!'

'No, Harry, no,' she whispered. 'Please don't tell him. Promise me you won't!'

'That you, Harry?'

With Hugh's awakening, April shot Harry a pleading look. He nodded reluctantly before answering his mate. April stifled her sigh of relief. Much as she had fantasised over pursuing Hugh with a more aggressive, liberated attitude, it just wasn't her. That time up at the cove had been an unusual situation, a spontaneous temptation she hadn't been able to resist. But in the cold light of day she knew she had too much pride to throw herself at Hugh's feet. And too much sense. For even if he capitulated, and had an affair with her, it wouldn't last. It couldn't, unless he truly loved her back.

After Harry's return, conversation was kept to what they were going to do when Hugh got out of hospital. Everyone sounded relatively normal but at regular intervals a short, strained silence would descend, betraying their underlying tensions.

Hugh's doctor made an appearance shortly after three. A tall slim man, still in theatre garb, he breezed in with the ward sister and, without further ado, began removing Hugh's bandages. April found herself holding her breath, so taken aback was she by the doctor's speed and efficiency.

'Everything went well, Mr Davies. We'll take these off for a few minutes then replace them for a couple of hours. After that they can stay off, but I would suggest you wear your dark glasses until your eyes stop watering under glare.' He didn't even slow down as the last bandage dropped away. 'There we are. Now open your eyes, Mr Davies.'

Understandably, Hugh didn't spring his eyes open as fast as the doctor ordered. April watched in petrified hope as both eyelids flickered, then blinked, then rose. Can you see? she wanted to scream at him. Say something, Hugh! Oh, please, don't let him still be blind.

His eyes were on her...surely. Staring at her... Was he really focusing, or was it some cruel quirk of fate that made him appear to be looking in her direction? And then his lips moved.

'Blue *and* beautiful,' he whispered.

'What is, Hugh?' she murmured, moving closer.

'Your eyes...'

'Oh...' The tears flooded into those blue eyes with such a rush even she wasn't prepared for them. They spilled over, ran down her cheeks, trickled down the back of her throat, choking off any further speech. She turned her face away with a muffled sob.

'Things have been a bit tense around here,' Harry said in an explanatory way. 'Fact is, I feel a bit like crying myself.'

Oh, kind, kind Harry, April thought as she pulled herself together and turned back, mopping at her eyes.

They were all waiting for Hugh to say something more but he seemed frozen, stunned almost, his gaze jerking away from April to stare almost blankly at Harry's beautiful flowers. Suddenly he blinked, his eyes finally focusing on the various colours of the glorious display. He shot Harry a heart-warming glance.

'Your eyes feel OK?' the doctor asked. 'They appear to be watering a little.'

'They're fine.' Hugh's voice was thick. 'Can't I leave the bandages off?'

'Well, I——'

'Please...' The plea echoed in the room, and even the hardest heart in the world could not have been unmoved.

The ward sister cleared her throat. 'If we turned off these lights and brought in a lamp,' she suggested kindly, 'he should be all right, Doctor.'

'Hmm. It's a mite irregular, but I suppose it'll be all right. Best draw the curtains.'

·April hurried to do so and the ward sister went in search of a bedside lamp. She was back within a minute and the doctor was satisfied with the results.

'I'll see you in the morning, Mr Davies,' he rapped out as he walked quickly away, the nurse in harried pursuit.

'He should be a truck driver,' Harry quipped after him. 'He'd never be late with a load, that's for sure.'

Hugh smiled for the first time but he was looking at Harry, April noticed, not herself. 'I gather you're the one responsible for transforming my room into a Garden of Eden?' he teased.

'Who said?' Harry blustered.

'A little bird told me.' Hugh laughed, giving April a lightning glance. Why did she have the awful feeling that he didn't want to look at her? Was he embarrassed now that he was forced to put a face to the voice that had tried to seduce him?

'I thought you might like to see all the colours you've been missing,' Harry muttered. 'The only one I couldn't buy was blue.'

Hugh's eyes turned almost reluctantly back to April. 'That colour seems catered for already, don't you think?'

'You mean girlie's eyes? Yes, I have to admit that it's hard to top them.'

'Oh, go on with you!' she said impatiently. 'It's Hugh's eyes we should be talking about. Isn't it wonderful, Hugh? Aren't you happy?'

Those grey eyes which she'd imagined so long ago to have been blue as well flickered with the strangest expression. She tried to grasp its essence but it eluded her. There was a hint of distress, then frustration, then finally...nothing. She could no longer hope to see it. He had shut out the light, drawn the curtains across his soul.

'Of course I'm happy,' he said in an oddly taut voice.

April glanced at her watch as she came downstairs that evening. Ten past seven. Time to be leaving for the hospital. She hastened her step, popping her head into her uncle's study before she left. 'I'm off now. Thanks again for the loan of the car.'

Guy glanced up from his writing and pushed his reading glasses up on to the top of his head. 'Let me have a look at you.'

April moved into the room with some reluctance. She had gone to a lot of trouble with her appearance, thinking that Hugh might not have been impressed with her baggy jeans and simple T-shirt that afternoon. 'I'll be late,' she said with a nervous laugh.

Her uncle cast a discerning eye over his niece's comely figure, shown to advantage by a lemon cotton jersey dress. It had a rolled collar, cut-in shoulders and a slim, curve-hugging fit. The white leather belt slung around her hips matched her high-heeled white sandals, all of which contrasted with her black hair. A pale bronze lipstick outlined her full lips and a whiff of perfume wafted from her pulse-points.

Uncle Guy sniffed, then frowned. 'You're rather dolled up for a hospital visit, aren't you?'

'Do you think so?' she answered carelessly.

The grey eyes narrowed. 'Yes, I do,' he said curtly. 'What exactly *is* your relationship with our Mr Davies?'

'R-relationship, Uncle? Why, we're just good friends.'

'Just good friends,' he repeated slowly. 'Somehow I don't feel reassured by that comment, my dear. Remember, I *am* responsible for your welfare. I hope you realise that Hugh Davies is a grown man?'

'Yes. As I'm a grown woman,' she countered with far more assertiveness than she usually showed to her uncle.

He looked taken aback for a second, but then he nodded. 'So I see...'

'I must go, Uncle, or I'll be late. Bye.'

April felt quite proud of herself as she hurried off. She could appreciate her uncle's concern, since Hugh was far older than the boys she usually dated, but after all she would be twenty-one shortly, and it was *her* life. April *knew* she loved Hugh, knew it wasn't a silly adolescent infatuation as Max had been. Of course, what would happen from this point on she *didn't* know. That was up to Hugh. But nothing was going to stop her from doing her best to impress him as a grown-up young lady, not some flighty girl just out of her teens.

The visiting-bell sounded as April dashed up the steps of the hospital, so she wasn't late. She stopped at the shop in the foyer where visitors could buy gifts for the patients. April waffled over fruit or chocolates and finally compromised. With a box of fruit jellies in her hand, she made her way up the stairs to the first floor, her pulse-rate leaping into overdrive as she approached private room 7b.

April should not have slowed near Hugh's room. If she'd walked right in without hesitating she wouldn't have had to live through such a painful experience. As it was she stopped to catch her breath and steady her nerves, and in that brief span of silence a woman's voice drifted, clear as a bell, through the open doorway.

'Hugh, I can't tell you how much it means to me to see you looking so...fit and well. And to think you can see again. I can hardly believe it.'

'Really, Cynthia?' April's breath caught at the name, and the hard sound in Hugh's voice. 'Forgive me if I say your good wishes are a trifle late.'

'Oh, Hugh... Hugh... Don't be like that. You've no idea what I've been through... The agony... The guilt. It's been hell.'

'It hasn't exactly been a picnic for me either.'

'I know, I know. And you've no idea how sorry I am at the way things turned out. If only I'd been stronger, but when I saw you after the accident, so still, blood all over your face... At first I thought you were dead...' The words shook with emotion. 'I sat with you in the emergency ward at the hospital for hours and hours. I never left you for a minute. You were unconscious most of the time but occasionally you'd half wake in a sort of delirious fog. All you said was..."I can't see, I can't see"...over and over in some kind of ghastly litany. Hugh it—it tore me apart...'

Cynthia's voice broke for a moment, but when she continued it rang out, warm and overwhelmingly sincere. 'I couldn't bear it, Hugh. To see you lying there, broken and bruised. And the intern said you were blind. Nobody told me that there was even the remotest chance you'd get your sight back. I suppose—looking back—that there hadn't been time for them to do the appropriate tests, to bring in the specialists...'

The voice faltered, then resumed, a desperate note trapped in every word. 'Try—please try—to look at it from my point of view. I felt terribly responsible. I... I'd had a couple of vodkas before I came to pick you up that night. I thought you'd hate me for having caused your blindness. Knowing how much your art means to you, I couldn't envisage our relationship lasting. Every time you felt frustrated about not being able to do the things you wanted to do, you'd blame me.'

'Cynthia, I——'

'No, wait! Let me finish. I have to say it all, make you understand. I...I had a nervous breakdown. Daddy sent me to a rest-home overseas. I was there for months. I've only been home a little while. Don't ever doubt that I loved you, Hugh. I did. I loved you. I still do. Even if you never want to see me again...'

April's hand flew to her mouth, stifling the sob that had risen to her lips. She leant back against the wall, her breathing a series of rapid, shallow pants. She wished with all her heart that she had never heard the words Cynthia had just spoken, never heard the undoubtable truth each syllable contained. She said she loved Hugh, and the worst thing was...April believed her. Her action of deserting him had been a disturbed emotional reaction, not the heartless cruelty April had imagined. And if, as April suspected, he was still harbouring feelings for the woman, it wouldn't be long before she was back in his life again.

April could not bear to stay another moment longer. She levered herself away from the wall and hurried along the corridor, the box of jellies clutched to her chest. She fled down the stairs, along another corridor, past the shop, into the foyer. As she hurried towards the open main doorway her progress was halted by a big, rough hand closing firmly over her slender wrist.

'And where do you think you're going?'

Startled, April stared up into Harry's rather angry-looking face.

'Are they for Hugh?' he went on, tapping the box of fruit jellies.

She swallowed and nodded.

'Hmph!' Harry snorted. 'Don't tell me. You took one look at dear old Cynthia and bolted. Am I right or am I wrong?'

April's stricken eyes dropped to the tiles on the foyer floor. 'Sort of,' she husked.

'For pity's sake, don't leave the poor bloke in that bloody woman's clutches!'

April's head snapped up, her eyes flashing. 'What else do you expect me to do? She loves him, and he probably still loves her.'

'Poppycock!'

'Oh, Harry, you're prejudiced!'

Harry clenched his teeth together and looked like thunder. 'Maybe I am,' he muttered, 'but I can recognise a sincere person when I see one. And that Cynthia female is definitely a fraud!'

'Believe what you like, Harry,' April sighed.

'I certainly will! You should have been there when she sashayed into the room a few minutes ago. She looked at me as if I were something that had crawled out from under a stone. Just because I'm dressed like this.' His hand waved over his shorts and singlet. 'She's nothing but a bloody snob,' he went on fiercely. 'Dismissed me as if I were a servant. Said she wanted a private chat with Hugh. And let me tell you something else, April. She'll have a hard job convincing Hugh she really loved him...I saw the fury welling up in those newly opened eyes of his when she walked into that room. Our Hugh's a lot less trusting than he was a year ago, I can assure you.'

'Believe me, Harry,' April said wearily, 'she was coping very well when I left.' She pushed the box of jellies into Harry's hands. 'Here, give these to Hugh, and for God's sake don't tell him they're from me.'

'But he's expecting you.'

'I'm sure you can think of a plausible excuse. Say I was sick or something.'

'Oh, girlie, you're making a big mistake.'

She sighed. 'Harry, I've been making one big mistake after another, ever since I met the man.'

CHAPTER NINE

APRIL was sitting alone at the kitchen table the following morning, forcing some muesli down her throat, when the phone rang. She dashed to answer it before it woke her uncle, who hated being disturbed before nine. 'Hello?' she asked rather breathlessly.

'April?'

Her heart did a complete somersault at the sound of Hugh's voice. Goodness, what was he doing ringing her at this hour? It wasn't even eight o'clock. 'Hugh, what is it? Is there something wrong?'

His light laughter brought instant relief. 'My, but you're a little worrier, aren't you? Nothing's gone wrong. Everything's fine now.'

Fine that he had his eyesight back? Or fine that Cynthia was back in his life? 'Then why are you ringing?' she said far too tautly.

'You mean you don't know?'

'I have no idea.'

'You little fibber! There I was last night, waiting with bated breath for you to arrive, and what happened? All I got was a box of fruit jellies and some pathetic message that you hadn't wanted to intrude when you saw I already had a visitor.'

April was too rattled by Hugh's flirtatious manner to be angry with Harry for not covering

119

for her. 'Your fiancée is hardly any old visitor, Hugh,' she said shakily.

'My *ex*-fiancée,' he reminded her.

'From what I overheard her telling you, that might only be a temporary status.'

'Don't be ridiculous!' he suddenly snapped. 'I wouldn't take Cynthia back in a million years. I don't know who she thought she was, thinking she could walk back into my life after all that had happened and expect me to forgive and forget.'

'But she still loves you!' April gasped, shocked by his angry outburst.

He made a harsh sound that reminded her of one of Harry's grunts. It only confirmed her suspicion that, underneath his anger, Hugh might still be in love with the woman. 'She sounded very sincere,' April said with her stomach churning.

'Look, let's forget about Cynthia, shall we?' he growled, reinforcing April's fear. 'I'd rather talk about you,' he added in a much lighter tone.

'What about me?'

'For one thing, when am I going to see you?' His voice was seductively soft, dangerously sexy. 'I missed you last night, April.'

She swallowed convulsively. This wasn't happening to her. It *couldn't* be real! It was far too close to her dreams, to what she had hoped would happen once he got his eyesight back. Her mind whirled, wanting to believe the emotion vibrating in his voice, but at the same time wary of it. The last thing she wanted was for him to turn to her on some sort of rebound.

'I'm getting out of hospital tomorrow morning,' he went on when she said nothing. 'And I can't wait! I'm dying to get back to work after all those wasted months. But first...'

'First?' she repeated, her heart in her mouth.

'First, I have to buy some new clothes. I have nothing that fits me except a couple of pairs of Bermuda shorts. Harry's come up with some jeans and a sports shirt I can wear out of the hospital, but I can hardly live in those. Would you come with me, April, give me your expert female advice? Harry says his taste in clothes is as pathetic as mine and I need a woman's opinion.'

Now April was confused. Was that all Hugh wanted from her, help with selecting some new clothes? Her heart sank. No doubt she'd misinterpreted his earlier behaviour as flirting. He'd merely been on a high from being given the good news about leaving hospital.

'I'd like to, Hugh,' she said with a sigh, 'but I have to go in to the university tomorrow and buy my textbooks for this semester. If I don't they'll all be gone.'

'Couldn't you go today instead?' he persisted. 'I really want you to come with me.'

'I... I suppose so. But I'll have to miss your afternoon visit. I can't come tonight, either. Uncle Guy needs his car and he won't let me use public transport at night.'

'I fully agree with him. Don't worry about any visiting today. Now that I can see again, it's not so lonely. Harry insisted on renting me a TV.'

'Where do you want me to meet you, then, on the Thursday?' she asked. 'In the city, or at the hospital?'

'How about we meet in the hospital foyer at ten-thirty? I'll get Harry to leave my Rover in the car park.'

They spoke for a few more minutes over nothing consequential but he made her laugh a few times. It rather disturbed her, this new relaxed Hugh. In a way April preferred the short-tempered mocking individual she was used to, for she always knew where she stood with him, firmly in the role of likeable kid and platonic friend, with no chance of anything more. Now she wasn't so sure...

Maybe he *had* been flirting with her earlier. Perhaps Cynthia's turning up had merely confirmed in his mind that he was over her. Maybe Harry had been right, April pondered. Now Hugh had seen she wasn't such a kid, he might want more from her than just friendship.

April was still considering the possibilities when a bleary-eyed Uncle Guy came into the kitchen just after nine. 'Did I hear the phone before?' he asked with a yawn. 'Was it for me?'

'Er—no.' She bit her bottom lip, feeling nervous over her uncle's reaction to her continuing friendship with Hugh. 'It was Hugh, telling me he was getting out of hospital tomorrow and asking me to go clothes-shopping with him.'

Uncle Guy gave her a sharp look. 'And you're going, I suppose.'

She turned steady eyes towards him. 'Of course. Why not?'

He shrugged. 'You're asking for trouble going out with a man as old as that.'

April's chin lifted. 'Hugh's a decent man,' she defended.

'But still a man!' Her uncle snorted. 'And I suppose you're going to ask him to your twenty-first birthday party as well.'

Her coming-of-age was on the following Saturday week, and, while her parents had promised her a big celebration when she went home soon at Easter, Uncle Guy had insisted on giving her a party on the actual day. 'I . . . I'd like to,' she admitted.

His expression showed resignation. 'Very well. I've always held the opinion that when a young person reaches the age of twenty-one it's time they assume full responsibility for their life. Just remember that also means you have to accept all the consequences of your actions.'

April cocked her head to one side and studied Hugh's reflection in the large mirror stuck on the wall. It was safer somehow than looking at the real thing. 'Yes,' she told him. 'That should do.'

What an understatement! Hugh was looking breathtakingly handsome in an outfit she had put together from the casual menswear department at a local department store. A loosely woven coffee-coloured top hugged his chest, the expensive knit fabric not wrinkling at all where it stretched across the broad muscles. Off-white stretch jeans skimmed across his hips then followed the shape of his powerful legs down to the cream canvas loafers on his feet.

The sales assistant who'd been helping them walked over with a jacket in his hands. 'This matches the jeans,' he said, slipping the modern, loosely shaped garment up Hugh's arms and over his broad shoulders.

It looked terrific, as had the other clothes they had decided upon. The pile already included a dark brown casually styled suit, assorted separates, a soft camel-coloured leather jacket, shoes, shirts, socks. But no ties. Hugh refused to wear what he called an outdated utterly useless item.

'Your husband looks well in just about anything, ma'am,' the salesman complimented.

April coloured. 'Oh, but he's——'

'You like this jacket, darling?' Hugh cut in, lifting his sunglasses for a second to wink boldly at her.

April tried not to show how taken aback she was. Since they had met up at ten-thirty in the hospital foyer Hugh had been friendly enough in his manner towards her. But there'd been not a hint of his wanting to develop their friendship into anything more, though wearing those sunglasses did preclude the eye contact a man and woman used to give that sort of message. Now here he was, suddenly expecting her to take part in a joke that implied a familiar intimacy between them.

April was bewildered for only a moment, however, quickly realising that this was just another form of Hugh's old patronising self. It was a type of teasing, putting her on the spot like this. Irritation made her decide to teach him a lesson.

'Oh, I don't know, dear,' she said, tapping a doubtful finger against her chin. 'It's very nice but haven't we spent enough already? The telephone bill came in yesterday and I have to confess it's a mite higher than usual. I suppose I shouldn't have rung Mother in Brazil so often last month. But I thought, how often does one's mother explore the far reaches of the Amazon? I mean, she might not come back, might she?' April directed towards the startled assistant. 'What value can one put upon a mother? I mean...'

Hugh strode over and clamped a firm hand over her elbow. 'Now don't get yourself all worked up, darling,' he said through gritted teeth. 'I have enough money for the telephone bill *and* the clothes. We'll take everything!' he informed the open-mouthed man standing beside them.

Hugh was still shaking his head when he pulled his grey Rover up outside his house at Mosman. 'That's the last time I take you shopping, you minx,' he said with a pretend growl, then laughed.

April surrendered to her own fit of the giggles. It had been rather fun, despite her initial pique. 'Did you see the look on that man's face?' she chortled.

'I certainly did. He threw me a pitying glance, I can tell you. Not that he should mind. I was a damned good customer.'

'You did spend a lot, Hugh,' April commented with a slight frown.

'I can afford it,' he tossed off. 'I rang my accountant this morning and it seems my modest inheritance has more than kept pace with inflation this last year. A genius at investment, that man. Besides, I haven't spent much on clothes for years. Come on, let's leave the parcels for the moment and go inside. I think we deserve some coffee. Not only that, I have something I want to show you.'

April laughed. 'Is this another version of "come up and I'll show you my etchings"?'

His face turned slowly towards her and her breath caught in her throat. 'And what if it were?' he asked quietly.

She gulped down, suddenly aware of nothing but the mad thumping of her heart and the knowledge that behind those glasses his eyes were definitely roving over her body. She was wearing the same yellow outfit he hadn't seen the other night and the knitted material now felt hot and clammy against her skin.

'I . . . I don't think I'd like it,' she said, her voice sounding strangled. But the admission amazed her with its truth. Up till this moment, she had thought she would willingly let Hugh make love to her whenever and wherever he wanted to.

She could see he was frowning now, his forehead wrinkling above the glasses. 'Hugh, I'm sorry if you thought that——'

He stopped her by reaching over and touching her hand. 'It's all right, April. Really. No need for any apology of any kind. I'm glad you're not the sort of girl who leaps into bed with anyone at the drop of a hat.'

'But Hugh,' she said, taking a deep breath, 'I don't think of you as just anyone. You know that. I wouldn't mind if you made love to me . . .'

He sucked in a startled breath.

'...but only if you really care about me. Not because you're missing Cynthia.'

He took off his sunglasses. His eyes were appalled. 'Is that what you think? That I would use you as some sort of sexual substitute?'

'Not intentionally...'

He gave an exasperated sigh. 'I thought I'd already demonstrated I wasn't that sort of man!'

She shrugged. 'You're only human, Hugh.'

His look was sharp and thoughtful. 'You really aren't so young, are you?'

Her heart leapt but she kept her eyes steady on his. 'I don't think so. But it's what *you* think that matters.'

'Just at this moment,' he muttered, 'I'm not sure what I think...'

'Then perhaps we'd better forget this conversation and go inside,' she went on, her composure the best piece of acting she had ever done. 'Didn't you want to show me one of your pieces of marble?'

Hugh's face showed surprise. 'How did you know what it was I wanted to show you?'

Her smile was wry. 'A person couldn't be around you five minutes without knowing your priorities in life. Your work comes first, second and third, in that order. Anything else would have to be slotted in at random.'

'Is that so?' A single eyebrow lifted, but his gaze dropped to her mouth and breasts before returning to her eyes. 'My priorities have been reassessed lately.'

April was shaken by the depth of desire she saw in Hugh's eyes. 'Come on, let's go,' she suggested nervously, her hand going to the door-handle. 'It's getting hot in here.'

Hugh was laughing as they both climbed out.

April blushed her confusion, unaware that she had made a *double entendre*. 'Did I say something funny?'

'Not at all. Not at all,' he hastily returned, but a drily amused expression lurked in his eyes.

As he led her over to the gate April realised what she had said, and flushed uncomfortably. How odd, she thought, that Hugh's coming on to her sexually should rattle her so! It was what she wanted, wasn't it?

The answer came back straight away. Not quite... She only wanted Hugh as her lover if he really cared about her, if any physical relationship between them was to lead to a more permanent one. Yet that seemed unlikely, for April could not see Hugh having a girl of her age as his girlfriend, let alone marrying her.

Both the gate and front door were locked, prompting April to ask where Harry was.

'He's out looking for a job,' Hugh explained as he ushered April along the cool hallway and into his work-room. 'He said I didn't need a minder any more and he had no intention of being a free-loader.'

April shook her head. 'Isn't that just like him? He pretends to be a hard man but he's not, is he? Perhaps one day he'll learn to trust women again, and fall in love.'

'I doubt it. He was hurt too deeply. Here, have a look at this,' he said, and swept a dustcloth off a piece of marble resting on the work-table. 'Tell me what you think of when you look at it. Tell me what you see.'

April took a deep breath and walked slowly forwards.

It was a roughly rectangular block, bluish grey in colour, with streaks and dots of white running through the top section. It was also completely unworked, a virgin block of stone waiting for the touch of the master.

'Well?' he prompted impatiently.

She ran a hand over the cold smooth surface and immediately it came to her. 'The sea...that's what I see... The surf in storm, with the waves curling upwards, foam along their crests just before they crash on to the shore...' Her voice trailed away and she turned to look at him.

He was staring at her, his mouth open. Then it snapped shut. He came forward and grabbed her, lifting her up and whirling her around the room. 'My God, you're a genius. A bloody genius!'

He plonked her down and dashed over to the table where he bent down to examine the marble from every angle, his hands never still on the object of his passion. April found her heart beating faster as she watched him. Oh, to be that piece of marble, she groaned silently, to have him adore her so thoroughly and so passionately.

'I'll let you name it,' he offered. 'Not now—when it's finished!'

He stalked around the table once more and April had the distinct impression that his creative fingers were already itching. 'I think you'd better take me home now, Hugh,' she said, 'so that you can get back here and go to work.'

His eyes flashed to hers, his expression surprised. 'You understand that I must? You wouldn't be offended?'

She could only smile. 'Would it make any difference if I were?'

'No.' He grinned.

April asked him to her birthday party during the drive back to Balmain, adding that she wanted him to ask Harry as well. Hugh accepted readily but expressed doubt about Harry, who he said hated crowds and strangers. 'I'll do my best to persuade him, though,' he offered.

April had expected him to just drop her off and go, but he asked to come inside and look at the marble basket her uncle had bought. She didn't mind, but she was a little nervous over what cryptic comment her uncle might make about her continuing friendship with Hugh.

No voice called out to her, however, when she let them both in. 'I don't think Uncle Guy's home,' she said with a relieved sigh. 'The basket's on the hall table along there,' she indicated to Hugh. 'Go on ahead. I'm coming. I'll just shut the door.'

He was standing looking at it when she joined him. He gave her a small smile, then deftly slipped the rings into two of the dips in the handle where they swung in perfect symmetry.

'Oh!' she exclaimed. 'Is that where they're supposed to go?'

'Not necessarily... Just another perspective.'

'Hugh Davies, you wicked man!' She laughed, giving him a playful tap on his arm. 'Won't you ever let me forget the stupid things I said and did up at the cove?'

He grabbed her wrist and slowly, ever so slowly drew her to him, his eyes locking on to hers. She stared up into them, instantly breathless. 'I don't want to forget any more,' he murmured. 'I want to remember everything. The way you felt, the way you responded to me. I've wanted to do this,' he rasped, his arms enfolding around her back and pressing her to him, 'since the moment I laid eyes on you yesterday.'

And then he was kissing her, bending her head back and kissing her, taking her gasping parted lips for his pleasure, sending his tongue between them, making her moan as a thousand stars exploded in her head.

'God,' he muttered when he released her mouth.

She looked up at him with a type of bewilderment and anxiety in her eyes. For much as Hugh's kiss had aroused her, it also brought apprehension. 'Hugh, I——'

He placed a finger against her lips. 'It's not what you think, April. My intentions are strictly honourable. I care about you, love, much more than I realised. Am I right in thinking you feel the same way?'

'Oh, Hugh...' She could hardly speak, so great was her joy. 'You—you know I do... I *love* you.'

Again that finger pressed against her lips. 'Let's not talk of love just yet, my sweet. Let's take things slowly. There's no need to rush things, is there?'

April's high took a small down-turn. Clearly Hugh was still worried about her age. 'I'm not as young as you think, Hugh,' she insisted. 'Country girls can be surprisingly mature.'

'So I've noticed.' He smiled wryly, his eyes glancing down at her prominent bust.

She gave him another playful thump. 'Stop that, Hugh Davies! I think that underneath your fuddy-duddy act you're very naughty!'

'Guilty as charged.' He laughed, and went to kiss her again.

The sound of the back door banging startled both of them. They were still looking surprised—and perhaps a little guilty—when seconds later Uncle Guy appeared at the end of the hall. 'Oh, it's you, April. I thought I heard something. I was out in the laundry doing some washing. Hello, Hugh...' Her uncle's rather cold gaze swept over him. 'Nice to see you again,' he said in a voice that held no pleasure. 'Glad to hear the good news about your eyes.'

'Thanks.' Hugh nodded, his swift frown showing he had noted her uncle's coolness. He gave April a thoughtful look. 'I think I should go,' he said. 'What date did you say your party was?'

'Sat-Saturday week,' she stammered, shocked that he meant it to be that long before he saw her again.

'And when does it start?'

'About eight,' she said, her face showing her confusion and dismay.

'Right. Thanks again for your help with the shopping, April. And the piece of marble,' he added. '*Au revoir*, Guy.'

'And you,' her uncle muttered before turning away. Hugh gave a dry little smile, took April's hand and walked slowly with her along to the front door. 'Your uncle doesn't approve,' he said ruefully. 'He probably thinks I'm too old for you.'

'He's just being over-protective!'

'Perhaps.'

'Hugh...' She lifted pleading eyes to him. 'Won't I be seeing you again before my party?'

He gave a frustrated sigh. 'I have months of work to catch up on, April. And your party's only nine days away.' When April went to protest he gave her a soft lingering kiss. 'Trust me,' he said on straightening. 'I want to prove to your uncle that what he's thinking isn't so.'

'And what's that?'

'Exactly what *you* thought. That all I want from you is your luscious young body.'

'But you don't! *Do* you?'

'We-ll...' He grinned. 'I *was* hoping it came with the package.'

Hugh left shortly after, April standing at the kerb, following him hungrily with her eyes till he had driven off and disappeared around the far corner.

She turned away, a groan escaping her lips. Nine days till her party. Nine interminable days. She didn't know how she was going to stand it.

CHAPTER TEN

APRIL returned to university on the Monday but wasn't able to put her mind to the lectures, sometimes a whole hour going by before realising she hadn't taken a single note. She scrambled around afterwards, begging notes from friends, but knowing if she didn't settle down soon her results at the end of the year might not be all she had hoped for.

Hugh delighted her by ringing on the Thursday evening, then astonished her by saying he had finished the surf piece. My God, she thought, he must have been working on it day and night since I last saw him.

'Now I'm on to a much smaller project. The type of thing,' he pointed out, 'that the ordinary person could put in an ordinary room. Some little bird once told me not to go making unwieldy sculpture.'

April laughed.

'By the way,' he went on, 'Harry can't make it to your party. He's taken a job driving coaches to Surfer's Paradise every weekend. He said he was sorry but I think he was relieved. Parties unnerve him.'

'That's all right. I understand. But if *you* don't come, I'll kill you. And don't be too late!'

'Wild horses won't keep me away,' he said, dropping to a low, intimate voice that sent prickles up and down her spine.

April's birthday dawned lovely and fine, her level of excitement increasing with the passing of the hours. She kept looking at the clock, counting off the hours till she would see Hugh again. The only dampener on the day was that she had wanted to buy herself something wonderful to wear but her stringent budget simply wouldn't stretch to party clothes. She would just have to dress up her best black skirt with one of her prettier tops.

By seven she had showered and shampooed her hair and was sitting at her dressing-table in a robe, putting on her make-up, when her uncle knocked on the door. He came in looking sheepish, trying to hide a large, gaily wrapped box behind his back.

'Happy birthday, my dear,' he said, grinning, and whipped the box to the front.

She stood up and took it with some bewilderment. 'I thought I wasn't going to open my presents till later!'

'Aah, but this one won't wait.' He beamed. 'Come on, open it up.'

She took the lid off the box and cried out in delight. 'A dress! Oh, Uncle Guy, you've bought me a party dress!' She drew the obviously expensive creation from the elegantly wrapped box. 'Oh, thank you, thank you!' she burst out and kissed him.

'It should fit,' he said. 'I snuck a dress out of your wardrobe to match your size. Don't let me hold you up, now. I have to go down and get the drinks and glasses ready, and put some music on. But you'd better be downstairs by eight in case we have some early arrivals.'

When her uncle closed the door April stripped off her robe and stepped very carefully into the dress. It was dazzling white, made of a fine cotton with a broderie anglaise border. The style reminded April of the type a tavern wench might have worn in Robin Hood's day, with elbow-length puffy sleeves, a low square neckline and tightly laced bodice. The skirt flounced wide then dipped almost to her ankles.

It soon became obvious that her bra would have to go. April discarded it freely enough and laced the bodice up. But when she glanced at her finished reflection in the dressing-table mirror, she almost died. Good God, she couldn't go downstairs like that, with two mounds of burgeoning flesh spilling out over the top of the neckline. It was almost obscene!

The only solution was to loosen the laces slightly, which settled her breasts into a lower, more comfortable position, though now showing a formidable amount of cleavage. April had never worn such a daring style in her life and, despite the fact that her uncle had bought the dress, when she did finally come downstairs she felt self-conscious in it.

Her uncle was standing behind the small bar in the corner of the front lounge-room, polishing glasses, humming away to a Bette Midler song, when she walked in. His humming came to an abrupt halt. 'Good God,' he gasped, his mouth staying open.

'Don't...don't you like it?' she asked shakily.

'Well, I—er——' He gathered himself quickly, his face falling into a resigned, though rueful, expression. 'You look lovely, April,' he complimented her. 'I'm just surprised how...different...it looks on you from how it did on the coat-hanger in the shop.'

The doorbell suddenly rang out, thereby bringing any further discussion on the dress to a swift halt.

'Someone's a bit early,' Guy muttered. 'It's only five to eight. Answer it for me, would you, April? I haven't finished these glasses yet.'

Her heart began to race as she walked out into the hall. Maybe it was Hugh. She hoped so. Perhaps he was as anxious to see her as she was to see him. She hesitated for a second before her hand went to the knob, taking a deep breath to calm a sudden burst of nerves. But when she saw what this did to her neckline she groaned and stuffed her overflowing bust back down, flattening it savagely with outspread palms. A quavering smile graced her mouth as she opened the door.

Max Goldman stood on the doorstep, a bunch of white carnations in one hand and a gift box in the other.

April's mouth fell open as she looked up at him. He looked as dashing as ever in a trendily printed shirt and cream linen trousers, his blond hair sporting a new semi-spiked hair-cut.

'Hmm,' he murmured, running speculative eyes over her as he stepped under the light in the hall.

He handed her the flowers and kissed her on the cheek. 'Happy birthday, doll.'

April was still standing there gaping when her uncle joined them. 'Max! You made it!' He came up and pumped Max's hand.

'I wouldn't miss April's twenty-first.' Max grinned down at her. 'It means she's officially an adult.' And ready for anything, he managed to convey.

April suppressed a groan. Why on earth hadn't she told Uncle Guy about her encounter with Max? It would have avoided this ghastly situation.

'Amuse Max for me, April. I have to get some ice out of the freezer.'

'I gather you weren't expecting me,' Max drawled when her uncle moved away.

'Hardly.' She made no pretence at being polite. She detested the man.

'I presume Guy doesn't know about us?'

'No.'

He laughed. 'So... You haven't forgiven me yet?'

She stared up at him, thinking what gall he had. But then came the realisation that in his pseudo-sophisticated world there was no such thing as sensitivity. All one could do to protect oneself from the Maxes in this life was to never let them get under your skin. 'Forgive you, Max?' She adopted a bored smile. 'Heavens, I'm grateful to you.'

'Grateful?' He looked amused.

'For saving me from the privilege of being the ninety-ninth scalp on your belt!'

He laughed again. 'You overestimate me, April.'

'I doubt that, Max.' She kept up the light bantering tone, thereby lessening the barbs. 'I will always expect the worst from you and I'm sure you won't ever disappoint me.'

He laughed again. 'Oh, April, you are a delight.' He traced her cleavage with an insolent fingertip, causing her to shrink back in outrage. 'Have you any idea how tempting a morsel you were? And still are... Tell me, then, since it's not me, who *is* the lucky fellow you're wearing this dress for?'

'Does it have to be for anyone?' she countered archly.

His knowing smile told it all.

'You two still standing there?' her uncle said as he bustled past. 'Bring Max in here and I'll get him a drink. April, why don't you open Max's present?'

They moved into the living-room together, Max drawing her down next to him on the enormous semicircular sofa that dominated the room. With a resigned sigh April placed the carnations on the coffee-table and tackled the wrapping-paper of the gift.

'Perfume! How thoughtful...' She smiled up at Max through gritted teeth.

His returning grin showed large white teeth. He reminded April of a vampire, a vampire who preyed on young girls' weaknesses.

'So glad you like it. Mother always said, if in doubt, buy perfume.'

'You have a mother?' April muttered under her breath.

Max wagged a finger at her. 'Naughty, naughty. There I was thinking you'd grown up at last and I find you've just become stroppy. This man of yours must have the patience of Job.'

'Bourbon for you, isn't it, Max?' Guy called from the bar.

'I've moved on to Bacardi, actually,' he drawled. 'With Coke.'

'I thought you'd be a whisky drinker forever,' April quipped, remembering how he had funnelled the Jim Beam down his throat all the time.

'And I thought,' Max whispered, leaning close, 'that you'd be a virgin forever.'

She looked up at him sharply and tried with all her might to stop the heat flooding into her cheeks. Best to say nothing, she thought frantically. Deny nothing. Max was just being Max. 'I'd better take this perfume to my room,' she managed in a splendidly casual voice then sped upstairs, not returning till some more guests had arrived.

By nine o'clock April was convinced Hugh wasn't going to come. She tried not to keep watching and listening for the doorbell by busying herself playing cheerful hostess. She fetched drinks, laughed at jokes and skilfully avoided Max, which was difficult, considering the crush of the crowd. Underneath, she felt sick with despair. If Hugh couldn't make it, he could at least have rung.

The living-room was literally filled to capacity, her uncle having asked a lot of people who had surprised them by all turning up. There were friends of hers from university, neighbours, a few people she played basketball with every winter, some of her uncle's older, more sophisticated set.

Some up-tempo music began to throb, and dancing couples overflowed into the hall, the study, even the kitchen. April was on her way down the hall for more potato chips when she passed Max sitting alone on the stairs, an empty glass in his hands. When he spotted her his free hand shot out, grabbing her wrist and pulling her down on to his lap. 'Come here, o, gorgeous one!' He discarded the glass and slipped his arms around her waist. 'How about coming home with me after the party? We'll celebrate your coming-of-age in style.'

'A few too many Bacardis, Max?' April snapped, and began extricating herself from his octopus arms just as the doorbell sent out its musical announcement.

'Hey, where do you think you're going?' Max growled, his arms tightening.

'That's the door,' she said, trying in vain to free herself.

'So? Someone else will get it.'

'But I——'

'For God's sake, April, will you calm down? You've been acting like a cat on a hot tin roof. Don't be so bloody obvious.'

'Obvious?' she repeated huskily.

'Yeah...obvious. When—and if—your prey arrives, try to be a little more subtle. There's nothing worse than a female falling all over her feet to get to a guy. Very off-putting.'

'And you'd know, I suppose,' she flung at him.

'Sure... Why do you think I was first attracted to you? Despite your sexy little body you had a touch-me-not quality that was quite challenging.'

'Oh, come off it, Max! You and I know only too well why you tried it on me. You'd been left flat and didn't like the prospect of going to bed alone. I just happened to be there.'

'Well, well . . . You have grown up, haven't you? I wonder how much?'

In true Valentino style he bent her backwards on to the stairs and kissed her.

When she went to beat at his chest, he grabbed her hands in a steely grip, holding them fast, using his free hand to grip the back of her head. He was a strong man with large, strong hands. She twisted her face from side to side but this only seemed to enflame him further, for she could feel his tongue probing even more hotly at her tightly clamped lips.

Her eyes widened as her panic increased. She peered over his shoulder, hoping to find someone to help her, and looked straight up into Hugh's face. In a matter of seconds his expression changed from shock to rage to total disgust.

That he would misunderstand the situation so completely gave April the strength to tear her mouth away. 'Max . . . *please*,' she choked out. 'Let me go. Hugh's here.'

Max drew back, his hand still gripping hers to his chest. 'Hugh?' He glanced over his shoulder. 'Good God, it's Hugh *Davies*,' he muttered, then raised his eyebrows. 'Well, well . . .' He released April's hands with an infuriating lack of speed and she hurried to her feet, aware that her face was burning.

She straightened her skirt and tried to stop her chest from heaving too deeply. 'Max was just giving

me a birthday kiss. Weren't you, Max?' she added
with an underlying plea in her voice.

'Naturally—what else? It certainly is a small
world,' Max drawled as he stood up. 'I had no idea
you knew April, Hugh.'

Hugh's gaze raked over Max, then herself. She
felt his regard sweep over her bold cleavage with
definite disapproval. 'The surprise is mutual, Max,'
he countered curtly.

'Oh, April and I are old friends, aren't we, love?
We met up at the cove about a year ago. I suppose
that's where you got to know her as well,' Max
rattled on. 'Well, you look as if your stay up there
has agreed with you, Hugh. Great tan! And your
eyesight's back. Didn't I tell you not to worry about
that? Doctors can perform miracles these days,
can't they, April?'

April made some noise of agreement, her eyes
not having left Hugh for a second. He looked
splendid in dark trousers and an open-necked blue
silk shirt, but it was what he was thinking that was
holding her speechless.

'How long have you been back from overseas,
Max?' he asked in clipped tones.

'Only two days. I was going to ring you next
Monday and find out if you've got your nose back
to grindstone again. After all, it's been almost a
fortnight since your operation,' he finished with a
sardonic grin.

'How well you know me, Max,' Hugh said drily.

'Oh, I don't know...' Max gave April a sly
sideways glance which made her wish the floor
would open up and swallow her. 'I have a feeling

you might have become a dark horse in some re-
gards . . . So tell me, did Cynthia get in contact with
you?'

April saw Hugh stiffen. She herself was startled
by Max's question.

'Cynthia?' Hugh said coldly.

'Yes, I ran into her at the airport in Paris a few
weeks back and told her about your impending operation. She seemed shocked and said she would
definitely go and see you. Did she?'

'She did,' Hugh admitted tautly.

'I gather her visit hasn't heralded an imminent
reconciliation,' Max drawled.

Hugh ignored this comment and turned to April,
who was standing there in a growing daze of terror.
She had the awful feeling that all her hopes and
dreams were disintegrating in front of her and there
was nothing she could do about it.

'I would like a private word with you, April,' he
announced with far too much composure.

Max chuckled. 'OK, I know when I'm not
wanted. I'll go help Guy prop up the bar. And don't
forget to give the birthday girl a kiss, Hugh,' he
called over his shoulder as he ambled off. 'I think
she's been waiting for it.'

They were left virtually alone in the privacy of
the narrow staircase, even though the party was
thrumming along all around them. Hugh stepped
up on to the stair April was glued to, his face instantly thunderous. 'You didn't wait long, though,
did you?' he snarled. 'One miserable bloody hour!'

For a few ghastly seconds April could only stare up at him, appalled that he would condemn her so quickly, without even hearing what she had to say.

'I wasn't kissing Max,' she burst out in defence. '*He* was kissing *me*. I didn't want him to. He just grabbed me.'

Hugh's laugh was dry. 'Look me in the face, April, and tell me that's the first time Max has kissed you. After all, when Max says he got to *know* a girl, he means it in only one way. Oh, I know you didn't sleep with him, not literally. But there's plenty of other activities for an imaginative couple.'

April's eyes widened, resentment at his unjust and hasty judgement fuelling a hot anger of her own. 'I've done nothing I'm ashamed of,' she denied hotly. 'I...I thought I loved him. I—— '

Any further explanation was cut dead by the look on Hugh's face. But it wasn't fury April saw there. It was total exasperation. And just a hint of despair.

'No more, April,' he said in a tight voice. 'No more. Here...' He handed her a small, rectangular gift, wrapped in pretty pink paper. 'Happy birthday.' He went to turn away but she grabbed the sleeve of his shirt. 'You're not leaving?' she asked, frantic.

His cold eyes made her flinch. 'You don't honestly expect me to stay, do you? I'm not a masochist.'

Tears welled up but she refused to let them spill, refused to show this man how much he was hurting her. 'Go, then,' she flung at him, finding some solace in lashing out verbally. 'Get out! I don't want you any more. I don't know why I ever wanted you. You're nothing but a coward!'

He rocked back in astonishment at her attack.

'Yes! A coward! You're afraid to have a real relationship with me. Afraid! Just because I'm young! But you're wrong, Hugh. Terribly wrong. And one day you'll know it. We could have been happy together. I know we could...'

Her voice broke then and tears flooded into her eyes. With a despairing cry she turned and fled upstairs. She slammed the door behind her and threw herself sobbing on to her bed, Hugh's present slipping from her fingers to drop silently on to the carpet.

CHAPTER ELEVEN

THERE were three sharp raps on her bedroom door. 'April? Let me in.'

She lay on her bed, sobbing, unable to answer him. Finally, she heard the door open and close, heard Hugh's footsteps cross the room, felt the mattress dip as he sat down beside her prostrate form. But he made no attempt to take her in his arms, or to deny what she'd accused him of.

'Don't, April. Please don't . . . You know I never meant to hurt you.'

'No, I don't,' she sobbed into the pillow. When he said nothing more she turned over and lifted her wet lashes, swallowing to gain more control over her voice. 'I love you,' she cried in a strangled voice.

Pain ripped across his face and he got to his feet, pacing across the room before spinning around and glaring over at her. 'You only think you do,' he said agitatedly. 'In a few months' time it will be someone else. You've already admitted that last year you thought you were in love with Max! For God's sake, April, if I thought there was a real chance for us don't you think I would take it?'

His hands raked through his hair. 'I want you, April. I want you like crazy! But I've seen what happens when an older man becomes involved with a much younger woman. I've seen the jealous scenes, the childish tantrums, the sexual manipulations. I don't want that. I want peace and security. And a sense of serenity. I need that for my work. I certainly don't want to have to worry if I'm going to wake up one day and find out that the woman I've given my heart to has grown tired of me, and wants out. Neither do I want one of those casual relationships based on nothing more than sexual gratification. I'm thirty-four years old. I want marriage. Marriage and a family. And a wife mature enough to stick it, even when things get tough.'

April sat up abruptly, her feet curling up underneath the billowing skirt of her dress. 'As Cynthia stuck it out when things got tough?' she pointed out mercilessly. 'Your mature old Cynthia?'

Hugh's jaw clenched hard and he looked away. 'There were mitigating circumstances in her case,' he ground out.

April was shocked that he would find excuses for the woman when he wasn't giving her an inch. 'My God, you're still in love with her, aren't you?'

His eyes jerked back to her, hard and angry. 'If you believe that then you're even younger than I thought! I'll have you know that Cynthia showed up on my doorstep tonight, just as I was leaving for your party. She begged me to let her talk, to explain further. I heard her out and I did feel slightly sorry for her, but that was all. Don't you see? I came here...to you...'

April couldn't see anything any more, except that it was all hopeless and futile. 'I don't know what for,' she said, her voice devoid of all emotion.

'Neither do I,' he pointed out coldly. 'I ought to have my head examined. But I kept telling myself that you were different. God! What a fool I am! At least I now understand why poor Garrick did what he did.'

A wretched despair snaked around April's heart. He hadn't believed a word she'd said about Max. He didn't want to believe her.

She gazed up at him, anguish in her eyes. Oh, Hugh...you really are still blind.

'Don't look so desolate, April,' he said harshly. 'A girl like you won't be lonely for long.'

She dropped her eyes again, not wanting him to see the misery in them. When she looked up again she had carefully replaced the misery with a type of offhand indifference. 'How right you are, Hugh.' She uncurled her legs and got to her feet, brushing the pretty skirt down into place. 'I've already had one proposition this evening. I might take Max up on it.'

His anger was so sudden and swift that April was caught unawares. 'You are not to have anything more to do with Max Goldman, do you hear me?'

Her chin flew up, her cheeks flushed. 'And who are you to tell me what to do? You're not my father or lover. You're not even my friend any more!'

He was glowering at her, his hands bunched into aggressive fists at his side. 'April—don't be stupid— Max has a shocking reputation ... I couldn't stand it if he——'

'If he what?' she cut in savagely, pain and resentment making her lash out. 'Took what you so nobly rejected?'

'For God's sake, April, you couldn't! Not a man like that!'

'Why not?' she argued blindly. 'I would think he'd be a good lover. He's had enough experience. A girl needs her first man to know exactly what he's doing, to...'

Her voice trailed away as she saw the control go out of Hugh's eyes. A manic determination had taken its place. He advanced towards her, each step full of frightening menace and passion. 'You can't give your virginity to a man like that,' he rasped. 'I won't allow it...'

She backed away from him till her legs touched the side of her bed. Her hands fluttered up to protect herself. 'Hugh...I didn't mean it—I wouldn't...'

But it was too late.

He grabbed her wrists and pushed her back on to the bed, covering her body with his body, her mouth with his mouth. His powerful legs pried her thighs apart and she could feel his arousal pressing against her even through her clothes. April was truly shocked. Shocked, and almost frightened. His lips were forcing hers open quite brutally, his tongue thrusting deep inside with a passion bordering on violence. She could hardly breathe as this onslaught on her mouth went on and on, punishing, bruising, suffocating...

With a desperate burst of resistance she dragged her mouth to one side. 'Hugh, no!' she gasped.

His head jerked back up immediately, and she was sure he was going to stop. But as he held himself above her, his body stiff and poised, she saw that his eyes were wide and glazed. Naked desire smouldered in their depths, a desire that was beyond reason, beyond conscience.

The knowledge that she could do this to him brought its own brand of insidious excitement. Her heartbeat quickened. Heat sizzled along her veins. From deep inside emerged the inevitable acceptance that she no longer wanted him to stop.

At first his gaze was riveted to her panting lips, but then it dropped down to where a single breast had half escaped its loosely laced prison. She also looked down, witnessing with a dry-mouthed fascination that the exposed tip was growing hard and erect even as they both watched.

She knew he was going to touch it; waited for his hand to move, a tremulous anticipation quivering throughout her body. But when his head began to descend and she realised what he was about to do, she found herself literally holding her breath. And when the tip of his tongue encircled the sensitive point, a shudder rippled through her, the long-held breath erupting from her lungs in a ragged groan.

Once again his eyes snapped up to hers, raking them with a blind anxiety. Surely he didn't think she wanted him to stop? came the dazed thought. If he did, she would die.

Her lips parted. 'Do it again,' she pleaded huskily.

He moaned, his mouth swooping to do as she asked, over and over again, sending a thousand shivery delights through her body. She felt her breast swell, the engorged nipple pouting ripely for his repeated ministrations. When he sucked the entire areola deeply into his mouth, a sharp pang of pleasure dragged at her womb, squeezing her muscles tightly inside. And in that moment she gained a tantalising glimpse of how it would feel to have him take her, fill her. She would welcome his hardness, enclose him round with the fierce possessiveness of love.

All of a sudden she wanted both her breasts free, wanted his hands on her naked flesh. She ripped at the bodice, the laces. Hugh caught her urgency, helping her push the now gaping material back over her shoulders.

'So beautiful,' he murmured, his hands reaching to knead both breasts softly, then more roughly.

April was in a delirium of desire. She didn't know what she wanted next, but when Hugh lifted her skirt and drew away her lace briefs her focus was soon on that moist pulsating part of her that she knew would not be still till it joined with Hugh.

When he touched her there she let out a ragged sigh, her body quivering as the most exquisite sensations rippled through her. She was soon liquid fire, burning with love for him, her arousal telling him more clearly than words of the intensity of her desire. But when he bent his mouth to her heated flesh, his kiss sent her mad, making her twist and turn in an agony of longing that was beyond bearing.

'No, no,' she gasped, and thrust him aside.

She tugged impatiently at his clothes, kneeling up to help him strip from the waist down. Her hand came out, quite unconsciously, to touch him, to marvel at his manhood. It seemed so natural to bend forward and kiss him, as he had kissed her, to show her love, to give him pleasure.

And it did give him pleasure. He closed his eyes, unable to suppress a deep, shuddering moan. When she did it again he grew still and tense, only the sound of his ragged breathing punctuating the electric silence.

The knocking on the door splintered the quietness like the crash of thunder.

'April? Hugh?' Guy's voice was crystal-clear through the door. And very impatient. 'Are you in there? April, your guests are waiting for you to cut the cake!'

April saw Hugh's eyes fly open, witnessed the horror of his appalled self-recrimination. 'Oh, God,' he groaned, and spun away from her. He reached hurriedly for his clothes. 'Fix your dress,' he threw over his shoulder.

'We'll be down in a moment, Guy,' he called, his words clipped.

'Don't be long,' her uncle shot back.

In the ensuing silence they heard his angrily retreating steps.

April felt embarrassed, shattered, confused. 'Hugh, I——'

'Don't say a word,' he snapped, whirling to face her as she was fumbling with the laces on her bodice. 'Not a bloody word!' He was already stuffing his shirt in his waistband.

She held the gaping sides of her dress together with trembling hands. 'But, Hugh, we love each other——'

'No!' He strode over to the door and spun round. 'No,' he repeated. But the anger had drained from his face, replaced by a bleak wretchedness. He turned the knob and yanked the door open. 'Goodbye, April.'

And, without a further backward glance, he left.

April would never know how she got through that night. Obviously there was a part of every person's psyche, some hidden survival mechanism that took over when one's pain became too much to bear, but when one had to go on.

She came downstairs, dry-eyed and smiling. She blew out candles, cut her cake, laughed at all the usual birthday jokes, even helped her uncle clean up afterwards, making some pathetic excuse about Hugh's departure.

Later, she sat alone on her bed, still dry-eyed. She didn't seem to be able to feel. But then her foot brushed something on the floor and she idly bent and picked it up. It was Hugh's present. Just as idly she ripped the paper off and exposed the exquisite little sculpture.

It was made of streaky black marble and looked like a figure eight lying on its side. There was a tiny card tied to it with a pink ribbon which had a word written on it. INFINITY.

April stared at the brilliance of the piece, the way it had been carved so that the grain in the marble followed the curves, never crossing, never ending, the material matching the concept.

Infinity...forever...never ending... Like her love for Hugh. Her crazy, hopeless love for Hugh.

The tears came then, gut-wrenching and loud. April turned and buried her face into her pillow.

CHAPTER TWELVE

IT WAS late on a Saturday afternoon in May, nearly three months after the party, when the phone rang and a paler, thinner April went to answer. 'Yes?' she asked lifelessly.

'April?' There was doubt in Max's voice. 'Is that you?'

'Yes. It's me.'

'You sound down, love. Anything wrong?'

April made a concerted effort to perk up and sound normal. 'No. Not at all. Why?' She had no intention of unburdening her soul to the likes of Max.

'No reason. You just sounded odd, that's all. Is Guy there?'

'Sorry. He's away for the weekend with some wine-tasting buddies of his. They've gone up to the Hunter Valley.'

'Damn. I was hoping he could pop in to my gallery later this evening. A few up-and-coming artists are showing selected pieces—tasty morsels of what the public can expect in years to come.'

'It's a bit late to be sending out invitations, isn't it?' April said archly.

'Yes, but I didn't know till an hour ago that Hugh would want to show something and I thought your uncle might give a critique of it in that column of his. He really liked Hugh's work the last time. But

156

don't worry, it probably won't matter in the long run. The way Hugh's going at the moment there might not be much more stuff of his to write about anyway.'

'Oh? Why's that?' April tried to sound mildly enquiring, but her heart had turned over at the mention of Hugh's name, and she was immediately worried by the concern in Max's voice.

'I gather things didn't work out between you and our temperamental artist, did they?' Max drawled.

'No,' she said tightly. 'They didn't. And what do you mean, temperamental? I would have thought now that Hugh could see again he'd be too busy for temperament.'

Max sighed irritably. 'Yes, I would have thought so too. But it appears that's not the case. That bruiser who lives with him tells me Hugh's been having trouble putting his mind on the job. Not sleeping well and generally being as miserable as sin.'

Just like me, April thought, and a weird feeling coursed through her body. If Hugh was so upset, wasn't it possible it was because of her, because he hadn't forgotten her any more than she had forgotten him?

'Then what is the piece Hugh wants to show?' she asked with her heart in her mouth.

'I have to tell you, April, it's simply the most fantastic thing he's ever done. It looks like the waves in a huge sea just before they crash on to the shore, all menacing power and movement. You can't stop looking at it as though any second the waves will come to life, curl right over and go thump!'

'What . . . what's it called?'

Max made an impatient sound. 'Nothing!'

'Nothing?' There was a tightness growing in her chest.

'Yes! An "unnamed work", he's labelled it. I tell you, April, he's turned into one hell of a difficult man. His looks might have improved but his manner certainly hasn't. He practically bit my head off when I tried putting some pressure on him to give a title to the thing.'

'And Hugh will be at the gallery tonight?' she asked huskily.

'Well, yes, but——'

'Would you mind if I dropped by instead of Uncle Guy? I could give him the low-down on everything.'

'Yes, of course, but——'

'What time?'

'Oh, any time after eight.'

'I'll see you later, then,' April said, and hung up.

Max frowned down into the dead receiver, wishing April hadn't rushed off like that. He'd wanted to tell her Hugh wasn't coming on his own tonight. He was bringing Cynthia with him. But then he shrugged. If April wanted to make a fool of herself then who was he to try to stop her?

April took a taxi to the gallery. Not because she could really afford it but because she had promised her uncle never to take public transport at night, particularly on a Saturday night.

Max's gallery was right in the city, down near the Rocks. It was as pretentious and tasteless as

Max, with revolving glass doors and marble columns at regular intervals, and not a hint of Australian style or culture about it. Yet it was called the Australiana Gallery. But Max knew all the right people and did very well for both himself and the artists who were lucky enough to exhibit in his mausoleum.

April had done the best with her appearance she could, choosing to wear a straight black skirt and a long-sleeved scarlet blouse that looked like silk but was really polyester. The colour suited her and put some life into her face, which was looking more than a mite peaked these days. Not even full makeup could totally disguise the drawn pallor of her skin, or the dark shadows under her eyes. But despite all this the taxi driver ogled her every step of the way as she walked up the steps to the glass doors.

The gallery was crowded, a haze of smoke greeting April as she stepped from the revolving doors. Her gaze travelled over the chatting, drinking, laughing, puffing groups, her stomach in knots. At that moment, she earnestly wished she hadn't come. Whatever made her think she would achieve anything? Even if Hugh had once loved her, it was *her* love he didn't believe in, not his.

It didn't take April long to see Max. His tall blond head was bobbing from group to group, an outlandish black and white striped shirt making it impossible to miss him. He spotted her standing there and started forward, his arms opening wide, a broad smile on his face. 'April! Darling!'

He addressed her so loudly that all the people nearby stopped and stared.

It was then that April saw Hugh near one of the marble columns. And the blonde clinging to his arm.

She had never seen Cynthia before. But she knew immediately who the blonde was. The hairs on the back of April's neck stood up as her eyes moved over the woman with the classic though cold face. She was wearing a slender black dress that had money written all over it, her blonde hair swept back and up, revealing an elegant gold necklace and matching earrings.

April watched Hugh say something and extricate his arm to walk towards her, looking incredibly male in his camel-coloured leather jacket and dark brown trousers, a cream silk shirt underneath. As he drew close though, April saw that the bones in his face looked stretched across his cheekbones. He looked tired. And angry.

'Hello, April,' he said tautly. 'What brings you here tonight? Is she here with you, Max?'

'Not at all,' Max admitted. 'Look, excuse me, will you? Someone is waving to me.'

'You don't have to stay with me, Hugh,' April said stiffly. 'Go back to Cynthia, by all means.'

Hugh's frown was immediate. 'I didn't realise you and Cynthia had met?' he asked, confirming his companion's identity.

'We haven't. I—er—saw her from a distance that night at the hospital.'

'I see ... Speaking of hospitals, April, you don't look well. Have you been sick?'

Yes, she longed to tell him. Sick at heart. For you, my darling. 'I...I did have the flu recently.'

'You need to eat up. You're too thin.' Thin or not, his eyes kept scrutinising her closely, and he appeared to have to drag them away.

April's heart began to pound when she saw Cynthia approaching. 'Darling,' the woman said, 'don't you think you should introduce me?' That hand went back to Hugh's forearm like a homing pigeon.

'Of course. Cynthia...meet April Jamieson. April...Cynthia Underhill. April was very kind to me during my blindness,' he added stiffly.

The woman didn't seem in the least bit embarrassed at being indirectly reminded how lacking *she* had been at the same time. Immediately, any belief April had once had in the woman's sincerity went out of the window.

'How very kind of you,' Cynthia was saying with a honey voice and eyes like ice. 'Hugh, there's a photographer here wanting to snap you beside your new work. Have you seen Hugh's latest sculpture, April?' she went on in a slightly condescending tone. 'Or aren't you interested in art? Most young people aren't.'

The woman's emphasis on the word 'young' brought April's hackles up. 'I wouldn't be here, Cynthia,' she answered sweetly, 'if I weren't. In fact I'm deputising for my uncle who writes the "Around Town" column.'

April got the distinct impression that this news soothed Cynthia somewhat, for she actually smiled—with her eyes this time. 'Oh, I see. Come on, Hugh. The photographer's waiting.'

April watched Hugh endure the photo session with barely held patience, after which he just stood and stared at his unnamed work while Cynthia drifted to one side to chat to Max. April stared too, a lump forming in her throat as she took in the way Hugh had made her suggestion into a living, breathing work of art.

She moved to stand beside him without even being conscious of doing so. 'It's truly magnificent,' she whispered.

He glanced across at her and their eyes met.

'Why *are* you here, April?' he asked abruptly.

She was going to repeat her excuse, but then she thought, Why bother? This was definitely her swansong where Hugh was concerned and it deserved the truth. Her smile was the epitome of grim resignation as her eyes ran over him, taking in his face and form as though imprinting them on her brain forever. She wasn't to know that she looked at him with a desperate desire that tore into his soul and shattered his bleakly held defences. 'I had to try one last time, Hugh. I had to find out if you still...' she went to say 'loved', then she realised Hugh had never said he loved her '...wanted me,' she finished.

'And if I do?' he bit out, his whole body stiffening in one last frantic attempt to deny what was sweeping through it.

'You know where to find me,' she husked.

'So I do, April.' He looked away from her, unable to bear looking at her for another second. 'But there again, I have all along...'

All her hope died. He might still desire her, but not enough. Not enough . . . She couldn't go on, an inner quaking beginning to take hold of her. She spun away, head held high, her partially blurred gaze searching and finding Max. She lurched towards him, ignoring a startled Cynthia, drawing Max aside with a trembling hand. 'Get me out of here, Max,' she choked out. 'Please . . .'

His strong grip fastened around her elbow and in seconds he had propelled her, not outside as she had meant, but into his private office. With the door safely shut he pushed her into an armchair. 'I'll get you a drink,' he said.

April could only nod and bury her face in her hands. She accepted the whisky with shaking hands, gulping it back on to an empty stomach. It burned like hell but in seconds she felt marginally better, certainly more in control.

But she jumped nervously to her feet when Hugh suddenly burst into the room. Max merely raised his eyebrows. 'Can I do something for you, old man?' he drawled.

'I'd like to speak to April. *Alone!*'

'Sure.' Max shrugged. But he took his time pouring himself a whisky and downing it before leaving.

April watched with a dry mouth as the door shut and Hugh started to pace up and down the room. He ground to a halt in front of her, his face in obvious torment. 'All right,' he growled. 'You win. Let's go . . .'

'Go?' she gasped.

'Don't play games with me, April. You knew when I saw you go off with Max that I wouldn't be able to stand it. It was your final gambit, wasn't it? Make the sucker so jealous he'd no longer be able to think straight. But what the hell? It worked. So come on . . .' He grabbed one of her hands and began dragging her towards the door . . .

She wrenched her hand away, stopping with face aghast. 'No!'

His face hardened, if that was possible. 'No? You dare to say *no* at this point?'

April was all hot fluster. 'Well, I . . . I . . .'

'You want me to make love to you, don't you? That is why you came here tonight, isn't it? That is what this is all about?'

April gaped at him.

'Don't tell me you're angling for *marriage*?'

April was totally speechless. This wasn't her Hugh talking. This was some sort of madman!

'I didn't think so,' he scorned. 'Marriage is for stuffy old fuddy-duddies. But don't worry, I've changed my mind on that score. I've decided to join the modern generation and give in to what I want, when I want it, without strings, without commitment. And I want you, April Jamieson, naked and willing in my bed. I want to make love to you for hours on end, I want to take your virgin body and make it respond to me in every possible way I can think of.' He grabbed her then, wrenching her hard against his heaving chest. 'Is that what you wanted to hear?' he rasped. 'Is that what you wanted me to say? I'll say anything you want me to say as long as I can have you . . .'

He groaned then, his mouth claiming hers, covering and possessing it with the passion and hunger of a starving soul, drinking in the soft sweet moisture of her lips and mouth with ragged, sucking gasps. He kissed her over and over, ravaging her lips till they felt swollen and bruised.

Initially April was rocked by the violence of Hugh's passion, and the anger behind it, but she gradually realised it was directed more at himself than her. He'd been fighting her love since the beginning, fighting this deep-seated mistrust of it. But the protective shell he had put around himself had been well and truly pierced now, and April had no intention of letting Hugh retreat behind it ever again. She would bind him to her sexually, make him need her body and the pleasure he found in it. And slowly, eventually, he would learn to trust, and the sort of love she really wanted from him would flower and grow openly in his heart.

She began stroking the back of his neck, kissing him back, letting her body speak for her. I love you, it said. Love you...

Hugh pulled away from her mouth with a moan, his hands trembling as he pressed her head against his chest and raggedly stroked her hair. 'Do you have any idea what you do to me?' he rasped. '*Any* idea?'

'Yes,' she whispered, looking up at him with eyes wide with arousal, lips parted with expectation.

'God...' Hugh let out a quivering sigh before tasting those willing lips once more. 'I want you, April,' he murmured against her mouth. 'Now...tonight. Come away with me. We'll go somewhere private. I'll ask Max for the keys to his beach-house. We can be there in a few hours. There'll be no traffic.'

A shiver of wild exultation ran through her as she thought of being totally Hugh's at last. 'Yes...oh, yes,' she cried.

'Wait here,' Hugh commanded. 'I'll go and speak to Max. Now don't move!'

CHAPTER THIRTEEN

THEY were over the Harbour Bridge and on the expressway heading north when April finally remembered Cynthia. She looked over at Hugh, who'd said nothing since he'd bundled her into the Rover and taken off. 'Hugh?' she said nervously.

'Mmm?'

'What about Cynthia?'

'What about her?' His glance was sharp. 'I asked Max to take her home.'

'And she didn't *mind*?'

'Why should she?' he almost snapped.

'Well, I . . . I . . .'

'There's nothing going on between Cynthia and me, if that's what you're thinking,' he elaborated with a degree of exasperation. 'I only brought her along tonight because Max insisted I bring someone and she's the only woman I could think of. She was well aware it didn't mean anything.'

'But she called you darling!' April reminded him. And dripped all over you, she didn't add.

'Cynthia calls everyone darling. April, I told you that I would never get involved again with Cynthia,' he went on impatiently, 'and I meant it! I never did entirely swallow her story. Oh, I think she felt guilty enough but as for her so-called nervous breakdown . . . I have it on good authority that she

167

spent quite most of her time overseas at ski resorts and on the Riviera.'

April sat in shocked silence.

'Cynthia, I've come to realise since, is a cultural groupie. She likes mixing with people of an artistic bent. Marriage to an up-and-coming sculptor was right up her alley.' He slanted April a sardonic glance. 'Women like Cynthia don't really love. They make suitable choices. Not that I can talk. I can see now that I never really loved her either. She fitted my idea of the perfect wife. Attractive, intelligent, independent, socially competent. Supposedly mature. Perhaps I deserved what I got.'

'I don't think so, Hugh. No one deserves to have done to them what Cynthia did to you. That was cruel.'

His eyes flicked her way. They grew amazingly warm and loving as they scrutinised her, and April's remaining doubts dissolved on the spot.

'I know you wouldn't have left me like that,' he said thickly.

'Never,' she whispered.

A tiny black cloud passed across his face. 'Tell me, April, have you been seeing Max at all?'

Her heart sank till she realised that what Hugh was asking was fair enough. Hadn't she worried that he'd resumed his relationship with Cynthia?

'I haven't seen Max since my party, Hugh. To tell the truth, I haven't been out anywhere except to university since that night. I haven't wanted to.'

Hugh's expression conveyed both relief and surprise. And a new respect. 'I haven't been at my best either. You know, April, I haven't been able to work. I haven't been able to do much of anything.'

'I...I noticed you didn't name that surf piece,' she said somewhat gingerly.

His sigh was oddly soothing. 'Ah, but I'd promised that to you.'

'But...'

He gave her a look that melted her insides. 'Deep down, I must have known I would come for you, April. Eventually...'

'Oh...'

'Now shut up, darling, and let me drive. I'm beginning to get a mite impatient...'

'It's cold,' she said as she climbed stiffly out of the car five hours later. They had made the trip in remarkably quick time but to April it had seemed to last an eternity.

Hugh looked thoughtful as he joined her. 'Max's place will be like an ice-box.'

April shivered. 'I know where Uncle Guy keeps a hidden key. His place is much smaller and he has two quick-heating radiators. He wouldn't mind.'

They walked quickly across the loose sand, arm in arm, their breaths showing mist under the sharp moonlight. A fresh breeze ruffled April's hair.

'I'll make us some hot chocolate,' she offered, once they were inside and the heaters were on. But as she went to walk away Hugh caught her wrist, bringing her back to enfold her into his chest. April's hands slid around and up his back and, when she looked up at him, her heart was hammering against her ribs in breathless anticipation.

The trip up, the having to wait, all the time knowing what was at the end, had brought her to a height of sexual awareness that the longest foreplay could hardly match.

'No hot chocolate,' he said with surprising calm. 'No more waiting...'

'I... I'm a little nervous,' she admitted.

'No need,' he murmured, one hand coming up to brush her hair back, to hold it there on either side of her face while he bent to kiss it. First on the forehead, then her eyelids, then her nose, each cheek, her chin, before sliding down her throat.

'Hugh,' she groaned, her lips parting impatiently.

He gave a low sexy laugh but didn't kiss her. 'No,' he refused, three fingertips pressed against her tingling lips. 'I've spent five hours regaining sufficient control over my body. I don't want to waste it. And I will if I kiss that rapacious mouth of yours.'

'Rapacious?' she repeated with a frown.

'Yes... Rapacious. Greedy. Insatiable.'

'But I want you to kiss me,' she moaned.

'I will—at the right time. First I want to undress you, to see all of you, touch you. With my eyes open this time...'

His hands went to her red blouse, easing it out from the confines of her waistband before starting at the bottom button and working slowly upwards. April tried to stay as calm as he seemed to be but she didn't feel calm. She could hear her heartbeat in the silence of the room, feel a trembling running up and down her thighs. 'Shouldn't we go into the bedroom?' she asked breathlessly.

'If you like,' he said and led her into the smaller room, which was already comfortably warm with the large strip-heater on the wall on full.

He turned her to a standstill at the foot of the low-slung water-bed, her calf muscles resting against the wooden frame. The last button gave way to his questing fingers and he drew the two sides of the blouse apart, his eyes narrowing with concentration on her as he pushed the garment back off her shoulders and peeled it down her arms. There was a slight hitch when it reached the cuffs, which were still done up, but with a brisk tug the sleeves finally lurched over her wrists and Hugh tossed it aside. It fluttered to the floor in a corner.

'That happens to be my best blouse,' she reproached huskily.

'I'll buy you a hundred blouses,' he said, his voice now almost as thick as her own.

Light fingers feathered up her arms and over her shoulders, then across the bones at the base of her neck, then finally downwards to trace the swell of her breasts. Hugh made no attempt to remove the confining skin-toned bra, seemingly fascinated by the way her full curves were lifted and pressed together by the light silky harness. 'You have beautiful breasts, April,' he murmured, moulding his hands around the cups like a human bra.

She swallowed against the tumultuous feelings that were clamouring to be set free inside her, feeling impatient with Hugh's slow lovemaking. But eventually she recognised and surrendered to the strangely addictive pleasure contained in such a gradual build-up of tension. In the end she wanted to wait as long as he was making her wait. She could well imagine these incredible sensations growing and growing till she would be nothing but a trembling incoherent creature who would allow any caress, any intimacy, anything at all. For this was the way she loved him. Totally, madly, mentally and emotionally, physically and sexually. She wanted what he wanted, and if he wanted to take forever making love to her then she wouldn't object.

But that was before his thumbs started rubbing over her nipples, before those normally small, soft buds suddenly burst into hard, swollen instruments of the most exquisite torture. 'Oh, God,' she moaned, and swayed beneath his touch.

He steadied her with a firm grip on her upper arms, watching her with such hot, smouldering eyes that she closed hers, blocking out the evidence of his desire. Hers was bad enough to cope with. His would only make it worse. She almost sighed with relief when she felt his hands on the back of her bra, felt the clasp give way and the garment drawn from her.

From her dark, sightless world she was surprised at the awareness she had of her unfettered breasts. They felt extra heavy and deliciously sensitive, their aroused state craving the return of Hugh's attention. But of course it wasn't his hands she wanted on them. She yearned for those throbbing points to be sucked into his hot moist mouth where they would be nipped and tantalised till she would practically scream for him to stop. She could almost feel the wet lips now, keeping each nipple imprisoned in turn while that wet flickering tongue encircled and licked with a relentless intensity.

Her moans came as a surprise, and her eyes flew open, shocked to find that her fantasy must have stopped being a fantasy some time back. Her hands went to his bent head, her fingers twining through his hair, holding him there, pressing her knees back against the bed to keep from sinking to the floor.

Finally that tormenting mouth abandoned her breasts and travelled downwards, Hugh sinking to his knees and kissing her stomach while he freed her of her skirt, then her shoes, her tights, and finally her bikini briefs. There was no shyness in her as she watched him throw them aside. She wanted to be naked before him, wanted his hands on her most secret places, wanted whatever he wanted.

She felt his hands parting her thighs, felt the knowing intimate touch of his lips and tongue. And then she was moaning and shaking, so much so that he stopped what he was doing, bringing a whimper of disappointment to her lips.

But once Hugh stood up and smiled down at her she was glad he had stopped, glad he had saved that ultimate pleasure for when his body was joined to hers. He scooped her up into his arms and lowered her gently to the swaying surface of the water-bed. 'Just relax,' he told her, and began stripping off his clothes.

But telling her to relax was like telling her not to breathe. Her love, her need, had made her only half of the whole. She was not going to be content till they were as one, till she had been satiated with the ecstatic sensations she knew she would find in his body.

Her hunger grew as he revealed himself to her eyes so that by the time he joined her on the wildly undulating bed she clasped him to her with frantic hands. His need seemed to be equal to hers now, for he didn't return to any aggravatingly slow exploration of her flesh. He positioned himself between her thighs, his elbows on either side of her chest, his hands cradling her face. 'I thought I could last longer,' he rasped, a rueful smile coming to his lips. 'I can't.'

'Good,' she sighed.

He laughed. 'You are a wicked little devil, do you know that?'

'Yes,' she agreed impatiently, arching her body up to rub herself against him. 'Yes, yes, yes!'

His raw naked groan was music to her ears. 'I don't want to hurt you,' he rasped.

'You won't,' she assured him.

April welcomed him. She closed her eyes tightly shut, waiting for the pain. But no cry was torn from her lips this time, only a gasp of surprise at the relative ease with which he entered her.

'Open your eyes, April,' he said thickly, and when she did he captured her parted lips in that long-awaited kiss. Her eyes widened as he began to move in her, his tongue and body thrusting as parallel forces, filling her, driving her mad. With swift savage surges she was transported into another world where straining bodies reached blindly and instinctively for those magical and sometimes elusive moments which had kept man and woman coming together since time began.

They struck with incredible intensity, April's body being gripped by the most sharp, piercing sensations. Her flesh convulsed and contracted around Hugh's, impelling him immediately into an explosive climax. He gasped away from her mouth, shudder after shudder running through him from his toes upwards, ending with an animal cry being punched from his throat.

And then he groaned—a deep, contented groan. And April knew he was feeling as she was feeling, as if she were sinking, sinking, her muscles all heavy languor, her mind a lazy haze of utter bliss. He sagged down on top of her and she held him close, stroking his passion-damp skin with tender hands, telling him how much she loved him.

April woke to find herself alone. There was a note on Hugh's pillow. 'Gone for a walk,' it simply stated.

She lay back on her pillow and sighed, but it was not the sigh of a woman in any distress, or with any regrets, more the sigh of a woman who had been made love to very, very well. April's heart contracted as she thought of how many times they had already made love, and of the various erotic ways Hugh had pleasured her.

The clock on the bedside chest said it was two in the afternoon. She had been asleep only a few short hours but she felt marvellous, simply marvellous.

April stretched and climbed out of bed, aware of her body in a way she had never been before. Her breasts felt heavy and extra sensitive, her skin flushed and tingly. There was a slightly swollen feeling between her thighs. She made her way slowly into the shower, knowing full well that Hugh would only have to touch her and in an instant she would be ready for him again.

The water played over her head and she shut her eyes. Her hand groped for the shampoo, finding it at last on the shelf. But before she could pour any on to her hair the bottle was taken from her hand.

'Let me do that.'

Her eyes flew open to see a naked Hugh standing there, smiling at her.

She laughed. 'Did you go for a walk like that?'

He glanced down at his body which was quickly becoming aroused. 'Well...not exactly like that.'

April laughed again. And Hugh stepped into the shower. She watched, suddenly dry-mouthed, as he trickled a small stream of the soapy liquid over her breasts. Gently, as though moulding a precious piece of clay, he began massaging, stroking the undersides, encircling one aureole at a time, then, finally, grazing lightly over the waiting, aching tips.

April moaned.

He bent into the shower stream that was running over her face and licked the water from her lips. 'You'll never guess what's happened,' he said between brief, tantalising kisses. 'I think my mental block is over. While I was walking just now, creative flashes just kept popping into my head. I could hardly believe it.'

She smiled up at him with adoring eyes. 'I'm so happy for you,' she whispered.

'Not as happy as I am. But I know who's responsible,' he said huskily. 'You are, April. You are... I love you, my darling. I love you...'

'Oh, Hugh...' April's joy knew no bounds.

His hand stroked her cheek. 'Without you I can't function, can't think. I want you in my life, dear heart. I *need* you. Not just for a weekend. But every day, every night...'

'I want to marry you too,' she choked out.

His groan was tortured. 'No, April. No... That's not what I meant.'

'Not...not what you meant?' she repeated, feeling sick.

'I won't marry you at this stage,' he explained haltingly. 'You—you're so young, my darling. So very young... You don't realise how much people can change in their twenties. Their ideas, their needs... It would be very selfish of me to tie you down at this point in time. Move in with me, live with me. And then, in a year or two...'

April stared up at him, finding it hard to hide her dismay. It wasn't her he was trying to protect. It was himself. He still didn't trust her love. Still...

She thought about the decision she had made last night and for a split second doubt and regret reared their ugly heads. But then she dismissed them. She loved Hugh. She knew she did. Eventually, he would know just how much.

* * *

'Oh, Hugh, it's simply wonderful!'

April was admiring his latest piece, a semi-abstract version of a horse and rider, called 'Rodeo', with the horse up on its hooves, back arched, trying to throw its rider. Hugh had been working on it all week, with April having barely sighted him.

April placed it down on the kitchen table then stepped back, looking at it from a distance.

'One of the best you've ever done!' she enthused. 'It even looks good in the middle of that old table.'

Hugh came up behind her and began nuzzling into her neck, whispering seductively what he would prefer to do on the kitchen table at that moment.

April's senses leapt in heady anticipation. It had been like that ever since they had returned from their weekend at the cove and started living together. Hugh would come out of one of his creative binges and immediately have this intense hunger for her. He was already turning her around and unbuttoning her shirt.

'It's just as well Harry moved in with Uncle Guy,' she murmured. Then gasped. Hugh's lips had found a nipple.

Guy had been furious with Hugh when he'd brought April home on the Sunday night and announced they were going to live together. But Hugh had asked to speak to Guy alone and, when they had come out of the study ten minutes later, it seemed they had reached some sort of truce. Though still not thrilled, Guy had given April his blessing.

April's parents, however, had not yet been informed, her hesitancy betraying a lingering fear that Hugh might not truly love her after all. Oh, yes, they were sexually attuned, there was no doubt about that. And their enjoyment in each other's company had increased with each passing day. But whenever she brought up the matters of marriage, or commitment, he deftly changed the subject, usually by making love to her.

So when April rang her family every week, she talked of everything else except Hugh, saying to herself that she would tell them about him, *after* she had graduated at the end of the year, and *if* she and Hugh were still together.

A black cloud passed over April's soul and she shuddered. Hugh stood up straight, holding her by the shoulders and staring down at her. 'Is something wrong? You seem ... tense.'

She thought of her visit to the doctor the previous day. 'No,' she said truthfully. 'There's nothing wrong.' The doctor had said she was the picture of health and that pregnancy suited her.

Of course April had suspected she was pregnant for some time, while Hugh had no idea. It had been easy to hide the possibility from him because he lived such an odd life, with odd hours. When he worked, he worked feverishly, only coming out of his studio for food. Days went by sometimes without their making love, which meant she hadn't had to explain her missing periods.

April looked at Hugh's dark frown and wondered what he would say when she told him. She knew he had assumed she was still on the Pill and it worried her terribly that the news would cause trouble between them. Her original idea that a baby would show the permanency of her love now seemed naïve.

The insidious thought came that she didn't have to tell him about her pregnancy yet. She was only two months. Pushing aside a rush of qualms, she reached up to kiss him lingeringly on the lips. 'Now, where were we?' she invited.

His relief was instant, his returning kiss unexpectedly fierce. She found herself edged back till her buttocks were hard against the table. Hugh's hands had returned to her breasts, caressing them none too gently. They were extra sensitive with her pregnancy, and it took all of her control to let him continue. The pleasure was mixed with unexpected pain.

When he suddenly stopped she almost cried out with relief. But he also stopped kissing her and was looking down at her breasts. 'You've put on weight,' he said.

April shut her eyes, her stomach twisting. She should have known he would notice. He was a sculptor after all, with a sculptor's hands, a sculptor's sense of shape and proportion.

'But I like them this way,' he murmured thickly. 'Lovely and full and heavy. You were too thin before.' He cupped one and kissed it with his eager lips. 'Luscious.'

Relief flooded her when she realised he hadn't jumped to any conclusion, but in no time she couldn't stand his energetic attentions any longer.

It was beyond pleasure now. 'Don't,' she cried, and wrenched away.

He jolted back from her as though she had struck him. 'Don't?' His face hardened, his eyes narrowing with suspicion.

April groaned with the realisation of how quick he was to misconstrue her rejecting him physically as heralding a deeper rejection.

'Oh, Hugh,' she sighed. A mental picture of his eternal mistrust of her love flashed into her mind, depressing her unbearably. She had been fooling herself all along. Their relationship wasn't going to work. It *couldn't* work. How could it without mutual trust?

'It's not that I don't want to,' she said, but her hands were slowly rebuttoning her blouse. 'But my breasts are terribly sore. You see, Hugh...' She lifted a resigned face to his. 'I'm pregnant.'

He just stared at her, his eyes oddly unreadable. Shock was all she could determine. 'Pregnant? But...*how*?'

Her smile was weary. It seemed cruel to say, 'The usual way.' Instead she explained quietly, 'I went off the Pill after my birthday party, Hugh. I didn't see the point in continuing with it at the time.' She had decided to see if her periods were still painful, since that had seemed the only reason left for staying on the drug, and had discovered that they were now much lighter, as sometimes happened.

He kept staring at her, but his shock had turned to thoughtfulness. 'So you knew...from the beginning...that you would probably get pregnant.'

'Yes.'

His frown darkened. 'Why didn't you tell me you'd gone off the Pill?'

She shrugged. 'You wanted me, Hugh. That night. As desperately as I wanted you. I had to make a snap decision. I did.'

'But April, there are other forms of contraception!'

Her sigh was an admission. 'I know... but I wanted everything to be... perfect. I didn't want——' She broke off, giving the matter some more honest thought before continuing. 'The truth is, Hugh, that underneath it all I wanted your baby. I love you, Hugh, and I know you love me, in your way, but I guess I didn't believe you would stay with me. I was afraid that one day you would find some reason for us to break up. I wanted to have a permanent part of you to love and keep. I know you will call that stupid and romantic and immature of me, but I don't look at it that way. I do love you. And I'm only sorry that you don't believe that my love will last.'

April was astonished at her composure. She had delivered her heart-breaking speech without a tear and as she watched Hugh, standing there dumbfounded, a special kind of satisfaction washed through her. She had sounded as mature and grown-up as she felt.

'Well, Hugh?' she prodded.

He looked down at her with a deeply thoughtful expression on his face. 'I have only one thing to say to that, April. Only one thing....'

'What?' she asked, her heart pounding.

A slow smile creased his mouth. 'Will you marry me?'

CHAPTER FOURTEEN

'DID you know today's our first anniversary?' April said to Hugh.

He gave her a puzzled glance.

'Since the day we first met,' she explained. 'Up at the cove.'

His laugh was light and happy. 'I thought you meant since our marriage.'

'It'll be our sixth-month wedding anniversary shortly,' she reminded him.

And what a wedding it had been! Nyngan had talked about it for weeks afterwards, Hugh having paid for the biggest reception the small town had ever seen. It turned out he was a good deal more well off than even he realised, that investor of his having brought off a recent coup on the commodities market.

'Hey—ssh!' Hugh darted a glance towards the busy hospital corridor then down at the precious bundle in his arms. 'You don't want people to hear we had a shotgun wedding, do you?'

April was still laughing when Uncle Guy and Harry stamped into the room. The two men were like the odd couple, she thought as she looked at them. One so dapper, the other a real navvy. But they had become good friends since Harry had moved into April's old room, the arrangement suiting them well with Harry taking over April's housekeeping chores in exchange for free board. He still drove buses every weekend and was in the process of building himself a small studio for his own sculpting out of the old laundry shed in Guy's backyard. April's uncle was also teaching him how to read and write.

'A little something for the bonnie babe,' Guy announced, placing several packages on the bed.

April glanced ruefully at the large teddy-bear Hugh had come in with, not to mention the other toys her family had brought when they'd flown down the previous day. She shook her head. 'Rachel is going to be spoilt rotten,' she announced. 'And she's only three days old!'

Uncle Guy raised his eyebrows. 'Nothing's too good for my great-niece,' he defended.

'And nothing's too good for my god-daughter,' Harry joined in, coming over to have a closer peep at the sleeping infant.

'Want a hold?' Hugh offered.

Harry looked appalled. 'Hell, no, I might drop her.'

'No, you wouldn't, mate,' Hugh encouraged him. 'Here—put one hand behind her neck, then another behind here...'

Harry succeeded at last, but looked so nervous and shaky even April was relieved when he handed the baby back.

'I think we'd better open these presents, don't you?' she suggested. 'Yours first, Uncle Guy.' She tackled the paper on a large box with gusto. 'I wonder what this is...' She lifted the lid and stared, then looked up exasperatedly. 'Now what do you think Rachel is going to do with a soccer ball, Uncle Guy?'

He was taken aback. 'I thought it was a netball!'

All the other presents were almost as silly, from the electronic robot to Harry's toy train set. 'Didn't anyone tell you that I had a *girl*!' April glared in mock disgust.

'Did you hear that, Hugh?' Guy huffed. 'You've married a sexist. Actually you're a brave man, Hugh, marrying her at all. Do you know what she said to me when I didn't approve of her moving in with you? She said she was going to, no matter what I said. She said she was grown woman, it was her life, her choice, and if I didn't like it then I'd have to lump it!'

'Oh, Uncle Guy,' April protested. 'I wasn't as bad as that!'

'Maybe not.' He grinned. 'Just as well Hugh reassured me that he was only giving you some time so that you could be sure. He said he would have married you that very night if it was only his happiness at stake.'

April turned wide eyes to her husband, who raised his eyebrows and smiled at her. See? his expression said. You were wrong about me.

She sighed and shook her head in wonder and happiness.

It was an enjoyable hour, but by the time Harry and her uncle left April was tired. Rachel, also, was getting fractious, having woken hungry.

'She needs a feed,' Hugh observed, when Rachel kept sucking her fingers ravenously.

'Yes, but ...'

Hugh smiled his understanding. He picked the baby up from the crib and handed her over to her mother. 'Here... Give the child what she wants.'

Not always, April decided privately. She had no intention of spoiling her children. But she conceded that this hardly applied to food. She pushed back her nightie, unhooked her maternity bra and offered her breast to the hungry infant.

April closed her eyes and breathed in sharply when Rachel started to suckle with even more vigour than usual.

'Painful?' Hugh asked softly.

Her eyes flew open. He was watching the whole procedure with undisguised fascination. 'Not so much now,' she admitted. 'It was bad yesterday. It seems the sucking helps the womb contract back into shape.'

Hugh shook his head. 'Incredible thing, nature.'

He resumed watching Rachel in studied silence.

April's loving gaze rested on her handsome husband, recalling the incredibly forceful way he had directed their lives once he had accepted the reality of her love for him.

They had been married within a month, but there was no honeymoon—April was to apply herself to her studies. Her career was just as important as his, he had said. During the next few weeks he had had the house renovated, with one of the bedrooms being converted into a nursery. He had taken over most of the housekeeping chores and learnt to cook, since April vetoed any help in the house. But the most astonishing decision he had made was not to do any sculpting in the months leading up to the birth, saying he would devote all his time to her needs for once.

And he had been as good as his word, April conceded, though she had detected a certain impatience during the last few days before she went into labour. She suspected he was itching to get his little chisel back to work.

April looked down lovingly at her baby, thinking to herself that she didn't regret giving up the job at the *Herald* to look after Rachel. She had the satisfaction of passing her final exams with distinctions and was very happy staying at home with Hugh and the baby for the time being. Perhaps later on she would...

Suddenly Hugh jumped up. 'I have to go.'

'Go where?'

'Home... I have this perfectly brilliant idea. You know that big chunk of light brown marble I've got? I'm going to do a large piece—sorry about that, I know you like small ones—I'll call it "Mother and Child", or something original like that... I see the woman with her head tipped back, her eyes closed, a look of controlled pain on her face. And the child at her breast, greedy, demanding... I must get at it...' He was already halfway out of the door.

'What about a goodbye kiss?' she protested.

His glance was full of passion. 'You'll have to wait for that,' he growled, then grinned. 'By the time I finish this, it'll be worth waiting for.'

April was left staring after an empty door. For a moment she was annoyed, and then she relented. He'd spoilt her, of course, these last few months.

Hugh was what he was and, after all, she and their child had been his inspiration.

She looked down at Rachel who had drifted off into blissful sleep. 'It's just as well we're going home tomorrow, bubs,' she said in wry warning. 'I have a feeling that if we weren't, we wouldn't see your father for quite some time.'

She rubbed her cheek lovingly over the silky down of her baby's head. 'But the end result is worth waiting for,' she murmured. 'All the best things in life are worth waiting for...' A sweet smile of satisfaction curved her mouth. 'Though sometimes you've got to give things a little push along. It's a matter of conviction...and love. Love is certainly worth pushing for.'

April sighed in contentment and closed her own eyes.

Rebecca Winters, an American writer and mother of four, is a graduate of the University of Utah. She has also studied at schools in Switzerland and France, including the Sorbonne. Rebecca is currently teaching French and Spanish to junior high school students.

Despite her busy schedule, Rebecca always finds time to write. She's already researching the background for her next Mills & Boon® romance!

BLIND TO LOVE
by
REBECCA WINTERS

CHAPTER ONE

PHILOMENA helped the two little girls into their coats and hurried them to the door. The bride and groom had left an hour ago. Little Sally, barely eighteen, going off bravely, her heart in the hands of the boy next door. Samantha, twenty, and her doctor-husband, Albert had been called away long since. Deborah, twenty-one, was waiting on the porch for her two little twins, while husband John brought the car around. The rest of the guests had filtered away into the late afternoon sunshine. That leaves one little Indian, Phil told herself as she leaned tiredly against the door-jamb and waved.

Stillness settled over the house like a shroud. It had never been this quiet before. Never. She smiled at her daydreams, seldom allowed. Miss Practical Pill, the younger girls had often said of her. That was before they could form the 'ph' sound, of course. Later too, when they were feeling just a little bit saucy. Phil smiled at the reminiscence. She brushed her shoulder-length straw-coloured curls away from her neck and walked slowly back into the house.

There was a musty smell about everything. The living-room was crowded with dirty dishes and glasses. The kitchen was awash with clutter. Neither of her younger sisters had thought to stay and help with the clearing-up. They had been conditioned by years of, 'Oh, Phil will do that'. And so she would. But not just yet.

She wandered back into the living-room, fingering the

5

furniture as she went, feeling the metes and bounds of her
world with tactile hands. The old armchair sagged to one
side, but it was comfortable. She sank into it, and the
stillness surrounded her again. *They were all married*. She
relaxed against the back of the chair, and the load placed
on her shoulders by her mother on her deathbed slipped
away. Phil had been seventeen that year. 'Take care of
the girls, Phil.' And with that faint whisper her mother
had gone.

The wind rattled at a loose shutter. It seemed as if the
house were trying to defy her. 'Mother,' she called as
loudly as she could, 'have I done well?' Her voice echoed
up the old staircase, bounced off the empty upstairs hall,
and returned without answer. She hadn't expected any.
Philomena Peabody shrugged her shoulders and went to
face the cleaning.

She was up at her habitual hour of six the next
morning, and it was not until she fumbled her way
downstairs that she remembered. There was no school
lunch to be made. No early breakfast for the three of
them. No laundry to sort and start. Nothing. Her pattern
of life had come unstuck. She went out into the warmth
slowly. It was mid-February, and the fog clung to the
valley as usual. Fog and low clouds were forecast in the
local newspaper, the *Sacramento Bee*. Light northerly
winds. High in the 50s, low in the 30s. High for the
Sacramento River, 5.3 feet at I Street Bridge.

Her elderly Subaru stood bravely beside the house, in
the shadow of a few scrawny old olive and almond trees.
It was a family joke of sorts. Her grandfather had farmed
one hundered and sixty acres. Now it was all reduced to
the old house and a half-acre of regrets. Urban sprawl
had conquered the rest. Sacramento was expanding

beyond its boundaries, and here in Rancho Cordova the future of farming was written plain on the wall.

Phil shook her head. The regrets were all hers. She would have given anything to keep the farm—but bringing up three sisters was expensive, and her talents never had leaned towards farming. She shrugged her shoulders and put it behind her. The treasured old vehicle started at the first touch. She drove slowly over to Folsom Road, and then on to Route Fifty for the long commute. 'Maybe I could get a flat in town,' she mused as she wheeled through the typical California traffic jam. 'Maybe.'

She was still pondering when she came to the turn-off, jockeyed her way over to Fifteenth Street, and made it safely up to P Street. The small modern building that housed Pacific Mines and Metals was just a couple of blocks south of the golden dome of the State capitol building, and parking was always a problem. Which explained why she arrived at her office an hour late to find that the world of work had come unstuck also!

Betty Pervis, young, moderately attractive, and a newcomer to the typing pool, was standing by Phil's supervisory desk, shaking. All the other eight girls in the office were bent over their word-processors, but the tag-ends of wild conversation hung in the air. Phil put an arm around the young girl's shoulders, and laughed wryly at herself as she did so. Here I am, the Spinster Aunt, she thought. Twenty-seven years old, and over the hill!

'I'm never going back up there again,' Betty whimpered. 'Never!'

'Of course not,' Phil encouraged. 'Where?'

'His office,' she hiccupped. 'Mr Wilderman. Never!'

'Of course not. Here, use my chair. Harriet, could you

bring Betty a cup of coffee?' Phil bustled aimlessly, knowing that the weeping woman needed time. When the paper coffee-cup arrived she pressed it into the twisting hands.

'Mr Wilderman isn't usually an—an ogre, Betty. He's too old for that. Was he ill, or something?'

'Ill? Foul-mouthed, abusive—and I don't know why you say old. He's——'

The internal telephone rang. Harriet answered it, blushed, and set it down. 'He says—he wants somebody else,' she reported grimly. 'And he's—wow.'

Phil patted Betty's shoulder and looked around the room for volunteers. Every head ducked. 'So all right,' she sighed. 'I'll go myself.' She nodded to Harriet, gesturing in Betty's direction, then picked up a notebook and a handful of pencils. It had been some months since she had taken direct dictation. Just to be on the safe side she reached into her desk drawer for her micro-recorder, and slipped it into the upper pocket of her blazer.

The lift was the only fast-moving thing in the building. It chuckled to a stop on the ninth floor and seemed to spit her out on to the gold carpet. Which reinforced one of Phil's long-held beliefs. *Anybody who was not an engineer rated as nothing in this business, and even the lift knew it!*

It was quiet up here. Even the air-conditioning equipment only dared to whisper. Six widely spaced office doors, all closed, glared at her. 'You can't intimidate me,' she murmured at them as she went down the corridor. An adjacent door opened and two men came out. They stared at her as if they had heard.

The door at the end of the corridor was half open. Phil smoothed down her navy skirt, checked the recorder in the pocket of her jacket, and pushed into the room. She knew the outer office, having visited with Mrs Simmons a time or two, and once had actually substituted for the regular secretary for a couple of days.

The outer office was empty. Mrs Simmons favoured an electronic typewriter. It stood mute, covered, and her desk was bare. So Mrs Simmons was out today. Phil shrugged her shoulders. One piece of the puzzle had just fallen in place. Now, to beard the lion. She moved resolutely forward, taking deep breaths, building confidence. She rubbed the perspiration off her hand before she turned the door knob to the inner office.

The room was dim, with curtains pulled across the four wide windows. A man was slumped in the swivel chair behind the highly polished desk, with his back to her. She took two or three hesitant steps across the thick-pile rug, and stopped. The man, whoever he was, was not Mr Roger Wilderman. *That* worthy was sixty-five, bald on top, slightly rotund. The present occupant of the executive chair sported a full head of raven-black hair. The rest of him was huddled out of sight in the gloom. Phil cleared her throat as loudly as she could manage.

'Well, it's about time.' A deep voice, vibrating off the beige walls. A voice that brooked no arguments. 'Lost your tongue? Dear God, what do we hire these days, a bunch of rabbits? Sit down.'

Bully, Phil commented under her breath. Just the sort of man who required a little trimming. She settled herself into the chair beside his desk. He must have heard the rustle of her skirts, but he did not turn around.

'Letter to McPherson,' he began, and the words flowed. Phil had ten years of practice behind her pencil-point. It skated across the paper just a trifle ahead of his comments, pausing on occasion to let him catch up.

Three letters in a row, right off the top of his head. She acknowledged the expertise with a wry grin. With his back turned it was hard to see what notes he was using. He stopped. 'You've got all that?' The tone doubted it.

'Yes,' she said quietly. His chair half-turned, as if he could not believe it, and then returned to its former position.

'A memorandum to the entire staff,' he began. This time he spoke sharply, moving along faster. And at the end of each of the following memoranda, he increased his speed. Phil smiled again, grimly this time. He was waging war, and she had no intention of losing the battle. He stopped to organise his thoughts. Phil tucked her pencils neatly into her pocket, turned on the tape recorder, and settled back. After another ten minutes of racing, he stopped. 'You've got all that?'

'Yes,' she acknowledged. This time the chair turned around all the way, and he sat up out of his slouch.

'You're sure you have all that?'

'Positive.'

'Read me back that last paragraph.'

There was a moment to look him over. There was nothing in him of the Mr Wilderman she knew. Husky, in his early thirties, she thought. A mass of black hair that kept falling down over his right eye. A stern sort of face, that would have been more at home in a Western movie than in a boardroom. And wearing dark glasses!

'Well?' She snapped back to attention. One finger fumbled for the replay button on the recorder in her pocket, and his words rolled off the tape effortlessly. His head came up as he listened, and a smile played at the corners of his mouth. 'Smart,' he commented as the tape came to a hissing end. 'I don't know you, miss?'

'Peabody.' She gave it the New England pronunciation of her ancestors—Pee-buddy. It drew a chuckle.

'Miss Peabody,' he mused. 'You're a long way from New England. An immigrant?'

'Isn't everyone in California?' She was using her most prim voice, a soft contralto. He nodded as if acknowledging the comment.

'And what do you do for me, Miss Peabody?'

'I'm the supervisor of the typing pool,' she returned. 'But I don't do it for you. I do it for Mr Wilderman. I don't know who you are.'

'And that bothers you?'

'Among other things.' The words snapped out as if she were biting their tails off.

'Do I detect a little censure there?' His laughter was a low rumble. Pleasant, but also threatening. Philomena squared her shoulders and plunged into battle almost happily.

'You certainly do hear censure,' she snapped. 'I don't allow anyone in this corporation to yell and curse and storm at my girls!'

'Ah!' That chuckle again. 'Protecting your little lambs, are you, Miss—Peabody?'

'Very definitely,' she returned primly. 'Betty Pervis is downstairs crying. I'll have to send her home. We have a large workload. Failures of this kind by the executive staff cost the corporation money. It's something that's just not done, Mr—whoever you are. In addition, our union contract prohibits this sort of thing, Betty could file a grievance.'

'Ah!' It was almost as if he were licking his lips, relishing the fight to come. 'I do believe you're threatening me, Miss—Peabody. What the devil is your first name? I can't spend all day calling you Miss Peabody.'

'I—I don't think you really want to know,' she murmured.

'That bad, is it? Well, Peabody, I don't take well to threats, Maybe you should have your shop steward contact me.'

'Maybe I should,' she returned bluntly. 'Here I am.'

'Here you am what?' Was there a little laughter behind the words? Phil strained to think, to measure.

'Here I am, the shop steward,' she announced. 'I represent all the clerical and staff employees of this headquarters.'

'And?'

'And I think you owe Betty—Miss Pervis—an apology.'

'Or else? Lay it on the line, lady. I can hear the "or else" hanging in the air.'

'All right, if that's what you want to hear.' She squirmed in her chair. One does not throw lightning bolts casually, but having been cast they must be followed up. 'Ninety per cent of the people in this building are union members,' she said very coldly. 'It's conceivable that the union could strike over an issue like this. We had a strike three years ago, and——'

He waved it all aside with a casual hand. 'I've heard,' he said. 'Man, have I heard. So OK, lady——' He fumbled across the desk searching for something. 'Where the hell is that telephone——' Phil slid the internal telephone over beneath his hand. He grunted an acknowledgement. 'What's the number in your lion's den?'

'Lioness,' she muttered as she dialled the number and

handed the telephone back to him.

His gruff character disappeared the moment he started talking on the telephone. Warmth and charm flowed down the wires. Apologies were offered, spirits were soothed, and he hung up. 'There,' he groused. 'I hope that satisfies?'

'Yes,' she acknowledged grimly.

'That's all—just yes?'

'Yes.'

'You are without a doubt the least talkative woman I've met in ten years or more,' he returned. 'My grandmother was like that. To the point. I like that.'

Well, I don't particularly like you, she told herself. And restraining comments were pure torture. Luckily her ten years as a substitute mother had taught her to guard her tongue. She cleared her throat again. 'Will that be all, Mr——?'

The question hung in the air between them until he laughed again. 'I wish I could see what you look like,' he pondered. 'This damn eye problem—well. For your information, Peabody, my name *is* Wilderman. Penn Wilderman. I suppose you know my father?'

'I——' He had caught her off guard, almost to the point where her real personality was showing. She struggled to suppress it. 'I don't really know him,' she said, truthful to the detail. 'I did substitute for Mrs Simmons twice in the past five years, but I don't really know him. I'm not an executive, or anything like that.'

'So you'll have a chance to know me,' he snapped. 'My father has been overworking. My mother laid down the law to him last Friday. They've gone on a three-month cruise. So I flew home to take charge.'

'I'm sorry to hear that.'

'Sorry that I flew home?'

'No,' she snarled, 'don't twist my words. I'm sorry that your father isn't well. He is well liked.'

'Now what do you know?' he chuckled. 'A kind word from the guardian dragon. You must be years older than those light-brains I've seen. What do they call you down at the typing pool? Battleaxe?'

'Something like that,' she admitted. 'What's the trouble with your eyes?' she offered as a tangential thought.

'Snow blindness,' he returned. For a moment she was afraid he would refuse the bait, but he relaxed again and settled back into the deep swivel chair. 'I was doing some advisory work down at Little America, the South Polar station. We were caught in a blizzard, and a stupid female technician lost her protective glasses. I gave her mine—and before we could make it back to the base camp I got burned for it.' He fiddled at the frame of the dark glasses over his eyes, and then removed them. Both eyes were covered by small medical pads, taped in place across the bridge of his nose.

Phil would normally have reacted with sympathy. One thing held her back. That phrase, stupid *female* technician. With the emphasis on *female*. As if, had the technician been male, no catastrophe could possibly have occurred. She offered a non-committal 'Oh'.

'Don't be too enthusiastic,' he grated, replacing the glasses. 'It's not permanent. Three or four weeks more, perhaps, and then maybe I can figure out the horrible mess the corporation is in. How soon will you have that material ready?'

Phil looked down at her notes and considered. 'Perhaps two or three hours,' she offered.

'Perhaps? Is that the best you can do?'

'Yes,' she snapped. He leaned forward over the desk as if he were about to argue—or demand—or order. And then he thought better of it.

There's something funny going on here, Philomena told herself. Not with or about him, but with me. Why do I have this crazy itch when I look at him. He's a strange sort of executive, but I've seen stranger. What's wrong? Her logical mind could find no answer. She stood up, brushed down her clinging skirt, and started for the door.

'Peabody,' he called. She froze, with one hand already on the door knob. 'Come back here.' This wasn't his real voice. It was the smooth charmer of the telephone call. It doesn't really affect me, she told herself quickly. I'm not little Betty Pervis, to be soothed by a telephone call. But her feet carried her back to the side of the desk. She stood there, silently.

'Peabody?'

'Yes?'

'I couldn't even hear you breathe!' Which is not surprising, Phil told herself. I haven't been breathing since he called me back! The imprisoned air boiled out of her in a long deep sigh.

'Peabody. Ever done any nursing work?'

'Me? Of course not.'

'Funny. You sound like somebody's mother——'

'Oh, that sort of thing? Band-aids and Solarcaine? I've brought up three——'

'Just what I meant,' he chuckled. 'I need some drops in my eyes. Would you?' He gestured towards the side table. Phil walked over without thinking. Eyedrops and a syringe, all neat and tidy. 'Three of them?' he queried. 'Must have been quite a family.'

'Yes, it was,' she returned wryly. 'But they've all grown up, and the last one was married off just yesterday.' She picked up the syringe and came back. 'Lean back in the chair,' she ordered. He took off the glasses and settled back. She picked at the edge of the tape, and managed to free it. Black eyes, almost as black and deep as his hair. She hesitated. The past few minutes of conversation were whistling around in her head.

'Well,' he complained gruffly. 'I don't want major surgery.'

'No,' she returned. *What do they call you—battleaxe?* He must think I'm fifty years old—an old hag who cracks the whip down in the cellar of the building. Well, it serves him right! The drops cascaded out of the syringe. One or two lucky ones hit his eye. The others ran down his neck.

'Hey, I didn't ask for a bath,' he roared.

'It's all right,' she soothed, in the same tone she had used time after time with the girls. It worked. He settled back as she tidied up the mess with a tissue. 'And now the other one. Don't blink like that. I can't get the drops in while you flutter your eyelashes.' Long lashes, she noted. Curling up at the ends. I'd give my right arm for real lashes like that! Three precise drops flooded his other eye. He spluttered, blinked and reached up a hand. She stopped it in mid-flight.

'None of that,' she ordered. The hand stopped. She dabbed at the excess forced out on to his cheek, then carefully replaced the pads and the tape from the fresh supply on the table. 'There now.'

'That's a good boy,' he chuckled as he sat up. 'You forgot that part. You could be my mother, the way you talk.'

'I doubt that very much,' she sighed. 'And you can't see a thing?'

'Shapes. Light and dark. Movements,' he said. 'It's nothing permanent. So you wouldn't want to be my mother?'

'I should hope not.' It was hard to keep the disapproval out of her tone. And I really don't have any reason for disapproving, she reminded herself. He acted like a boor and a bully, and he apologised very nicely for it all. So either he's the world's biggest fake, or he's been raised with the nicest manners, or—lord, I don't know, do I?

'Thank you,' he offered. She jumped. While she had been debating, he had left his chair and was standing directly in front of her. He was not a huge man. Slender, whippet-like, and about a head taller than herself. Which isn't any great height, she told herself. But tall enough for me. If he hugged me, the top of my head would fit just under his chin! It was a fine supposition, but she was more than startled when he proceeded to demonstrate how true it was.

'What are you doing?' she snapped. It wasn't a gut reaction. She had some experience with hugging. From time to time over the past ten years she had found time to date a man—and to fight off a hug or two. Three times, to be exact. Raising three girls took a great deal of effort!

'I can't see you,' he grumbled, 'and I need to know something about you. I have to do it in Braille.'

'That's a good excuse.'

'I'm glad you think so.' He hadn't noticed her sarcasm, evidently. 'But I do wish you'd stand still. I can do this all by myself. You needn't wiggle against me.'

'I wasn't wiggling *against* you,' she stormed. 'I was wiggling—stop that!'

His hands had wandered through her hair, surrounded her pert round face, touched on eyes, nose and mouth, and were now diving over her chin and off into space. They landed on the tops of her well rounded breasts, paused for a second, and then trailed down her sides, over her swelling hips, and——'

It had taken her that long to recover from the surprise of it all. From the surprise, and from the shock of wild-running senses which his touch had evoked. Her hand moved automatically, bouncing off his cheek with a satisfying thud, driving him back a step or two.

'Hey,' he protested.

'Hey is right, Mr Wilderman,' she stormed. 'I don't allow people to take liberties with my—with me. I don't see any reason why you should want to get to know me better, because I doubt if I will be seeing you any time in the near future. Mrs Simmons——'

'Mrs Simmons will be out for the day,' he returned. 'For a sweet little old lady you've got some marvellous figure.'

'And a strong arm,' she threatened. 'And I never said anything about being a sweeet little old lady.'

'No, you never did,' he chuckled. 'I'll strike out the *sweet*, if you object. Why don't you run along to your little cell and get that work out?'

'Yes,' she snapped, happy that he couldn't see the rose hue that coloured her face. Blushes she had never learned to suppress. She started for the door.

'You even walk softly,' he called after her. I'm darned if I'll take that at face value, she told herself. The man had a tongue that's hinged in the middle. One side sweet, the other sour. She reached for the knob.

The door was one that swung inward. Just as her hand

moved forward the door swung open, catching her in the stomach. She staggered back a step, lost her balance, and sat down on the floor with a thump. 'This makes my day,' she groaned.

'Now what?' he asked. She turned to look at him. He had left the security of the desk and was fumbling his way across the room.

'Don't do that,' she called.

And behind her, at the door, a young voice. 'Don't do that, Dad!'

'Robert? What the devil are you doing here at this hour? And what happened to Peabody?'

Phil turned around. A boy stood in the door. A teenager, from the look of him. Painfully thin, blond hair neatly combed, wearing a suit and tie. A thin face. You could almost count the bones. Dad? He was a carbon copy of the man, in every way.

'Robert?'

'I—I think I knocked your—your lady over. She's sitting on the floor.'

'Well, help her up—or—come over here and lead me to her! Hurry up. She has fragile bones!'

Oh, do I? Phil ran a hand up and down her 'fragile bones'. Everything seemed to be in order, but her bottom gave notice of bruising to be reported later. The boy sidled around her as if she were a poised rattlesnake, and hurried to his father. The pair of them came over to her. 'Give me your hands, Peabody,' the father commanded.

She reached up hesitantly. 'I can get up for myself,' she said quietly.

'I'm sure you can,' Wilderman returned. 'Hands!'

She offered them both, smiling as they were swallowed into his. He might not be a big man, she thought, but his hands are for giants. How would you like them to——

He interrupted her wandering mind by moving around in front of her. The boy was doing his best to fade into the background. 'Put your foot up against mine,' he ordered. It hardly seemed worth a protest. She complied. 'Now, upsy-daisy.' His hands tightened on hers and up she went, as effortlessly as if he had been handling a five-pound parcel. 'There now. OK?'

Those darned hands again, sweeping up and down her body, brushing at her skirt, touching her in places where they had no right to be. She slapped at the hands, and he withdrew them.

'That's better than the last time.' He was so close that his whisper echoed in her ear.

'Don't press your luck,' she retorted. But his hands dropped to her shoulders, and before she could duck out of the way he planted a light kiss on her forehead. 'Don't *do* that,' she muttered through clenched teeth.

'Robert?' He turned Phil around in the approximate direction of the boy, who moved a step or two closer.

'Robert, I want you to meet Miss Peabody. She's the nice lady who has been helping me out.'

'She looks like——' the boy started to say. His father silenced him with an upraised hand.

'Don't say it,' he was admonished. 'She's a lovely lady. Shake hands.'

Phil worked up a smile, and offered her hand. The boy moved away and clasped both hands behind his back. Like that, huh, Phil thought. Shake hands and come out fighting? Well, have I got a surprise for you, sonny. I don't give a darn!

'I want you two to be friends,' his father said, evidently thinking the handshake had been effected.

'Yes, I can see that,' Phil retorted. 'And now if you *gentlemen* will excuse me, I have work to do.'

His ear caught the sarcasm this time. He looked down at her, puzzlement written all over his face. She shrugged herself loose from his hands, picked up her scattered pads and equipment, and rushed out of the door, leaving it open behind her.

'But, Dad, she looks like——' The boy was trying it again as she whizzed down the corridor. All of a sudden, the upper reaches of the Pacific Mine and Metal Corporation had taken on a threatening atmosphere. She dived for the protection of her own little empire on the ground floor.

CHAPTER TWO

BY the time the weekend rolled around, Phil was happy to stay at home. Her trip to the executive suite had not been repeated, but images had hung in her mind. Strange images, that caused her more than one dreaming moment when she should have been working. His face, bad manners and all. His eyes, that pulled at her pity, his hands that stabbed at her raw emotions and left her wriggling on her chair. The boy. Thirteen going on fifty-five. Rigid speech, formal airs, and an unhappy shadow trying to hide behind his eyes. A strange pair.

To keep them out of her hair on Saturday she house-cleaned. Polished, scrubbed, dusted, until the old house sparkled. There was nothing to be done outside. Even in California, February spells winter, and many a night the temperature would be down to thirty degrees, just below the frost line. So she had bedded all her flowers in early December, burying them under a load of seaweed imported up the Sacramento River from the ocean, ninety-five miles away.

A walk through the remains of her orchard helped a little. There were branches on the ground from the ancient olive trees and the equally ancient walnut trees. The orchard was so small as to make harvesting, except for her own use, a complete waste of time. At the end of her land she stopped for a breath. The fog had lifted shortly after noon, and there was a sweet clean smell about the earth. She rested one hand on the gnarled tree-trunk nearest, and glared out to where another high-rise office building was under construction. Sacramento was surely expanding, like a rising loaf of bread gone mad.

Sunday was a lazy day. She slept late, then drove down into Rancho Cordova to St Clemens, the Episcopal Church on Zinfandel Drive. And then it was Monday.

'He wants you.' Betty Pervis, in early for a change, with a wide smirk on her face.

'He?' Phil struggled out of her jacket and swiped ineffectually at her fog-damped hair.

'Him. That Mr Wilderman.'

'What would he want me for? Don't tell me Mrs Simmons is out again?'

'No. I saw her come in twenty minutes ago. He wants you, Phil. I bet the minute he saw you he flipped.'

'Stop it, Betty. That's fairy-tale stuff. Besides, he never did see me. His eyes were bandaged all the time I was there.'

'Well,' the young girl pouted, 'it's happened before, you know.'

'What?' Phil was still trying vainly to control her curls. When wet they coiled up like little springs all over her head, and then jingled and bounced as she walked. 'What's happened before?'

'You know. The millionaire boss marries the typist?'

'Oh, sure he does. Daydreamer. So what did he say? What did he want?'

'I told you. He said he wanted you—and then he hung up like to burst my ear-drum. You'd better hurry up. He hates to be kept waiting.'

Mrs Simmons was in her appointed place, every iron-grey hair in place, her mannish tailored suit impeccable, her

hands poised over the keys of her electronic typewriter.
'He wants you,' the older woman said, and nodded
towards the door.

'That's getting to be the most hated quotation of the
century,' Phil returned, smiling. 'He wants me for what?'
Mrs Simmons shrugged her shoulders and smiled back.
Phil shook her head in disgust and headed for the inner
office.

His hearing must have improved. He heard the door as
it opened. 'Well, damn it, isn't she here yet? How far is it
to that typing pool?' A papa-bear growl, from an office
almost as dim as a cave. He was at his desk. His son
Robert was sitting on the divan in the corner. The boy
got up silently, with not a wisp of a smile on his face.

'Yes, she's here.' Phil replied in her most serene tone.
'The typing pool is on the ground floor, a hundred miles
from here.'

'Oh, a wit, no less,' he growled. Phil had already lost
her desire to prick his bubble of conceit, regretted her
poor attempt at humour.

'Well, you're half right,' she said wryly. She stood
quietly in the middle of the room, eyes swerving from
father to son, waiting. The boy was fidgeting, moving his
weight from one foot to the other.

'Come over here.'

'Yes, Mr Wilderman——'

'Penn. Mr Wilderman is my father.'

Silence. Phil could think of nothing to say.

'You can't manage a simple name like that? Let me
hear you say it. Penn.'

'I—Penn.'

'That's a start,' he laughed. His entire appearance
changed. The worry-lines disappeared from his face,

taking years off his age. The dark glasses, sited at a jaunty angle on the bridge of his nose, seemed to be laughing at her. Not maliciously. Happily. Breathe, Phil commanded herself, and relaxed as air poured into her lungs. His fingers beckoned. She moved slowly towards the desk until she was up to the typist's chair that stood beside it.

'No further?' he asked.

'No.' It wasn't exactly a whisper, neither was it a full-blown statement. I'm losing my nerve, Phil snarled at herself.

He was up from his chair before she could assemble her defences. Up and in front of her, inches away, with both hands trapping her head between them. Fingers moved up her cheeks, into her hair, and paused. Her agitation ceased. The hands were stroking, calming. Altogether—wonderful, she thought, and blushed at her own statement.

'Good morning, Peabody,' he said softly. 'The records tell me it's Philomena—is that right?'

Tongue-tied, Phil struggled to reply and gave up. His fingers read her struggle, and moved down to cup her chin. 'Do I frighten you?'

'Yes,' she managed. And then more bravely now that the dam was broken, 'Yes. I wish you would stop pawing me, Mr Wilderman—Penn. I——'

She managed to get to the chair as his hands dropped away. That uneasy feeling crowded almost everything else out of her mind. It bothered her because she could not define it, and definition had circumscribed her life for so long she felt lost.

'What do you want of me?' she asked impatiently.

He went back to his chair and sat down. He moved

with more confidence, more agility than he had the previous week, she thought. He stood a little taller, straighter, and there was an aura of power surrounding him. 'How are things in the typing pool?' he asked.

It was not what Phil had expected. She squared around in her chair, set both feet flat on the floor, and stiffened her spine. 'Work is slow,' she said in her office voice. 'On Monday it's always slow. By Tuesday, when the engineers have had a chance to think, work picks up.' And now what? Did he want to fire a couple of the girls? Save a little money in the over-inflated budget?

'That's good,' he said. Which again was not quite what she expected. Executives about to fire somebody don't usually start off with 'That's good'. She stole a quick glance at the boy. He had sat down when she did. Better manners she had never observed before in a teenager. And that was one of the problems. He was just too unnaturally quiet for an American teenager!

'We have a problem.' Penn broke in on her thoughts.

'*We* do?'

'Robert and I. We have a problem.' And I'll bet that's the understatement of the year, Phil told herself. She sat up even straighter, not willing to contribute a comment, and waited.

'You don't seem to care?'

'I'm sure you'll tell me about it when you're ready,' she returned primly. To emphasise the point she put her pencils away in her pocket and folded her hands in her lap. He cleared his throat, as if not accustomed to such rebuttal.

'Robert is growing out of all his clothes. You can see that, I suppose.'

'Yes.'

'I'm not boring you, am I, Philomena?'

'No, but nobody calls me that. I——'

'I should call you Miss Peabody? By the way, it *is* Miss, isn't it?'

'Yes. I mean, yes it is, not yes you should——' Another tangled tongue. She swallowed hard to clear the obstruction. 'I mean—you should call me Phil. And yes, it is *Miss* Peabody—Phil.'

'I'm glad we've settled that,' he chuckled. 'How in the world did you last as a *Miss* all this time? You seem to be a nice companionable lady.' Phil almost strangled over the words that wanted to pour out.

'Oh, never mind,' he conceded. 'None of my business, is it? What I want, Phil, is for you to take Robert out on the town this morning and get him a new outfit.'

'I——'

'No, I know it's not in the union contract. I'm asking for a favour.'

'I wasn't going to say that,' she retorted angrily. 'All I meant to say is I don't have any experience buying for men. All my expertise is with girls!'

'Boys, girls——' he grumbled. 'This is the unisex age. I don't see what difference that makes.'

'A lot you know,' Phil told him. 'The unisex age is almost over. The pendulum is swinging madly in the other direction. Girls look for the very feminine. Boys look for the very masculine.'

'And skirts are longer this year,' he chuckled. 'Or so they tell me. Why any woman with good-looking legs would want to wear skirts at mid-calf is more then I can reason out.'

'Perhaps that's to keep them from being ogled by men,' Phil said primly. 'And all that is beside the point. We were talking about Robert's clothes. He's old enough to pick out what he wants for himself. At most, you might have his mother go along with him to supervise.' A silence settled over the room. Penn Wilderman drubbed his fingers on his desktop. Robert Wilderman was staring at his father, his eyes wide open, and an anxious expression on his face.

'Robert,' the father finally broke the silence, 'would you please go out to Mrs Simmons' office for a moment. I need to speak privately to Peabody.'

'About my mother?' The belligerence was unmasked. The boy had no intention of sharing his mother's secrets with another woman, Phil thought, and he was making no bones about it.

'Robert!' A stern command that snapped like a whip, but left all the scars internally. The boy got up slowly from his chair, looked as if he might voice an objection, and thought better of it. He slammed the door behind him on the way out. The whole thing was too mediaeval for Phil to accept.

'I don't want to hear any of his mother's secrets,' she exploded. 'That's a terrible way to treat a child of his age. Terrible!'

'I didn't ask you in here to criticise my life-style—or my family's,' he snapped. 'Just shut up and sit down.'

'I am,' she fumed. 'And don't tell me to shut up. I can always get another job. Sacramento is crying out for experienced secretaries.' Just for emphasis she stuck her tongue out at him, and then had a hard time smothering the giggles brought on by her own silliness.

'I don't doubt you could get a hundred jobs,' he thundered. At least it seemed like thunder. It wasn't very loud, but it shook the furniture—and Phil—in a manner she was not eager to repeat. 'In fact, I might offer you a better job myself. Now just listen. OK?'

'OK,' she whispered, her fit of rebellion suppressed. Despite what she had said, it wasn't all *that* easy to get a new job—and she had worked for Pacific Mining for almost ten years now.

'My wife and I are divorced. Robert is our adopted child. My wife was awarded custody. Now my former wife has remarried and Robert had become an— obstruction, I guess you would say. So she shipped the boy to me, not even waiting to find out whether I was in the country or not. My son is a bright young man, but so thoroughly stamped down that he hardly appears normal. I'm sure you've seen that?'

'Yes,' she admitted. It was a hesitant agreement. His world of darkness seemed to be closing in on her, disordering her usually logical mind. Just for a minute she wished she had the nerve to get up and open a curtain. Outside the window Sacramento roared and chugged and whined its way into the future. Inside, she was swathed in a thousand veils that shrouded and blinded her to all but this man. This man who was suddenly turning from grouchy bully to loving, concerned father.

'So now I have a difficult problem,' he continued. 'I can't stand this man my wife—my former wife—has married, and I wouldn't want Robert to be within a hundred miles of them. Yet, to get the court order rescinded, I have to be able to provide a home life for him myself. And today is a beginning. You are obviously the motherly type. You don't think yourself too old for Robert?'

'Me?' she gulped. There it was again, that obsession he

seemed to have about age. 'Why—why no, I don't think of myself as too old for Robert, but I—I would hardly classify myself as a motherly type.'

'Come off it,' he chuckled. 'You brought up three girls——'

'Three sisters,' she insisted firmly. 'They were my younger sisters.'

'So all right, your younger sisters. Children none the less. You saw them through their scrapes and bruises and teens?'

'I—well, yes, so to speak.' It was technically not true. Sally was only eighteen—but his statement was close enough to the truth to be accepted.

'Then there you go,' he nodded. 'The motherly type. No, I don't see this as being any big thing. Your department is in the doldrums. You hop in the car, take Robert to some place where clothes can be had, and outfit him. Easy.'

'Not that easy,' she sighed. 'What sort of outfit? How many things? How much money are you willing to invest in all this? Children's clothes come higher priced than adult clothes these days.' Again that prim maiden-aunt tone. And I wish I could wash *that* out, she told herself fiercely.

'I want him to have a complete wardrobe,' Penn rumbled. 'It's up to you what he gets. As for money, there's a company credit card in my wallet here.' He squirmed around to reach his wallet out of his back pocket and laid it out on the desk. 'Take it with you. I don't really care how much things cost. Spend what you need to. Anything up to five hundred dollars, I would say. If you need more, give me a call from the store.'

Phil almost swallowed her tongue. Accustomed to

nursing money as if it were a sick relative, she could have outfitted three boys the size of Robert for five hundred dollars. And have change left over. She fumbled for the card.

'I—I guess I could manage,' she returned softly. 'I'll take him over to the K-street Mall in my car, and we'll——'

'Nonsense,' he said. Again that roll of thunder, that threat hanging in the background. 'My car is downstairs. Harry is probably ruining his lunch by chewing on doughnuts in the cafeteria. He'll drive you. Off you go.'

Off she went, indeed. It was like being swept out of the kitchen by a particularly big broom. Robert was standing at Mrs Simmons' desk, having said not a word, apparently. When she tapped him on the shoulder he followed. Not until they entered the lift did he speak.

'You're really going to buy me some clothes?'

That disdainful look, meaning *how can a mere female buy clothing for me?* His father's look all over again. The pair of them would be great candidates for monkhood, Phil told herself. I'd like to give them both a hot-foot to upset that darn dignity. How can a thirteen-year-old boy be such a stick? 'No,' she responded. 'I wouldn't dream of buying anything for you I'm going to take you somewhere where you can buy yourself some clothes— and your father's going to pay for them. Do you have any objection?'

He thought about it until they reached the lobby. 'No,' he said, as they stepped out of the lift.

A short bandy-legged man was leaning against the reception desk. He looked like an out-of-work jockey with grey hair and no semblance of uniform. When he saw Robert he sauntered over to them, spread both feet apart, and issued a challenge.

'You the broad gonna take Robbie shopping?'

She glared at him, eyeball to eyeball. It wasn't hard. They were both about the same height. 'Yes,' she snapped. 'I'm the—er—broad that is taking Robert shopping. Are you Harry?'

'Who else?' he sighed. Another woman-hater, Phil noted. That makes three. They must be a close tribe, the Wildermans. I wonder if there are any more at home? 'Well, c'mon,' the little man drawled, 'I don't have all day.'

'Do you not really?' Phil drawled in return. 'Have to get your bets in at the track, do you?'

'Well,' he stuttered, embarrassed by her directness. 'I—hey, the car's out front in a no-parking zone.'

'Where else?' She did her best to present a royal cold stare, but just the doing broke her up. When she giggled he smiled back at her. Out of the corner of her eye she could see the boy smiling too.

The car was one of those stretch-Cadillacs, two blocks long, with shaded windows for one-way viewing. Hollywood style. Phil classified it all as she scrambled into the back seat. Robert dithered a moment or two, and then desire overcame manners. He scrambled in up front, next to the driver. Mark it down, Phil, her subconscious demanded. He's really a thirteen-year-old kid. Give him the chance and he'd have the engine out and in pieces on the pavement. All that dignity is faked!

'Where to?' The little man needed a pillow under him to see over the steering-wheel. His voice had the gravel-sound of those who do a great deal of shouting in their lives. 'Where to, Miss——?'

'Peabody,' Robert told him, using his father's inflection.

'To the lower K-street Mall,' she said. ' I don't rightly know how you'll get there. They're tearing up that whole area to put in the Light Rail vehicles, and——'

'I know,' Harry grunted. 'Been drivin' in this town for twenty years or more.' That seemed to be that. Phil buttoned her lip and relaxed into the soft springy seat, planning her strategy. Unfortunately she found it hard to give Robert's needs her full attention. His father's face seemed to haunt her. *And I don't know when I've met a more despicable man,* she insisted to herself.

Harry proved to be some sort of driving genius. He managed to deliver them to the back of the Mall without scraping a fender, or killing anyone in the middle of the mad traffic jam which normally haunted the Capitol Mall when the California legislature were in session. Phil began to breathe again when Harry pulled over to the kerb in a no-waiting zone and opened the door.

'Lose your breath, lady?' he asked as he handed her out.

'I always do when someone else is driving,' she apologised. A real smile was her reward. 'I don't know how long we'll be,' she hazarded. He shrugged his shoulders.

'Makes no mind,' he returned. 'I'll be around here somewheres. You come out, I'll find you.' Robert climbed out without assistance and stood fidgeting, as if he had never been in downtown Sacramento before.

'Over this way,' she called, and led him across the grass and tree-lined open mall. Her goal was the classic simplicity of Macy's, but before they made it to the front doors the boy stopped and stared.

'What's that?' he asked in awe. Phil looked up. As a perennial shopper she tended to ignore the obvious these days. The boy was standing almost underneath the Indo Arch, a mass of steel formed vaguely in the pointed-arch shape of an Indian Temple door. Soaring forty feet above the surrounding mall, it was the starkly symbolic gate between the modern State capital and the rebuilt park area known as Old Sacramento.

'You've never been here before?' she asked.

'I've never been anywhere around here,' he returned bitterly. 'There never was any time. My—she was always busy at something or other. She never had time.'

How about that? Phil mused. She spent a few minutes explaining about the arch, and the reconstructed Old Sacramento.

'I'd like to see that some day,' he said. Not enthusiastically, just a general comment. Which made it even more strange to her when she heard herself say, 'Maybe we could come. I'd be glad to take you.'

He looked at her as if she were some curious sea-monster. As if he had heard but could not believe. 'You mean that?'

'I said it,' she said grimly, wishing she could take it all back. They marched into the store without another word. From long practice, Phil knew her way around. She led him unhesitatingly to the Men and Boys clothing area, and then stopped him with a small hand on his wrist.

'Now you have to decide just what you want to wear,' she told him. He was the slightest bit taller than she, and it was unnerving to see how his grey eyes studied her. I wonder what colour his father's eyes are, she pondered as he thought out an answer.

'You really mean that? I can decide for myself?'

'Why not? You have to live in them. What's your favourite?'

'Jeans,' he replied immediately. So what else is new, Phil chuckled to herself. Give a kid enough rope and he'll buy—blue jeans. She waved her hand towards the proper aisles, and followed as he plunged down them like a young colt just unleashed into fresh pastures. Jeans. They come in all size and all styles and all colours, and he just couldn't make up his mind.

'If you're sure of the size,' she prompted, 'try on one pair, and then take a couple of each.' That broke the log-jam. He actually smiled. With his whole face *and* his eyes, he smiled. As with his father, it changed his whole appearance. The solemn formal stick figure turned into a glowing teenager. He was gone into a fitting-booth before Phil could add another word.

She sank into a chair, glad to rest her feet. If this expedition were to be anything like a shopping trip with her sisters, she would need arch-supporters before the day was done. It was—pleasant—just to sit there, watching people buzz around her like a hive of angry yellow-jackets. She was surprised when Robert came out of the booth and stood in front of her.

'Do you think this would do?' he asked hesitantly. She smothered her smile. This was not the time for it. The waist band was comfortably loose, although the jeans clung to him like a second skin. The legs were a little too long, but a quick needle would turn up the cuffs with ease.

'Do you like them?' she countered.

He strutted back and forth, did a couple of deep knee bends, all without bursting out of the pants, and then came back. The smile was flickering, as if he expected a denial. 'I like them,' he said fiercely.

'So we'll get—oh—six pairs,' she commented casually. 'Choose the rest of them, but make sure they're this same size.'

He flashed away again, thumbing through the racks as if he were a seasoned shopper. In fifteen minutes he had accumulated an armful, and the smile seemed permanently fixed.

'And now shirts, socks, and underwear,' she announced. He nodded happily. 'And one suit, for dress-up.' She expected rage, and got acquiescence. It took another hour to complete his outfit. The credit card was somewhat more worn than when she first received it. *But*, Phil told herself, *if it were Sally, we would have one dress by now, and I'd be exhausted.*

It was warm outside. The sun had finally broken through and dried off the fog. Aircraft seemed to be stacked to preposterous heights, waiting to be called in to the landing pattern of the Metropolitan Airport, to their north. A few pigeons, paying absolutely no attention to the sanitation rules, were dive-bombing the pedestrians. And Harry was waiting for them beside the Arch.

'Bought a lot, did you?' the little man asked. For some reason the gravelly voice seemed more friendly than before. He came up to Phil and relieved her of all her packages, without offering help to the boy at all. *And he's doing that on purpose*, she told herself. Robbie was tired. She could read that on his face. But there was a stubborn determination there too. The first one to offer him help would get a first-class set-down! But women are entitled to be tired, she chuckled to herself, and put on such a demonstration that they both believed it.

The ride back was different. When Phil climbed in to

the back seat, Robbie was close behind her. Harry took the long-cut, around the Capitol building and the park that lay behind it, then wandering eastward past the reconstruction of Sutter's Fort, north around the cool green of McKiney Park, east again to circle the scattered buildings of the Sacramento branch of the University of California, and then back in a twisting path through the back streets, until they were in front of the Pacific Mining and Metals building.

'Leave them packages in the car,' Harry instructed.

'Someone has to do a little sewing on the trouser legs,' Phil told him. 'They need to be taken up about an inch. Can you get it done?' He looked doubtful, but helped her out of the car and then drove off.

'I know your mother would have been a better help for you,' she told the boy. His face hardened. She fumbled to a stop.

The boy was bursting with something he wanted to say. It tumbled out in all the bitterness of a thirteen-year-old mind. 'My mother hates me,' he announced, and strode off towards the front door of the building.

'Now wait just a darn minute,' she called after him. He stopped. She walked over to confront him. 'Don't you ever say anything like that,' she lectured. 'You don't know everything there is to know about your mother and the world. What do you suppose your father would say if he heard that!'

The boy was close to tears, but his pride was bigger than his frame. 'He wouldn't care,' he said. 'He hates me too.'

CHAPTER THREE

PHIL made sure that Robbie got to the right lift, then turned back and hurried to the typing pool. It was after one, and the girls were gradually drifting back to work. 'While the cat's away, huh?' She grinned at them and headed for her own work station. A surprising amount of work had come in, for a Monday morning. She thumbed through it all and made a distribution among them.

'Not El Dorado again,' Harriet groaned as she scanned her assigned workload. 'It's a devil of a note when a company can't take gold out of its own mine!'

'Type,' Phil chuckled. 'Yours not to reason why. El Dorado county had become a suburb since the old days. The new residents are householders, not old miners. You can't blame them for not wanting us to reactivate the old mines.'

'I can,' Harriet returned. 'I don't make enough money to move out there. Why should I feel sorry for them? They work on the idea that *I've got mine, and to hell with anybody else*. They don't want to listen to the fact that the mines on the Mother Lode were there before *they* were.'

'Oh, wow,' Phil laughed. 'That sounds definitely like sour grapes. Or is it Lionel again?'

Harriet waved her comment aside. 'Lionel is long gone,' she said, bending over her word-processor keyboard. 'It's Frank now. And yes, he's a pain in my—stomach. Oooh!'

'Oooh?'

'Look who just came in!'

Phil whirled around. The entire room was quiet. Only one keyboard clicked. Penn Wilderman stood at the door, his hand resting lightly on Harry's shoulder. It was the first time she had seen him in full light. His face, screened by the inevitable dark glasses, was narrower than she had thought. The black hair tumbled in some profusion, to curl slightly at the back of his neck. He went from broad shoulders to narrow hips, reminding Phil of the boy. There was an aura about him, a feeling of poise, of command. His grey three-piece suit was immaculate. His tie, slightly loosened, flamed red against the white of his shirt. Not a huge man, not at all, but big enough.

Harry led him down the narrow aisle that separated the work positions. 'Peabody?' Penn said.

'Yes?' Her stomach quivered. She took a deep breath to calm it. You've been doing a lot of that lately, her conscience nagged.

'Lunch,' he announced. The keys in the background stopped clicking, as all the typists listened unabashedly.

'I—I have a packed lunch,' she stammered. 'The boy——'

'The boy is on his way home to try out his new clothes. And now you and I are lunching. There's something I want to talk over with you.'

'Oh!' Well, what else do you say? To Phil's certain knowledge the boss of Pacific Mining had never ever come down into the typing pool. Neither father nor son. And now, oh so casually, *lunch!*

'Mr Wilderman——'

'Penn.'

'Ah—er—Penn. I don't go out for lunch, and it's——'

'I know. It's not in the union contract. But you'll come anyway because it's a favour.'

'I—yes.' It wasn't a question of making up her mind. That area was totally vacant, spinning around in an upset such as her twenty-seven years had not known before. And tumbling out of the vacuum her voice had given its own answer.

His hand transferred to her shoulder. 'Get the car, Harry,' he ordered, and then urged Phil down the aisle towards the door. Behind them a buzz of conversation rose. 'They'll have enough gossip to last a week,' he told her softly as the door sighed shut behind them.

'Well, I don't relish being the subject of it,' she grumbled. His hand squeezed her shoulder—partly warning, partly command. She stepped off briskly towards the front door.

His magic carpet of a Cadillac whisked them over to L street in a matter of minutes, and into Frank Fat's restaurant, the favourite eatery of the Republican administration. He must have called ahead. A table was waiting for them. They moved through the crush like an elephant train, first the *maître d'*, then Phil, and slightly behind her, hand on her shoulder for a guide, Penn. He seemed to have a good many friends in the late-lunch crowd. People called out to him from both sides as they passed, but he signalled her forward.

'I'm really hungry,' he said as he fumbled at the back of her chair, then trailed a hand around the table to the opposite side. 'The Beaumonts quit this morning. That's the third couple I've lost in six weeks.'

'I'm not surprised,' she muttered.

'What?'

'I said I'm surprised,' she lied cheerfully. The frown on

his face indicated disbelief.

'Yes, well—I want the steak, please. The special, with onions and oyster sauce. Philomena?'

'Please,' she cringed. 'Someone might hear you. Phil is my name. And I couldn't possibly—oh, bring me the Chef's Salad, please, and a cup of tea.'

'Now, where was I?'

'The Beaumonts quit this morning?'

'Yes. And Harry is such a terrible cook.'

'Didn't you know that slavery is against the law? It seems to me that Harry is around day and night.'

He smiled at her, tilting his head in a truly attractive move. 'Harry and I go a long way back,' he told her. 'He's one of my father's old war buddies. I think he's shared everything I've ever done—except for Vietnam. Ah, I love the smell of Fat's steak special. Sure you won't have some?'

'Of course not,' she sighed. 'I'd be a balloon in three weeks if I ate like that.' After a moment she stopped eating, staring at his dexterity. He attacked his food with vigour—just as he does everything else, she thought. That hank of black hair kept sliding down over his forehead. Phil squeezed her own hands together to get rid of that traitorous impulse. Leaning across a table to brush the hair out of his eyes was just too much to expect of an employee!

He managed about half of his steak, then laid his utensils aside and dabbed at his mouth with his napkin. 'Well?'

She was caught by surprise again, idly tracing the line of his chin with her eyes. 'Well? Well what?'

'So are you going to help us?'

'I—I guess I don't understand, Mr—er—Penn.'

'Robert and Harry and I are living in a big house. We need help.'

'Oh. Yes, I suspect you do. You want me to find another couple to take care of the house, is that it? I'm not really in the personnel business, but I suppose I could ask around and see if something can be arranged. There must be *somebody* willing to put up with you!'

And there goes your big mouth, she yelled at herself. What sort of a way is that to talk to your boss? *Somebody might be willing to put up with you. Hah!* 'I—I really didn't mean that, Mr Wilderman,' she stammered. 'I don't know what came over me.'

'I do,' he rumbled. 'You've got a terminal case of honesty. That's one of the several things about you that I like.'

'But——' She gave thanks again that he couldn't see her mad blushes. If there were anything about herself that she hated, it was that blood-surging blush that gave her away in many a tight corner.

He was off on his own hobby-horse. 'I like you because you're quiet,' he enumerated. 'You tell me the truth. You are eminently practical. You know how to handle children. You know how to handle grouches and bullies. You know how to handle other women. You're a fine figure of a woman. And you're old enough not to be bothered with all this first flush of love and emotion. You are altogether a fine person, Philomena.'

Her first confused reaction was, 'Hush, people are listening'. And then her flustered mind marshalled all his statements, everything seemed fine until she ran into *and you're old enough to*—that was the phrase that stuck in her craw. She threw up her hands in disgust, and pushed her plate away.

'Finished eating?' He had returned to the work at hand, and was proving to be a fine trencherman.

'Yes,' she sighed. She put both elbows on the table and rested her chin on them, trying to read his face. She waited until he had completely dismantled the lunch, and then, 'Just what is it you want me to do?' She tried to keep her voice cool and low. The couple at the next table were taking an inordinate interest in *their* discussion.

'Simple,' he said. 'I want you to come live with us.'

'You want me to *what*!'

'Hey, keep your voice down,' he chuckled. 'We don't want everybody in the place to know what we're talking about, do we?'

'I—no!' Phil collapsed back into her chair and dabbed at the residue of the overturned water glass, a victim of her outraged jump to her feet. 'No.' More softly, but hissing with her anger. 'Say that again. You want me to what?'

'I said, we want you to come and live with us. Surely for someone of your age and charm that's not a surprise?'

'Well, a lot you know,' she hissed back at him. 'What has my age and charm got to do with it! I——'

'All right. Don't blow a fuse. It's not all that complicated. I thought you wouldn't mind coming over and looking after our house—and us. You have kept house before, haven't you?'

'Yes,' she snapped, 'for my own family. All girls. And you have the nerve to—I——'

'I didn't think it took a great deal of nerve.' She flashed a look. His face was solemn. There might be laughter behind the words, but his face was solemn. Her hand waved in her natural gesture, and she looked at the upset glass by her plate.

'I—you startled me,' she sighed. 'I spilled——'

'I hope it's water,' he interrupted. 'It's running down the leg of my trousers.'

'Oh, my,' Phil gasped. She snatched at the two other place napkins and rushed around to his side, madly sponging at his trouser-leg.

'I think I'd rather be wet than notorious,' he grumbled. 'I suppose now that everyone in the restaurant is looking at us?' Phil's empty hand flew to her mouth as she straightened up and glanced around. Everyone was. Clutching desperately at the wet napkins she sidled around the table and back to her seat.

'I—I'm sorry.' She had to make do with a whisper. It was all that would come out. 'They're all—staring. I'm sorry!'

'For God's sake,' he returned. 'I'm not asking you to give up the world and enter into seclusion. You have a holiday coming, don't you.'

'I—yes. Four weeks. But I thought I would save it for the summer, and then I could help my sisters with——'

'So give me two weeks of it now. Your job will be protected for you—and at the end of that time we could see how it's going.'

'I——' She closed her mouth with a snap. If I give him a word off the top of my head I'll regret it, she thought. It's too easy to say yes to this—this aggravating man. He seems to have some sort of mind-control over me. Or have I been missing someone to care for these days? All I know is that I want to say *yes*, but I'd better not! So she compromised.

'I think that's too much for a quick decision. Mr Wilderman—er—Penn. I'll have to think it over very carefully.'

'Why?' He was going to pound at her defences, and she grew more wary because of that. 'You know me. I'm the world's biggest grouch, right?' Phil shook her head in agreement, and then thanked heaven that he couldn't see. 'Are you afraid of me?' She shook her head again. 'Can't say anything?'

'I—it's Robert I don't know. He could be a bigger problem than all three of my sisters combined.'

'I don't see why you say that. He's just a normal thirteen-year-old kid.'

'Hah! A lot you know!' She hadn't meant to say that. It slipped out. But having said it, the rest had to follow. 'Robert is a mixed-up child. He thinks his mother hates him.'

'She does. Almost as much as she hates me. That woman would do anything in the world to do me in. Well, maybe that's an exaggeration. I think she would draw the line at hiring a hit-man to get rid of me. That would be like killing the chicken that lays the golden eggs.'

'Goose,' she advised absent-mindedly. 'Goose that laid the golden eggs.'

'Yeah,' he noted. 'Our divorce settlement gave her a quarter share in Pacific Mining.'

'I—but a mother can hardly hate her own child. That's just biologically not an in-thing.'

'Robbie is an adopted child,' he reminded her. A chill seemed to gather around Phil's heart. The way he talked about his wife was pure venom. But this casual reference to Robbie was like a chunk of ice. *It's true*, she told herself. *He hates the boy too! And they look so much alike. Carbon copies. His illegitimate child?*

'I—I need to think about it,' she maintained stubbornly. His sigh shook them both.

'All right.' He wadded up his napkin and threw it down. 'Then there's no need for us to remain here, is there?' He hardly waited for an answer, but scraped his chair back and stood up. The waiter hurried over.

'Madame did not care for her lunch?'

'What the hell—didn't you eat anything?'

'I wasn't hungry,' Phil said quietly. The waiter held her chair as she stood up. 'Shall we go now?' She moved over to him, and lifted his hand to her shoulder. It lay there for a second, and then closed in a harsh grip that hurt her. He seemed to be in the grip of some strong emotion. She bore it until a whimper was forced out of her, at which point the grip relaxed. No apology came. Phil struggled to control her facial muscles. It would be adding to the gossip if she led him through the crowd with tears in her eyes. He waited patiently.

The Cadillac carried them painlessly back to the office building, where Penn scrambled out. Phil followed, helping him to the door. 'The reception people will take me the rest of the way,' he said gruffly. 'You go home. You've some considerable thinking to do.'

'But it's only two-thirty,' she said. Being late, quitting early, shirking the hard jobs—these were just not the things that the Philomenas of the world did. But he insisted.

'I do believe I have a little influence with your boss. That's Henderson, isn't it—in Administration?'

'Yes. I had to take two days off for my sister's wedding, and Mr Henderson won't like it if——'

'Mr Henderson will think it's just grand,' he chuckled. 'He'll be so pleased he'll do handsprings. Go home. Harry?' The wiry little man came over to them. 'Harry, take Miss Peabody to her car. And while you're at it, check the damn thing over. I hear that most women in this town drive junk.'

'Well, I really——' Phil stamped her foot and prepared to give him a piece of her mind, but it was too late. He went through the doors, and the two receptionists were fawning all over him. Just watching turned Phil's stomach.

So, like Cinderella, Phil rode around the corner in great style, to be deposited beside her rusty old car. The coach had turned into a pumpkin faster than any fairy godmother could swing a wand. Harry got out with her and circled the ancient Subaru, making *tch tch* noises as he went. Phil stood by the driver's door, key in hand, waiting as if she expected a death sentence from him.

'It's an old car,' he commented as he came up to her.

'I know that.' It's hard not to *sound* exasperated when one is. She did her best, but he caught the inflection.

'If it was a horse we would've shot it four years ago.'

'You don't have to be a critic,' she snapped.

'Brakes work OK?'

'Of course they do.' Righteous indignation, followed by an immediate amendment, because the truth must be served. 'Well, perhaps they're a little bit—soft?'

'Turn on the engine.'

She slid into the driver's seat, flustered, and was unable to find the ignition lock. 'Take your time,' he offered sarcastically. Which made her angry enough to do just that.

The key finally achieved its purpose. The engine rumbled, turned over a couple of times, and then caught with a ragged roar. The car body shook, It was all so normal that Phil smiled. Until the little man stuck his head in the car window.

'Four-cylinder engine?'

'Yes!'

'Only runnin' on three. Been that way a long time, I suppose?'

'I—leave me alone,' she muttered as she reached for the gear-lever. He backed away, looking as if it would all blow up when she moved it.

'Lights work?' he yelled as she moved slowly out of her parking slot.

'Yes,' she roared back at him. It was a definite lie, but since she never drove after dark, she felt it could be marked down as a minor misdemeanour. She snatched a quick look at him in the rear-view mirror. He was laughing.

'Darn nuisance,' she muttered as she turned right on Fifteenth Street and headed for Route 50. During the entire trip home to Rancho Cordova she spent ninety per cent of her time painting images of the jockey and his boss in her mind, and throwing mental darts at them. Which left only ten per cent of her brain to navigate the car—about par for the course with California drivers.

The car squealed to a halt in the familiar driveway, throwing up pebbles and dust in all directions. She got out and walked around the steaming vehicle, trying to see what Harry had seen. It wasn't hard. She was driving a piece of junk, she told herself. She kicked at the left tyre to relieve her anger.

Supper was as simple as one could get. Two fried eggs shoved into a sandwich, and a glass of cold milk to go with it. Then back out to the living-room to ponder. Channel 13 news was on. She watched it with half an eye, deep in thought. Come live with me. Of course, he didn't mean it the way it sounded. Give up your typing job, and come and be my housekeeper was what he meant. Which gave it all an entirely different slant. She loved her job. On the other hand there was something to be said for staying at home and keeping house. I wonder where he lives. What *kind* of a house is it that needs keeping? The questions piled up, while the answers receded.

Along about ten o'clock the telephone ruined her chances to see—again—the old black and white movie, *Raffles*. She snapped off the set with a twinge of regret and went out into the hall to answer the call.

'Phil, this is Debbie.' Phil groaned, Debbie lived about five miles away, on the edge of Fair Oaks, and only called when she wanted something. As in this case.

'Phil—John and I have a chance to take a wonderful trip up to Tahoe on the weekend, but we can't take the girls!' *I'll bet you can't*, Phil thought. *Two more monstrous kids I've never seen. Real hell-raisers.* 'So we thought we'd let their aunt really get to know them,' Debbie continued. 'How about if I bring them over on Friday night, and we'll pick them up Sunday night late?'

And that will shoot my weekend for sure, Phil thought. *A whole lovely weekend baby-sitting for somebody else's children. So their aunt can get to know them? Their aunt knows all she wants to know about them. They expect me to clothe them and feed them and nurse them, and nobody will ever say a word about payment.*

John is a senior architect, and they're looking for a free baby-sitter! Good old dependable Phil! It was hard to tell which one of the sisters was most surprised at the answer. The little family push had been just enough to make up Phil's mind for her. She would accept Penn Wilderman's offer—because she was curious, and to please herself for a change. Just herself, no one else. Because she wanted to find out what would happen. And here was the perfect opportunity to burn her boats before she could change her mind back again.

'I'm really sorry,' she said, 'but I won't be available this weekend.'

'Oh, Phil!' Under the usual procedure. Debbie would cry a little, Phil would simmer, and then relent. *Not this time, sister.* 'But Phil, we counted on you!'

'How about the week after?'

'Not then either, Debbie. Why don't you hire a baby-sitter! There are plenty available.'

Deep silence from the other end, then an off-telephone conference. John came on the line. 'Phil, you just have to do this for us. Debbie needs a vacation, and——'

'So do I, John. I haven't had one in ten years. But I intend to take one now.'

'Hey Phil, what's got into you?'

'It's hard to tell.' She managed to work up a chuckle. 'But whatever it is, I like it. Do have a good time, John. Call me when you get back and tell me all about it—oops. I forgot. I won't be here. Well, I'll be in touch.' She laid the receiver down on to its cradle with a broad smile on her face. Her brother-in-law was still spluttering as she disconnected.

'One nail in my coffin,' she teased herself as she went for coffee. 'Now, if the family grapevine is working——'

It was. No sooner had she made her mug of instant coffee and added the skimmed milk than the telephone rang again. *They'll push me over the top, to where I can't possibly back out!* She smiled as she picked up the instrument.

'Phil, just what are you up to?' Imperious Samantha.

Being a doctor's wife was next door to coronation in Sam's mind.

'Up to?' Phil queried. 'Why, I can't honestly say that I'm up to anything much. What makes you ask?'

'Debbie called me. She's all upset, Phil.'

'Is she really? How terrible.'

'Phil, you *are* up to something. I can smell it.'

That's some nose. Phil wanted to say, but didn't. Samantha and her husband lived downtown, adjacent to Mercy Hospital, more miles away than the crows cared to fly in a California winter.

'I can't imagine what gave you that idea,' Phil coaxed. 'The truth of the matter is that I'm tired of having all of you lean on me, Sam. I almost feel as if my life stopped when Mother died—and I took her place. Now it's ten years later, I'm twenty-seven, and people treat me as if I were fifty. I want something more out of life, Sam.'

'Phil! You've lost your head! And besides—what will we all do without you?'

For the first time a serious note crept into Phil's voice. 'Why, I guess you'll all learn to grow up just a little bit more,' she sighed. She was going to have to use stronger ammunition to make them see things her way, Phil decided. And the language they all understand and respect is: 'I've found a man,' she said softly. Her sister made a curious noise at the other end of the telephone and hung up.

'And now,' Phil announced to the house at large, 'they'll both be over here tomorrow to bring me back to the straight and narrow. But neither of them gets up early enough to catch me before I go off to work, so all I really need to do is be gone by the end of the day. The coward's way out, Philomena. Just exactly what I need!' That night, still dithering, she packed a bag. And so to bed.

The day blessed her decision. The sun was up bright and clear. The early morning fog had dissipated before seven o'clock. The highways were cluttered, but not jammed. One or two dare-devil sparrows could be heard above the hum of civilisation. Phil started earlier than usual, just in case either of her sisters made the supreme sacrifice. Which was just as well.

The doors to the building were already unlocked, but nobody was in reception, and the typing pool was still locked. She fumbled with her key and propped the door open while she felt the inside wall for the light switch. The rows of fluorescent lights flared. And the voice at her elbow said, 'Miss Peabody, they don't fit.'

She dropped her bag, startled, and whirled around. Robert was directly behind her, a rebellious look on his face. A dirty face, at that.

'What don't fit?' She was struggling for time. Never an early-morning person, Phil required a little prompting to get moving.

'The trousers. They don't fit.'

'But that's only the cuff,' she said solemnly. 'I told you yesterday. Every pair of jeans has to be turned up. It won't take but a minute or two with a sewing machine, and not more than ten to fifteen minutes by hand.'

'Really?' A faint appeal stalked that thin face. *And that's something I can do for him*, Phil told herself fiercely. *He hasn't an ounce of confidence in himself! Or anyone else, for that matter!*

'Really,' she repeated. 'What did your father——'

'His father said why didn't you stop at the tailor's.' Penn Wilderman came stalking in from out of the dimly lit lobby. 'So why didn't you.'

'Because I don't think Macy's has a tailor on tap,' she said fiercely. 'And even if they did, this isn't the sort of thing you need a tailor for. Anybody can sew a cuff. Anybody!'

When he laughed she knew he was laughing at himself, and her happy grin flashed back at him. 'Evidently not quite everybody,' he returned. 'I tried last night, and Harry did too.' He looked down at her with his head tilted—that crazy boyish look on his face—and only the dark glasses to distort the happy picture. She was mesmerised by that smile. It tugged at her heart, and her head had no chance.

The water's too deep, she whispered to herself. Way over my head. But she dived in anyway. 'When we get home tonight I'll fix it,' she said.

CHAPTER FOUR

PENN allowed Phil all morning to straighten out the affairs of the typing pool, and to leave Harriet a notebook full of advice. That, of course, left her no time to call either of her sisters. Which helped her guilt feelings immensely. They could hardly interfere when they knew nothing about what was happening. Robbie, demonstrating his confidence in absolutely nobody, sat near her in the work-room. 'To make sure I don't escape?' she asked him.

He returned a tiny smile, and continued to play around with one of the spare word-processors. He did generate a little stir when, along about ten-thirty, he managed to break the corporation's access code and went wheeling and dealing among the corporate memories. Phil caught the action out of the corner of her eye and hustled over to him.

She leaned over his shoulder and turned off the set. 'And just what do you think you're up to, young man?'

'Nothing.' He sat there rigidly, hands still on the keyboard.

'Nothing? That access code is designed especially to keep people out of our records.'

He swivelled around in his chair and looked up at her. His narrow face was flushed. 'It's a stupid code,' he announced. 'Any *hacker* could solve it in twenty minutes.'

'But you took a whole hour?'

'Well, I'm only thirteen, for goodness' sake. What do you expect of a kid?'

'Yeah, kid,' she chuckled. 'Don't do it again—today, that is. Promise?'

He studied her for a moment, looking for—something. 'Well, OK. Promise.' And still those eyes staring, judging. Phil walked away, trying to look confident, but actually keeping her fingers crossed. *Too bright,* she told herself. *He may be adopted, but he's a chip off the old block for all that. What am I letting myself in for?*

There was no more time to ponder. Penn arrived at eleven o'clock. Phil was not watching, but the sudden silence was enough to announce his appearance. She finished the sentence, gave Harriet a quick 'God bless', and headed for the door.

'I have my car in the car park,' she said. 'I'll follow you.'

'Suitcases?'

'In the boot.'

'Harry, transfer the suitcases and have someone bring her car along. Robbie's waiting in the limousine, Peabody. Let's get a move on.'

She was still fumbling with 'But I' when they reached the lobby, his hand firmly on her shoulder. Harry had already disappeared. They were out on the pavement before she could muster up a 'This isn't right.' And even then it hardly contained enough indignation to make it worth while. He pulled her to a halt. 'The flowers,' he asked brusquely. 'What kind?'

She sniffed the air. From long usage she had forgotten them, sited in large pots on either side of the entrance inside the lobby.

'Camellias,' she said. 'It's like a little artificial garden.

Your father loves them, they say. The gardener keeps changing them whenever the cold gets to them. There's a greenhouse somewhere. Haven't you ever been here before?'

'Not me,' he laughed. 'I was always the kid they sent out into the field. When my father decided I was seasoned enough to run the company I was no longer interested. I wouldn't have come back—except my mother laid it out for me, too. A very domineering woman, my mother. Come on.'

'Wait,' she said softly, and slipped out from under his hand. The blooms were profuse. She picked one of them and was back at his side.

'Now what?'

'Stand still,' she ordered, stretching for his lapel. 'Darn. You modern men have ruined a good custom. No button hole in your lapel. Here, I'll tuck them into your jacket pocket.' His warm hand closed over hers and carried both up to his lips. It was a fleeting kiss. Just a touch of warmth that made her shiver. 'You're a strange one, Peabody,' he chuckled. 'Whoever would have thought? Flowers in February. I'll have all my suits altered. Button holes coming up!'

'Now *you're* being silly,' she laughed. 'Robbie is getting impatient. Come on.' As they went across the wide walkway she kept cadence to herself, 'Button holes, button holes, button holes.' And for some strange reason it warmed her heart.

The ride was smooth, like drifting in a canoe down a slow-moving river. It was comfortable, too. She was in between Robbie and his father, and the width of the seat provided plenty of room. 'As soon as we get home I need you to put those drops in my eyes,' he said as they circled around down the one-way maze that led to Fifteenth Street.

Phil had already lost track of their route. 'Does it hurt much?'

'Hardly,' he grunted.

'And you can't see a thing?'

'Hey, don't work up that pity bit,' he chuckled. 'I can see. Shapes, outlines—but everything is a little fuzzy. It's getting better. The doctor says it's sort of like getting a bad sunburn. Another three weeks and I'm sure everything will be cleared up. These pads are just a precaution.'

'That's a relief.'

'You were worried about my dad?' The boy was trying to puzzle something out.

'Of course I was worried.' Phil tried to keep it all on a casual basis, but for some reason that was becoming a hard thing to do.

'But two weeks ago you didn't even know him.' The boy had the bit in his teeth, and meant to run with it.

'That doesn't stop me from worrying now that I *do* know him.'

'You're funny.'

Penn's hand came over and squeezed hers. *A warning, or a comfort? Maybe both?* At least I can hope, she thought.

They were in a part of Sacramento Phil had never seen. A little enclave of winding roads, scattered houses. A sign said South Land Park Drive. Another, swathed in old trees, said 12th Street. Directly ahead was the Sacramento River, masked by the trees. They were in the old section of the city, where residential land sold by the foot, not by the quarter-acre. They turned left.

'You don't live here?' A hesitant question begging for denial.

'I believe I do,' Penn answered.

'But—this is where all the millionaires live!'

'I do believe you're right.'

'I——' The car turned off the street, through a set of wrought-iron gates that opened on a small circular drive. A stone wall circled the block-long property. Bushes and trees hid the house from the street. The car came to a stop in front of a massive building that sparkled with windows.

'You don't live here!' An angry statement, defying an answer.

'I do believe I do.'

'Well!' A large sigh to accompany. 'How in the world do you think I can housekeep such a monstrous house all my myself?'

'My mother did.'

'Well, she must have been some sort of—I don't believe it. It's just not possible. For a house like this you have to hire half a dozen servants!'

He was pushing her out. 'Not quite. Only five, I think!'

'But you—you—said that Mr and Mrs Beaumont had quit and that you wanted me to——' She turned around and faced up to him. Nose to chest, so to speak. The closer she got the taller he seemed to be. 'I think you had better tell me just what you want *me* for, Mr Wilderman!'

'To fix my trousers,' Robbie answered from behind her.

'That's one good reason,' Penn chuckled. 'There are half a dozen more. What I really want is for you to get these people of ours organised so there's some order and efficiency and quiet in this crazy house. I don't expect you to peel the potatoes and make the soup or sweep the floor. Organisation, Philomena!'

'Oh!' She bit at her lip, wished that her car were there for a quick get-away, and alternately wished she had worn sharp-pointed shoes, so she might kick him in the ankle.

'Now, shall we go in?' He tucked his hand under her elbow to emphasise the fact that the invitation was purely rhetorical. The house was a stranger to the Sacramento area. Built along the lines of an old Spanish *hacienda*, it would have fitted better into the softer climate of southern California. But the walls, the trees, the isolation, hid it from all its neighbours, of whom there were few. Pillared arches provided a porch, and swept around the sides of the house to form an open mall. The house itself was deep-set within this portico, with wide arched windows flanked by huge wooden shutters. Around the entire second floor a narrow balcony ran, railed with filigree iron. Phil could barely see the curved red tiles of the roof, topped with four sets of twin chimneys. Penn seemed to read her mind.

'Conspicuous consumption,' he said. 'My great-grandfather had it built, when gold was still pouring out of the Mother Lode. Impressed?'

'Frightened,' Phil returned. 'I just keep wondering what happens to me at midnight. Pumpkins and mice?'

He chuckled and hurried her into the house. Robbie trailed behind them, while Harry struggled with her bags. A young girl was waiting for them in the bright hall. Seventeen, perhaps, or eighteen. Short curly black hair, held precariously in place by a white ribbon. A round full face, with smooth tan complexion. Mexican, somewhere in her background, and pretty, Phil concluded.

'Philomena, this is Cecily. Where's Mrs Waters?'

'In the kitchen. She's doing lunch.' A touch of liquid accent, the soft caress of Spanish mingled with the drawl of the American South-west. Altogether nice, Phil thought. Her smile was returned four-fold.

'Mrs Waters is our cook, Philomena. You can meet her later. Cecily works the morning shift. Mary comes on from three until seven. Frank is the handyman, and George is the gardener. They'll all be around the house somewhere, after lunch. Why don't you go up to your room and settle in? Cecily?'

The girl nodded and headed for the broad sweep of mahogany stairs that curved gently around to an upstairs landing. There was a painting on the wall, half-way up. A portly pirate, with short black beard, piercing eyes, and a gold watch chain prominently displayed across a half-acre of stomach. It almost seemed there should be an earring in one of his lobes, but of course he wasn't that sort of pirate.

Harry, right behind Phil, with the bags, said, 'The old Boss. He built the place. Been nothin' like him in the family until Penn come along.'

And I can surely believe that, Phil thought. Isn't that the claim—there's a throwback in every family come the third generation? The room to which she was led was almost at the head of the stairs. Cecily threw back the double doors with a touch of grace and stood aside. Harry stopped behind them in the hall. Both waited for Phil's reaction.

'Oh, my,' she murmured as she walked slowly to the centre of the room and looked around. 'Oh, my goodness.' Cecily smiled broadly. The bedroom was four times the size of her own, back home in Rancho Cordova. The walls were pink, the wall-to-wall carpet beige, and the bed covered with a Coat-of-Joseph quilt. Four floor-to-ceiling windows made up one wall, facing west towards the river. The windows stood slightly ajar, inviting her out into the sunshine on the balcony. She resisted. There was too much to be done, too much to be learned.

'I think you've made a mistake,' prim little Philomena said. 'I'm the housekeeper, not the daughter of the house.' But you don't want to change to something else, Phil, her conscience shrieked. Don't be so darn positive!

'No mistake,' Cecily laughed. 'The best room in the house, yes. Mr Wilderman picked it out himself. This one, he said, this one is for Peabody. He calls you that?'

'Yes', Phil laughed. 'But everybody else should call me Phil. You too, Harry.'

'Sure,' the little man said as he swung her bags up on to the bench in front of the dressing-table. 'He hears me call you that and the balloon goes up for sure. Well, maybe when he's not around.'

'The lunch is in twenty minutes,' Cecily offered. 'You want help to unpack?'

'Me?' Phil could just not hold back the giggles. 'I don't have enough in those bags to—well, I don't. But please do stay. I want to ask a question or two.'

Harry took the hint, and left. Phil opened her cases, and transferred the dresses slowly into the huge armoire that took up one corner of the room. It was true, she hadn't brought many clothes. And those she had brought were of two kinds, simple suits for office work, or take-aways from Good Will Industries. At least they looked that way. Cecily watched, somewhat disappointed.

'Tell me about Robbie,' Phil asked. 'Does he go to school? Does he ever see his mother? Is he happy here?'

'Ay Dios mio,' the girl laughed. 'First, yes, he goes to school. But they have vacation. A private school, no? The boy is too sharp. He knows everything. And in his room the computer—you wouldn't believe. He is in trouble once. The police came. Something about tapping into the City's computer system illegally. He—his mother—that is hard to say. His mother has the right to him—you know—the court control. The guardian? But I don't think—especially now that she is remarried—well.' She shrugged a very expressive shoulder. The girl sat down on the corner of the bed. 'It is money, I think. The mother has an income from the Company. The boy also. His mother can't stand to have him around—until she needs money. His money. Then she comes here with much noise and loud argument, you know? And takes him back. Mr Wilderman, he tries now in the court to get permanent control of the child. But the lawyers say you must have family. There must be the home life, and parents. It is a puzzle. There must be action quickly. The court is—ruling? Next week.'

'You mean the case has to be decided as quickly as all that?'

'Yes. I think so. Mr Wilderman, you know, he don't tell us, but we hear. And Mrs Wilderman—well, I don't know. She does not want the boy for love, you understand. She would rather he live with his father. But then she would lose the money. I think—it has been peaceful here for a week. I think something is bound to explode very soon.'

'And Mr Wilderman? He really wants the boy?'

'Of course.'

'For an adopted child he looks very much like Mr Wilderman.'

'But of course. I—oh—the bell. I must serve the lunch. Excuse me—I forgot to say, Welcome.'

'Thank you, Cecily. I'll be down in a minute.'

It took much longer than that. She stopped long enough to scrub herself in the white and gold bathroom, then slipped into one of her better cotton dresses. It was a distinct contrast to her working clothes. A dress warm enough for the mild winter, but sparkling in spring buttercup. Her head was already starting to ache with all she had learned—and had not learned. She pulled out the pins in her hair and unbraided it, setting it straight with a few quick passages of her brush. It made a world of difference to her appearance, but that was something she had failed to notice in the haste of the past ten years.

Fifteen minutes later, she started back down the stairs. Sunlight glittered off the stair-runners and played echo off the little glass squares suspended from the massive chandelier. Behind, on the darker wall, another picture hung. A life-sized oil, it appeared, of a young woman in the spring of her life. She was dressed in a long ball-gown, and was poised looking to her right, a happy smile on her face. Something tugged at Phil's mind. There was something about the picture—but she could not place just what it was. A young woman, with golden hair, smiling at the world! She shrugged her shoulders and went down.

Robbie was waiting for her. 'The dining-room is at the back of the house,' he said. 'When are you going to fix my trousers?'

'Just as soon as we finish lunch,' Phil said casually.

The boy looked at her sceptically, his solemn thin face a mixture of hope and doubt. He stood there for a moment, then turned and walked away down the hall.

Phil was distracted as she followed him. There were more paintings on the walls. Not family pictures, but works of some merit, hung too high for her to read the names of the artists, but not so high that she could not appreciate their excellence. When she turned her attention to where she was going the boy had disappeared. At the end of the hall were a pair of double doors, closed. She was looking down the lateral corridor, wondering where Robbie had gone, when she reached for the knob and went in. Actually she was half-turned, not paying attention to her path. And she smashed into Penn.

His arms came out, almost automatically, and kept her from falling. More than that. They wrapped themselves around her and pulled her in solidly against his vibrant strength. All his actions seemed programmed, not real. He held her close, muttering something she could not make out. She relaxed against him, enjoying the feeling.

One of his hand wandered to her hair, tumbling through it like a leaf in a mill-stream. The other moved to the small of her back and pulled her closer, ever closer. The warmth and comfort of it all had taken her completely by surprise. The hands moved up to cup her head, and his lips brushed across hers gently.

Gently, at first. They came again, insistently, demanding, drawing out of her all the emotions she had stored for twenty-seven years. Stored and never shared. Until now. It was too much of a demand. Her own hands were trapped against his chest. She wriggled them loose and felt them follow the flow of his ribcage, around his back as far as she could reach. And then, as suddenly as the assault had begun, he pushed her back, away from him. 'Who?' he asked bitterly. And all her castle of dreams collapsed.

'Philomena,' she quavered.

'Damn!' He stepped away, widening the gap beyond touch. 'I don't know what came over me,' he sighed. 'I was thinking of something, and there was the smell of your perfume—damnit, Peabody, it reminded me of someone. I'm sorry.'

She had managed to regain her breath by then, and some semblance of her mind. There was a feeling of loss involved—what had tasted so sweet was bitter. But she was determined not to let it show. 'No need to apologise,' she said primly. 'I've been kissed before. To be honest, I rather enjoyed it.'

'That's kind of you,' he chuckled. 'And honest. I like that. But I want you to know I don't run around the house assaulting elderly ladies.' He offered an arm. For himself, she knew, but it felt warmingly good. 'They're about to serve lunch.'

She led him to the table, wrestling all the way with her own thoughts *Elderly lady!* Good lord, he's got *me* thinking that way now. Philomena Peabody, twenty-seven going on fifty! It was nice, that kiss. She *did* enjoy it. She had been kissed by men before—but so long ago she could hardly associate name with face in her memory. And I mustn't let him think—what he's thinking.

'I'm not really *that* old,' she told him. If he wants to pursue the subject, now's the time!

'No, of course not,' he rumbled. 'Sit over here next to me.' He held a chair for her. Phil slipped into it, biting her lip in disgust. He *didn't want* to pursue it—or her, for that matter. Why should that seem important to her? A gong sounded out in the hall. Robbie came in, thumping, in his seven-league boots. Harry was not far behind.

And there's another question answered, Phil thought. Harry eats with the family. So he's not a servant, he's a—what? And Robbie, sitting all hunched up at the far end of the table, looking as if he expected to be poisoned by the cook. His hands were grimy, and there was a streak of something—chocolate?—on his chin. Phil's household soul rebelled. She beckoned to the boy. He looked sullenly, then got up with much reluctance and came around the table to her side. She pulled his head closer so she could whisper in his ear.

'I do the trousers, you wash the hands,' she said. 'And the face too, for that matter.'

The boy considered. He had his father's habit. His head was tilted to one side as he thought, but not an inkling of a smile crossed his face. 'OK,' he said, and thumped out of the room.

'OK?' Penn, looking at her but not seeing, the pads behind his dark glasses still fixed in place. Silence. 'I know it has to do with Robbie. I never realised how noisy he is when he walks. What's going on?'

'He's doing me a favour,' Phil replied. 'We have this bargain going. And all teenagers sound like a herd of buffalo. Even the girls.'

'At least he didn't yell. You're a good influence on that boy, Peabody. You could have been his mother.'

She had her water glass at her lips when he said that, and almost drowned as the fluid went down the wrong pipe. He bent over the corner of the table and patted her back a couple of times. Patted, in his style, Phil thought.

A couple more of those and he'll break my back. *I could be the child's mother?* Robbie is thirteen and I'm twenty-seven. So it's biologically possible, I suppose. But again, that urge to tell him—if he wanted to know. 'Me being Robbie's mother is faintly possible,' she offered with a touch of whimsy in her voice. 'But just barely so. There's this matter of age between us.' And having thrown out the gauntlet for the second time, she relaxed in her chair, waiting to see what he would do.

Cecily came in at that moment with a serving-tray, and set it down in front of him. 'Don't go on about your age, Peabody,' he said firmly. He reached for the carving-knife, and, as Phil held her breath, did an adequate job of carving the roast. And that, she told herself, is the last time I'm going to bring up the subject. When they take the pads off his eyes he'll know better, and I'll be back at my word-processor faster than he can say *who the hell are you*!

She ate more than she had intended. Lunch was usually a sandwich. Mrs Waters was obviously a cook *par excellence*. Phil wandered out to the kitchen for an introduction. The cook was a good advertisement for her wares. Short, well-rounded, flushed cheeks, grey hair. Somebody's mother, looking for a family to love. 'Been here thirty years,' she admitted. 'Mr Waters was the gardener here—before George. But, the war and all, and we never had children, so I stayed. I seen Penn grow up. He was a happy kid—and a happy young man, until his sister died. Since then—well, he's changed. Needs some lovin', that man.'

'His sister died?'

'Boating accident. The pair of them used to race up and down the river in those speedboats and all. Neither one never listened to what nobody had to say. Hit a piece of driftwood, she did. Turned the boat over, broke her neck. She was racing him. He never forgot that. Killed her man too. But he wasn't a Wilderman.' The tone of voice gave to indicate that *therefore the husband didn't count in the scheme of things*.

Robbie came through the swinging doors. 'I washed my hands,' he said. 'And ate all my lunch. Now?'

'Now,' Phil laughed. 'Thank you again, Rose. We'll talk later on. Come on, Robbie.' When the door swung shut behind them Rose Waters stopped what she was doing, put her hands on her hips, and contemplated the back of the door. 'Well,' she said 'I *do* declare. Make a nice housekeeper, that one—make a better wife!'

Not even dreaming of such a fate, Phil and Robbie tumbled up the stairs and into her room. Cecily had resurrected an old pedal Singer sewing-machine from somewhere in the attic, and it stood rather forlornly in the middle of the beige rug. But it worked. 'Up on this chair now, Robbie,' she ordered. The boy, still suspicious, climbed up on the low flat chair and moved as she directed. While she measured and pinned she tried a little conversation.

'When does your school open again, Robbie?'

'Pretty soon.'

'Like it, do you?'

'Ummph.'

With a mouthful of pins Phil could hardly question him at length. 'What do you want to be when you grow up?'

'An adult.'

She looked up quickly, and caught him in a smile. He did his best to erase it, but failed. The grin spread gradually across his face as she made a mark in the air with her finger. 'One for you,' Phil told him. 'But watch yourself, wise guy. Two can pun as easy as one.'

'Well, stupid people keep asking me that,' he returned. The sulky expression was back.

'And that puts me in *my* place,' she chuckled. 'Skin out of those trousers now, and I'll get them sewn.'

'I—I didn't mean you, Miss Peabody,' he defended. 'And I don't take my trousers off when there's girls in the room.'

'Thank you on both counts,' she chuckled. 'But I'm not a girl—I'm a woman.'

'I—I don't think I know what the difference is.'

'I don't think I do either,' Phil returned. 'Scoot out of here now. I'll have all of these ready in about an hour.' The boy managed one more tiny smile, and was gone.

Her first major task of the day finished, Phil decided to wander. She saw Cecily leave, driven off by Frank the handyman in a very plebeian Ford. The sun was bright outside. At the end of February, in the sun, the temperature stood at seventy degrees. It would get colder at sunset. Even worse if clouds settled down from the mountains to the east. There was snow in those mountains, deep snow. Lake Tahoe was under a blizzard, the weatherman had said at midday. And that only a couple of hours away by road. But now it was worth a walk. Phil strolled out on to the veranda, and wandered around to the back of the house.

It was all too confusing, this house, the Wildermans—husband and wife fighting over the boy. Not exactly what you could call a tug-of-love case. Maybe Robbie was right. Maybe they both hated him. But why? He was an adopted child, but he resembled Penn so closely—

could that be the source of the bitterness? And if Mrs Wilderman was intent on getting the boy back, what would she do next? I just hope, Phil told herself, that I'm done and gone from here before the inevitable explosion.

CHAPTER FIVE

THE remainder of the week was a string of little scenes, as Philomena put her hands to organising the household. There was the early morning uproar that brought her up in her bed. It came from behind the connecting door which she had noted but not checked. She slipped into her robe and padded barefoot in the general direction of the problem. The door was unlocked, and on the other side Penn, dressed only in pyjama bottoms, was vainly trying to avoid Harry's ministrations. The bedroom was dim, almost dark.

'I don't want a bath,' Penn said grimly. 'For God's sake, Harry, can't you get the eye drops closer to the eyes?'

'I could if you would stop wigglin' around like a fish on a hook.'

'Oh, so now it's my fault?'

'Look, boss, it's been your fault for two weeks. I hadda refill the prescription four times already. Everybody in the drug store thinks I'm drinking it.'

'Ah. Afraid of your reputation, are you?'

Phil ghosted across the floor. 'Let me do that,' she told Harry. He surrendered the dropper without an argument. 'Sit still. Stop acting like a little baby,' she warned Penn. Harry almost swallowed his tongue, and faded out of the room.

'Baby, is it?' He was a tiger now, all sleek and deadly. She paid his objection about as much attention as she had

71

her sisters' under similar conditions.

'I call it as I see it,' she said firmly. 'Hold still.' Her thumb forced his eyelid up, and two precise drops fell on to his eyeball. 'Is that any better?'

'Lucky,' he grumbled. 'So you got it all. Lucky.'

'You bet,' she chuckled. 'We'll try for two.' Her thumb went out again. He shrugged away, and almost got the digit in his eye. 'I said sit still,' she commanded.

'Yes ma'am.' A very docile comment, that foreshadowed troubles to follow. A tiny grin flicked at the corner of her mouth as she repeated the eyedropper exercise.

'There now, that wasn't too bad, was it?'

'No, Mommy.'

'Don't be a smart-aleck,' she warned.

'Or you'll turn me over your knee? How about a little retribution?' He lunged at her, managing to find one wrist, and pulled her down across his knees. 'Now, Miss Know-It-All, try this one for size.'

It wasn't her time of day, frankly. She did anything better in the afternoon. But there wasn't a great deal of time to object. He had her trapped, pinioned, and crushed up against his naked chest before she could catch her breath. It was about as close as she had ever been to a naked man, and the lack of experience told on her. What followed replaced at least two of her normal three cups of coffee. His lips came down on hers again, softly, gently. His breath smelled like warm clean breezes. *And I haven't even brushed my teeth,* she thought wildly. It didn't bother him. The gentle assault became mental torture. He sealed her off from every outside contact, forcing her to concentrate on him, and him alone. Her nerves filed complaints—rioting complaints. They were ignored. The hand behind her head was no longer needed to lock her in place. She had totally surrendered. And then it was over.

She struggled to sit up. At least it was affecting him also, she noted. He's as out of breath as I am. And something more. That strange expression on his face, as if he had tried something awful and found he liked it!

'Damn it, Peabody,' he muttered. 'You've done it again!'

'Of course,' she returned, as the experience whirled from pleasure to bitterness. 'It's all my fault, right? I took advantage of you.' Her hand reached out against her will, and stroked the curling hair on his massive chest.

'Right,' he grunted. His two hands under her armpits lifted her straight up and set her down on her feet. 'For the sake of my peace of mind, please get the hell out of here!' She fled back into her own bedroom, slammed the connecting door behind her, and frantically fumbled with the key.

It spoiled the whole morning, but the next day, and every day thereafter, he appeared politely at her door, eyedrops in hand. She would lead him over to her bed, sit him down comfortably, and administer his daily dose. And as each day passed, she wished crazily that he might pull her down into his lap again.

With Robbie, things were a little different. The first three days the boy gloomed around the house in his new jeans, disappearing into his room whenever she tried to make conversation. 'Hiding with his computer,' Cecily told her. 'It talks back, but it can't give him any orders.'

On the fourth day she trapped him in a corner and refused to let him go. 'I mean to talk to you, Robbie,' she insisted. 'And if it means that I have to follow you all over the house, even to the bathroom, I'll do it.'

'I'll go in my room and lock the door,' he muttered.

'I've got a key to every room in the house,' she returned, jingling her key-ring at him. He thought about it for a minute or two, and then gave up.

'So talk.'

'Don't you have any friends, Robbie?'

'Not around here. In St Louis, yes. I talk to them through the computer network.'

'Lord, that must make a tremendous telephone bill.'

'He doesn't care so long as it keeps me quiet. Didn't you know that?'

'I know that your father is very worried about you,' Phil snapped. 'Between the lawyers and the court case, he's about to go through the roof. Do you *want* to go back to your mother?'

'No. No, I don't.' The defiance had disappeared. He was just a lonely little boy.

'Then you have to help, Robbie. You have to get out in the sunshine—get a little exercise. How about touring the city with me?'

'Well—I'd rather play with my computer.'

'I'll pull out all the fuses in the house if you don't get outside,' she threatened.

'Why are you so serious about all this? I'm nothing to you.'

'Of course you're something to me. Everybody is something to everybody. Don't they teach you *anything* in that school of yours?'

'No, they don't. I don't understand you. Women are like my mother—and you're not. I think you've got a crush on my—on him!' Those dark eyes bored through her like daggers. She caught her breath.

'That would be a likely way to commit suicide,' she returned, even though her heart wasn't in it. 'Get yourself a jacket while I see if I can rustle up a car.'

'You are funny, Peabody—er—Phil? You rustle cattle, not cars.'

'Not where I come from, buddy. The clock is running. Scoot.'

Phil's life had been marvellously improved by the reappearance of her car. It arrived three days after her, and seemed to have been—perhaps resurrected would be the best word for it. The engine had been tuned, the brakes re-lined and adjusted, it sported four—no five— new tyres, and the whole rackety thing had been re-painted. The only thing she could object to was the colour. An ancient Japanese car masquerading in Kelly Green was just not her cup of tea. But it ran.

They made their first visitation to Sutter's Fort. Once it had stood on a hill, distant from the confluence of the Sacramento and the American rivers. Now the city had grown up around and past it, its ruins had been reconstructed by the state, and it stood its vigil just a short distance up Capitol Avenue from the State House.

The wall around the fort looked newer than it ever had in Sutter's time. The original wall had been eighteen feet high, made of adobe. The replacement was lower, of painted brick. The central building, the trading post, glowed in a new coat of paint. And the low workshops that stood against the inside of the walls now sold souvenirs. Robbie was impressed but not very. His reaction fell into that gap that Phil defined as 'under-whelmed'.

'Junk,' he commented. 'Tourist stuff. And I read somewhere that John Sutter was a fake.'

'Did you now,' Phil chuckled. 'I thought the jury was still out on that. So maybe he wasn't a Swiss nobleman.

You can't dispute that he established the first white settlement in Northern California, and if it hadn't been for the Gold Rush in 1849 he would have been a very wealthy man.'

'That don't make sense, Phil.' She smiled at him. Her name had come out naturally—and that was a start. 'How could he go broke because of the Gold Rush?'

'It wasn't hard,' she returned. 'Thousands did. But John Sutter had his own way. He wanted to make his money from wheat. There were plenty of customers. Bread cost a fortune in the Gold Rush days.'

'So what was the problem?'

'Wheat has to be planted, tended, and harvested. In the end every labourer that Sutter recruited gave up the agricultural work and went off to pan gold for themselves. Sutter went so far into debt that there was no escape. Want to see some more?'

'Like this?'

'Well, it's hard not to be like this, Robbie. Everything from the old days went to wrack and ruin. It's only been in the last few years that things have been reconstructed. But there's a lot to learn. How about if we go down to Old Sacramento?'

'It's your car,' he grumbled, but she could actually see him relax. So she drove west, skirting the traffic problems on the Capitol Mall, the wide expanse of road that ran from the Capitol building itself down to the river, on the order of the great boulevards of Paris. She also had to dodge the traffic around the K Street Mall, a shopping district that was being overhauled to allow the use of LRV's—light rail vehicles.

They left their car parked in the underground facility in the mall and walked across into the Embarcadero area, the flat plain between Route Five and the river. Reconstruction of the old city was not yet complete, and might never be, but as they walked from block to block they saw it all as it might have been when this little corner of the world was the gateway to the goldfields. There were drapers and drugstores, grocers and hardware, mixed together with saloons, gambling halls, and banks. Not to mention the Hastings building, and the statue which marked the Western terminal of the Pony Express.

'You mean to tell me that they actually lifted the whole town up over fifteen feet?' Robbie's scientific mind found it all improbable.

'More than that in some places,' Phil laughed. 'You know the original city was almost swept away several times in the early days. But instead of just moving away, they dredged the river, lifted all the buildings with hydraulic jacks, and filled in underneath them. And if you think all of that is fairy tales, young man, just run across the street there. You can still look down at the original building, below the present street level.'

Phil stayed where she was and watched as he ran the gauntlet of traffic to have a look. She had had enough. Her feet hurt. If the Bee had suddenly predicted a twenty-foot rise in the river level, Phil was prepared to stand and drown rather than move another step. Robbie walked back slowly.

'Convinced?'

'Yeah. I'm convinced. It's hardly believable though, is it? How could they afford all that?'

'You have to remember that in those days, Robbie, practically all the gold mined in the United States flowed through this city. And a little of it stuck on every hand it passed through. So now, what have you learned?'

He pulled himself up out of his normal slouch. 'I've learned that sightseeing is hard work. My feet hurt.'

Which led them back to the house in a companionable mood, about four o'clock in the afternoon. 'I'm gonna go watch television,' the boy commented. He made himself up a bologna sandwich and a glass of milk, and wandered off.

'Television?' Phil asked. 'I didn't see any antennae on the roof. Have they run the cable out here yet?'

'Nope,' Rose laughed. 'Satellite antenna. Out behind the swimming-pool it is. Gives us one hundred channels twenty-four hours a day, and not a worth-while programme on any of them.'

'But Robbie likes it, I suppose?'

'He sure does. A mite more companionable, the boy is,' Rose commented as she prepared the dinner. 'Roast lamb tonight. Can I give you a hint, Phil?'

'You bet, Rose. Shoot.'

'Maybe you ought to,' the cook muttered. 'Shoot, that is. Find out what Mary is doing.'

'Well, according to the schedule she's supposed to be cleaning the downstairs rooms. Cecily does the upstairs in the morning and serves lunch. Mary does the downstairs in the afternoon and serves dinner. No?'

'That's what the schedule says.'

'I see.' Phil bit her lip. The only thing she hated worse than trouble was letting a little trouble go long enough to become big. 'I'd better go change and clean up,' she said. 'And then I'll see.'

'You bet you will.' Rose was not going to say any more, so Phil got up, stretched, slipped off her shoes and went off, not expecting to find that there was a serpent in the Garden.

The house seemed very still as she made her way up the stairs. *It's like one of those Gothic horror stories,* she told herself as she paused in front of the portrait on the wall. 'You wouldn't haunt me, would you?' she asked the picture. The old pirate seemed to grin back at her. With that reassurance she went, barefoot, up the rest of the stairs.

The door to her room was closed. She could not remember shutting it, and Cecily had long since gone home. So perhaps the wind blew it, she thought, as she pushed her way in. Across the room a figure was bent over the bureau, and all Phil's clothes were lying in disarray on the floor.

'What in the world are you doing!' She was across the room like an avenging angel. This surprising invasion of her own privacy was almost as bad as a physical attack. Sick to her stomach, Phil clutched at the woman's shoulder. It was Mary Treadway, the second maid. A middle-aged thin woman with iron-grey hair, Mary was the sort of person who could easily be someone's spinster aunt. Instead she was the mother of a large family, always in need, always complaining.

'I—I was just cleaning up,' the maid stammered.

'Cleaning up? Here? It looks as if you're *making* a mess, not cleaning one up. And why up here? You know the programme. Your job is to clean downstairs. Cecily takes care of everything up here.'

'I—I must have forgotten.'

'How could you forget? It was only yesterday that I went over the complete list of duties with you!'

'I don't have to listen to any talk like that.' The thin

face was diffused with anger. Real or false, Phil asked
herself.

'No, you don't,' she returned quietly. 'You can always
quit.'

A flash of alarm came over the woman's face. 'I—I
can't do that,' she almost cried. 'I need the money.'

'Then I think you'd better get yourself downstairs and
do the work you're assigned.' Phil felt grim, and her voice
reflected her feelings. She watched as the older woman
hurried out of the door.

And what do you suppose that was all about, she
thought? She forgot? Not a chance. It's true she used to
clean this room, until I changed the schedule, but forget?
Never. So then what? Checking my clothes? To what
purpose? Or maybe it's just snooping; an incurable urge
to know everything about everybody. If so, all she found
out is that I like expensive underwear. How about that?

Still puzzling, Phil stripped off her clothes, took a
quick shower, and climbed into her working-clothes. She
made a quick tour, as she did every day, of all the rooms
on the second floor. They were immaculate, as usual.
Cecily was a cheerful and thorough worker. Phil left
Penn's room for last. Because it stands next to mine, she
told herself. It was as good an excuse as any.

His room was slightly smaller than her own, with none
of the frills. Its colour-scheme was bronze and gold. The
windows opened up on to the same balcony. His clothes
were hung neatly, all in a row, more suits than she wanted
to count, but all in what she classified as 'Corporation'
colours—navy blue, grey, pinstripes. As with his son,
until Phil had worked over the boy's wardrobe, he tended
towards formality. And yet, he was not always formal.
She had a few glimpses of the man beneath the disguise.

Wonderful glimpses, that left her staggered. She sat down on his bed, and then fell over on to his pillow.

There seemed to be some residual comfort from it all, some warmth. Left over, of course. He had been gone from the house for hours, and the pillow cases had been changed. What *are* you diddling about, she accused herself, and could not find the answer. A wry smile played on her mobile face. *Back to the salt mines, lady!* She laughed at herself as she swung her feet back on to the floor, brushed down the counterpane, and went downstairs.

There was that feeling again, that mood of Gothic doom. She stopped in the bend of the stairs, concentrating this time on the painting of the young woman on the opposite wall. There was some ethereal vagueness about the girl. She looked like someone. *Someone I know!* Again it escaped her, and she went on down.

Robbie was in the game-room at the back of the house, glued to the ten thousandth re-run of a Tarzan movie. A youthful Johnny Weissmuller swung through the vines, chasing after Jane. Phil stayed for a moment. She liked the really old movies, and the dialogue was just right. 'Me Tarzan, you Jane.' What a lovely bunch of writing that was! Chuckling quietly she ruffled Robbie's hair and headed for the door. To her surprise the boy followed her movement, and smiled.

Her tour of inspection swept on, through the dining-room, where there was dust on the sideboard, into the living-room, where the cushions were in some disarray, and out into the hall, hunting Mary. And found her.

The maid was talking to someone on the telephone. Talking softly, swiftly, with her eyes continually sweeping the hall. As soon as she saw Phil appear she downed the telephone and did her best to look industrious. Phil was tired of being the disciplinarian. She swept by Mary without saying a word, and went out into the afternoon sunshine looking for Mr Yu, the gardener. There was something very comforting about sharing the old man's garden—and his dry wit.

Dinner that night was more relaxed than meals had been since she came to this—palace. Penn was in a good mood, allowing her to administer the eyedrops before the meal with not a single quibble. 'Things went well today?' she hazarded.

'They surely did,' he said, 'but I can't carve this darn roast.'

'I'll do it,' she offered. 'You don't have to be totally independent. Not here.'

He tendered her the carving-knife and fork, and a big smile. The last so startled her that she almost dropped the other two. He leaned back in his chair. 'We settled a part of that business out at the Mother Lode,' he said. It was the first time he had ever introduced business into a casual conversation. Two firsts for the day, Phil crowed to herself. Robbie smiled at me, and Penn said a few nice words!

'I never did understand what it was all about,' she tempted.

'You know, of course, that we own a dozen or more small mines in El Dorado county. They were open into the 1930s, but the costs of extracting gold were just booming, so my Grandfather closed them. There's plenty of gold left there, mind you, but it just cost more that it was worth to get it out. The United States government had pegged the price of gold at thirty-five dollars an ounce, and there it stayed. Now, things have changed.

The government no longer tries to control the price of gold. Of course extraction costs have gone up, too. But today, one ounce would cost us about one hundred and sixty dollars to extract—and gold prices are pretty firm in the neighbourhood of three hundred and thirty dollars an ounce. So, it could be profitable.'

'But?'

'Yes, there's a *but*. But the people who live in El Dorado county are suburbanites. They don't want the massive machinery that we would need for open-pit mining. Well, some of them don't. Today we made agreements with three of the towns which allow us to reopen four of the mines, provided we don't go to open-pit mining. I think we can still make a profit. How did your day go?'

'I think I wore out a pair of shoes,' Robbie interjected. Another surprise. To that moment he had never said a word at table. 'She took me sightseeing. I must have walked fifty miles!'

'Poor you,' Phil teased. 'I think it was more like five.'

'But I got even,' the boy returned, grinning. 'I think her feet hurt more than mine did.'

'That must have been a sight to see, all by itself,' his father commented. The two of them launched into a heated discussion about places they had been and admired, leaving Phil sitting in a conversational back-water, happy to hear them making real family talk. Harry was out of it too. She caught him once with a big smile on his face, and he winked at her, as if *she* might be responsible for breaking the log-jam. Which of course I'm not, she told herself regretfully.

At the end of the meal she threw them a bombshell, without meaning to at all. 'Tomorrow is Sunday,' she said as a reminder. 'All the help has the day off, and——'

'All except George Yu,' Penn told her. 'He comes into the house and we eat Chinese for the day.'

'Well, that had me worried,' Phil said. 'I have to go home tomorrow.' A heavy silence fell at the table. All three of the men laid down their utensils and stared at her. 'Did I say something terrible?' she asked.

'Yes,' Robbie returned.

'I think so,' his father added. 'We hadn't expected you to leave us, as if you were hired help.'

'Well, that's what I am,' she returned defensively. 'And besides, it's only for the day. I have to check up on my *own* house, and pick up some more clothes. And my sisters! Sally will be back from her honeymoon, and the other two will want to beat me up, I'm sure.'

'Well, I won't let them,' said Robbie, his face flushed, both fists formed and resting on the table-top.

'I'm just joking,' she hastened to add. 'I don't mean they'll beat me up—I'm older than they are.'

'And they respect your grey hairs,' Penn chuckled.

'She don't have any——'

'That's enough, Robbie. If Philomena needs a day off to go home, we must consider ourselves lucky to have her the rest of the week. What time do you want to go?'

'Early, I suppose,' she said, trying to hide her own groan. 'There's nothing I like about the word early, but I've a lot to do.'

'I'll bet there is,' Penn said. 'By the way, I brought your pay-cheque home.' He handed her an envelope. She tucked it under her plate for the moment, and waited for dessert to be served.

Despite her hatred of things early, she was up and dressed by six-thirty. There was a noise at her door by seven. Penn, wanting his eyedrops administered before she disappeared. 'Just a week and a half more,' he said quietly as she went about the job with dispatch. 'Dr Morgan says everything is coming on fine, provided I just don't rush things. I can see much better.'

'Well, he's right,' she sighed as she applied new pads. 'After all this time it would be silly to take chances. Whatever took you to the Antarctic in the first place?'

'Government secrets,' he chuckled. 'They were looking for coal, so they imported a mining expert.'

'But—coal isn't your line!'

'Hey,' he laughed. 'After ten years in our typing pool and you don't know that Pacific owns open-pit coal mines all over the West?'

'Well, I don't read all that stuff,' she huffed. 'I just type it. Most of you people write as if you had swallowed a dictionary. You need more warmth in your correspondence!'

His hand trapped hers, and his other joined, sliding over the softness at her wrist, and up her forearm. 'Warm, like you,' he muttered. He was looking at something beyond her ken, feeling something more than her arm, dreaming something? It would have been simple for her to pull away. Robbie had come out of his own room and was staring at them. But Phil just did not want to. There was too much pleasure to be had from his hands. Pleasure like nothing she had ever experienced before.

'Well, I won't keep you.' He disengaged her gently, lowering her hand rather than dropping it. 'Have a good day.'

'I will,' she promised softly, and stared after him as he made his way back to his own bedroom, using the wall as a guide. It amazed her how proficient he was. How strong. How gentle. How—'Dear lord, Phil,' she muttered to herself. 'It isn't as if you were going to *eat* him.'

'What did you say?' She turned around, startled. Robbie was still standing there, fully dressed.

'Nothing,' she improvised. 'I was—just clearing my throat.' She managed a dismal hacking cough to illustrate. 'And what brings you out so early, young man?'

'You.' He partnered her as she went down the stairs.

'Your car is out front.' Mr Yu, dressed in slacks and white shirt, held the door for her. 'Frank filled up the tank and checked the oil.'

'Silly,' Phil remarked, but was warmed just the same. After all, she had only driven the car forty miles since the last time Frank had checked it out. She strolled down the stairs. Robbie went right along with her. As she reached for the door handle she looked over at him. I do believe he's growing like a weed, she thought. His eyes are dark grey! Dark, intense eyes.

'And just what are you up to?'

'I'm going with you.'

'Not *may* I go with you?'

'No. Just I'm going. You need somebody to look after you. Dad said last night you are really a *little* thing.'

'I'm not all *that* little.'

'Well, I'm going anyway. You're a girl—a woman. Whatever. Somebody's got to look after you.'

Phil knew when she was beaten, and surrendered gracefully. 'How kind you are.' The boy seemed to swell up just the slightest bit. He ushered her into the driver's seat, closed her door behind her, and went around the car to climb in. As she drove away a peculiar thought hit her.

The boy. Is he going just to keep me company, or to make sure I come back? Is it possible that I mean something to him? As he means something to me? She chewed on the idea all the way out to the house in Rancho Cordova.

'That's an old house,' Robbie said as they drove up into the yard. 'Funny kind of a house to see in the middle of all this.' Phil followed his waving hand. It *did* seem that a dozen more high-rise buildings had come into existence in the short time she had been away.

'It's a farmhouse,' she said as she led the way up to the front door and fumbled for her key. 'When I was a little girl this was all a big farm, and my daddy was a farmer.'

'But it's not now?'

'No,' she said softly. 'My father had no sons—only girls. It takes a great deal of muscle to be a farmer. Muscle and brains. And Dad left so many debts we had to sell the land. But that's last year's news. Come in, Robbie.'

He stepped over the pile of mail lying on the floor behind the mail slot. She stopped to pick it all up. Bills, advertisements, magazine subscriptions—she sorted them all out on the way to the kitchen.

'Now the first thing we do,' she told the boy, 'is open a few windows. The house smells as if it hasn't been lived in for years!' And so the day began. There was dusting to do, some washing—somehow the living-room furniture had accumulated jelly fingerprints—and some laundry to be done. Robbie followed her around like a shadow. It wasn't until midday that Phil got around to the mail. Most of it was disposable. But there were four or five hand-delivered envelopes, with no stamps. She tried the first.

'We're home,' the first note said. Sally. 'I'll have to call her,' Phil told Robbie. 'That's my youngest sister. The baby of the family.'

'How about that,' Robbie returned. 'I'm the oldest *and* the youngest in my family. I wish I had a little sister.'

'It could happen,' she told him absent-mindedly. 'Your Dad's still a young man. He could marry again. Look at this!' Four of the envelopes were identical. 'Call me!' the first one said. 'Call me !!!!' the fourth one said. And the ones in between were the same, but with fewer exclamation marks. 'My sister Samantha,' Phil explained to a giggling Robbie. 'She's impatient.'

'Me too. No lunch way out here?'

'Not much,' she returned. 'A can of spaghetti? I never keep lunch stuff around.'

'I'll take it,' he said enthusiastically.

While he was eating she dialled Sally's new number. The response was electric. 'It's wonderful,' the girl gushed, and then invested ten minutes in the details, concluding with, 'Phil, you've just *got* to get married!'

'And who would have a spinster like me?' Phil returned through the forming tears. 'I've got a mint of work to do before I go back, Sally.'

'You're at home?'

'Yes, for a little while.'

It should have been no surprise, but when the doorbell went at three o'clock, and she opened it to all three of her sisters, Phil was almost in a state of shock. One at a time she could handle—three were just too many. She fell back into the living-room, and all three of them started yelling at her at once. There came a terrible clatter down the back stairs, and Robbie was standing close in front of her, fists half-raised, his face flushed.

'Don't you yell at Philomena,' he roared. They all

stopped, with mouths half opened. After a pregnant moment Samantha said, 'And who in the world is this?'

Phil put both hands on the young man's shoulders. 'This is Robbie,' she said warningly. 'I told you I had found myself a man, didn't I?'

'And you'd better leave her alone,' the boy threatened, 'or I'll get you all.'

'Phil, I just have time,' Deborah interrupted. 'Our trip to Vegas is on, and I can bring the girls over here in no time. We'll be back on Wednesday.'

'I hope you don't,' Phil said firmly. 'I won't be here. Robbie and I are leaving in about twenty minutes——'

'And she's never coming back,' the boy threatened. Debbie managed an impatient laugh.

'Come on, Phil, the joke's over,' she grated. 'Let's get life back to normal in this family.'

'And Phil,' Samantha interrupted. 'Albert and I have just got to talk to you about the terms of the Trust. He—I—want enough money to open a new office in a better district, and——'

'Sally,' Phil ordered. 'Take Robbie out in the kitchen, will you.' She watched as her baby sister complied. 'Now, you two. Things have changed around here. I don't *want* to go back to the old ways. I have my own life to lead, and it doesn't include baby-sitting, or trying to break the terms of Daddy's will. You two tear at my heart. You know Mother told me to take care of you. I've done a terrible job. I don't know when I've met two more selfish people in my life.'

She stopped to stab at a tear forming in her eye. 'Now you both have families to look after, and jobs to do. Just go and do them. When I get back on an even keel I'll contact you. But don't hold out any wild hopes. Things have changed permanently.'

The two of them stared at her for a moment, and then picked up their bags and left. Moments later Sally came out of the kitchen. 'Atta girl,' she said softly, kissing Phil on the cheek. 'You should have done that years ago. You know what Charley and I want from you?'

Phil's tears were really rolling now. She looked at the blur that was her youngest sister and waited. 'What *we* want is to love you.' And with that Sally was gone too. Robbie came out of the kitchen.

'You forgot this,' he said, waving another envelope at her. She managed to dry up the storm, and tore open the plain white envelope. Inside was a cheque, made out in her name, for four times her usual salary. The tears started again. She dropped into the armchair and let them flow. Robbie came around in front of her, with both hands in his pockets.

'What's the matter now?' he asked patiently.

'I don't know,' she admitted. 'I just don't know.'

'Girls are funny,' he said conclusively. 'Let's go home now.'

CHAPTER SIX

PHILOMENA devoted the drive back to the city to deep thought. Robbie climbed into the car without a word, his face relapsing into his typical teenage scowl. The inbound traffic was light because it was Sunday afternoon, but they were still serenaded by the city-dwellers' bird-song—the whiz and hum of tyres as cars passed, the rattle of gratings as heavy vehicles hit the overpasses at speed, the blinking of headlights as fools tried to exceed the fifty-five-miles-an-hour speed limit, and the occasional blasting wail of a horn as one bad driver signalled curses at another.

It was all background. Phil had her own problem. She went back over all that was said between sisters, and still believed herself to be right—but at a painful cost. Little sisters don't become spoiled by themselves, she told herself fiercely. It takes two to tango. They are what I made them. And now, having laid down the law to my own, I'm darned if I'm not running off to somebody else's family, all set to take up the burden again! And how big a fool does that make me?

Harry waited for them at the bottom step. He opened her door. Robbie made some sort of grunting noise that might, under the wildest circumstances, be interpreted as a 'Thank you,' and then scrambled out of the car. Phil required a great deal more care. Before she left the house she had changed into one of her best dresses, a light wool that matched each of her curves gently, and clung just above the knees. Which made scrambling out of tiny cars something of an adventure. Harry tried to act as if he hadn't noticed the large amount of thigh on display. She tendered him a wry smile, and went up the stairs ahead of him.

It had been a long hard day, and Penn was not quite able to assemble it all. A day set aside out of the rush of time. The sort of splendid day that could be spent outdoors, in the heated pool—damn those eye pads—or just piddling around and listening as George Yu commented on the world, the planets, and the Raiders. Until they had insulted half the world by moving to Los Angeles, the Oakland Raiders football team had been the old man's pride and joy.

But there had been no relaxation in it all today. Mr Yu seemed grumpy. Something about his camellias, and the up-coming flower festival. Something too about how quiet the house seemed without Miss Peabody in residence. And just hearing it said had startled Penn into breaking away and stomping off into the house. 'Bad enough, for God's sake,' he muttered as he fumbled his way into the lounge, 'to be thinking stupid things like that myself, without hearing everybody else in the house come down with a terminal case of Peabody.' He splashed what he thought was Scotch into a tumbler, discovered it was Bourbon, and sipped at it anyway. The whole picture bothered him. Her reaction to Robbie, and to himself, and—his reaction to her. Damn, it bothered him.

Along about four o'clock in the afternoon Harry found him, slumped down in the old Morris Chair in the front sitting-room, still nursing the same glass of Bourbon, down more in spirit than in spirits.

'Ain't nobody set in here since the old man died,' Harry commented softly.

'I know.' There was a time of silence, punctuated by the clink of ice in Penn's glass. 'Have something, Harry?'

'Not me. You know what the doctor said.'

'Yeah, I remember. No wine, no women, and not much song?'

'That about covers it. Funny feeling around the house today.'

'No, don't *you* start that. That's all I've heard all day from George Yu.'

'Crazy Chinaman.' A soft comment, not a criticism, but more like the underlining of a long-held pleasantry.

'Like a fox, Harry. He could have been a stockholder in Pacific Mines and Metal, but he didn't want it. Too much responsibility, he said. I remember him arguing with my father about that. Responsibility brings ambition, ambition brings worry, and—I forget the rest of it. Some Chinese philosopher before Confucius' time. Where the hell is she?'

'Who?'

The glass in Penn's hand seemed to crumble, spreading shards all over the carpet. His reflex action knocked over the bottle of Bourbon at his elbow. It fell to the carpet beside the glass, dumping its contents over his coat sleeve and trouser leg. 'Damn!' Harry moved rapidly over to his side and picked up the flaccid hand.

'Just a nick,' he reported. 'Needs a plaster. What's bugging you? The hearing?'

'Among other things. Next Thursday, Harry, and it's going to be one tough struggle. These bandages don't come off until three days later. I'll walk into that courtroom, the Juvenile judge will take one look at me, and everything goes down the drain. All I've got going for me is character witnesses and past history. Nobody in their right mind would give custody of a child to a blind man. What I need is—damn it, Harry, if I had my sight it would be no problem at all. I'm sure of that! But——'

'But what?'

'Her. What do you think, Harry?'

'I wish I knew what the hell you're talking about, Penn'

'Peabody, damn it. Philomena. What do you think?'

'Nice lady. The kid don't let on, but he likes her. Nice shape. Built classy, not one of these skinny broads. Always used to hate those skinny ones. Every time you try to hug one you get splinters. Not this girl.'

'She's hardly a girl, Harry. And that's the problem. What about the age difference between us?'

'Oh, I don't know, boss. It's hard to tell with a good-looking broad. I'd say there can't be more than eight or ten years between you both. Nothing to worry about. Hardly anybody would notice, these days. Just what are you thinking about?'

'I'm thinking—you'd better find me another glass. And put Scotch in it. I can't seem to find the Scotch bottle.'

'OK, if that's what you want, but that's her car coming up the drive now, and you——'

'And I stink of Bourbon. Good lord. Get this coat off me. Do I have anything right here?'

'That smoking-jacket thing—the one you swore you'd never wear because——'

'Never mind what I swore I'd never—give me the damn thing and get out there and make her welcome!'

All of which brought Harry to the front door all in good

time, and left Penn to fumble around madly trying to rid
himself of the Bourbon smell, and at the same time stuff
himself into the scarlet smoking-jacket his former wife
had given him. The jacket clung, and so did the smell.
Draconian measures, he told himself, as he poured the
carafe of water over his trouser leg. Better water-wet than
Bourbon-wet. It had suddenly become important to
make a good impression on a certain lady.

Phil looked back towards Harry as she moved up the
stairs. 'You're sure it's OK to leave my old car parked in
front of the house?' she asked. There wasn't time for an
answer. Moving faster than usual, for some reason she
still did not fathom, she cannoned off the solid steel of
Penn's chest, rattled around a time to two, and was
finally rescued by those arms. For a second she was about
to relax, to let it all happen. But then he seemed to pull
her closer, to bury her nose against the soft suede of his
smoking-jacket. And the smell hit her.

'My lord,' she muttered, wriggling furiously until his
surprised arms unfolded and turned her loose. 'Drunk by
Sunday evening?' It was hard to hide the disgust in her
voice. Drunks and smokers were her favourite hates, and
she had no plans for staying close to either category.

'No, I am not,' he returned indignantly. 'I've had one
drink today, and managed to spill it all over myself. And
just supposing I were? Who are you to—dammit!' She
could see him try to suppress his words. His angry throat
seemed to choke up in sympathy with his swollen angry
cheeks. It was a momentous struggle. She watched, spellbound, having never seen an autocratic man swallow his
own words. Her moment of anger had passed. But
perhaps the chuckle was a mistake. His hands seemed to
find her by radar and fastened on her shoulders, holding

her stiffly at arms' length.

'Funny, Peabody?' he asked warningly.

'Er—no, of course not.' After all, he was the boss. She
had never held a doubt about that. 'I—I think you must
have spilled something,' she offered tentatively, a sort of
good-will gesture. It was amazing how quickly he
snapped up the olive-branch.

'Yes,' he returned gently. The hold on her shoulders
became a gentle squeeze, and then a tentative caress.
'We've missed you, it seems.'

There was nothing she could think of to say. Especially
when he leaned forward on a straight line, kissed the
fringe of her hair, then corrected his aim and lightly
touched her lips. 'Dinner's ready,' he grinned. 'Won ton
soup and Mandarin chicken. Mr Yu's been worrying
about it all day.'

It was the grin that undid all her resolves. So he
smelled like the Jim Beam Distillery—that lopsided little
grin took years off his age, charmed her prejudices,
soothed her worries—and gave her something to say.
'Great,' she enthused. 'I'm sick of my own cooking! Give
me ten minutes to freshen up.'

'Better make that twenty,' he chuckled. 'I need to do
some freshening myself.'

'We're going in the same direction,' she chuckled,
taking his arm, 'so why don't we share a stair?'

'Poetry?' he groaned, but followed her lead into the
house and up the stairs. From the kitchen she could hear
a great banging of pans, and a few delectable Chinese
phrases that required no translation. As usual, her eye
was caught by the haunting painting on the opposite
wall. The girl-woman's eyes seemed to follow Phil as she
came to a gradual stop. The artist had caught an

expression—was it happiness—congratulations? Almost it seemed as if the girl in the painting were at least wishing her well.

'What is it?' he asked, tugging at her arm.

'The painting. The girl——' She struggled for words and found none. His massive head swung in the direction she was looking. It almost seemed that she could see tears beneath the eye-pads, but that was ridiculous. Phil started them up the stairs again. 'It's just that the—she——'

'Robin,' he said in a low tired voice. 'Her name was Robin.'

'Was?'

'Yes.' A blunt word, that cut off the conversation. She escorted him to his door, then returned to her own room. A quick brush-up, that was all she wanted. A quick wash, a struggle with comb and brush through her long curly hair, the briefest of touches from her lipstick, and a knock on the connecting door. Startled, she walked over to it. In all her time in the house she had never thought to lock the connecting door into his bedroom.

'More drops in your eyes?' she asked as he came in.

'Well—it wouldn't hurt, I suppose.' It was the first non-positive statement she had ever heard him make. He was a man who made up his mind quickly, and spoke it immediately. And now, 'I suppose,'—as if there were other objectives to be reached.

'Sit here on the edge of my bed.' She guided him around the furniture. He dropped down, and the old four-poster seemed to groan at the weight. Phil smiled at the thoughts that ran through her brain. He couldn't see, so there was no need to hide the hungry look in her eyes. And he couldn't read minds—she hoped.

Phil feasted on him for a moment, then went over to her own dressing-table where she kept eye-droppers and his prescription. On the way she detoured by the windows and drew the curtains, darkening the room. The dosage was as usual, but her hand shook just the slightest amount.

'Lost your nerve, doctor?' he chuckled.

'It does seem so,' she returned ruefully as she re-loaded the dropper. Make conversation, her mind demanded. But it was hard. He was beginning to have an effect on her that puzzled her. 'I had a little squabble with my sisters,' she offered as an explanation. 'Well, with two out of three. Don't blink, for goodness' sake.'

'Well, don't stick your thumb in my eyeball,' he snapped. 'Two out of three? That's not bad at all.'

'Shows you what a really terrible mother I turned out to be,' she quipped, turning his head so that she could get at the other eye. 'I raised two adult delinquents. This darn pad is sticking to your eyebrow. Whoever put it on this morning wasn't too careful. That didn't hurt, did it?'

'Of course it did,' he laughed. 'You tore off half my eyebrow there, lady.'

'Just not my day,' Phil mourned. 'Hold still, for goodness' sake! You're worse than a basket of kittens!'

'Nobody's ever told me *that* before,' he said as she returned the medications to their proper place. 'Come sit by me, Phil. There's something I need to say to you.'

Her skirt rustled as she complied. The bed complained. 'I'm not sure this bed was made for two,' she teased. Her thumb ran over the edge of his eyebrow, smoothing down the hairs. 'I didn't really pull any hairs out at all,' she mused, accusingly. 'You made that up. Can you see any better today?'

'If you've got all the lights on I'm losing ground,' he said.

'They're not,' she laughed. 'I don't have a single light on, and the curtains are drawn.'

'In that case I'm making marvellous progress. Monday week, that's when the doctors promise the great unveiling.'

'A week from Monday?'

'That's what I said—Monday week.'

'Stop wriggling, or this pad will have the rest of your eyebrow,' she threatened. Her fingers gently smoothed the pad in place, and then, for luck, she kissed the tip of his nose. He reached out for her, but she dodged, giggling.

'I'm not your fourth sister,' he said darkly.

'Oh, do I ever know that,' she sighed. He waited for an explanation—which she had no intention of giving. Why confess to this—this arrogant man—how much he had come to mean to her? She longed for the privilege to brush the hank of hair out of his eyes, to kiss each of his damaged eyes, to—and of course, that was the problem. When the day came to remove those pads, the day when he was fully restored to the light of the world he ruled, Philomena Peabody would become just one of the dull shadows in his life. Someone unnoticed until needed, and then in an absent-minded way. And then what will I do, she asked herself. Go back to my sisters and apologise?

'What are you thinking about?' Again that gentle fumbling sound, as if he had a point and hadn't the courage to come to it.

'Oh, nothing,' she sighed. 'My sister Sally, Won ton soup, Robbie's next protest march—I don't know.'

'Sit down here again.' He patted the bed beside him.

She sank down gracefully, closer than before, and tucked her legs up under her.

'I have a problem with Robert,' he said. 'A legal problem.'

'Yes, I know.' Almost unconsciously she captured his hand and moved it to her lap, between her own warm sympathetic fingers.

'There aren't any secrets in the world?' he asked.

'Not in the kitchen.'

His fingers squeezed hers gently. 'I don't get rid of my blinders until Monday next,' he repeated softly, as if re-telling an old story. 'The Juvenile Court hearing is scheduled for this Thursday.'

'Yes?'

'If I go into court on Thursday I've two strikes against me. First, I can't see; secondly, I don't have a real home for Robert. God, who could believe it would all end up this way?'

'You might as well be honest,' Phil added quietly. 'You've three strikes against you already.' He sat up, rigidly, waiting. 'Robbie thinks you hate him.'

'Oh God, not that too,' he muttered. 'You know this?'

'He told me. He thinks both of you hate him. Both of you.'

'He tells you lots of things?'

'Whoa up,' Phil chuckled. 'It's not that way. He's a crazy upset adolescent. He doesn't like me any more than any of the rest of you—he just sort of—hates me less.'

'But you do get along with him. And that's more than I can do.'

'Or his mother either?'

'I told you once before. His mother's dead.'

'Yes, well, that's more confusion than I want to know

about—please don't explain anything more to me about it. What did you really want to talk to me about?'

'I——' He coughed to clear his throat—or his mind. It was hard to tell which. 'I'd like to hire you for another job, Philomena.'

'I——' A sudden fear clouded her mind. 'I'm only a typist,' she moaned. 'I—what other job?'

'I want that boy.' His hands snatched at hers to emphasise. Her little whimper brought him back to reality. 'I'm sorry,' he said bitterly. 'That's all I seem to do—hurt the people closest to me.' And then it all came out, in a machine-gun burst of words, without pause for breath.

'My only hope is to walk into that court on Thursday with a capable, happy wife on my arm, and a son willing enough to go along with the gag. My only hope. By Thursday morning I've got to be married. That's a pretty hard thing for a temporary blind man to do when he's been away for a long time, has no available choices, and no time to ponder about it. I need somebody who will act the part, is on the scene.' He paused for a moment, his head cocked to one side as if waiting for some comment. She offered nothing. He took a deep breath and continued. 'Somebody who—er—is willing to accept the temporary nature of the whole affair, and that's why I want you to marry me, Philomena.'

She took a deep breath to match his own. 'You want me to——?'

'Marry me. On Tuesday, if I can arrange it.'

Well, she sighed to herself, at least he didn't call me 'Peabody'. That's one step in my favour!

'Well?'

'I'm thinking,' she blurted out angrily. 'Surely you

don't expect a girl to hear something like that and promptly fall at your feet in rapture? I'm thinking.'

'I'll wait.'

'Don't be *that* darn patient,' she snapped. 'I don't expect to get through thinking about it in the next thirty minutes. Why don't you go downstairs and have your meal. I can hear Harry coming up to look for you.'

'We'll both go.' He stood up. The bed creaked in relief. He tugged at her hand, but she refused to budge.

'Go ahead,' she sighed. 'I'm suddenly not hungry any more.'

'But you are thinking about it?'

'I am. But—from where I sit it's all for Robbie, and I have to talk to him first.'

'It's not *all* for Robert,' he returned. 'I'll see you right in all this, Philomena. I—I seem to like you very much. When I get my bandages off, I'll fix things for you. You'll never have to work again, believe me.'

'Ha!' she snorted. 'You think being a mother to Robbie Wilderman is some sort of lead-pipe cinch. And with *you* thrown into the bargain besides?'

'I swear there will be proper compensation for it all,' he said. There it was, that pompous 'I am the head man' tone again.

'Yes,' she snapped. 'I'm sure there will be, and it's only temporary, and now before you really make me angry, go get your supper.'

He mumbled something about 'women' under his breath as he stumbled towards the door. She made not a move to help him, but Harry was just outside, in the hall, and rescued him. Phil sat where he had left her, and tried to think it all out.

Men! He hadn't even attempted to put icing on the

cake. He just set it out there in front of her and dared her to accept. Marry me and save Robbie. A most objectionable man, with a most objectionable son. Good lord, am I some sort of masochist? I've put up with a decade of playing mother—and didn't do too good a job at it, either. And now I'm supposed to dive into a worse mess. How long is temporary? What happens when he takes those darn pads off his eyes and really sees me? And having learned to survive through adolescent sisters, is any of that experience transferable to a sulky-boy type? Oh lord.

She sat there for more than an hour, knowing all along that there was something she had not entered into the equation. It had something to do with *him*—and every time she approached the subject her mind shied away from it like a nervous mare! Finally, about seven o'clock, she gave up the argument and went to do the one thing she knew had to be done.

Robbie's room was just a few doors down from her own. A stereo system was blasting at high intensity from within. Although all the walls were thick, almost sound-proofed, this penetrated. Phil shrugged her shoulders. Only four years ago Sally had been swept up into hard rock—heavy metal as it was known as on the street. She knocked on the door without response, gave it a moment or two, and then barged in. Robbie was sitting at his computer table, hard at work on some word-game. The stereo blasted away from a desk beside him. His right foot was tapping on the rug matching the primitive rhythm of the music. His unruly hair looked as if it had been exposed to perhaps ten seconds' worth of shower. He was wearing a blue pyjama top and his favourite jeans. When she leaned over his shoulder and flipped the stereo off he jumped.

'Hey,' he yelled, and then stopped in mid-sentence when he recognised her. He dropped back into the chair again, and went on punching keys on the computer board.

'I need to talk to you, Robbie,' she said softly. That sullen look swept over his face. He refused to turn around. Phil looked around for the power switch, and shut it down. The computer rumbled a couple of times, its internal blowers slowed to a stop, and quiet reigned. He turned around. A swivel chair, she noted. A poor under-deprived kid.

'Now I've lost the entire computer program,' he growled, but avoided her eyes.

'You'll think of it again some day,' she said very complacently. 'I have some questions, and I need some straight answers. Listen up.' The last two words had a snap to them that brought him up to the mark. It works on boys too, Phil noted, with some pleasure. Maybe I learned how to be a mother after all!

'So?' A touch of insolence, but overlaid by curiosity, and curiosity was winning. Phil looked around. There were four chairs in the room, all loaded with clothes, books, videotapes, and what-have-you. She picked the nearest, dumped its computer magazines on the foor, and sat down.

'Hey,' he protested again. Her eyes roamed around the dishevelled room. He had the grace to blush. 'So it's not neat,' he grumbled. 'I can't have those *women* coming in here every day and getting everything out of order.'

'You sound like your father,' she commented softly, showing just enough steel in her voice so that he knew it was there. 'Starting tomorrow you pick up in here, or

Cecily will, or *I* will.' He got the message. If Phil had to come in and clear things, shortly thereafter there would be hell to pay.

'Is that all you came for?' he grumbled. 'Breaking up my program just about that?'

'No,' she said, showing more steel. The boy was becoming agitated. He moved back into his swivel chair as if to re-establish his position. She didn't give him the time he needed.

'Your father,' she said. 'For some reason he likes you.'

'No, he doesn't,' the boy returned bitterly.

'He does,' Phil continued relentlessly. 'He told me so. I don't know why he would. You're a real cactus.'

Robbie's head snapped up. 'What's that mean?' he demanded fiercely.

'Well, look at you,' she continued. 'When you love people you want to hug and kiss them once in a while. Look at you. You're just like a cactus, loaded with spines and prickles. Some hugger you'd make! Let me tell you something, Robbie. The world is full of people who don't want to be loved—so nobody loves them. You have to give a little to get a little.'

The boy turned all this over in his mind. She could see the gears creaking. 'My father likes me?'

'Of course he likes you. Why do you think he's going through this fire-drill with the court?'

'Because he needs the money,' the answer came.

Phil stifled a giggle. You can be hard with adolescents. You can be direct. You can be bitter. But you can't laugh at them. 'Your father's got enough money to buy out the US Treasury,' she commented. 'And maybe a couple of other countries to go with it. He *wants* you. I don't know why. Do you?'

'Yes,' he returned after a pause. 'I think I do. I haven't been hugged since—since a long time. I suppose that's something you have to put up with when you have women around the house?'

'I suppose so. And you've got a problem, Robbie.'

He watched expectantly.

'Your mother wants to keep you, and she has a new husband. You like him?'

'I can't stand him,' the boy returned. 'He doesn't like to go fishing or swimming or anything. And he don't know a thing about computers. Can you imagine that?'

'Yes,' Phil returned. 'I can imagine that. So you don't like your mother's new husband, and——'

'She's not my mother,' he interrupted bitterly.

'Ah. I had forgotten.' Another moment of silence. 'Did you know that your Dad is planning to get married again?'

The little head snapped around. 'To a woman?'

'Well, that's the usual thing.'

'No, I didn't know.' There was a look of appeal in his eyes. 'I know I won't like her.'

'Well, that *is* too bad.' Phil got up, brushed down her dress, and moved toward the door. 'I thought you and I might become—well, perhaps not friends, but——'

'You mean he wants to marry *you*, Phil?'

'Is that so bad? So I'm not a movie queen. Yes, he wants to marry me.'

'I—and are you going to?'

'I don't know, Robbie,' she told him bluntly. 'It all depends on you. If it's going to start a revolution, then no, I won't marry him. If you and I could live peacefully together, why I thought I might give it a try. What do you think?'

The boy was up from his chair, moving towards her. Awkwardly, but with a hint of his father's feline grace. Thirteen, and he was already an inch taller than she. Much taller, if she slipped out of her two-inch heels. She did just that.

It was just the right touch. Suddenly towering over her, bigger, she could see his face lighten as he came closer. The dominant male, she giggled to herself. At all ages. Now what?

He took her by the hand. 'I want to show you something,' he said. She followed him out into the hall and down towards the stairs. George Yu stood at the bottom.

'You don't eat?' he called up to them. 'Neither of you to eat, and the boss all grumpy. You two come down to the kitchen. I got left-overs. The soup is still hot.'

Phil stopped at the head of the stairs. Robbie looked down and actually smiled at her. His tugging hand led her half-way down, and stopped at the bend.

'There.' He pointed across to where the painting of the woman was half hidden in the shadows.

'There? I like that painting very much. Who is it?'

'That's—that's my mother.' There was a catch in his voice, as if he had some trouble with his throat. Phil dropped to the stair and pulled him down beside her. They both stared at the painting through the interstices of the banister.

'So that's your mother,' she sighed. 'There's something about her—the picture—that's bothered me for two weeks. Something familiar—but I know I've never seen her.'

'Me neither,' the boy returned. 'She died when I was one year old.'

'So long ago,' Phil sighed. 'And you've never been hugged since then, I'll bet.'

The boy cleared his throat, and relaxed his stiffened back. 'No,' he whispered, 'I guess not.' It must have been an unconscious movement. He slid over on the stair until he was touching her, and then suddenly he collapsed in a heap, tears streaming down his face, his head close on Phil's shoulder. Her arms went around him, comforting. She murmured consolation in his ear, and he cried it all out, there on the stairs.

The storm went on for minutes, then gradually decreased to a hiccup, and blew its way out. He fumbled for a handkerchief to wipe his eyes. Dirty, Phil noticed, as any good housekeeper would. He coughed a couple of times, and cleared his throat.

'You didn't get any prickles,' he said, 'so I can't be a real cactus.'

'I guess you can't be,' Phil said in pseudo-amazement. 'Could I have been wrong? I was wrong once before—let me see now—that would have been eighteen years ago.' He managed a chuckle. She flowed gracefully up to her feet and pulled him with her. He wrapped both arms around her, and pulled her close, her soft cheek against his, for comfort.

'I still don't see why that picture bothers me,' she repeated a moment later.

He released her, laughing. 'It's because you look just like her, Phil, didn't you know?'

'I like this hugging business,' she returned. 'How could she look just like me?'

'Well, maybe not *just*,' he said, 'but kind of—well, you know!'

'I'll have to take your word for it,' she giggled. 'And

now I'm really hungry. Why don't we both sneak down to the kitchen and try some of the left-overs?'

'And what are you going to tell my father?'

She was all solemnity again. 'What *should* I tell him?'

'I think—I don't know. I suppose you might make a nice mother for some kid. I don't need one myself, but you'd make a great mother.'

'But not for you,' she probed. That stubborn, sullen look flashed across his face. 'Well, at least have a little sympathy for my elderly bones,' she sighed. 'Take me to your kitchen and feed me—before I have to decide what to tell your father. You won't advise me?'

'Nope.' He went over to the table and sat down, burying his face behind a huge soup spoon. Phil stood in the kitchen doorway, both hands on her hips. Well, I *almost* got you. And there's always a next time, kiddo. She had already decided what she was going to say to Penn.

CHAPTER SEVEN

WHAT with one thing and another, it was late evening before Phil tracked Penn down. The warmth of the sun still lingered. He was lounging out behind the house on a comfortable swing-sofa, with no one else around. She stopped on the edge of the grass to absorb the picture of him. He was leaning back in the swing, both feet planted firmly on the cement that surrounded the pool. His sports shirt was unbuttoned, his raven hair flopped to one side, and worn jeans clung to his supple hips. There was a little frown tugging at his mouth. Altogether too handsome, she told herself. The fingers of his right hand came up and tugged at the pads that covered his eye.

'No!' The half-scream was involuntary. She dashed across to where he sat. 'Don't do that!' she ordered.

'Don't do what?' He was laughing, and that boyish look was on his half-tilted face.

'Don't touch those pads,' she gruffed, doing her best to swallow her fears. 'It's just a week to go. If you take those pads off out here in the bright sun you'll—you'll——'

'I'll what?'

'Don't tease me,' she muttered. 'You know darn well I don't know what would happen. I'm not a doctor or a nurse. But I'm sure you'll——'

'But you're sure I'll do something wrong?' Definite laughter. The frown was gone. And then he gave her a set-down. 'I don't remember any of my employees who worry about me the way you do, Peabody.'

One of his employees, that's the way he thinks of me. So much for all those lovely dreams last night! She stood silently beside the swing, her hands twisting nervously behind her back.

'So you came to tell me something.'

'I came to tell you—I—I talked with Robbie about—about—what you said.'

'So it all depends on Robbie, does it?'

'Well, doesn't it? That's what you told me in the first place!' He reached out a hand in her general direction. Without even thinking, she put her own in his. He tugged at her gently, until she settled down into the swing, as far from him as she could get.

'I put it all very badly, didn't I?' he said softly.

'Yes, you did,' she returned grimly. His hand still held hers, and it disturbed her in some way which she couldn't comprehend.

'I'm not much for speech-making, Philomena. It wasn't *all* for Robbie. Some of it was for me. I need a wife, need one very badly.'

'And that's what you'll get if you make blind choices,' she snapped. 'You'll get one very badly.'

'Low blow,' he returned gravely. 'Blind choices? Semantics, Peabody, or do you mean it?'

'I—I'm sorry. I wasn't thinking. I—'

'Just blurted it all out?'

'Yes.' She had composed herself by this time. Both his hands were on her one, toying with it. 'I'm sorry. You were saying?'

'I was saying I need a wife, Philomena. A woman like you. I happen to like you very much.'

And that, she told herself, sounds about as exciting as a peanut butter sandwich. But it was better than nothing,

wasn't it? Because I—I like him very much too. Her
resolve returned. She added her other hand to the pile. 'I
came out to tell you that if you still want it, I'll marry
you—Penn.'

'Ah.' There was a whole host of satisfaction in his one
word. He slid over on the swing, agitating it as he moved,
until he was sitting hard up against her. *Which was just
the way she wanted it.* His hard thigh crushed up against
her, his warm arm around her shoulders, gently
squeezing. She used her free hand to snatch at the sofa
arm as the swing jerked and bounced. Her feet no longer
reached the ground, but for some stupid reason her heart
was as high as the clouds that temporarily brushed across
the sun.

'So now we're engaged?'

'I—I guess so.'

'Good. Now where the—where did I put that thing?'
His struggle to get a hand into his pocket without moving
away from her was agitating her—not the swing. His
elbow kept brushing against her breast, sending shivers
up her spine. 'Ah!' The hand came out of his pocket with
a small box. He snapped it open with one hand, and held
it out to her.

She stared at the diamond ring, stunned, not knowing
what to say. It was a small but perfect diamond, set in a
circlet of sparkling diamond chips, the whole gleaming
on a platinum ring.

'This is where the heroine says *For me*?' she managed.

'That's the line,' he chuckled. 'See a lot of movies, do
you?'

'No.' She had finally managed to clamp down on her
emotions, and her usually cheerful spirit was leaking
through. 'No,' she repeated, 'but I read a great many

books. What do I——'

'Now you don't do anything,' he said. His strong tactile fingers snatched the ring from its nest and held it out towards her. Wordlessly she extended her left hand. He fumbled for the right finger, found it, and slipped the ring on.

'It just fits,' she reported, astonished.

'Of course,' he chuckled.

There, she told herself. Of course it wouldn't dare not fit. Not if Penn ordered it! But instead of that surge of anger that had teased her for weeks in such situations, this time she felt marvellously better—happier.

'It's lovely,' she managed to breathe.

'Of course,' he commented.

'Did you ever think that if you keep talking like that somebody might just—hit you?'

'Somebody will, I'm sure,' he agreed. 'But not you, Peabody.'

'No,' she sighed, giving up the war after one battle. 'Not me, I guess. Were you *that* sure of me?'

His arm was around her shoulders again, tucking itself under her left arm, with the tips of his fingers just inches from her breast. She leaned over against him, resting her head under his chin. 'Sure of you?' he said. 'I don't believe I've taken such a risk in many a day.' She started to raise her head. 'No,' he ordered, 'don't move.' She dropped back, sighing. It was pleasant to be coddled. His free arm came across her, resting on her stomach, hand clutching at her hip.

'You're a great deal of woman, Philomena,' he whispered into her hair. 'A great deal of delightfully designed woman. We'll make a good pair, you and I.'

Surely we will, she told herself fiercely. Until my

option runs out, we'll make a great team. And after that—well, I won't think about that. Not right now. She snuggled closer, pulling her legs up under her. He used one foot to start the swing rocking gently. Somehow or other his right hand had moved from her hip and was cupping her breast, weighing it. The pleasure of it all overcame her reluctance, but only for a moment. When her hand moved his away from her breast back down to her waist he sighed deeply.

'Not accustomed to giving samples?' he asked. There was something wrong with his voice. It sounded as if some—passion—were choking him, fighting him. 'Not even for your fiancé?'

'How could I know?' she answered, her own voice husky with strain. 'I've never been engaged before. Perhaps I just don't know the drill?'

They rocked back and forth for minutes. Her muscles relaxed as the tension faded. She lay against him, savouring the warmth, wondering whether she should have—but the chance had passed.

From out of the mist of her day-dreams his voice finally penetrated. 'And then on Tuesday we can be married,' he was saying. 'Judge Caldwell will do it for us in Chambers, I'm sure. Then comes the hearing, followed by a short honeymoon at home. I'll send Robbie off with Harry, and give the others a vacation.'

And that, she told herself, puts a period to all the dreams. Orange blossoms and a long white gown, and music—'Here comes the bride—'All down the drain. She nestled closer to him, and hid her face against his shirt. After all, he's only a man, she thought fiercely. What can he know about a girl's dreams!

'God,' he muttered. 'I don't understand what you do to

me, Peabody. We'd better go into the house and—tears? Why?'

She sniffed back the last drop, and used a knuckle to clear her eyes.

'Why?' he repeated.

'Nothing,' she stuttered. 'Sometimes women feel like crying. It isn't every day that—that one gets a proposal—or—oh lord, I can't hold it in!' The tears came again. She wrestled free from his embrace and raced back to the house as fast as her feet could carry her. Blinded, she fumbled her way down the hall and into the kitchen, where George was still at work.

'Why, what's the matter?' the old man asked, as he opened his arms and Phil came into them.

'I—Penn and I——' she stammered through the tears. 'We're going to be married.'

'Which is certainly a good reason for a girl to cry her heart out,' Mr Yu murmured, laughing over Phil's bent head.

Penn made all the arrangements. Or perhaps his super-efficient secretary did. In any event on Monday Doctor Hanson came to the house, took a blood sample, gave her a smile of approval, and went off mumbling to himself about laboratory schedules and tons of work to be done. But Harry, who drove the doctor to the house, gave Phil a wink as if assuring her that all medical men have such troubles.

And so when Rose came to her at one o'clock in the afternoon with a puzzled frown on her face, Phil saw no real problem. 'So if your niece is that sick,' she assured the cook, 'Frank can drive you down to San Francisco right away. No, it's no real problem. Harry said he and—

Penn—would be home early, and Mr Yu is out at the back somewhere.'

Frank managed to combine his errands. He took Cecily home on the way, and promised to stay in the city until Rose was sure he was not needed.

That left Phil rumbling around the house until Robbie came in from school at two o'clock, with Mary, the afternoon maid, right behind him. At which time, Philomena told herself, somebody has to get dinner for the master of the house, and that somebody is obviously me. And off she went to the kitchen.

She heard the noise in the front hall at about three o'clock. The big front door slammed, and feet echoed down the hall. A quick smile flashed across Phil's face. She wiped flour off her hands on to one of Rose's super-sized aprons. Penn was home earlier than she had expected. Her hands fumbled with the ties of the apron. Ordinarily when she was cooking she thought nothing of welcoming guests in an apron. But Penn, on the day before their wedding? Nothing doing! She struggled, but the loop around her neck got caught in her hair, and it was a pretty dishevelled housekeeper who finally made it to the hall. It wasn't Penn.

Mary stood in the alcove leading into the library, a strange couple stood at the foot of the stairs, and Robbie was frozen in position half way down.

The woman was tall and aristocratic, her blonde hair piled up on her head in the latest fashion, wearing a mink coat despite the heat. The man was tall, thin, trying to hide a narrow face behind a full beard and moustache. Not one of that kind, Phil moaned, as she positioned herself between Robbie and the intruders.

'And you are?' she inquired in her best deep voice.

'Oh, none of your business,' the woman stated flatly. 'I don't have to dispute the world with the hired help. Come, Robbie, we're leaving at once.'

'No,' the boy shouted, backing up the stairs. 'They can't make me go, Phil?'

'No, they can't make you go,' she answered.

'I'm the boy's mother,' the woman snapped. 'Come down here, Robert. At once, do you hear.'

'So that's it,' Philomena grated. 'Possession is nine points of the law? Well, Mrs whatever your name is now, *that's* the boy's mother.' She gestured over her shoulder to the picture that gleamed against the wall. 'And there's no way you're going to get Robbie out of this house without his father's approval.'

'We don't have to put up with this nonsense,' the woman returned. 'Donald. Get the boy. Now.'

'Mary, call the police. Report an attempted kidnapping,' Phil called. All eyes turned to the maid. She was standing just by the hall telephone, but made no effort to pick it up.

'Eloise?'

It was obvious that Donald really didn't want to play the game. 'Get the boy,' the woman snapped. 'They're all alone in the house.' She turned her attention back to Phil. 'And don't think we don't know about you. Living in his house. In the next room, for that matter. You just wait until the Judge hears about *this*. We've got pictures!'

Donald had finally made up his mind. He moved past Eloise and headed for the stairs. Phil backed up directly in front of him, slowing him down. 'Robbie,' she called over her shoulder. 'Into your room. Lean out the window and yell for Mr Yu.'

Donald stopped, one foot in the air. 'Mr Yu?' he asked over his shoulder.

'The Chinese gardener,' Eloise supplied. 'He's eighty years old at least.'

Robbie had gone by this time, his boots clattering on the stairs as if heralding the Light Brigade. Donald put his foot down on the next riser. Phil backed up slowly, directly in front of him. 'You'd better change your mind, Donald,' she told him softly. 'You're the one who's going to get hurt. Although when I get through with you I might save up a punch or two for your lovely wife. That would sound good in court, wouldn't it?'

He hesitated again. 'Get on with it,' his wife ordered. He began the pursuit. This is silly, Phil told herself. Here I am being stalked by a rabbit! But he is big. What I need is a weapon. They were in the second-floor corridor, inching gradually down toward Robbie's room. She could hear the boy yelling out of the window at the top of his lungs. His bedroom door was open. Phil backed into the room, and found exactly what she needed.

It was something one finds in every American child's bedroom, girl or boy, when they get to a certain age. A baseball bat. She hefted it, found the balance, and moved briskly back to the door. 'Don't bother, Robbie,' she called over her shoulder. 'Everything's in good order now.'

'That's what you think.' The man in the door was trying to show a little bravado. He hadn't seen the bat as yet. 'I intend to take that brat with me, little girl, and— oooh.' The bat, wielded like a quarter-staff, had just slammed into his solar plexus. He dropped to the floor, gasping for breath.

More footsteps clattered on the stairs. High heels.

Eloise stormed down the corridor, her face rigid with anger. 'Get up, Donald, and get that child,' she screamed. 'Donald? What happened to——?'

'You'd better pick him up and go home,' Phil grinned at her. 'Donald has suddenly decided not to do any kidnapping today.' The worn end of the bat wiggled in her hands. Eloise carefully started to back down the hall.

'You'd better take Donald with you,' Phil insisted. 'They don't collect garbage in our neighbourhood for another two days.'

'I—wait until I tell the judge about this,' Eloise threatened. 'Now I'm sure we'll get custody of the boy.' She had been sliding steadily towards the stairs, ready to abandon her new husband, when she backed into George Yu.

The old man had sufficient strength to force Eloise back up the hall, and sufficient wit to take in all the evidence. 'Kidnappers,' he chuckled. 'You want me to use judo on them? I could break a few bones?'

Eloise paled, her face so white that the patches of rouge on her cheeks gleamed like fire. 'No, no,' she gasped. 'We're going. It was all a terrible mistake. Get up, Donald.'

Donald looked as if he would rather stay where he was, but when Mr Yu bent over towards him he scuttled along the floor a few paces and staggered to his feet. The Chinese gardener pointed toward the door, and the pair of them fled. The three conspirators waited until they heard the front door slam, and then broke into laughter.

'Would you really use judo?' Phil asked through the giggles.

'Me?' the old man returned. 'What do I know about judo? I spent all my life in California. Baseball I know—

judo, no. That's Japanese stuff. Besides, what did you need me for? I was busy with the camellia beds. Exhibition next month. I *have* to get the blossoms ready.'

'Well, I'm sorry,' Phil said very primly. 'I couldn't find the baseball bat, you see.'

Mr Yu smiled, bowed, and retreated down the hall. He moved like a shadow, without a noise. What a marvellous man, Phil told herself, and then, unable to contain it, told Robbie, 'He'd make a wonderful grandfather.'

'Mr Yu?'

'Who else?'

'Why did you do that?' the boy asked. 'You didn't have to fight him just for me. He was a lot bigger than you.'

'Yeah,' she giggled, 'but I had the bat.'

'And you did it just for me?'

'Just for you. Hurts, does it?'

'Yeah. Sort of. I'm not accustomed to——' That tiny smile edged at the corners of his mouth. He saw his reflection in the wall-mirror and quickly replaced the smile with his normal frown.

Philomena whistled as she took the stairs two at a time, stopping to pay tribute to the Pirate King, and Robbie's mother. Mary was struggling into her coat by the front door.

'Leaving?'

'I—I guess I'd better,' the maid replied. 'I——'

'I know. You've been spying on us for them all the time.' There was no bitterness in Phil's voice. She understood the woman's need. 'They paid you to call them?'

'Yes. I—I needed the money. I hate to lose my job. It's the baby.'

'Yes. I know all about it, Mary. I looked into it all last Friday. It wasn't such a terrible crime, what you did, provided it doesn't happen again. There's no need to give up your job—unless you can't stand us here.'

'No need to——?'

'No need to. And next week, when things settle down, I want you to sit down with Mr Wilderman and see if he can't work something out. I know it's all been a shock. Go on home. Take a few days off, and come back when you're ready. Nobody need know except you and I, and I have the most atrocious memory you ever saw.'

There were genuine tears in the woman's eyes. She thought for a moment, nodded her head, and turned to the door. 'I'll be back Wednesday,' she said softly, and went out.

'And that leaves the whole blinking house to me,' Phil lectured herself. There was a smell invading the hall. 'Oh my heavens,' she wailed as she ran for the kitchen. 'My pies!'

There was no need for her elaborately prepared explanation, concocted over a tray of hot biscuits to go with the salmon loaf. Robbie clattered down the stairs as soon as Penn's car purred to a halt, and poured the whole story into his ear before Phil could even get her apron off.

Dinner went well, but there were so many questions to be answered that Phil hardly managed a bite before everyone else was finished. The whole affair was topped off when Frank stomped into the house in the middle of the meal.

'Wasn't any emergency at all,' he grunted. 'Nothing wrong with anybody in Rose's family. Somebody's playing games with the telephone. Rose nearly blew a fuse when she found out. I brought her back and left her at home.'

Later that night, exhausted, Phil tumbled out of the shower, slipped into her shorty nightgown, and stood by the window to watch the full moon chase the evening star across the sky. Up in the mountains, forty miles away, it was snowing. Down in the protected valley where the Sacramento and the American rivers flowed, spring was showing signs. By craning her head she could see the reflected light of the dome of the State Capitol. And this is how the rich people live, she chuckled to herself. Here I am in the middle of the city and it looks more like country living than actually being out in the country.

Behind her there was a light knock on the interconnecting door. She left the view behind her reluctantly. There was no need for a robe—Penn couldn't see anything. She opened the door and extended her hand.

'What are you doing?' he asked casually.

'Just looking—the window,' she murmured. He came to her as if he had all his faculties, slipping one arm around her waist, and walking her back to the window. There was nothing at all wrong with his sense of touch, she told herself, alarmed. His hand was broadly open, resting in that declivity where her narrow waist swelled outwards into her rounded hip. His finger tips moved.

Not a sweeping caress, just a sensuous application and release of pressure, almost as if he were playing a drum. And if his fingers were the drummer, her skin came taut under the pressure, as if she were the drum.

'So you hit Donald with the baseball bat,' he murmured into her mass of hair.

'Well, it seemed the logical thing to do at the time,' she

returned. 'She said—that it would help *their* case in court.
I hope it doesn't?'

'I don't think it will,' he reassured her. 'The more I
think of it the funnier it all seems.'

The conversation seemed to be going on at two levels.
The verbal she could handle—if she put her mind to it.
The other, the pleasing assault of his fingertips, was
beyond her experience, and her automatic response,
moving closer against his side, did nothing to help her
resolution. Her nightgown, lightweight, felt almost as if
it were not there. His hand rested just inches above its
hem. She felt a crazily mixed feeling—remorse and
relief—when it lifted and moved higher. And gasped as it
kept going upwards, to rest on the lower slope of her
breast. And the conversation went on.

'Tomorrow is our wedding-day.' A casual statement of
fact from him that caused her mind to somersault. In all
the madness of the day she had forgotten!

'Yes——' she managed to stammer, 'Yes, it is. I—I
hope the weather's nice.'

'That's my girl,' he laughed. 'Tomorrow is our
wedding-day and you want to talk about the weather?'

'It—it seemed to be the safest subject.'

'Ah. I never thought of you as wanting to be safe.'

'Well, I do,' she insisted. 'Every woman does. It isn't
the same for a woman as for a man.'

'What isn't?'

'Getting married. It's too wrapped up in responsibili-
ties and—and passions——'

'I understand.' Those pernicious fingers smoothed the
firmness of her breast, touched lightly on its proud peak,
and faded away. Regretfully.

'I just wanted to say good night. Everything will be all

right, Philomena. I shall keep you safe. Guide me back to the door.'

'I know you will,' she sighed as she led him back to his own room. There was no sleep to be had that night. She tossed and turned, feeling the trail of those fingers all night long, wishing mightily that there could have been no need for him to stop.

She came down to breakfast with him on Tuesday, before he went off to work. They were all quiet. Robbie squirmed in his chair, almost smiling. Harry was his usually gloomy self, and Penn seemed to be wrapped up in something deep in his mind. As she had done for weeks now, Phil picked up the morning paper and began to read him the headlines. But none of the stories caught his interest, and when she stopped short of the whole reading, he didn't urge her on.

'I'll send the car for you,' he told her briefly. 'Along about midday, I suppose, and I'll meet you there.'

She stood in the door for ten minutes after the car had gone. What a wedding, she groaned to herself. I'll meet you there. Well, I suppose when you stretch the truth a little, that's what happens at a *normal* wedding, right? The groom waits at the church, and the bride comes to him. *Normal*, hah!

So it was all rather a surprise when the doorbell went at about ten-thirty, and Cecily, a big smile on her face, ushered her sister Sally into the living-room. Sister Sally and half a million packages.

'Well, you certainly fooled us all,' her sister said as she slumped down on the couch to catch her breath. 'Lord, I've been running around like a head with its chicken cut off. That man is crazy, Phil.'

'That man?'

'That man that you're going to marry. Now we'd better try everything on. Mrs Ralston is waiting just in case something needs to be adjusted.'

'Mrs Ralston? Waiting where?'

'She's the head seamstress from Balmain's, silly——'

'And she's up in your bedroom,' Cecily interrupted. 'And she don't look like a wait-around person.'

'But you——' Phil sighed as she took her youngest sister's hands. 'Stop just right there. What the devil is this all about?'

'Well, you could have knocked me over with a feather when he telephoned me yesterday morning. Of course I had all your measurements. So he sent that sexy car around after me, and he and I went down to Balmain's—boy, is he a choosy guy. It took hours. For me they never would have stirred a stump. For him they jumped every time he opened his mouth. What the devil does he do—own a gold-mine?'

'Several dozen,' practical Phil inserted deftly. 'And I still don't know what you're talking about. Let's go upstairs—at least we shan't keep Mrs Ralston waiting for whatever it is.'

Her bedroom had been taken over. Mrs Ralston had brought two assistants, who were busy emptying boxes, and stuffing their contents into her wardrobe, and her bureaux. Noting her anxious look, the seamstress said, 'Your future husband insisted on a complete trousseau, Miss Peabody. A little of everything, he specified. And this, of course.'

A dressmaker's dummy stood by the open window, and Phil's heart did a sudden jump at the dress it displayed. Orange blossom and white lace, demurely seductive, revealing a little, promising everything. She could almost hear the wedding march being played in the background. A tiny gold coronet—pure gold it would be—the idea broke through her trance, and left her giggling like a fool. A long train, the veil, everything! It was too hard not to cry—and when she started they all joined in—all except Mrs Ralston, who had other things on her mind.

A few alterations were required. Well, Mrs Ralston thought they were, and Phil had given up the struggle long since. It was easier to just drift down with the tide. 'Just a little lower in the cleavage,' the dressmaker insisted.

'A little more and I'll get pneumonia,' Phil protested feebly.

'The lace will protect you,' the practical answer came. Sure, Phil thought. The lace was like a transparent film, hardly real enough to stand a fingerprint. Sure it will protect me. You bet!

And when it was finally completed, they all insisted she take it off again. And come down to lunch!

'I couldn't eat a thing,' she sighed for the tenth time.

'Got the willies?' Sally laughed. 'Me too. But if you think it's bad now, wait until tonight!' They all laughed.

'Very funny,' Phil groaned.

'So eat something,' Rose insisted. 'It takes a lot of strength to be a bride.'

'Yeah, sure.' But she did manage a pink grapefruit, the smallest corner of the steak she was served, and a piece of toast. 'And Penn did all this?' she asked again.

'All this,' her sister assured her. 'With his fingers, no less. He felt everything from top to bottom, then had me describe the whole ensemble. What a lucky girl you are, Sis. You just wait until he gets those pads off his eyes.

Now, I've got to change too. Upstairs, lady.'

'You too? For a wedding in a——' Shut up, Phil, she yelled at herself. You don't know what's going on. Just shut up and do what you're told. You just wait until he gets those pads off his eyes—yeah. You're not what he thinks you are, and nobody, but nobody fools around with Penn Wilderman's sensibilities! There'll be a day of reckoning, little Miss Peabody! She shivered, and Mrs Ralston complained of it as they slipped the magic dress down over her head again, set the train, adjusted the veil, flounced out the fulness of it all, and led her gently down the stairs. The limousine was waiting.

'There'll be a reckoning,' she told herself as she stepped carefully into the big interior. 'But not today, lady. Enjoy.'

The car whispered away, like a magic carpet. She closed her eyes. For some reason she didn't want to see where the judge's chambers were. The ride was longer than she had expected, and the bridal party was tense. The bridal party. Herself, Sally, Cecily, and Rose. Mrs Ralston had gathered all her troops and disappeared.

'We're here.' Sally made the announcement, nudging her sister. Phil opened her eyes. 'It isn't the guillotine,' Sally chuckled. 'Or if it is, you're riding in one fancy tumbril, sis. Get moving. We're five minutes late. And I don't think the man you're marrying is much of a waiter-around either.'

And so she opened her eyes. The car was parked directly in front of her own parish church, Saint Clement's Episcopal. The doors were wide open, waiting. Sally handed her the tiny bouquet of orange blossom, they all fussed with her dress and veil, the organ sounded, and she walked down the aisle towards the altar, where he and Harry and Robbie waited, all kitted out in formal wear. Her arm shook in the crook of Mr Yu's elbow. Her entire frame shivered until that moment when she came close enough to feel the aura, and Mr Yu transferred her hand into that of Penn. Then suddenly it all became a dream, a warm comforting dream, and the shivers left her.

The ceremony passed completely over her head. She must have made the proper answers, because the organ was playing again, and Penn was folding back her veil to kiss her. She walked back down the aisle with him, proud and puzzled. At the door of the church he stopped and kissed her again.

'What's the trouble, Philomena?' he asked softly.

'I—I was surprised,' she sighed. 'The dress, the church. I thought we—you—I was just surprised.'

'I'm not altogether insensitive,' he whispered in her ear. Her hands crept up around his neck, and she pulled his head down to hers.

'Thank you for everything.' And the tears came in little driblets.

'Crying on your wedding-day?' he teased. 'I thought only the bride's mother did that. What's the matter now?'

'I—nothing,' she mumbled, and ducked her head into his shirt front. She had finally puzzled it all out. What a stupid place this was to discover that you've fallen in love with your husband!

CHAPTER EIGHT

THE party was a small one. The group of Penn's friends who had been at the church came home with them. Sally's husband Jim had joined, apologising for missing the ceremony. The old house welcomed her. It seemed to smile, gap-toothed, through its arches at her. Confused, wildly happy and at home, she needed a clean up and a respite from the tight coronet that held her veil. When she went up the lady in the picture smiled at her.

'Wish me luck,' Phil begged as Sally hustled her up the stairs.

'Who, me? I already did that.'

'Not you, sis. The girl in the picture. I have a sort of feeling that if——'

'Don't let it worry you, love. Look at that leer on the Pirate's face, over here. Now if *he* got you alone in some dark corner you'd have something to worry about!'

Phil dappled her face with cold water while her sister looked over the room in awe. With coronet and veil off, she took down her hair, brushing it out into a gleaming sheath of wild curls. 'Be careful of the dress,' Cecily admonished, giggling. 'You'll need it for your daughter.'

'Yes. Of course.' Why not dream? Phil challenged herself. What law is it that says I can't delude myself if I want to? And so she stood carefully still while her two attendants rearranged the beautiful wedding-gown. One question bothered her, and she could not help but ask. 'How did you know about the wedding, Sally?'

'The wedding? Your—Penn, is it?—Penn telephoned.'
And then, in a more serious tone, 'Deborah had already
gone. They found a baby-sitter for the week, and took off
for Lake Tahoe.'

'Who in the world would willingly watch those two for
a week?'

'John's mother and father. I don't say they were happy
to do it, but they're doing it.'

'And Samantha?'

'I—I'm sorry, Phil. Samantha and her husband have
decided that you are purposely keeping them from *her*
inheritance. Sam said—well, she wouldn't come. And
after all you did for them! Dammit, Phil, sometimes
relatives can be worse than enemies!'

'Don't let it bother you,' Phil said softly. 'I'll survive,
and one day they'll get over it. You'll see. Hadn't we
better go down?'

The group downstairs was making enough noise for
twice its number. Phil hesitated on the bottom stair, took
a couple of deep breaths to steady her nerves, and strode
into the living-room looking as complacent as if she had
done this sort of thing every day. Or at least once a week,
she amended as they all turned in her direction and her
composure slipped away from her.

Penn was standing in the middle of the room, a glass in
his hand, his ears perked. 'Philomena?' She went directly
to him, a rush of affection assaulting her. He smiled
when she stretched high enough to kiss the tip of his nose,
then surrounded her with one arm. Somebody in the
crowd filled her hand with a chilled champagne glass.

'A toast,' Penn announced. 'To the loveliest bride ever
to come into the Wilderman family.' There were cheers
as the wine went down. Not used to wine at all, Phil

emptied her glass, and then hiccupped as the sparkling liquid hit her stomach. Penn pulled her close. 'What did you say?' he whispered in her ear.

She hiccupped once more. 'What I said,' she whispered back, 'is that you haven't the slightest idea what you're talking about, Mr Wilderman.' Someone filled her glass. She clinked it against his. 'And here's a toast to the true descendant of the Pirate King,' she whispered back at him. The second glass went down as quickly as her first, but nobody was counting—or noticing—until he handed his glass into the nearest passing hands and swooped down on her with both arms. Her own glass fell to the floor, and there was considerable cheering as his lips touched hers gently, moved away, and then almost as if compelled by outside forces, came back passionately, demandingly, sweeping her out of herself with sweet abandon. It left her weak, trembling, leaning against him for support. He gathered her up again, coddling her head against his chest gently.

'And that's what happens to uppity wives,' he whispered into her hair. 'Want to try for two?'

'I wouldn't dare,' she quavered. 'Not here, with all these people watching!'

'Now that's the right attitude,' he chuckled, releasing her. She didn't want to go. 'We have to mingle,' he chided.

'I—I'd rather do it right where I am,' she confessed, but he gently pushed her away, and she mingled.

An hour later they had all gone. Rose provided a buffet supper for the family. The lobster was delightful, the heart-of-palm salad equal to it, but everything else Phil noted was some hazy world whose borders were too ill-defined for her to recognise them. Never-never Land, she asked herself? What have I done to me? She was seated between Penn and Robbie, and they both looked so—so huge, so handsome, so——

'So now *you're* my mother.' Robbie, bending close to her ear.

'It looks as if,' she returned, having trouble with all the syllables. 'Eat your heart out, kid.' The lobster salad splattered all over her beautiful dress.

'I dunno,' the boy chuckled. 'I like neat people.'

'What are you two arguing about?'

'We're not arguing, Penn. We never argue. We occasionaly—did I say that right?—we fight might, but we don't argue.'

'How much champagne have you had tonight, Philomena?'

'Counting this one?'

'Yes, counting that one.'

She gulped it down thirstily and giggled as the bubbles tickled her nose. 'That makes—three,' she managed. They were both laughing, and she could see nothing funny about it at all, as her earnest face showed. 'Compared to all the champagne you've drunk in your lifetime, that's hardly a drop, love.' She shivered at the word. Love. Delicious. If only it were true. Why is my mind so hazy?

She wanted to be sure he understood her. 'Yes, three,' she said sleepily.

'Yes,' Penn chuckled. 'I understand. You're sleepy, and you've had three glasses of champagne tonight.'

'No, no.' She waved her hand in front of his face to get his attention. 'I've had three all of my life. Only two tonight.'

She had spent the whole evening sitting up straight,

being the lady. And now suddenly the table was at an angle, falling slowly up at her. Things were all just very confusing. The salad bowl kept falling up at her, faster and faster, until Robbie yelled, and Penn caught her by the shoulders, then climbed out of his chair and swung her up in his arms. 'Whoever would have thought of it. She doesn't drink alcohol. Wow!' He shifted her weight in his arms, so that her head rested on his shoulder. One of her arms was around his neck, and a contented smile marked her face.

'She's smiling,' Robbie said softly.

'Is she really? Well, we've got to get her to bed, Robbie. It'll have to be a two-man job. I'll carry and you guide. Right?'

'Right.' They started slowly for the stairs, doing each tread slowly. Half-way up one of those huge eyes of hers opened.

'Penn,' she managed, waving towards the painting. 'Who was that lady?'

He stopped, shifting her weight again, looking over his shoulder. 'I thought I told you before,' he said gently. 'That's my sister Robin.'

That's my sister. That *was* my sister. *That's my mother,* Robbie had said. The words haunted her confused mind. She squeezed the eye shut again and tried to move closer to him.

'Stop wriggling,' he complained softly. 'You'll have us both back down the stairs. I'm not one of these macho Hollywood stunt men.' She became rigid in his arms, which made it worse, and then went limp as he carried her into her room and stretched her out gently on the bed. They *shushed* each other as the door closed behind them.

She squeezed one eye open. 'Shower,' she muttered.

'Wedding night.' The floor rocked abominably, but she made it to the bathroom, shedding items of clothing as she went.

With more luck than skill she managed to cram her curls under her shower cap, and stepped into the cubicle. The hot water sprayed ice-cold, shocking her out of her comfortable daze. Her blank mind began to spin, and even the gradual warming of the water could not help.

'Wedding-night,' she muttered. 'Happily ever after!' The thought twisted like a knife to her heart. He had already set the boundaries to their marriage. Just until he could see again. It would have worked, she thought bitterly, if I hadn't gone and fallen in love with him. Now *that's* a real laugher, Philomena. Poor slow-witted Philomena.

One day soon he'll be able to see again. What will he expect? An old battle-axe? Five-foot-two of stern matriarch? You little fool. He doesn't even know how tall you are. Five foot two, provided you wear two-inch heels. Grey hair. How can he possibly know that it's straw-blonde, that the curls are real, not ironed in? He's braille-read my face, but all he knows is that it's round. He can't tell that I've got green eyes, and a dimple in each cheek. And a too-wide mouth that couldn't be stern if it wanted to. What a mess!

She shut off the water and stepped out into the steamy bathroom. The full-length mirror on the wall confronted her with more than she wanted to see. No, he can't know all that, her mind screamed at her. That's something he'll never see. The freckles on my shoulders, and across the bridge of my nose. The pale white skin that burns when I'm not careful. The full, firm breasts. If I were older he would expect *something* to sag a little?

The narrow waist? No, I stopped him when he got that far in his *research*. The comfortable hips, the tapered legs? Nothing. He'll look for a woman of comfortable age, inches taller than I am, and he'll pass over the little thing I really am, with all my fears and prejudices and *ordinariness* written on my face, and he—and he won't even know me. Or want to know me. And that's what will break your heart, won't it, Philomena Wilderman? Her mind was too muzzy, too filled with fears and tears to continue. She dabbed at herself with the towel, discarded the shower cap, and stumbled back to bed.

The pale light of pre-dawn was outlining the window when she woke up. She was lying flat on her back in her own bed. See, she told herself, you went and got yourself fool-drunk, and nothing bad happened. Here you are, totally naked in your own bed—totally naked? The thought startled her, and she tried to sit up. It proved impossible. A heavy brown arm was thrown completely across her body, locking her into position. The attached hand had taken complete possession of her left breast. When she tried to gently remove it there was an instant groan of protest in her ear. She inched her head sidewise, and found herself nose to nose with a man.

It was something she had not expected. Something she had not even thought about. Which proves what an idiot you are, Philomena Peabody, she lectured herself. She wriggled slightly to try to break away. The movement brought another protest, and the hand slowly and gently kneaded her breast, until its roseate peak sprang to full proud life. It brought something else too, a wild incessant hammering at the door behind which she had locked all her passions. And just another minute of this, she knew,

would show how weak that lock was. She froze in
position again. The hand gradually came to a stop. She
stared at the pads that covered his eyes, wishing mightily
she might see them without them seeing her.

What have I done? Nothing unusual, her practical
mind insisted. That's not just a man—that's your
husband. You remember, Phil? Orange blossoms and
lace, and *I, Philomena take thee, Penn*. Remember? Harry
couldn't find the ring because Robbie had it, and Cecily
caught the bouquet, and you stepped out into the
sunlight, right in the church doors, and discovered you
loved him? Remember? Well, there he is. The man in
possession. He's the *possessor*, and you're the *possessee*,
lady, and there's no way to back out of it—because you
don't want to! He needs a shave. He's got such a heavy
beard. Funny I had't noticed that before. I wonder how it
feels to kiss a man with a beard? Well, it's not really a
beard, just a little—lord, isn't it rough! That was her two
fingers, exploring, reporting, drawing back quickly when
the dragon almost opened an eye. And we're in my bed
together, and it's almost morning and he—good lord, he's
as naked as I am!

So what I'll do, she decided, is to lie here quietly,
making believe I'm fast asleep, until he—but he didn't.
Not for another three hours, and by that time Phil was
indeed sound asleep again, dreaming wild dreams,
sighing sweetly in the toils of the dragon.

On Wednesday morning it was another noise, another
male, who brought her up out of the darkness. Sleepily
she forced one eye open. Robbie was sitting on the foot of
the bed, bouncing. The mattress shook.

'Hey,' the boy called. 'Dad's downtown. He called and
told me to get you up. They've moved the hearing up a

day. We have to be in court by eleven o'clock!' She gave him a glare and then a smile, and pushed him in the general direction of her door.

She dressed slowly. What does one wear to a court hearing in the morning? Something judgmental? Dark, sober? Her hand reached automatically for one of her two old light blue trouser-suits. Her office uniform, no less. But a sudden intuition stopped her. Instead she chose a demure white blouse with a Peter Pan collar, and imitation gold studs at the wrists. A sturdy corduroy beige skirt, and a pair of dark brown half-boots completed the outfit. She brushed her mass of hair diligently, and let it hang free. A touch of pink lipgloss, a bit of powder on her nose, and she was ready. 'Into the valley of death——' she quoted haphazardly as she squared her shoulders and went down.

The hearing was to be held in rooms in the Hall of Justice, 'because of alterations in the regular Juvenile court,' Frank explained. They drove down I street, past the City Hall and the Post Office. There was construction everywhere. The city was growing almost before her eyes. Which she could open now, she found. The aspirin had already begun its work. There wasn't a parking place to be had. So what else is new, she asked herself.

Frank drove the limousine right up to the front of the building, parked in the No Parking zone, and held the door for them. Harry was waiting for them on the steps. 'The boss has gone up already,' he said. 'He and the lawyer. Better hurry up. This judge, she don't stand for nonsense.' He took the crook of Phil's arm and hustled her up and into the building.

'She?'

'Yeah. Judge Irene Mulrooney. Not too well liked by

the lawyers. She doesn't care for long-running cases.'

'Like this one.'

'Yeah. Like this one. You don't look old enough to be married, Mrs Wilderman.'

'Well!' It was all she could think to say. Twice in one hour. Well! She squared her shoulders and reached back for Robbie's hand. It came into hers. Reluctantly, but it came.

The hearing room was larger than she had expected, but plain. A bare desk in the middle of the room for the judge, with a high-backed swivel chair, and two sets of modern armchairs, facing each other on opposite sides. The empty space in the middle looked like the bullring, waiting. Blood spilled? she asked herself. Will it be one of *those* battles?

Penn knew she was there. Perhaps the sound of her heels, she considered. But she was wearing boots, and the heels were soft leather. But he knew, and he stood up, a smile on his face, and arms extended.

For the audience, she supposed. The opposite side of the room was crowded. Eloise and Donald, and what must have been a whole platoon of lawyers, all glaring at her. Play the game, she told herself fiercely. Play the game.

Her feet did not require orders. They sped up, leaving Harry behind, and in a moment she was safe again, squeezed inside his arms, almost as if it were all true. It *is* all true, she insisted to herself. It is! We're married—and even if only one of us is in love, there's enough here for two. More than enough. Her sigh gave her away.

'Something bothering?' His lips were at her ear.

'I—I don't know,' she sighed. 'I think I—I'm just not a morning person—and changing the date surprised me. I don't like surprises. I like—neat, orderly—well, some-times I do.'

'Sounds a little confusing there,' he chuckled. 'I'll see what I can do about providing a safe orderly life for you.'

'Can you do that?' she sighed.

'You sound suspicious.'

'I don't know a great deal about *happily ever after*,' she confessed, pressing her nose into his chest. There might have been more lovely words, but at that moment Robbie caught up to them, exchanged a very adult handshake with his father, and sat down. Harry pre-empted the lawyer's seat in the first row, and relegated that worthy to the second row. Penn offered a brief introduction. 'Mr Whirlmount,' he nodded backward. Phil barely caught a look at the middle-aged blue-eyed man behind them, before Penn seized on her attention, drawing her down beside him.

She scanned his face for some sign that he knew yesterday had been different, and last night had—what? Those gauze pads stared back at her.

'Are you peeking?'

'With these things on? Don't be silly.'

'Did you get your eyedrops this morning?'

'Is this what it means to be married?'

'Yes, it does,' she snapped indignantly. 'I'm entitled to worry about you!'

'Yes. I admit that,' he laughed. 'One of the pads fell off last night. Harry fixed everything this morning.'

'One of them fell off?' Panic. Last night? She squirmed in her chair. 'What—what did you see?'

'A dark night,' he whispered. 'Was there something I should have seen?'

'Oh no!' The judge and bailiff came in at that moment.

She jumped to her feet, spilling her purse and its contents all over the floor. The judge looked over at her as she bent to recapture her wordly goods. Judge Mulrooney. About sixty, white-haired, gold-rimmed glasses, tall for a woman. She nodded at both sides of the case with equal chill, and sat down. Phil, still scrambling for her lipstick and key-chain, half under the chairs, decided to leave things where they were. She stood up, brushed down her skirts, blushed an apology at the judge, and sank into the chair next to Penn, hoping she might sink competely out of sight. The judge rapped on the desk top with the rounded end of a ballpoint pen. Her recorder rushed in and handed her a large envelope. She opened it with some disdain. 'The Case of Wilderman Versus Wilderman,' the judge announced. Her court recorder bent over her shoulder and whispered in her ear.

'I stand corrected. The case is amended to read Wilderman versus Worth. Do I understand, madam, that you are the former Mrs Wilderman and are now Mrs Donald Worth?' Eloise's platoon of lawyers signalled agreement.

'I'm sure she can speak for herself,' the judge commented wryly.

'Yes,' Eloise returned. Her voice was high and shrill, on the point of breaking.

'And your former husband, Mr Wilderman, is suing for custody of an adopted child, Robert Penn Wilderman.'

'Yes,' Penn nodded.

'You, Mr Wilderman, charge your former wife with neglect, child-abuse, and failure to comply with prior court orders. Now, let me hear the lawyers.' And she did. For an hour and thirty minutes, like a battle royal, as Phil slipped lower and lower in her chair, trying to dodge the verbal bullets. The judge handled them skilfully. Probed, when questions seemed half answered. Tapped her pen occasionally when things seemed to be getting out of order. And then——

'And now, Mrs Worth, I see you have added to your charges, alleging that your former husband is now, along with his other problems, guilty of lewd and lascivious conduct, by reason of living openly and immorally with another woman. Who?'

'That one. Right there,' Eloise screamed. 'They've been at it for weeks, with the boy in the house too!'

'Well,' the judge sighed. 'What is the quotation—there are none so blind as those who will not see? You, young lady. Are you cohabiting with the plaintiff?'

'Me?' Phil squeaked. 'Am I what?'

'Are you living in the same house as Mr Wilderman there?'

'I—yes.'

'All right, sit down, I won't bite you.'

The devil you won't, Phil sighed. Penn's hand closed on hers again, gently. It did a little bit to soothe her spirit, but not much. The judge was tapping her pen on the desk monotonously.

'I think I understand everything so far,' Judge Mulrooney said softly. 'So now we'll hear from the third party involved. Robert Wilderman?'

The lawyer reached over the row of chairs and tapped Robbie on the shoulder. The boy stood up. In spite of the suit, the tie, he looked like an accident on its way to happen. That sullen teenage scowl was back in full force. He spared one quick look over his shoulder at Phil, and she could see the unspoken appeal in his eyes. She shifted over to be as close to him as possible. He heard the chair shift, and one of his hands reached behind his back. Phil leaned forward and tucked her own in his. It continued to surprise her. Thirteen years old, and his hand was bigger than hers. Bigger and stronger. It closed around her like a vice. The boy backed up, as close to his chair as he could get, and hung on.

'Robert Penn Wilderman?'

'Yes sir—ma'am.'

'Don't be embarrassed. What do your friends call you?'

'Robbie.'

'Well then, Robbie. You've lived with your mother, the present Mrs Worth.'

'She's not my mother. My mother is——' The bitterness rolled out of him. The judge tapped the desk.

'Yes, I understand that. But Mrs Worth is your mother by adoption, as your uncle has now become your father by adoption.'

'That's it!' Phil clamped her hand over her mouth as everyone in the court glared at her. But that was it. She remembered. He was carrying her up the stairs, when they looked at the painting. *That's my mother, Robbie had said.* And *that's my sister, Penn had said.* No wonder they look alike. He's not—how could I have thought that Robbie was his illegitimate child! How could I have thought that! She wanted so badly to apologise to the silent man sitting straight and true beside her, but the judge was watching.

'To continue,' Judge Mulrooney said, 'If I may, young lady?'

'Yes. I—I'm sorry,' Phil stammered.

'And then, Robbie, you lived with your father for some time?'

A very defensive, 'Yes.'

'Now, Robbie, there are three sides to this case. It's your life we are dealing with. You *do* understand that?'

'Yes, ma'am.'

'Good. Now, given your own choice, Robbie, would you prefer to live with your mother?'

'Her? No. I don't want to live with her. She hates me. Her and that—that wimp she married.' More taps with the pen.

'All she's interested in is that I need to be living in her house at the end of each quarter, because that's when the company pays my dividends, and she takes all the money. That's all she's interested in, my money. I'd let her have it all if I didn't have to live with her.'

'All right, son. Mrs Worth, is it true that you receive all the child's stock dividends? One eighth of the company stock?' The judge peered at some papers. 'Eighty thousand dollars a year?'

'Well, I—yes,' Eloise began. 'But you know how expensive it is to feed a child these days.'

'Yes, I'm sure I do,' the judge snapped. 'I have three myself. Eighty thousand dollars. How much of that is banked for the boy's future?'

'Banked?' Eloise's troops were in confusion, muttering among themselves.

'Well?'

'None, your honour,' her lawyer interjected.

'But next year we expect to start an investment programme for him,' Eloise shrilled. 'My—Mr Worth is an Investment Counsellor.'

'Next year?' The judge grinned. There was nothing

happy about it. It looked like the grin a wolf might offer when meeting Little Red Riding Hood.

'All right, Robbie,' she continued. 'So you would prefer to live with your father?'

The boy agonised for a moment, then shook his head negatively. 'No,' he managed. 'I—he's a nice man, but—my mother was his sister, you see, and he thinks I'm a *responsibility*. I don't want to live where I'm just a responsibility. He's—he's busy, and works hard, and goes places where I can't go, and he never stops to play with me, or anything—but he does send me to a private school.'

'I see. He takes his responsibility seriously, though?'

'Yes, ma'am.'

The judge thought for a moment. 'You leave us with a difficult situation, Robbie,' she finally sighed. 'You don't want to live with your father, and you don't want to live with your mother—by adoption,' the judge hastily qualified as the boy stirred into objection. 'Do you have any ideas?'

'Sure,' the boy proclaimed. 'I've got a perfect solution. I wanna—excuse me—I want to live with Phil.'

A deadly silence fell over the entire room. 'And who the devil is Phil?' The judge leaned forward over her desk to stare at the boy. Philomena shrugged her shoulders. After all, they had outlawed the death penalty. So what else could happen to her? She stood up, still clutching at Robbie's hand.

'I'm Phil,' she announced in her soft ready-for-battle voice.

'And I wanna stay with Phil because she wants me,' the boy interjected swiftly. 'She doesn't have any responsibility—about me, that is, and she doesn't want my money—she just wants me. And that's what I want. I want somebody who wants me.' And with that he slumped back in his chair, pulling Phil down with him, clutching at her hand as if defying the world to separate them.

'Now let me see if I've got this right,' the judge sighed. 'This woman is cohabiting with Mr Wilderman, and you want her to be your legal guardian?' From behind, the lawyer nudged Phil sharply. She turned around. He gestured towards her left hand.

'Your honour,' she offered tentatively. 'If you mean I'm living with Penn and that's a bad thing, it's not, you know. It's really very nice.' Chuckles surrounded her. 'I forgot to tell you my full name. I'm Philomena Peabody Wilderman. Penn and I are married, and I think Robbie should live with us—because—because Penn is the nicest man I've ever known, and it takes two parents to bring up a teenager, and I know because I've had lots of experience in that field, and so—I think Robbie should go home with us.' And she collapsed into her chair again, and tried to shrink into a smaller package than she was. Another hand trapped her, on her left side. She was thoroughly surrounded. Penn on one side, holding her gently; Robbie on the other, clutching desperately, so that her hand ached.

The judge looked at all of them, one at a time, counting, assessing. And finally she tapped on her desk a couple of times with the top of her pen. 'I think maybe you're right,' she finally said. 'So ordered.' That pen again, an extra rap, and the judge billowed out of the courtroom, followed by her marching legion.

Luckily the room had two separate exits, or there might have been blood on the sand after all, Phil thought.

'I'll appeal!' Eloise yelled after them, as half her lawyer-platoon held her from making a frontal assault. 'I'll appeal!' They could still hear it echoing down the hall as they headed for the stairs.

Robbie was still clutching her hand, and it ached so much that she finally could not suppress a whimper. Penn turned around in a flash. He had been walking ahead of them, his arm on his lawyer's.

'It's only my hand,' she said quickly. 'Robbie doesn't know his own strength.'

'Gee, you should have said something,' the boy returned, releasing the pressure. 'Oh, what a mess I made!'

'It's not a mess,' she assured him. 'It just needs a massage and a——'

She stopped in mid-sentence. Penn had turned away and was going down the stairs. She could read anger in the set of his shoulders. It was still there when she followed him into the back seat of the limousine. Robbie—a smiling Robbie—jumped into the front seat, and was quickly lost in conversation with Harry—about machinery, of course. Phil settled back into the seat, and made an attempt to lift up the arm-rest. Penn's heavy hand kept her from doing so.

'So don't bottle it all up,' she said quietly. 'Whatever it is, it belongs out in the open. You won the case. Robbie is yours.'

'No,' he said bitterly. 'I didn't win the case, and Robbie isn't mine.'

'Penn! What are you trying to say?'

'I'm trying to tell you the truth,' he muttered. 'I didn't win the case. You did. The judge didn't appoint *me* to be the boy's guardian, she appointed *you*. And in any case, you were right a week or so ago. You said he hated me, and obviously he does.'

'He doesn't hate you, Penn. He defended you in the court. He laughed with you, and——'

'And he also told the absolute truth,' her husband grated. 'All I ever did was put a roof over his head and feed him. Nothing more. I was always too busy—too wrapped up in the Big World. I kept him away from the river because I remembered how his mother died. I couldn't go with him, so no Little League. No Boy Scouts. With the finest mountains in the world within forty miles of us, I've never once taken him camping. It's all damn true, but it took you to bring it all out, Peabody. Sometimes I'm not sure whether meeting you was good or bad for me.'

The bitterness was more than she had expected. She tried to defend herself. '*I* didn't win the case,' she sighed. 'The judge misunderstood. I was speaking for you!'

'I know that,' he grunted. 'Maybe I could have better spoken for myself!'

It was a cold, flat statement. For the past few minutes she had been hugging herself, congratulating herself, and now suddenly it all exploded in her face. He settled back in his seat, a frown on his handsome face. She studied him. He had the look of a man troubled beyond his capacity. And then, just as suddenly, his muscles relaxed, the frown disappeared. One of his warm hands fumbled for hers, squeezed it gently, and held on to it as the car moved out into traffic on the way home.

'It's not your fault, Philomena,' he sighed. 'It just seemed for a moment that—well, it's one problem out of our way.'

'But your—but Eloise—she said they would appeal.'

'So let them,' he said wryly. 'I can afford to hire more lawyers than that damn St Louis wimp. We'll lead them a merry chase before they get *that* decision overturned. You did a good job, old girl!' Congratulations, but the taste was bittersweet.

How can I be so high up in the air on one side, and so low down on the other, she asked herself. Congratulations—old girl. Darn. I *should* have told him the first time the subject came up. And now I don't know *what* to do! She was still deep in thought when the car drew up at the front door.

CHAPTER NINE

THE atmosphere of tension was still there when she came down to dinner. Robbie appeared with clean face and hands, and something that might be called a smile on his face. Harry was his usually glum self, and Penn had withdrawn somewhere inside that darkness of his, and no amount of conversation would bring him out. After the meal Harry guided him into the library, and before the door closed behind them she could hear the hum of conversation.

'So that leaves you and me, Robbie,' Phil offered tentatively. 'Or have you got something on too?'

The boy shrugged his shoulders. 'I was going to watch *Dr Who* on television, but if you and—Dad—I thought both of you would like to be alone for a while, so——'

'No, don't disturb your plans,' she returned hastily. 'I've got a million things to do. You just go ahead.'

He proffered a real smile this time, and when he walked by her chair he stopped long enough to kiss her cheek. 'It takes some getting used to,' he said, 'but maybe I could like having a real mother around the place.'

'Well, don't get over-enthusiastic,' she returned. 'Who knows? Given enough time I might be able to put up with you.' She reached up, ruffled his hair, and giggled.

'You don't plan to disappear now, do you?'

'It all depends on how you mean that,' she said. 'I *do* intend to disappear. Out into the garden, before it gets dark. Run along, kid.'

It was still light outside, in those minutes after the sun

149

had gone but before the dark had taken over. She wandered slowly down into the garden, towards the hot house. Mr Yu was still working inside, and she was in no mood for casual chatter. She turned back and sat down on the sofa-swing. The tip of her toe barely reached the ground. The whole construction was adapted for long-legged men, she accused. Two blue jays refused to accept her comment, and fled, flying low over the shrubbery in the direction of the park. In the background she could hear Mr Yu singing. She braced herself and gave the swing a shove, then coiled her legs up beneath her and tried to relax.

Being a wife, if only a temporary one, was proving more nerve-racking than she had thought. His offer had puzzled her as much as her own acceptance—until that moment on the steps of the church. But the fact that she loved him was no guarantee that he felt the same. Something temporary, he had said. Until the problem with Robbie was disposed of, and he gets his sight back. Well, Robbie was—settled, not disposed of. And on Monday morning the doctor would remove his pads for the final time. And then what?

Her mind balked at the jump, and left her wandering around in her head as the gold on the western horizon began to fade into the blue and purple that heralded the end of day. Although she was in the centre of the city the trees and purposefully curved streets cut out the traffic noises, and left only a certain empty tranquillity on her ears. The swing squeaked a little as she lowered a foot and gave another push. Mr Yu's song had a haunting familiarity about it, but the name escaped her. She nestled back in the corner of the swing, and wrestled with her devils again.

'Mrs Wilderman?' Harry, standing on the little ridge

that overlooked the pool area. Just a shadow now.

'Here,' she answered softly. The little man sidled down the hillside in a rush of gravel.

Mrs Wilderman? What a nice sound. She had heard it so seldom these last two days. 'What is it, Harry?'

'I have to go now.'

'I—what?' Harry was a part of the family. A fixture in the house. Every minute of every day, where Penn was, there was Harry. It was almost impossible to think of Harry as having to 'go now'! She dropped her foot to the ground and braked the swing to a stop. 'You have to *go*?'

'A ten o'clock flight,' he returned.

'But you—how the devil can Penn get around if you——?'

'He has you now.'

An overwhelming statement. He has *me* now. If only it were true! 'I—I don't understand, Harry.'

'It's simple enough. I have to make a trip. I'll be gone two or three days—well, to be exact I expect to get things wound up by Sunday. But my plane leaves in a couple of hours, and he needs you now.'

'I—yes. Yes, of course, Harry. Where is he?'

'In the living-room.'

'I'll go in at once. And Harry?'

'What?'

'Have a safe trip.'

The little man had disappeared before she could gather her wits about her. Mr Yu was making closing-for-the-night noises down in the greenhouse. And Penn was waiting for her? She jumped up, setting the swing into a wild creaking and groaning. The gravel of the path crunched under her sandals as she made her way back up to the house.

The house was quiet, as if it had gone to sleep. Penn

was sitting on the big couch in the middle of the room, facing the door. Somehow he sensed her. She stopped to scan his face, uplifted in her direction. There was something dear about it, something heartwarming. She floated over the distance between them. He was holding out a hand. She took it, and followed his direction as he tugged her down to sit beside him.

'Well, Mrs Wilderman.' The second time in one night! She pinched herself, just to make sure, and then settled back. His arm automatically came around her shoulders.

'Well, Mr Wilderman?' she sighed.

'What we need now is a nice fire in the fireplace.'

'Yes.' She snuggled closer to him. 'What fireplace?'

'The one right in front of us.'

'That's a door,' she offered.

'You need more imagination,' he returned. 'A big stone fireplace. And the flames? They're blue on the top, a flickering blue.'

'Silly. It's still a door. A double door, I grant you, but there aren't any blue flames.'

'Pragmatic Philomena?'

A deep-throated chuckle. 'The girls called me Practical Pill.'

'Pill?'

'Well, it was hard to say Philomena when they were young, and then when they got older, they thought Pill was more appropriate.'

'Tell me about them.'

So she did, emphasising the good, making herself the butt of the bad, not knowing how clearly she silhouetted her own loneliness, demonstrating how quickly her youth had fled. 'And now it's your turn,' she concluded.

'Not much to tell,' he assured her. 'Compared to you I'm practically a stay-at-home. Although they did call me

the "Wild Man" when I was younger. A dare-devil fool,
that's what my father called me. Up until——'

'Until your sister's accident?'

'Ah. You know about that too?'

'Kitchen gossip,' she said, feeling a compassion for
him that went beyond all bonds.

'She never would have gone out on the river if I hadn't
teased and dared her. Never could let things alone. She
always had to do everything big brother did. And the
race was the most stupid thing imaginable. There was
debris in the chanel. She must have been going ninety
miles an hour when her boat hit the floating tree trunk. It
threw them both almost a hundred feet. They were both
dead before—well—it was all my fault, and the cloud has
hung over me ever since. If only I could have that little
time to live over again.'

'And that's what drives Penn Wilderman?'

He crushed her against him with one strong arm. She
could feel his fingers sink into her shoulder. 'And that's
what drives Penn Wilderman,' he said bitterly. 'I'd better
get to bed.'

His hand relaxed. Phil rubbed her shoulder where the
fingers had dug craters, and then stood up. As soon as he
heard her move, he came up too. Holding his hand, she
guided him up the stairs and into his own bedroom. Still
holding her, he took himself to the big armchair next to
the bed, and sat down.

'Eyedrops,' she offered, trying to get a little normality
into her voice.

'Yes, please. Not many more times to go,' he
answered. 'Lord, doesn't that sound good?'

She dimmed the overhead lights, found the drops on
his dresser, and administered them. 'Hey, what's the
hurry?' he grumbled. 'No sooner do you get the pads off

than you flood me. I wanted to get a look at you.'

And that's just what I *don't* want, she told herself.
We've gone this far in the dark, and I want to keep it that
way until the last possible minute! 'Don't touch those
pads,' she warned. 'It's just a few days before the grand
unveiling, and all will be revealed!'

'You make it sound like a Hallowe'en project,' he
complained.

'Well, this is no time to ruin weeks of work,' she told
him. 'Be optimistic, Penn.'

'Oh, I am,' he returned. There was just a touch of
sarcasm, just a touch of despair. 'But have you ever
thought—suppose I go down to the doctor on Monday, in
all my darkness, and he takes the pads off—and the
world is still dark?'

'It won't happen,' she assured him. 'I just *know*
everything will be OK. Here are your pyjamas, at the foot
of the bed. I have to check up on Robbie.'

'Damn that kid,' he said. 'You married me, not
Robbie.'

'I know, but he needs somebody to——'

'So do I,' he snarled at her. 'Go ahead!'

The depth of his anger reached her. She reacted by
running. None of her experience had taught her how to
deal with an angry husband. But kids——

So Robbie, still following a horror movie on Channel
Six, was quickly disabused of the notion that his sweet
lovable mother would let him sit up until midnight. She
hustled the boy into the shower, picked up the clothes he
had strewn across the floor, and went back to her own
room.

An hour later, bathed, perfumed, but not yet calm, she
stood by her window. Her translucent pink nightgown,
the one that reached her ankles, but hung loosely at her

shoulders on two shoe-string bands, flared around her. Half dreaming, she watched the star patterns. There was a noise from next door, a strangled cough.

Surely Penn must be asleep by now, she told herself, but could not stop the movement that carried her through the connecting door into his bedroom. Penn was in bed, apparently asleep, but the lights were still on. And *his* clothes were strewn around the room. He has an excuse, she told herself fiercely as she bent to the task, and then laid out the clean things he would need in the morning.

He stirred in the bed as she finished. She froze in position, sure that her vague movements, her mutterings, might have awakened him. When he became quiet again she edged cautiously over to the door and flicked off the light switch. The change from light to dark blinded her. She blinked her eyes, holding fast until some of the darkness became less dark, some of the shadows became more distinct. Gently, she whispered across the rug towards her own room, then stopped and came back to kneel beside him. Her gentle hands brushed the lock of hair back from his forehead, and offered a loving kiss. And before she could move both his hands snatched at her.

'Gotcha,' he whispered, pulling her closer.

'Darn you, I thought you were asleep! I——'

'I wanted to see you.'

'I'm not going to have you take those pads off your eyes,' she stormed at him. 'You're worse than Robbie is, for goodness' sake!'

'I don't need to see you with my eyes,' he contradicted. 'Be still.' It was a command she could not refuse. She didn't want to refuse. His hands had given up their imperious grip on her upper arms, and were now shaping her face, running through the softness of her long hair.

She knelt there beside the bed, ignoring the complaints from her leg muscles. Hardly receiving them, for a fact. All the lines of communication to her brain were tied up in the sensual assault those hands were making as they dropped gently down on to her shoulders, pushed the straps of her nightgown away, and coursed down on to the proud pulsing mounds of her aroused breasts. Somewhere in the distance she could hear the hiss of his breath as he caressed and measured the fullness of her, the proud upward tilting of her womanhood.

One of his hands slipped downwards brushing the gown off her hips, as it explored the softness of her rib cage, the sharp inward curve of her waist, the burgeoning outward bulge of her full hip. And then back upwards again, to torture her breast.

Madness raced through her mind as she fought herself. One half of her screamed for more. The other half kept at a litany. *It's only a temporary marriage. It's only temporary!* There was little doubt which half might win—until he laughed. 'No doubt about it, old girl,' he commented, 'You are a whole lot of woman.'

'No doubt,' she whispered bitterly as she scrambled away from the bed and restored her nightgown. Dear old girl. There's nothing special about *this* man, she told herself. He's just like all the others. All cats look grey on a dark night! Damn him! It was hard to lock in the whimper of anger and frustration.

He sat up in the bed. She could see the shadows moving, and took another step backwards. 'I didn't mean to make you cry,' he said sombrely. 'Come back here.'

'Well, you managed to, no matter what you meant!' She retreated into her own room and slammed the door behind her. It wasn't *all* his fault, her conscience proclaimed. Maybe not, she thought angrily, but if I don't blame *him*, I have to blame myself—and I don't want to do that! Wearily she stumbled across the room in the dark and flung herself down on the bed.

It was a wasted effort. She tossed and turned all night, but sleep would not come. When the fingers of dawn light touched on the trees outside she gave it all up, went for a quick shower, and hastily crammed herself into fresh underwear, a pair of old dungarees and a T-shirt. Rose and the maids were off on vacation. Harry had gone. Frank lived out in an apartment over the garage, and Mr Yu would be coming in. The old man would make the dinner, but breakfast and lunch were in her hands. Make-up was not worth the effort, but she did take time to brush out her hair before she went down to the kitchen.

The only solution, she decided, was to keep her fingers busy and her mind empty. She scavenged up utensils, broke half a dozen eggs, and scrambled them. Sausages went into the microwave. Bread went into the toaster. The coffee pot began to bubble. She scattered a few plates on the huge kitchen table, added coffee mugs, and plodded determinedly back up the stairs to serve as Penn's guide. He hardly seemed to need one. She went into the room and closed the door behind her. He was just coming back into the room, followed by a spiral of steam from his shower. He was using his towel to scrub at his unruly hair.

It was a sight she had never seen before. The dominant male, in all his naked glory. A week ago she would have screamed and run. Today she stood with her back against the door, trying to breathe so softly that he could not hear. And admired. He was every bit as male as she was female. Sleek, muscular, broad shouldered, narrow hips.

Strong heavy thighs—and everything else, beautifully proportioned. He fumbled for a moment at his clothing, and she almost broke away from the door to help. Almost. His groping hands found everything where she had placed it the night before. Very slowly, it seemed, he balanced on one leg at a time and struggled into his shorts. Slacks followed, and then a sports shirt.

She was congratulating herself on not being discovered as he bent to lace up his shoes. 'Enjoy the show, did you?' he asked casually. He stood up and brushed at his slacks as he turned directly toward her. Startled, she looked at his eyes. The pads were still in place.

'Damn you,' she muttered.

'The door squeaks,' he told her as he started to move towards the sound of her voice. 'See everything you wanted?'

He was within reach at that moment. Her hand seemed to move involuntarily. It jumped to his forehead, and her fingers combed through his hair, smoothing and shaping it. 'That's nice,' he said. 'We must do this more often.'

There was just enough sarcasm in his voice to bring her back to reality. She snapped her hand back. Her finger tips were burning. 'I suppose you've come to take me to breakfast?'

'Damn you,' she sighed. His hand dropped on her shoulder. She turned, opened the door, and led him out into the hall and down the stairs. Robbie clattered up behind them, half shouting a greeting, passed them on the stairs, and hesitated just long enough to give his 'new' mother a light kiss. He was gone into the kitchen before the pair of them reached the bottom step.

'Damn kid,' Penn commented. She almost jumped, startled by his first words outside the bedroom.

'Don't talk like that,' she retorted fiercely. 'He's a sensitive boy—and both words are operative.'

'Me too,' he chuckled. 'I'm a sensitive boy too. And he's stealing my act.'

'I don't know what you mean,' she snapped. He demonstrated. But his kiss wasn't aimed at her cheek, and in no way could it be called fleeting. When they both came through the kitchen door Robbie, who was half-way through the scrambled eggs, laughed like a fool.

She guided Penn over to his chair, and then glared at the boy. 'What are you laughing at, you——' She stamped her foot on the hard floor, too late to remember she had no shoes on.

'You and Dad,' the boy chuckled through another mouthful of food. 'You don't *hafta* hide in the hall to get kissed. I know all about that stuff. Why is your face so red, Phil?'

'Because you don't know all you think you know,' she snarled. 'And there's nothing I hate worse than cheerful people in the morning! Leave your father some sausages!'

Robbie and Penn spent most of the morning together in his library. Conspiring about something, Phil thought as she rushed through a brief dusting and rearranging, and then went upstairs. I'm angry. Why? At whom? And had no answer.

Robbie had heard the 'cleanliness' message. His room was as neat as a new pin, bed made up, magazines put away, clothes on hangers. And we'll see how long that lasts, Phil snorted, as she made her way down the hall to Penn's room. Everything was as it had been earlier—except that that magnificent body was missing. She picked up the wet towel. It was a crazy thing to do, but she rubbed it gently against her cheek before dropping it into the clothes hamper. His pyjamas were still huddled up at the foot of the bed, unused. She re-folded them and put them back in the drawer. And then the bed.

It was a very difficult bed to make. Not that it was over-large, oddly formed. Every time her hand reached for a pillow or a sheet or a blanket it just seemed to linger, as if some sustenance could be drawn from its emptiness. 'Come on, girl,' she told herself. 'You're going down with something. Get to work.' It might have taken something more than words—horse whips, perhaps—but a thump of feet on the stairs served instead. She finished making up the bed in twenty seconds flat, and ran for her own room. She spent the rest of the day trying to avoid everyone else who lived in the house. And since they all suddenly appeared to be very busy, it wasn't too hard a job.

Saturday night Robbie served as his father's guide. Phil could hear them from her hiding-place next door. There was considerable laughter. It served to warm up a very tiny portion of her chilled heart. For all the muddling, all the interference, all the upset she had caused, at least one good thing had resulted. Robbie and his father had come to appreciate each other.

Exhausted from a sleepless night and a fugitive day, Phil went to bed early, slept the sleep of the just, and awakened to a household already in motion. She could hear multiple thumps up and down the stairs, banging noises from the area of the kitchen, and motor noises from a car at the front door. She checked her bedside clock. Seven o'clock. Sunday morning? It seemed impossible. She threw back the covers, snatched at her heavy blue robe, and cautiously peered into Penn's room. Empty.

Through his room, just in case, and out into the hall.

Empty. Down the stairs and into the kitchen. Robbie was stuffing his face with buttered toast. His father, fully dressed, across the table from him, was deep in thought. Harry was back, standing by the sink, a big smile on his face.

'Tarpon?' the boy asked through a mouthful of bread.

'Bonito,' Harry returned. 'Everything.'

Robbie looked up just in time to catch Phil standing in the door. 'Isn't it great, Mom?' he cried.

The two adults turned in her direction. 'Yes,' she managed. 'It's great. What?'

'Fishing,' Robbie said. 'Dad's arranged for me to go down to Catalina for a week of deep-sea fishing! Harry's coming with me, and we'll camp out on the boat and— wow!'

'Wow indeed. You'll need more breakfast than that.'

'I can't wait. The plane leaves at eight o'clock. We've only an hour to get to the airport, but I'm all packed, and—Mom? Didn't anybody tell you?'

'No, I guess not.' Phil tried to sound cheerful. It was bad enough to have to smile at seven o'clock on a Sunday morning, but—no, nobody had told her, had hinted, had even suggested. Tomorrow his father comes out from under the bandages. Today we ship Harry and Robbie off for a week of deep-sea fishing. Mr Yu is too old to travel but lives in his own little house out at the back. Frank is required to take Penn to the doctor's. And that leaves only me, she thought. What about me?

But none of her agitation showed in her voice. 'No, that's OK,' she told the boy. 'I get seasick just thinking about water. A whole week. I'll bet you'll have fun.' She slipped into the chair between her two 'men' and snatched at the last piece of toast on the plate. Harry thumped a mug of black coffee down in front of her.

'Yeah, well, women have that kind of trouble,' Robbie pontificated from the depths of his thirteen years of experience with life. 'Only—I wish Dad were coming. But of course, with his eyes and all—next time, Dad?'

'Next time, Robbie.' It was the first time Penn had spoken, and it didn't sound all that enthusiastic—or is it something else, Phil asked herself. She was straining, these days, to register nuances—to read behind the words. And there was definitely something there to be read.

'We gotta go,' Harry contributed. 'All the stuff's in the car. Come on, kid.'

The car was moving before Phil could get to the front door. She waved a belated goodbye to the back of the vehicle, and was rewarded when Robbie stuck his head out the window and blew her a kiss.

Penn was still at table, nursing his coffee-mug, a dour look on his face. Phil plumped herself down in the nearest chair and pulled her mug over in front of her. The coffee had cooled just about to the edge of drinkability. 'It'll be all right,' she said softly. 'He'll enjoy every minute of it. And he will be safe, won't he?'

'He'll be safe,' he returned gruffly. 'Happy, I don't know. Safe, I'm sure of.'

'So what brought all this on so suddenly?' She leaned both elbows on the table, the coffee-mug treasured between her hands. Penn was wearing that office mask, a look of non-committal interest that gave nothing away. His fingers were drumming on the table-top. She remembered where they last had drummed, and blushed. 'Is there something wrong, Penn?'

'Wrong? How the hell could there be anything wrong?' he roared at her. His chair fell over as he moved violently away from the table. 'I'm going back upstairs. You needn't come. When Frank comes back from the airport send him up to see me.' He stomped out.

She heard him stumble on the stairs, and repressed the urge to run after him. Somehow or another, she knew, he was not prepared to accept any help from her this day. This is strange, she told herself as she started to clean up the kitchen. Sometimes I feel very married, and sometimes I feel—like a stranger in their midst.

It was another sunny day—the first day of March, for a fact. Spring was hustling about in the valley where the American and the Sacramento rivers met. She snapped on the kitchen radio as she worked. Ski-ing conditions were still perfect up in the mountains, forty miles away, with deep-packed snow. She stretched up on tiptoe to look out of the small kitchen window. Mr Yu was transplanting flowers out of his greenhouse into the beds in the back garden. In the middle of the garden a pair of robins were strutting. She felt the need to share, dropped the rest of the dishes hastily into the dishwasher, and dashed upstairs to dress.

She wandered around the gardens all the remainder of the morning, and then went back in, having promised Mr Yu that she would see to the evening meal. The house was like a tomb.

As she headed for the kitchen Frank came out of the living-room and started for the front door. 'He's in the library,' he said in passing. 'He tells me to get out and take the rest of the day off. You be OK?'

'Me? Oh, yes.' Just to be sure, after Frank had left Phil went along to the library and cracked the door slightly open, just enough to see her husband sitting at his desk, a glass paperweight in his hands, and an almost-lost look on his face. As gently as she knew how, she closed the door and went back out into the kitchen.

They shared dinner in the kitchen. 'It's not worth carrying everything to the dining-room just for the two of us,' he said when she went to get him. He looked tired, as if all the little tensions had become one big one. There was no discussion at the table. He ate the Western omelette she put in front of him, drank the coffee, enjoyed a slice of the apple pie, and said nothing.

An hour later, having stood the silence as long as she could, she got up and started on the dishes. It was growing dark outside. She took a quick look. Thunderclouds obscured the setting sun. She could hear the boom and rumble in the distance, as the storm did its work.

'It looks like a bad storm,' she commented. 'I think I'll have to put the lights on.'

'Yeah, you do that,' he said bitterly. 'At least one of us might as well be in the light.'

'Oh Penn,' she sighed. 'Please. It will all be over tomorrow. You'll see.'

'You're damn well right,' he returned. 'Everything will be over tomorrow. I'm going upstairs.' Fighting the chill in her heart, Phil came around the table and offered her hand. He brushed it aside. 'I don't need any guide dogs,' he grumbled as he pushed back his chair and felt his way along the wall to the door. 'Just keep out of my way.'

She collapsed in a chair. It was worse than she had ever expected. *Just keep out of my way! Tomorrow it will all be over!* Her head ached, as if the storm had shifted to the inside of her head. 'Oh, Penn,' she moaned as she dropped her head into her arms on the table. The tears that followed upset her more than anything else. Practical Philomena just didn't cry. The world was too full of things to be done. There was no room for crybabies. She knuckled the last drop of water from her eyes, and marched out into the living-room.

By nine-thirty she had read the same page of her novel over for the twentieth time, her headache had abated slightly, and she hadn't heard a sound in the house since seven o'clock. 'Well, there's no use struggling,' she lectured herself. 'Staying up late won't put off tomorrow. It's going to be, come hell or high water.'

Phil got up, stretched mightily, and then performed the nightly ritual, going around the house, locking windows and doors, and setting the burglar alarm. It was something that Harry usually did—and just the doing of it reminded her that Harry and Robbie were far away. Another little stab in her heart, that. If Robbie were at home perhaps they might have talked together—played games—built up some camaraderie? She turned off all but the night lights, and went upstairs slowly, feeling like some old hag whose days were numbered. There was no sound from Penn's room. The thunder was still working its way around the basin of the valley, and rain was thundering for admission. Not one to be plagued by storms, she felt something different in this one. Some evil, trying to reach out and pluck her from the safety of her home.

She closed her door behind her, then trailed clothes across the floor—doing just what she hated most when Robbie did it. By the time she reached the bathroom she had completely stripped.

The hot water revived her. Shower cap tucked tightly around her mass of hair, she revelled in the beat of the water on her skin. The sounds of the shower shut out the storm—and everything else. The soap felt sensuous as she lathered her hands and rubbed them up and down her body—and dreamed. If it could be Penn's hands? Penn's arms? Too much to hope for. She reached for the cold water and smashed the dream to bits under an icy deluge.

The bath towels were immense. She used one to dry herself, then wrapped the other around her, sarong-fashion. Her hair was dripping at its ends, where the shower cap had failed its mission. A little brushing, she assured herself, and walked out into the dark bedroom. There was someone there. Penn. Standing by the windows, listening to the rush of water against the panes.

'Penn? You wanted something?'

'My eyedrops.'

'Oh! I thought you said yesterday that you wouldn't want another——'

'Well, I do.' How could everything that seemed so warm and loving turn into such coldness, she asked herself. Have I done anything to deserve all that?

'All right,' she returned, using her softest voice. 'Sit on the bed here, and——'

Whatever it was he wanted, it wasn't eyedrops. He seized her proffered hand and yanked her up against him. She backed away and he followed. Backed until the inside of her knees banged into the side of the bed. 'What—I don't understand,' she managed. 'What do you want, Penn? Have you been drinking?'

'Not a drop. You don't really understand, Philomena? I'm your husband, and it's dark inside here. I want a little comfort.'

'Inside? You want me to put on a light?'

'I want you to *be* a light, Philomena!' He pushed. Trapped against the bed, she fell over backwards and suddenly he was on top of her.

'What—Penn!' The towel was gone. Ripped away and discarded over his shoulder. His robe followed. 'Penn!' Not a scream, but a soft reproach. 'I didn't expect this. It wasn't part of our——'

'Bargain? This is a marriage, not a bargain. Did you expect I could lie there next door to you and never have an inclination?'

'Is that what it is, Penn? Just an inclination? You need someone to pick on, and I'm the nearest? Is that why you sent Robbie and Harry away?' It was getting harder to talk, to reason, than she had ever supposed. His hands were roving over her face, along the line of her neck, down to her breasts. His weight was no longer a burden, but some sort of promise. That's all you need do, she told herself fiercely. Talk to him, be calm, keep cool. But her traitorous body wanted nothing of the kind.

She could hardly suppress the moan as his hands shifted lower, to her hips and below, and his lips took their place at her breast. The breath blew out of her as wild spasms shot through her nervous system, and reported in to her brain. So many feelings, so many reports, that her control centre was at the point of overload.

'Don't. Please, Penn—don't.' A weak effort—her strained voice trying to give one answer while her rolling hips gave another. His hands stopped.

'You don't want this?'

'I—no!' That last word took all her remaining control.

'Then fight me off,' he snarled.

She was fully stretched out, her nerves jangling, perspiration pouring from her, her legs spread. 'I won't fight you,' she sighed. 'I can't. But it isn't part of our bargain *or* our marriage, Penn.' The hands started moving again, his lips followed. Not a mad physical assault, but a teasing that drew her out from herself, sent her tossing and turning out of control.

'You don't want me to do this?' A hiss out of the darkness. Her eyes were shut tight. She could not muster

an answer, but her tossing, squirming body told him all
he wanted to know. Those lips teased at her, nibbling her
ear-lobes, running channels of fire down to her breasts,
across her stomach, until she could stand no more. Her
hands snatched at his hair. He hesitated for a moment in
his wild pursuit. But instead of pushing him away she
pulled him closer, hard against the softness of her. Her
mouth was half open. It was hard to breathe. When he
came into her it was like a benison.

There was a sharp momentary pain, hidden quickly in
the glory that followed, as their wild passion drove them
up to and over the edge. She screamed at the joy of it,
wrapping arms and legs around him, refusing to let him
go. After that one last surge he was strangely quiet, his
hands holding his weight up off her. The fever in her
mind gradually subsided, until she recognised the real
world. *So that's what it's all about, she told herself. How
wonderful!* She felt a tiny chill as air moved across her wet
skin. *What wonders marriage can bring. I love him more
than ever.* The glory of it filled her. And then he spoiled
everything.

He rolled away from her and sat up on the edge of the
bed, holding his head. 'Penn?' she queried. 'It was——'

'I didn't mean that to happen, Philomena,' he groaned.
'I didn't expect that you would still be a virgin—not at
your age. I—I'm sorry. I'll try to make it up to you.'

She sat up carefully behind him, feeling the ache in her
bones and muscles, feeling the despair sweeping over
her. *It was all a mistake, that's what he's telling me now?
He may have wanted* it, *but he doesn't want* me. *Oh,
God!*

'Make what up to me?' Her voice was like glass, ready
to shatter at any moment.

'All of that,' he returned. 'I don't even know what to call it.'

The glory had gone out of life. She felt as deep in blackness as he must, behind those terrible pads. He wanted a woman, she told herself fiercely, and I'm the only one available! 'The word they commonly use is rape,' she said, and the bitterness rolled off her tongue, poisoning every word. 'Rape,' she threw after him as he stumbled off in the darkness to his own room. 'Rape,' she whispered against the door that he slammed behind him. It wasn't rape, and she knew it without question. Seduction, yes, but not rape. She was trying to hurt him with words as much as he had hurt her. He had turned all that beauty, all that wonderful experience, into something that animals do, without feeling. Something precious had died in that dark room. She wept for it.

CHAPTER TEN

DESPITE the agonies, the tears, the recriminations, Phil finally fell asleep, and when she awakened the California sun was bright in the sky. She sat up quickly. The room and bed showed the ravages of the previous night. Her bedside clock reported ten in the morning. All she could think of was Penn. This was the morning he was to have his eye pads removed. She had to be gone before he came back. The idea rolled over and over in her troubled mind. She had married him to help keep Robbie in Sacramento, and that task had been accomplished. He had always said it would be a short marriage—a temporary device. But she had not counted on falling in love with him!

And last night, wasn't that the confirmation? He had taken her to emotional peaks of which she had never dreamed, and then cruelly dumped her off the mountain. She dressed hurriedly. Slacks and sweater, her long curls tied back carelessly into a pony-tail, and low-heeled shoes. A few personal items crammed into a case. Leave the rest, but hurry! Down the stairs for the last time, pausing to salute the Pirate and squeezing out one last tear for the Lady. Steal by the kitchen door. Rose is at work, singing at the top of her lungs. Hurry.

No time for goodbyes. Robbie would just have to understand. Out of the door into the sunshine, around the house to the garage. Her little car, shining like new, started immediately. As soon as the engine settled into a regular beat she drove around the house to the front door.

Up the stairs, into the hall, where her suitcase waited. Back to the door—too late. She could hear the imperious purr of the Cadillac as it swept around the drive and halted just behind her own car. Too late. Her hand moved towards the doorknob, but before she could grip it, the door flew open. Penn.

He stood in the doorway, staring at her. The pads were gone. A pair of dark sunglasses covered eyes that could definitely see. Eyes that followed her as she shrank against the left wall, out of his reach, out of his way. He had that facial expression that one sees on the statues of Caesars—autocratic, commanding, solemn.

'You can see again,' she managed to whisper.

'Who the hell are you?' he snapped. He took off the glasses. Dark brown, almost black eyes searched her up and down. 'What's going on?' he snarled. 'I know you, but——' Some thought snatched his attention away, he strode down the hall and started up the stairs. She heard him stop, half-way up.

It was worse than she had expected. 'Who the hell are you?' I guess that's a great way to sum up a marriage, she gibbered to herself as she grabbed the suitcase and ran. She was in the car, engine running, when he came back to the door. 'Hey, you!' he yelled. The old car jumped as she jammed it into gear. Gravel spurted as the wheels spun. She accelerated down the drive, one eye on her rear-view mirror. He came down the stairs, hastily restored the dark glasses to the bridge of his nose, and watched, hands on hips as she turned left and disappeared from sight.

Traffic was heavy, as it was every Monday morning in the centre of the city. Phil found it hard to concentrate.

'Running away from your husband.' The phrase kept repeating itself, pounding in her ears like a dirge. 'Yes,' she yelled to the world at large, 'and if he catches me——' And then she came to her senses. What do you mean, *if he catches me*? Whatever gives you the idea that he is even going to try? You know where you rate, Philomena. But just in case!

Just in case, she swung the wheel hard left on P Street, heading westward towards the river. The parking lot at Pacific Mines and Metals seemed full. She pulled up in front of the building and parked in the No Parking zone. A guard came out of the building, waving his hand, and came to a full stop when he saw who she was.

'Good morning, Mrs Wilderman. Will you be here long?' Listen to the anxiety, she told herself grimly as she powered past him into the building. He's helping me break the law, and doesn't dare do otherwise because of Penn. If it were not for Penn, he would have thrown me in the river and had my car towed away. The idea made her angry, and anger overcame fright. She stalked into the typing pool as if she were a queen. All the noises stopped. She gave them all a vacant smile, a quick wave, and slid into one of the empty booths. Her fingers were slippery with perspiration. Phil wiped them off on her slacks, punched up the computer terminal, entered the Personnel Access Code, and sat back as the computer unrolled all the names of employees starting with the letter P. P for Peabody. She slapped at the stop key.

And there I am, she snarled at herself. One entry in a thousand. Peabody, Philomena Mary. File Number 621. Address and telephone number. Date of first employment. Pay increases. Promotions. Commendations. Health record, next of kin. Ten years of work, all summarised in green on the display panel. She glared at it, doing her best to hold back the tears. You can't drive in California while crying, she told herself. It's against the law.

'Phil?' She looked up over her shoulder. Harriet, the new supervisor, stood there, and the last thing I need, Phil told herself, is a long conversation—or someone looking over my shoulder to see what I'm doing. The screen glittered at her as the electronic circuits waited for further instructions. Her hand moved to the keyboard and typed Peabody, Philomena Mary, File Number 621. ERASE. She slapped down hard on the command. The computer ruminated for a second, then flashed a message: 'Are you sure?' She dragged her hand back for just a second and typed 'Yes'. *Peabody Philomena Mary*, glared at her for a second, then disappeared from sight and from memory. Just to be sure, when the computer displayed the query sign she ordered it to search for Peabody, Philomena Mary, File Number 621. The machine grumbled for a second, then reported 'No such file exists'. Now—he'll never find me, she told herself as she turned off the terminal and struggled to her feet. *If he ever wants to!*

'Have to hurry,' she mumbled to Harriet as she brushed by her and headed for the street. 'Double-parked.'

It was a long slow drive out along Route Fifty, heading for Rancho Cordova. Twice she had to pull off the highway to wipe her eyes. 'I won't cry,' she told herself. Nobody seemed to notice, not even the Highway Patrolman bustling by her on his motor-cycle. Crying on the highway was *not* a crime, it appeared. A stop at the local shopping mall brought enough food for her to

hibernate for a few days. At one o'clock, when she let
herself into the old farm house, she was dead tired. Too
tired to carry in the groceries. She snatched out the milk
and the frozen orange juice, put them in the freezer, and
stumbled off up the stairs to bed. And that took care of
Monday.

Gloomy Tuesday. The skies were packed with
thunderheads, close enough to rattle the windows in the
old house. Philomena managed to climb out of bed and
paddle her way down to the kitchen. Coffee was the only
answer. Her head felt as if an elephant had stepped on it.
Her nose was stuffed up, cheeks red, and eyes rimmed
with black. 'Change the bed,' she reminded herself as her
hands fumbled for the makings. 'You've cried the pillow-
case to death.' As the pot perked she huddled herself up
into a little ball on the window seat, and stared out to
where the garden once had been. All gone. The garden,
the farm, the clump of willows that stood by the creek.
And even the creek itself, diverted to make room for
another high-rise.

Her conscience nagged her. 'Rape,' she had shouted
after him, and it hadn't been. Seduction—well, yes—but
there's no law against seducing your wife. And she had *so*
enjoyed it all. All except the last five minutes, when his
words had spoiled all his deeds. But it wasn't rape, and
her accusation had no foundation. 'I owe him an
apology,' she told herself as she reached for the
telephone. Her hand stopped before she picked up the
instrument. Talk to him? I'd sooner wrestle an alligator!
I don't *dare* to talk to him. Or face him, for that matter.
I'll—I'll write him a nice letter?

Thirty minutes and two cups of coffee later she was
still reaching for the telephone. I've *got* to call somebody,

she told herself as she dialled her sister Sally's number. There was no answer. She tried it again three times during the day, with the same result. Disgusted with the world, she suddenly remembered the groceries, still stacked in the car. Wrapped in her faded old green robe, she ventured out. It was raining as if someone had broken a dam somewhere in the sky overhead; coming down in sheets.

'Sunny California,' she muttered as she dodged back into the house, dressed, squeezed herself into her heavy rainwear, and went back for the groceries. And felt as stupid as she must have looked. While she was forcing herself into her sou'wester coat the thunderstorms had rolled on towards the mountains, and the sun was sparkling at her.

By Wednesday she felt well enough to eat a decent meal. Put it all behind you, she ordered. It's time for Practical Pill to get her feet on the ground and go about living. She had a place to live, no job, and not a devil of a lot of money in her bank account. The house—well, it belonged to all the girls, not just to herself. To sell it would require action by the Trust, a couple of bank officials whose names she had already forgotten. So the first order of things must be to get a new job. She settled down with copies of both Sacramento papers and began to scan the sits. vac.

A very hard job that, scanning the ads. The print was small, and behind it lurked Penn's face. Smiling, laughing, accusing, pursuing, loving Penn. His face swam in miniature behind the advertising, then grew and grew until it filled the page, and held her, bound her, until the tears came to blot it all out. When she dried her eyes, the cycle started again. She threw the paper down and dialled Sally. Still no answer.

There were still two sisters left. But Deborah had gone to Tahoe for a ski-ing vacation, and if Samantha were actually at home she was not the person with whom Phil could share a confidence. So she put the telephone and the papers away and threw herself into a fury of house-cleaning. Her mind steadied under the diversion. At four o'clock that afternoon the doorbell rang, and she found herself running down the stairs in eagerness, almost singing. He had finally come!

She threw back the lock and opened the door expectantly. And there, standing on the bottom step, so that his eyes were just at the level of hers, was Penn. She brushed away the tears and stared. Black eyes, focusing on her, sending out pulses of anger, massive anger.

'Mrs Wilderman, I believe,' he said, in a voice that sounded like a steel rasp at work. She backed slowly away from him as he came up the steps and into the hall. It was as if Penn's anger were a terrible wind, forcing her backwards step by step down the hall, until she ran into the back wall. *I need to make a decision,* she screamed at herself. *No you don't,* that inner voice assured her. *The decision was made for you, a long time ago.*

All of Phil's resolution and fierce independence disappeared in one crashing collapse. She abandoned dignity and pride. With tears streaming down her face she ran straight ahead and threw her arms around her husband's waist. 'Oh, God, Penn,' she groaned into his sweater. 'I need you.'

He stood rigidly still for a moment as she huddled herself against him. *He's going to refuse me, she thought in panic.* But she was mistaken. His arms came around her, pressing her even tighter into the safe nest. His lips brushed lightly against her hair. So lightly that she could barely feel it. 'It's all right, love,' he said. 'I'm here. Everything will be all right.'

And she knew it would be so.

It took more time for the tears to slow and all the time he held her close, crooning into her hair.

'You didn't forget,' she finally stammered. 'I thought you had forgotten me!'

'I've never forgotten anything about you, since the day we met,' he said, suddenly very solemn, very believable. 'Everything except what you looked like, Philomena. You've been a rascal, *young* lady.'

'Yes,' she admitted freely. 'I—I didn't know how to tell you, and——'

'No matter,' he laughed. 'If I fell in love with you blindly—how much easier it is to love what I can see. There's an old Roman poem that goes something like *How much stronger Love must be, sweeter the touch, the kiss, the mind, if Love be blind*. You're a beautiful woman, Mrs Wilderman. Come on. Blow.' He offered her a handkerchief that seemed half an acre in size, then tucked her under his arm. She squeezed up against him, unwilling to be an inch from her anchor.

'I'm sorry,' she offered tentatively.

'I'm sorry? Is that all I get from my run-away wife? I'm sorry?'

'I—I don't know what else to say.'

'If it's conceivable, after all the things I've done to you, Phil, for you to say *I love you*, that would be a good place to start. Can you forgive me?'

'I—I don't need to forgive you.' Happy for the first time in days, she almost giggled at his serious face looming over her. 'I love you. I'm pretty stupid. I didn't find it out until the day we were married, Penn, but—I love you.'

'That's enough for now,' he returned as he leaned over and kissed her gently. 'Let's go home, wife.'

'Whatever you say,' she said, and did not recognise the proportion of her surrender until they were at the front door. The telephone rang behind them in the living-room. She stopped, and used the momentary break to quell her panic.

'Leave it alone,' he grumbled, reaching out for her.

'I—I can't,' she stammered, stalling for time to regain control of her very scattered senses. 'I—I have this thing about telephones. If I don't answer it, I'll have bad luck all the rest of the day!'

'That's about as crazy an excuse as I've heard,' he chuckled. 'The telephone is your servant, not your master. You don't *have* to jump every time it rings at you.' He did a quick scan of her worried little face. 'Or maybe you do. Well, I'll give you two minutes to get back out here.'

'Or else?'

'Or else I'll come and get you, wife.' He added a small push in the middle of her back to get her moving. She ran the rest of the way.

'Phil? It's Sally here. I think you're in a lot of trouble. Phil? Are you there?'

'I'm here, dear. What trouble could I be in?'

'Well, we just got back from our trip to Los Angeles about three hours ago, and the telephone was ringing when we drove up to the house. Your husband, it was. Mad as a hatter. Wanted to know where the family home was. I gave him the address—Phil, if you're in trouble, you'd better get out of there quick. He means to get you.'

'You're too late,' Phil giggled nervously, not quite sure of the status of things. 'He's already got me.'

'What in the world is going on, Phil?'

'I—you wouldn't believe it if I told you, Sally. I—I think I've managed to get him just where he wants me. I can't talk now. He hates to be kept waiting. Call me here tomorrow. If I answer you'll know I'm in a *lot* of trouble. G'bye.'

She barely managed to get the instrument back in its cradle. Her feet were busy running before her hand was finished 'putting down'.

'Relax,' he said, catching her on the fly, like an expert outfielder. 'You've still got thirty seconds.'

'Oh,' she sighed, out of breath and courage at the same time.

'But there's no need to waste all that allotted time,' he continued smoothly, and proceeded to kiss her very thoroughly. Even more shaken than before, she leaned against his arm as he helped her out to the Cadillac. Frank held the door for them. It was not until they were enclosed in the moving cocoon, out on the highway, that she regained a little aplomb.

'You used more than thirty seconds,' she accused him, doing her best to glare. 'What if we were really in a hurry?'

'First, lady, you need to remember that the boss doesn't have to account for his time. Got it?'

'I—yes. I—I've got it.'

'Good. Secondly, Robbie and Harry will be back tomorrow morning on the nine o'clock flight.'

'But that's—that's hours away.' The spirit was willing to dare, but her shaky voice demonstrated her weakness.

'Yes, isn't it?' A broad grin spread across his face, and

a devilish look gleamed in those dark, dark eyes of his. She shivered. Whatever it was he was planning was bound to be—bound to be! She shifted uneasily in her seat, clenched her hands together in her lap, and did her best to admire the scenery.

They were back at the mansion before she could account for the time. Penn helped her out of the car, and before she could muster the scream that ought to have followed, he swept her up in his arms and carried her up the stairs to the door. 'Put the car away, Frank, and take the rest of the day off,' he called over his shoulder.

Murder, she thought wildly? He's getting rid of all the witnesses? He's going to kiss me to death? Phil's head kept spinning as he kicked the front door closed behind them and bustled her into the living-room. The couch bounced as he dropped her there.

'Now then, Philomena.' He pulled one of the straight-backed chairs over directly in front of her, reversed it, and sat down with arms resting on its back, almost nose to nose with her.

'Yes?' Calm, cool Philomena—well, almost. With those pads on his eyes, and then his glasses, she had never noticed how neat and precise his nose was. How— Roman? It was irresistible. She leaned forward and planted a kiss on its end.

'Now cut that out,' he growled. 'First, we have a great deal of talking to do, you and I.'

'Dictatorial,' she muttered. 'Pompous. What you mean is you're going to talk and I'm going to listen, right?'

'No, it's not right,' he sighed. 'So I'm a little pompous. You're a whole lot impulsive. And neither one of us is really going to change.'

'I—suppose so,' she returned apologetically. 'Mama

always said you can't marry a man, meaning to change him to what you want. What did you want to talk about?'

'You and me,' he said. 'Your mother was some smart cookie. How old were you when you became housemother?'

'I—seventeen. I was old for my age, though.'

'Of course you were.' His hand ruffled through her loose hair. 'And you kept on being older than your age, didn't you? That was a mean trick you played on me.'

'I—I didn't,' she returned indignantly. 'It was all in your mind. I never said I—you decided right away that I was some old biddy—what Harry called me, an old broad!'

'But you knew what I was thinking, and you never set me straight. Why?'

'I—at first I thought it didn't matter. We wouldn't have met again, ever. Until you suddenly had to have a new wardrobe for your son. It's all your fault! How did I know Robbie needed clothes, for goodness' sake?'

'He didn't.' There—in the background. He's laughing at me, she thought. I can hear it. Her temper was climbing, rescuing her from being a shrinking violet. A blush flooded her cheeks.

'What do you mean?' she said very slowly, very firmly.

'I mean Robbie had a cupboard full of clothes that we had to get rid of. It took me two or three days to think up that excuse.'

'Excuse? You sent me off with that little—with that boy as an excuse!'

'I had to think of something to get us back together again,' he chuckled. 'You have no idea what you put me through, Philomena Wilderman. There I was with this crazy feeling, for some—old broad—that I couldn't even see. I *had* to find some excuse to keep you close by until I could get all those crazy feelings under control. Instead, I kept getting deeper and deeper in the mud. But that wasn't the height of my scheming. The wedding—that was my centrepiece. A real out-and-out scam, that almost backfired.'

'You—you—rascal!' she gasped. 'You—the wedding—it wasn't because you needed a wife for the court hearing?'

He got up and spun his chair out of the way, and sat down on the couch beside her. One arm went around her stiff shoulders, the other covered both her hands, twisting and straining in her lap. 'Oh, I needed a wife,' he whispered in her ear, 'but not just for the hearing.'

'But—but you said it was only temporary—that after the hearing and all—you said—you'd make it all worth my while. That's what you said!'

'Well, in for a dime, in for a dollar,' he chuckled. His hand had come off her shoulder, and was toying with her ear lobe. 'I somehow had the feeling that you wouldn't buy the package without an escape clause.' And then, much more seriously, 'Do you want to escape, Phil?'

'Me?' She was struggling between laughter and tears, and the laughter won out. She relaxed, and snuggled up against him. 'Not me. I never had it so good!'

About five minutes later, while she struggled to regain her breath, he tickled her chin. 'I love kissing,' he chuckled.

'Well, don't be too free with your favours,' she snapped. 'I don't share.'

'Hey now, love, I don't either. We were lucky, you and I.'

'Lucky?'

'Of course. Robbie was always a problem. There was no way our marriage could work if you hadn't won him around.'

'It wasn't all my doing,' she sighed. 'The poor mixed-up kid thought I looked like his real mother. That picture of your sister—it seemed to connect us all. It gave me a first advantage with Robbie. And it gave me my first bad opinion of you. I thought that Robbie might have been— your illegitimate child, or something. And it wasn't until we went to the court hearing that I found out you were really his uncle. You could have told me outright, you know.'

'Sure I could have,' he chuckled. 'And would have lost your interest completely. I knew the boy had your attention, and as long as you thought I was his father you were hanging in there. I had few enough strings on you to afford to let one go. But you're right in one aspect. The painting did tie us together. When I came home Monday without the pads on my eyes I just couldn't wait to find you, to see what you looked like. And what did I see? My sister Robin standing in the door. I thought I had lost my wits, or something, so I rushed up the stairs to look at her portrait, and by the time I came down again you were gone. I thought—well, I was high—on excitement, not alcohol—on Sunday night. And when you yelled rape at me and then ran away, I figured I had really blown the works.'

'It wasn't rape,' she sighed, and moved as close as she could. 'I knew it at the time, and I know it now. It was just that—well, afterwards—you seemed to be so disgusted with it all that I thought—I just wanted to hurt you back, and that's why—I'm sorry, Penn. It wasn't rape. I'm your wife, you were very gentle, and I did enjoy it so much. I—I never thought I could—I just didn't know about that sort of wonderful excitement.'

He heaved a sigh of relief after the explanation. 'I thought I really had done us in,' he told her. 'I thought I deserved to be miserable—that I ought to let you go.'

'I'm glad you didn't.'

'Well, that was only for a couple of minutes that I had that crazy idea,' he laughed. 'And then I called the office, and lo and behold, someone had erased all of Philomena Peabody's records. Who could have done that?'

'Who indeed?' she murmured in a very quiet voice. There were some interesting patterns in the wallpaper. She studied them carefully. Anything rather than look into those eyes.

'And then your sister—I had her telephone number, but nobody answered. Do you realise that I had two secretaries at the office do nothing for three days but dial your sister's telephone every fifteen minutes, day and night?'

'It must have cost you a fortune in overtime.'

'Don't be sarcastic,' he laughed. 'I'll get it all back. I'm a persistent guy.'

The wallpaper lost its interest. She turned around to face him, treasuring his face between her two soft hands. 'I'm very glad for that,' she confessed. 'I'm a very stubborn woman. I might have held off from calling you for—oh—at least another week. Maybe two.'

Confession is good for the soul, she told herself a few minutes later. My, doesn't he taste good! But there's something going on around here that I can't quite figure out. He's up to something! She shivered deliciously, in anticipation.

He raised his hand to check his wristwatch. 'Three

o'clock,' he announced. 'And Robbie will be back tomorrow. I should have arranged for the kid to spend *two* weeks fishing.'

'Why—that's unkind, Penn. That's my son you're talking about.'

'So it is. Well, I think you'd better run up to your room and have a nap, Phil.'

'Nap? I'm not tired. I'm so excited I couldn't sleep. I—why?'

'I'm glad you're not tired,' he chuckled. 'Scoot upstairs.'

She went, but reluctantly, dragging her feet, stopping to smile at his sister's picture, winking an eye at the Pirate King. By the time she wandered into her room he was right behind her, with two glasses in his hand. 'Champagne,' he said. 'Let's drink a toast to the time when the pompous overcome the impulsive.'

'Or vice versa,' she giggled, gulping the contents at one swallow. 'Oops, I forgot.' She hiccupped. 'What are you doing?'

'How does this damn thing come off?'

'There's a zipper in the back,' she whispered in a very tiny voice. The glass slipped out of her hand and fell, but did not break. Her blouse slipped off her shoulders. His warm breath on her skin started her quivering. He needed no other invitation.

An hour later, satiated, she lay stretched out flat on her back, all her limbs askew, like some wanton Eve. He lay on his side, facing her. Perspiration stood on his forehead. She used a finger to trace letters in it, then dried it off with her loose hair.

'What are you writing on me?' he asked.

'A message,' she responded. "Penn Wilderman Belongs To Me." I intend to have one made for each of your cars, and two to go in your office.'

'Are you really? Pretty possessive, aren't you, Mrs Wilderman.'

'I—yes,' she stated very firmly. Practical Pill was back in action. Everything seemed under control. Except—it had been a wild hour, but how could she know if it had been as wild for him as it had been for her?

'Penn?'

'Yes. I'm still here.' His hand was tracing circles in her hair.

'Penn, that wasn't too shabby for—for an old broad, was it?'

'For a beginner I'd rate that as a ten plus,' he laughed. 'Were you worried? I never would have thought that you would catch on so quickly. And that's enough with the *old broad* business.'

'I—well. I wanted to talk seriously—stop that!' His index finger was probing at the spot just under her ribcage—the only spot on her entire body that was ticklish. She squealed as she wriggled away from him and seized the punishing digit. 'Don't do that,' she giggled. 'I hate being tickled.' Her hand pulled his finger up to her mouth. She snapped her sharp little teeth at it without touching, and then kissed it gently.

'Hey, for a minute there——' He rolled over on his stomach, half on top of her.

'That's just to remind you that I don't put up with any foolishness,' she giggled.

'Even from your husband?'

'Especially from my husband. I wanted to talk seriously about something.'

'Now? Here? Boy, you can always tell who the

amateurs are, can't you.'

'Amateurs? I thought I had just become a professional. Stop that!' Two tickling fingers this time, one on either side. She snatched them both up and held them. Talk fast, you fool, she told herself. Talk fast.

'It's about Robbie.'

'Oh.' His fingers stopped wriggling. 'Even in our bridal bed? *What* about Robbie?'

'It's just that—I think it's a bad mistake, having an only child in the family, and I'm not really getting any younger, so if we intend to do something about it we'll have to be fairly quick, and—what are you doing?' A *frisson* of alarm in her voice, as he rolled over again, on top of her, and began that tickling assault.

She did her best to squirm away, but his weight pinned her in place like a butterfly in a showcase. 'What are you doing?' Barely forced out, this time, because of the wild giggling she could not suppress. He stopped.

'What am I doing?' That Voice of Doom tone of his, suddenly broken off in the deep bass of his own laughter. 'You presented me a problem. Robbie needs a little sister. These things don't come easily. I may have to work on it for some time to come.' Those hands again, not poking, not tickling, moving slowly up to the undercurve of her breasts.

'You silly man,' she said in a soft, love-filled voice. The fingers moved on and his lips came down on her. Everything else was lost as her world dissolved in flames.

MILLS & BOON®

Makes any time special™

Bestselling themed romances brought back to you by popular demand

Each month By Request brings you three full-length novels in one beautiful volume featuring the best of the best.

So if you missed a favourite Romance the first time around, here is your chance to relive the magic from some of our most popular authors.

**Look out for
Conveniently Yours in February 1999
featuring Emma Darcy, Helen Bianchin
and Michelle Reid**

*Available at most branches of WH Smith, Tesco,
Asda, Martins, Borders, Easons,
Volume One/James Thin
and most good paperback bookshops*

This month's
irresistible novels from

ENTICING EMILY Gina Wilkins

Southern Scandals

Emily McBride was fed up with always being the 'good girl'.
But she never expected to end up on the wrong side of the law,
even by mistake. Then Wade Davenport, the sexy new chief of
police, insisted he wasn't going to let her out of his sight—
maybe crime did pay after all...

PRIVATE PLEASURES Janelle Denison

Blaze

Grey Nichols wanted a *lover*, not a *wife* and Mariah Stevens
wanted a *husband*, not a *lover*. So, no matter how incredible their
nights were together, she gave him an ultimatum. No more
private pleasures without a public ceremony. Now all she had to
do was keep her side of the bargain!

SMOKE AND MIRRORS Lisa E. Arlt

Caris Johnson was having difficulty maintaining her ice queen
image—and suave, sexy Alex Navarro had *everything* to do with
it. No one had ever guessed that, beneath her sober business
suits, Caris wore sexy lingerie. But, on steamy Navarro island,
Alex was about to find out...

MANHUNTING IN MIAMI Alyssa Dean

Manhunting

Unfortunately, Miami didn't have the blue-blooded type of
people Victoria Sommerset-Hays' family married. So Vicky
hired detective Luke Adams to track down a suitable man. But
then she found herself noticing Luke's broad shoulders...Why
couldn't she keep her mind on finding a husband?

MILLS & BOON®

Next Month's Romance Titles

♡

Each month you can choose from a wide variety of romance novels from Mills & Boon®. Below are the new titles to look out for next month from the Presents™ and Enchanted™ series.

Presents™

Enchanted™

On sale from 5th February 1999

H1 9901

Available at most branches of WH Smith, Tesco, Asda, Martins, Borders, Easons, Volume One/James Thin and most good paperback bookshops

EMILIE RICHARDS

FUGITIVE

Tate Cantrell froze, the stranger wielding a
revolver was an escaped prisoner. He was also
badly hurt—and in desperate need of her help.
Carl longed to spend a life sentence in her
arms, but he had to keep running, or he might
not be the only one to pay with his life.

Available from February

RANDOM ACTS

TAYLOR SMITH

DOES IT TAKE A KILLER
TO CATCH A KILLER?

Available from February

JoANN ROSS

a woman's heart

In *A Woman's Heart*, JoAnn Ross has created a
rich, lyrical love story about land, community,
family and the very special bond between a man
who doesn't believe in anything and a woman
who believes in him.

MIRA®

Available from February

He's a cop, she's his prime suspect

MARY LYNN BAXTER

HARD CANDY

He's crossed the line no cop ever should.
He's involved with a suspect—his
prime suspect.

Falling for the wrong man is far down her
list of troubles.

Until he arrests her for murder.

MIRA® Available from 18th December 1998

ELIZABETH GAGE

When Dusty brings home her young fiancé, he is everything her mother Rebecca Lowell could wish for her daughter, *and for herself*...

The Lowell family's descent into darkness begins with one bold act, one sin committed in an otherwise blameless life. This time there's no absolution in...

Confession

MIRA®

AVAILABLE FROM JANUARY 1999

MILLS & BOON®

Makes any time special

**Enjoy a romantic novel from
Mills & Boon®**

Presents™ Enchanted™ Temptation®

Historical Romance™ Medical Romance™